THE LOST SOULS MC
SNAKE - BOOK TWO

Surrender

BROOKLYN CROSS

Trademark Acknowledgements

The author Brooklyn Cross acknowledges the trademarked status and trademark owners of familiar wordmarks, products, actors' names, television shows, books, characters, video games, and films mentioned in this fiction work.

 Created with Vellum

BROOKLYN CROSS

WARNING

THIS IS A DARK MMFM (WHY CHOOSE) MOTORCYCLE CLUB ROMANCE NOVEL AND IS INTENDED FOR MATURE AUDIENCES ONLY.

THIS BOOK IS FOR SALE TO ADULTS ONLY, AS DEFINED BY THE COUNTRY'S LAWS IN WHICH YOU MADE YOUR PURCHASE.

THIS BOOK MAY CONTAIN DARK HUMOR, EXPLICIT SEXUAL CONTENT, GRAPHIC VIOLENCE, COARSE LANGUAGE, KIDNAPPING, MULTIPLE KINKS, TRAUMA, MEMORIES OF ABUSE, PTSD FAMILY LOSS, DRUG/TOBBACO/ALCOHOL USE AND SCENES THAT DEAL WITH SENSITIVE AND MATURE SUBJECT MATTER.

FOR A COMPLETE BREAKDOWNOF THE CONTENT WARNINGS, PLEASE SEE BROOKLYN CROSS'S WEBSITE WWW.BROOKLYNCROSSBOOKS.COM

ALSO BY BROOKLYN CROSS

Lost Souls MC

(Motorcycle Club - Dark 3.5-4.5 Spice 3.5-4.5)

Malice

Surrender

Showbiz

Handcuffed

Other Books in the Lost Souls World by T.L. Hodel

Adversaries

Frenemies

Warfare (Coming 2023)

The Righteous Series

(Vigilante/Ex Military Romance - Dark 3-4 Spice 3-4)

Dark Side of the Cloth

Ravaged by the Dark

Sleeping with the Dark

Hiding in the Dark

Redemption in the Dark

Crucified by the Dark

Dark Reunion (Coming 2023)

The Consumed Trilogy

(Suspense/Thriller/Anti-Hero Romance - Dark 4-5 Spice 3-4)

Burn for Me

Burn with Me

Burn me Down (Coming 2023)

The Buchanan Brother's Duet

(Serial Killer/Captive Horror Romance - Dark 4-5 Spice 3-5)

Unhinged Cain by Brooklyn

Twisted Abel by T.L Hodel

The Battered Souls World

(Standalone Books Shared World Romance/Dramatic/Women's Fiction/All The Feels- Dark 2-3 Spice 2-3)

The Girl That Would Be Lost

The Boy That Learned To Swim (Coming Soon)

The Girl That Would Not Break (Coming Soon)

The Brothers of Shadow and Death Series

(Dystopian/Cult/Occult/Poly MMF Romance - Dark 3-4 Spice 3-4)

Anywhere Book 1 of 3

Backfire Book 1 of 3 by T.L. Hodel

Seven Sin Series

(Multi Author/PNR/Angel and Demons/Redemption - Dark 2-5 Spice 3-5)

Greed by Brooklyn Cross

Lust by Drethi Anis

Envy by Dylan Page

Gluttony by Marissa Honeycutt

Wrath by Billie Blue

Sloth by Talli Wyndham

Pride by T.L. Hodel

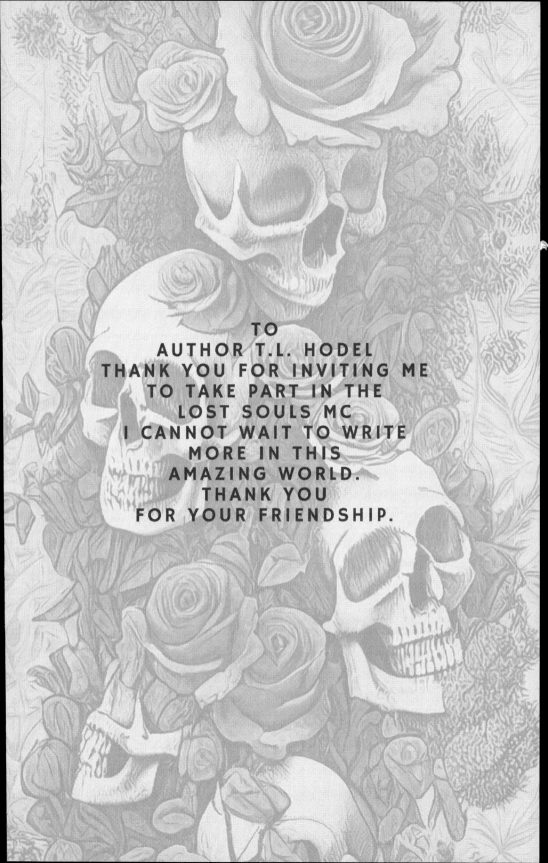

TO
AUTHOR T.L. HODEL
THANK YOU FOR INVITING ME
TO TAKE PART IN THE
LOST SOULS MC
I CANNOT WAIT TO WRITE
MORE IN THIS
AMAZING WORLD.
THANK YOU
FOR YOUR FRIENDSHIP.

AKNOWLEDGEMENT

IT IS WITH LOVE AND
APPRECIATION THAT I
SAY THANK YOU TO ALL
THOSE THAT HAVE STOOD
BY MY SIDE THROUGH MY
AUTHOR JOURNEY.
WHO PICKED ME UP
DURING MY LOWEST
MOMENTS AND CONTINUE
TO MAKE ME SMILE.
I COULD NOT DO THIS
WITHOUT EACH OF YOU.

PLAYLIST

PAGE 1

VENOM - EMINEM
A LITTLE BIT STRONGER - SARA EVANS
A LITTLE BIT DANGEROUS - CRMNL
BAD HABITS - ED SHEERAN
FORGET ME - LEWIS CAPALDI
BUTTERFLY - CRAZY TOWN
SURVIVOR - NATHANIEL RATELIFF
BUTTONS - SNOOP DOGG & PUSSYCAT DOLLS
I WANNA BE YOU - MANESKIN
BREATHE - SKITZ KRAVEN
LIMIT TO YOUR LOVE - JAMES BLAKE
SHE KEEPS ME UP - NICKELBACK
NEVER GONNA LET YOU GO - ESTHERO
YOU WORRY ME - NATHANIEL RATELIFF
PEACHES - JUSTIN BIEBER
GUNS+AMMUNITION - JULY TALK
BAD BUY - BILLIE EILISH
THE KIND OF LOVE WE MAKE - LUKE COMBS
MEMORY - KANE BROWN X BLACKBEAR
HOLD ON, WE'RE GOING HOME - DRAKE
THE NEXT EPISODE - DR DRE
ANTI-HERO - TAYLOR SWIFT
SOMETHING TO LOSE - LANDON TEWERS
SHIVERS - ED SHEERAN
I THINK I LIKE WHEN IT RAINS - WILLIS
RUN AWAY TO MARS - TALK

PLAYLIST

PAGE 2

NEVER LEAVE - BAILEY ZIMMERMAN
BURY A FRIEND - BILLIE EILISH
I WALK THE LINE - HALSEY
LAST RESORT - PAPA ROACH
TAKE WHAT YOU WANT - POST MALONE
HERO - CHAD KROEGER
APOLOGIZE - TIMBALAND
WRECKING BALL - MILEY CYRUS
FUNHOUSE - PINK
STERO HEARTS - GYM CLASS HEROES
TOXIC - BRITNEY SPEARS
CENTURIES - FALL OUT BOY
SUGAR, WE'RE GOIN DOWN - FALL OUT BOY
ATTENTION - CHARLIE PUTH
SATELLITE - GUSTER
OUT TA GET ME - GUNS N' ROSES
TREEHOUSE - HE IS WE
ME, MYSELF & I - G-EAZY X BEBE REXHA
COMING UNDONE - KORN
SEX AND CANDY - ALEXANDER JEAN
CONFETTI - CHARLOTTE CARDIN
PIECE OF MY HEART - JANIS JOPLIN
COMING FOR YOU - OFFSPRING
RESCUE ME - ONEREPUBLIC
SLOW HANDS - NIALL HORAN
SANGRIA - BLAKE SHELTON

Chapter 1
LOST
1%   MC
SOULS

Raine

The bus station was surprisingly quiet when I walked in, but it seemed all the strange shit wanted to follow me around lately.

"Penis," someone yelled, and I turned to look along with everyone else, quickly wishing I hadn't.

"Penis," the man yelled again. He looked like he might be drunk, but it was hard to tell. His hair was a mess standing in all directions, and the glasses were askew on his face. He wore a business suit that looked expensive, but the shirt was wrinkled and partially untucked, and there were no shoes on his feet. That wasn't the strangest part.... The open zipper with this dick hanging out had me pressing my lips together to keep from laughing.

It wasn't funny. He could've taken a party drug that went sideways. Might've even drunk too much or lost a bet. But he kept yelling penis like he was calling a dog and pointed at his dick like he was shocked to find he had one, and I couldn't stop the giggle.

"Penis!" He screamed again, and a woman exiting the bathroom with her two children turned them around and went back inside.

"Security, we have a 10-56. I repeat a 10-56." The person on the PA said. A few guards walked out of a door not far away and immediately went to surround the guy. The man had other ideas and wasn't interested in going quietly with the guards.

"Penis, penis, penis," he called out like he was in the midst of the game Marco Polo. It was like a train wreck I couldn't look away from as he took off in a run around the bus terminal. He hid behind shocked people, using them as shields and the large planters with small trees before sprinting toward the exit. "Penis," echoed back through the open door until it closed.

"I do hope he finds his pecker, terrible thing to lose it," the elderly man beside me said, and I couldn't hold back the laugh any longer. The man was dressed like an old English gentleman, from the wool cap on his head to the polished shoes on his feet and the wooden cane in his hand. He lifted a bushy white eyebrow and smiled before turning to face the front of the line once more.

"How can I help you?" The teller smiled as I stepped up to the glass.

"I need to get to Seattle," I said.

"We don't have a bus that takes a direct route, but there's a bus that goes from here to the Atlanta bus terminal. From there, you can take one bus the rest of the way or shorter distance ones if you want to stop along the way," she said.

"Sounds good. I always wanted to see Atlanta." I pulled out my wallet and was going to swipe my card but thought better of it and handed her cash. I had no idea what tricks Kai might have up his sleeve, but I wouldn't put it past him to track my cards.

I grabbed my ticket and wandered out to the bus idling on the curb. Seattle was the furthest place I could think of to put space between myself and all that had happened here and it was a spot I always wanted to see.

"Penis! No, you'll never take me alive." I looked toward the parking lot and saw security forcing Penis Man into the back of a police car. On the plus side, I wasn't starting my day in the back of a cruiser. I guess there was always a silver lining...

I hated this. I hated that once more, Kai found a way to terrify me. It didn't matter that it wasn't him that hurt me when I was fifteen. I'd still spent my whole life believing it. Then when he came back, it certainly wasn't to try and explain that it wasn't him. Then again, I don't know if I would've listened to him if he had knocked on my door. It was all so complicated.

No matter what I'd said to Kai, I was scared that my life would be forever living out of a backpack on the run from him and the rage that had built up like a volcano inside him. I realized that I could never be with anyone ever again. Whether it was five, ten, or even twenty years from now didn't matter. That shimmer in his eye had said it all—no one would ever be safe.

Maybe I just wanted to hurt, but I did what I ordered myself not to do and pulled out my burner phone. My finger hovered over the text message before giving in and tapping on the little dot. This would be my one guilty pleasure. I knew I wouldn't be able to resist when I sent myself the pictures. I had snapped some images of Avro and me at the beach and another that Avro insisted we take after Jace's concert with all three of us in it.

My heart ached for so many reasons, and I started questioning if I should be going.

"No, there is no point in dwelling on the 'what ifs,'" I mumbled.

Glancing at the time as a few people lined up, I realized I'd been staring at the photos for over half an hour. Stuffing the phone into my jeans pocket, I pushed away from the wall and made my way to the line of passengers slowly boarding the bus.

"Any big baggage needs to go around to the other side of the bus," the driver called out as the procession shuffled along.

The more I thought about it, the more it felt right to take the opportunity to spend a few days at each location the buses stopped to tour around. It would be my version of a hired bus tour. Besides, once I hit Seattle, I'd need to find a job and a place to stay. Who knew when I would get the chance to vacation again? I had enough money to keep me going for a while in my bag but not enough to live off of for a long time.

I handed my ticket to the man collecting at the door. My nose curled as I stepped inside, bombarded with the fake scent of coconut and pineapple. I normally didn't mind these particular flavors, but it was as if the smell had reached inside my nose and tried to choke me. Opting to sit as far away from the smell as possible, I wandered to the back of the bus and picked a spot with two empty seats.

Sitting by the window, I placed my bag in my lap and pulled out the pamphlets and maps I'd taken from the bus station. Of course, the first one I opened had an ad for Eclipse, and my heart fell.

My boss wasn't impressed with my impromptu departure. I told him it was an emergency that couldn't be avoided and recommended Avro take my place. He still grumbled and cursed into the phone about how no one could run the place as well as I had. It was a stupid statement, I hadn't been the manager for very long, but I promised that if I came back into town, I'd call.

My finger rubbed over the image, and I choked up. It felt like I was trying to contain the tide with my emotions raging and swaying one way and then the other. Never allowed to settle, never able to feel too safe before it all fell out from under me all over again. Like a bottle lost at sea forced away from shore only to tumble back and be yanked away once more, that was the story of my life.

. . .

I stared out the window, keeping my eyes on the butterfly floating around. Its brightly colored wings shimmered in the golden rays of the bright sun. A sun that had shined every day since my attack. A reminder that no matter what had happened to me, the girl in the bed beside me, or even the man in the room down the hall...the world continued to turn.

It was a terrible thing to realize that you were unimportant. I was nothing more than a blip on the radar or another grain of sand along the beach, blending in with all the others. I was no one special. The girl with cancer in the bed beside me was no one special. There wasn't a collective holding of breath to see if either of us survived. Only difference was, she had people that visited daily.

That reality was terrifying and freeing. I didn't matter, and no one cared, so I had no one to disappoint, but never being seen or understood and never being able to trust again was scary. I was now sixteen, having spent my birthday in the hospital, and it already felt like I'd lived three lifetimes and died twice along the way.

"Hi there, sweetie, are you all packed and ready to go?" The warm and cheery voice said from behind me. I smiled as I recognized Nurse Liz's voice. Pulling back on the wheels of the wheelchair, I slowly turned to face her. She always had the warmest smile. She nodded toward the wheelchair. "You're getting better," she said.

"Thanks. I'm still awkward, and I get mixed up on which way to pull and push to turn. It makes me feel stupid."

"Nonsense. A baby learns to crawl before it can stand and eventually walk and then run. You've only been able to get up and move around for a few days. You'll get used to it."

"Hopefully, I won't need it much longer. The doctor said that the wounds are healing well and the grafts are holding, so I can start walking around more."

Liz smiled and grabbed my packed bag, laying it on the bed. "You're not forgetting anything, are you?"

"I don't think so." I didn't have much, just a few changes of clothes and my journal. "Did my foster parents say when they would be coming to get me?" The bright smile slipped.

Liz looked away, and I knew something was wrong. "I thought you would've known," she said.

"Known what?" I wheeled myself a little closer, and Liz sat on the edge of the bed. She glanced out the door and lowered her voice as she spoke next.

"I guess I shouldn't be the one to tell you this, but it's Child and Family Services coming for you." My eyes went wide, and my heart tripled its pace.

"What? Why?"

I wouldn't say I loved the Collinses, they were both kinda cold and distant most of the time, but they were the only family I had left. I had loved Kai, or at least I thought I did, but he betrayed me and left me for dead. Now the Collinses weren't coming. What had I done to deserve this? Was I really that much trouble? Did everyone hate me so much that they wanted to hurt me?

"I don't know why, sweetie. I just heard that is who was coming to pick you up, so maybe they are just sending them to collect you or something," she offered, but I knew better.

I ignored Liz as she called my name when I wheeled out of the room and turned to roll down the hall. I didn't know where I was going. I didn't care as the tears hit and flowed down my cheeks. There was a small sitting room to my left, and I stopped the wheelchair and pulled into the small space, closing the door behind me. Breathing hard from the burst of exertion, I sat in the privacy of the four walls and covered my face to let the tears fall. Why did the world hate me so much?

It was then that I realized I was probably better off alone. No one could hurt me when I didn't let anyone in. I didn't need anyone anyway.

K aivan

I watched the black sedan turn around and ground my teeth together. The guy was gutsier than I pegged him for. Once I was sure Avro was out on the main road and out of sight, I closed the door and ran up the stairs.

"Fuck, I think he broke my nose." Pushing open the door to the bathroom, I paused to look in the mirror and assess the latest injury. It didn't look broken, but blood was running down my upper lip. I think my tear ducts were broken 'cause I didn't tear up anymore when I got hit in the face. Now all I got was more pissed off.

Grabbing tissues, I twisted them and shoved them up my nose to stop the bleeding. I definitely wasn't winning any beauty pageants looking like this. Aside from my nose, I had a black eye and a cut over my brow from Jace. There was another cut and long bruise—a nasty shade of yellow—on my jaw, and my knuckles were once more split open.

Since the cops weren't knocking on my door and hauling me back to prison, I assumed that Raine had won the argument with Jace and Avro...at least for now. It was stupid to storm into their home, but I couldn't let them have her. Raine was mine. She'd always been mine, and there was no fucking way I was letting her take off and disappear.

Stripping out of my relaxed clothes, I pulled on my road gear before slipping my arms into my leather jacket. I picked up my phone and turned on the tracker app, smirking when I saw the little blinking dot. I knew it was smart to put that in her go bag. Wilder came through. Crazy fuck.

She was on the move, almost halfway to Atlanta, and a shit load further than I thought she'd be. With her headstart, she would be there by the time I caught up if that was where she stopped.

Sweat suddenly coated my body, and my gut churned as I pictured her hitchhiking her way there. She could be in some creepy trucker's cab right now. I knew she didn't have a car, and if Avro was here with his that left bus or putting her thumb out. If someone else hurt her, I'd kill them.

Grabbing my gun, I held it up, and what she'd said last night came rushing back.

"Look at me, Snake," Raine yelled. She'd always refused to use the nickname given to me when I started fighting. She said it wasn't me, said that she could only see me as Kai and that Snake was some made-up char-acter to scare people. She said she never wanted to see me like that or be scared of me. It had divided us then 'cause I thought it was cool, and it hurt now to hear her use it.

"You're not Kai, not right now, not like this." Raine's eyes looked me

up and down, and under the anger and fear was disgust and, deeper yet, disappointment. That look cut like a knife to my heart. I'd never wanted to hurt her, but the anger had been riding me for so long that it felt like it was a whole other person and all I had left, at least until now. "I don't even recognize you."

"Don't call me that," I said softly.

"Why not? You want me dead anyway, right? That's what Snake wants. To destroy the person that made you this angry." She spoke like I was two different people, and maybe I was. I felt as conflicted as two people inside of me.

"Well, I'm right here." She said, giving me a clear shot to do what I'd dreamed about in prison and to take my final revenge. "Do it. Take the shot and end this, because I'm not living in fear of you anymore." A tear slipped from her eye, and I watched it trickle down her cheek. Why that one tear punched so hard, I couldn't say, but a well of emotion was trying to break free of the cage it had been locked in for years.

"I know now that it wasn't you back then, but I've lived the last eleven years a shell of who I was because of what was done to me, and I won't hide in my closet anymore. I won't triple lock my door and stay up all night with a knife by my bed. I won't close my eyes and see your face hurting me." She shook her head, and my heart constricted in my chest. "Not anymore."

I stared at the gun in my hands. The same gun that had taken countless lives since I got out of prison and the same gun that could've easily gone off and killed the only person I'd ever loved on this shithole planet. She wasn't running. She was in protection mode. Protecting Avro and Jace and probably even me from myself. I pushed her to do that. I saw the look in her eyes last night. She knew I was on the line and would've killed them and had been willing to take the hit.

"Fuck!" I yelled. Self-loathing apparently had a lower level, and I had just reached the bottom floor. My hand began to shake, and I squashed the unease trying to take hold of my mind as old memories flooded to the surface.

"What the hell do you mean, Jack?" Mom yelled into the phone at my dad. She stomped across the living room and back again. I wasn't supposed to be listening, but I couldn't stay in my room when she started yelling.

Sitting on the stairs, I saw her shadow moving around with the light from the setting sun coming in the window at just the right angle.

"I told you I didn't want to deal with this shit anymore. We have a son, for fucks sake." I could hear the mouse-like sound of my dad yelling back as she stepped close to the stairs again.

"Yes, of course, I know he's your son too, but he doesn't want to be in the club. You were supposed to be done after the last job. I don't care! You promised you'd leave. No, no, Jack. I don't care." I'd never heard my mom this angry before. I knew why she was pissed off. They'd been arguing for months about my dad leaving the motorcycle club he belonged to. I wasn't really supposed to know much about what the club did, but I knew. Just like all the kids of the members knew, even though we were only allowed inside the clubhouse for special occasions or when my father needed to pick something up and I was with him.

When we'd all get together for parties and holidays and other shit like that, you could hear the men talking. Also, did they think we were all stupid and didn't watch television or the news? It wasn't normal for people to always wear leather jackets to weddings with a giant, snarling dog head on the back. They always assumed kids were stupid, but we picked up on a lot more than they knew.

Mom wanted him to be done. She said that he was too old for this shit and was always putting us in danger. She wasn't wrong, although I knew even without asking that no matter what my dad said, he was never leaving the club. He acted like that place was heaven. Maybe it was. How was I to know? Things had come to a head when three weeks and two days ago, our house was broken into, and everything was smashed. A warning, 'Stay out of our business,' was sprayed on the wall. Dad would only say that one of the girls that worked at the club was roughed up. That's when Mom got really intense and insisted that Dad leave and for us to move.

"Fuck you, Jack. I've given over the best part of my life to you and that club. Even with all the shit you've done and the women you've fucked while I sat home and looked after our son, I still stood by you, but I'm not sitting here like a target and just waiting for their next move. I'm taking Kai, and we're going to my sister's house in Connecticut. If you decide to leave the club, then you'll know where to find me."

The words had no sooner left my mom's mouth when there was a bang and glass shattered. I covered my head, not sure what was going on, and thought for just a minute that my mom had decided to break one of the glass tables in the living room. There was a loud roar that I knew was a motorcycle, and my hair rustled like a wind was lifting it.

Jumping up, I ran down the few stairs and rounded the corner to the living room.

"Mom!" She was lying on the floor, and blood was seeping into the carpet all around her. Running to her side, I dropped to my knees. Her eyes were wide and terrified.

"I don't know what to do," I said, my hands shaking as I stared at the wound in her chest. "What do I do?" She grabbed my hand in hers.

"Run," she said, her voice soft as she wheezed out the single word.

All I could feel was the pounding in my chest as my heart hammered, and I looked around for the phone. I needed to call for help. It was still in her other hand, and I realized Dad was still on the phone.

Leaning over Mom, I pulled the phone from her fingers that didn't want to let go. I could hear my dad yelling for my mom to answer him.

"Dad? Help, it's Mom, she's bleeding, and I don't know what to do."

"Okay, Kai, listen to me. Is anyone else still there?"

I looked around, confused by the question. We'd been alone the entire time. "No, it's just me and Mom."

"Good. Now, where is your mom hurt?" I could hear motorcycles revving, making it hard to hear my dad.

"Her chest," I said as something warm trailed down my cheeks. "Dad, there is so much blood."

"Hang up, Kai, and call nine-one-one."

"But dad...."

"No arguments Kai. Hang up the phone and call now." The phone clicked off in my ear.

"But I'm scared," I gasped as the asthma attack gripped me. Fear made me wheeze, and my eyes returned to my mom's face. Her eyes were still open, but she was looking right through me. "No, Mom, you need to stay with me," I said, gripping her shoulder to shake her. Mom's expression never changed as her head rocked with the movement.

Her hand was still wrapped around mine, but I pulled it free to stand and stumble into the kitchen. My mom always kept my puffers in the cupboard. It was getting harder to breathe with every passing second, and I knew that I couldn't pass out or I wouldn't be any help.

I shook the inhaler and got a puff into me before I dropped to my knees and fumbled with the phone to get those three simple numbers punched in. The phone slipped as I picked it up from the slick blood coating everything.

"Nine-one-one. What's your emergency?" The guy on the end of the line said.

"It's my mom, I think she's been shot, and I don't know what to do," I said, barely able to keep the phone to my ear as it kept trying to slip through my fingers.

"Are you in danger?"

"No, it's not me. It's my mom," I cried. I hated to cry. In this house, if you cried, you were not a man, but I couldn't hold the emotion back as Mom laid there. I'd never seen someone die, but I was sure my mom was dying now.

I couldn't remember what the man said to me. Everything had become a blur. From the police arriving and the paramedics to my dad showing up *and yelling and crying like she meant everything to him. I stared up at him as they carried my mother's body out of the house, tears streaming down his face. All I could think was that he was a liar. I'd heard the fights and the names he called her. I heard the threats and the promises to kill her if she took off. That wasn't love, and if it was, then I never wanted to love someone.*

I sat on the stairs, no one watching me or even looking my way because my dad was making so much noise. Trying for a part in a movie was my guess. The house became still after everyone was gone. My head lifted and my eyes locked on the front door and the bloody hand print smeared into the crisp white.

Rising to my feet, I slowly walked to the closet that held the cleaning supplies and pulled out a bucket and soap. Tossing in a sponge and the brush I used to get the dirt out from under my nails, I walked into the living room. The blood on the carpet was shaped like a person with a giant blob in the middle. It reminded me of the art projects from school when we would put a bunch of paint on paper and fold it in half.

Lowering myself to my knees, I grabbed the sponge and started to scrub, but the stain wouldn't go away. Instead, it got larger but faded to a terrible shade of pink, and no matter how hard I tried, I couldn't get the red out from under my nails.

I hated my dad from that moment on. My mom was scared. She'd been terrified that something was going to happen, and he chose to keep us in danger. Then he abandoned me. It was his fault, she died, and I prayed hard that he would die a terrible death.

The last word my mom said to me was 'run.' I didn't run, but I should've.

My father left on a Monday night at seven-thirty-one and never returned. By Friday, I'd eaten everything in the house that I knew how to make. I tried to call my dad, but he didn't answer. At the age of nine years, two months, and three days at exactly ten-fourteen on Saturday morning, the knock that would change my life forever sounded at the door.

Three months and six days after my mom died, I was hauled away by social workers to live with someone else because my dad was arrested for three murders. I never saw him again. I had the choice to visit but refused every time until they stopped asking. He meant nothing to me. He wasn't my dad, just a man who had given me some of his DNA, and if I could, I would give that back.

The first three homes I went to were all rich people with fancy homes, and not one of them had been a nice person. I quickly learned that just because people had money didn't make them any nicer or loving than my old man.

Then I ended up at the Collins home, and my world went from shit to amazing in a blink—only to end in a shitstorm. I figured it was karma for all the crap my father had done and for wishing a horrible death on him. Whether he was alive or not, I couldn't say, but I wanted him to suffer, and in the end, it was me that suffered.

I shook my head, trying to rid it of the image of Raine lying on the floor, bleeding out like my mom. I was worse than my dad. At least he hadn't pulled the trigger.

I almost did.

Raine

Chapter 3

aine

Yawning as I walked, I sipped on the shitty coffee the rest stop offered. Why did every cup taste too dark and burnt? It didn't matter where we stopped. It was all the same. I'd thrown out the first few, but now I was desperate enough to drink it no matter what. I popped the last bit of burger into my mouth and climbed up the stairs onto the bus. Thankfully, it wasn't that busy, and as it turned out, no one sat beside me, which I was grateful for.

The emotional rollercoaster that started with the decision to leave hadn't gotten any better with the quiet ride. There was too much time to think, and I found myself going over the lyrics of, *Another Sad Love Song*. It seemed perfect for the story of my life. There were moments I was so livid that I wanted to jump off the bus and storm Kai's house to kick his ass. But I knew I couldn't do that, and the melancholy would settle in as I thought about how I'd put Avro and Jace at risk.

Pulling the backpack off, I plopped down into my seat and stared out at the darkness. I knew I needed to stop thinking about everything, but that seemed impossible. Just like I knew I couldn't shut off the emotions with a switch, my brain was no better. It seemed intent on torturing me with images and the memory of touches. Of sweet words and the taste of lips that made them tingle. I'd fallen asleep once, and I could've sworn I was back in bed, cocooned in the warmth of Avro and Jace. I woke up with a smile on my face, only to have it slip as the bus bounced and jarred me back to reality.

I saw someone step onto the bus but didn't pay them any attention until they sat down beside me. Startled, I jumped and looked at the man I didn't recognize. I glanced around the bus at the four other people soundly sleeping.

"Um...can I help you," I asked, confused.

"Nope," he said and didn't look my way. It was hard to tell his age, but he had shoulder-length hair that ran into a scraggly beard. He was gripping a large book to his chest while his eyes searched the front of the bus.

"The seats across from me are empty," I offered, hoping I didn't sound too pushy and yet wanting him to take the hint.

"Oh, that's okay. Did you want to see my family?" He pulled the large book away from his chest to reveal a photo album. Before I could respond, he flipped open the cover. I looked down at the smiling images of people cut out from a magazine. "This is my son, Jeffery," he said, tapping an image of a boy doing a cannonball into a pool. It still had the for-sale banner from the pool installation at a twenty-five percent discount.

I wasn't sure what to do. I didn't want to upset him, but I wasn't sure it was healthy for me to play along with whatever delusion he had.

"Jeffery loves soccer, but his sister Leslie hates it." He shook his head, a scowl pulling at the corners of his mouth and wrinkling his brow. He flipped a few more pages and pointed out travel ads for Jamaica and Ireland, telling me how they'd all flown there as a family.

"Do you like this photo?" He tapped one of a large mountain with a sunset in the background and a vehicle set up like it was camping on the top of the tall peak.

I nodded. "It's stunning."

The man smiled and flipped a few more pages. My eyes went wide as he turned to a page littered with Polaroids. The people all looked dead. I swallowed hard as I stared into the sightless eyes. It was a crash scene with cars in the background and glowing lights from the emergency vehicles. I had no idea how someone would even get their hands on pictures like this.

He smiled at me. "They're not actually dead. This was for a movie. They are great actors," he said, but out of all the images, these were the ones that I believed were real. Glancing up from the book to his eyes, they were shimmering with happiness, and I swallowed hard. "Jeffery is going to be a famous actor one day. He keeps saying that he wants to be on a crime show."

The man pointed to a woman on her knees in the background. "This is my wife. Isn't she amazing? The kids get their acting skills from her." Her face was covered in blood, but it was the pain in her eyes as she wailed that had my chest aching for this man. I could almost hear her cries.

"She's incredible," I said softly, and his face lit up with emotion, but behind the smile were ghosts that I understood. I didn't know what else to say, but I could feel his sadness in my soul, and tears pricked at my eyes.

The bus shook, and I looked up as two police officers stepped onto the bus and walked down the aisle to where we were sitting.

"Come on, Luis, we need to get you back to your place," the first officer said. His name tag said, Dolson.

Luis looked up at them and then at me. The shadows in his eyes mirrored the scars in my mind. The smile on his face fell, and I suddenly wanted to stand up and yell at them to leave him alone.

"I don't want to go back there," Luis said and gripped the album to his chest like a shield.

I expected Dolson to grab Luis and drag him off the bus, but instead, he knelt down and reached out, laying a hand on his shoulder. "Where are you going to go, Luis? Your family is all here. If you leave, then how will you see them?"

Tears welled in Luis's eyes, and the pain was so raw that I felt the stab to my heart as if the loss was my own.

"I don't want to leave them," Luis said.

"I know you don't. That's why you need to come with us. This bus is going to take you far away from them, Luis. I know you don't want that."

He shook his head slowly as tears trickled down his cheeks. "But the doctors are mean. They say that my family is gone. I want them to stop that. They're not gone," Luis said. If I hadn't been watching Dolson so closely, I would've missed the sadness in his eyes, but he was quick to cover it and nodded and smiled for Luis.

"You're right. They need to stop saying that. Come on, I'll speak to them for you." Dolson stood and held out his hand.

"It was nice meeting you," Luis said as he took Dolson's hand and stood.

"Can you take him out to the car," Dolson said to the other officer, who had been quiet the entire time. Dolson turned to look at me as soon as they were down the steps and out of earshot. "I'm sorry about my Dad," he said.

"Your dad? But...."

"That was my sister and brother. They passed away in a crash with an impaired driver. My dad was the officer that arrived first on scene. He…" Dolson looked over his shoulder to the police car sitting outside. "He hasn't been the same since." The corner of his mouth turned up, and I had the urge to jump up and hug him. "Anyway, I'm sorry if he scared you." With a nod, Dolson walked away.

Pulling on my hood, I covered my head as I fought the sadness threatening to overtake me. How many days had I laid in bed, convinced that I wouldn't be able to get up and function ever again? How often had it been better to dream of what I wished my life was rather than dealing with the pain I slugged through? How many times had my mind sat on the edge of that very precipice? It would've been so easy to give up and let the imaginary world swallow me whole.

The reality of how close I'd come to that felt like a noose tightening around my neck. I was no longer that girl, but the pain stuck with me. The memories and dreams of someone with a future laid out felt like they belonged to someone else. Someone that had died in that warehouse. My body had been rescued, but my mind never recovered.

The bus hissed and lurched as we started moving, but I kept my face buried in my sweatshirt. I could run, but I could never hide from my demons. Those would stay with me forever.

Snake

Chapter 4

Kaivan

By the time I rolled into Atlanta, my ass was sore. It had been a while since I took that long a ride. Just another reminder that I was almost thirty. I tapped at my phone in the waterproof holder and made the image larger. The dot hadn't moved for a few hours, and I zoomed in on the spot to get an accurate location. It was a motel, a good twenty minutes outside of downtown.

The time was eleven-eleven. She might be asleep or maybe paying off her ride. I quickly squashed that thought before it could take root and make me murderous.

Memorizing the directions, I took off and made it there faster than the map showed. I parked under a light near the office. The blinds were drawn, and a sign on the door said No Vacancy. This was a tough area, and I prayed that no one tried to steal my baby. If they did, I would put a piece of lead between someone's eyes. I glanced up at the motel. Pulling my phone out, I zoomed in as close as possible and realized that she had to be walking outside or could walk through walls. All the doors faced the outside, so I hopped off the bike and began stalking my little dot to cut her off.

I still had no idea what the hell I was going to say to Raine. There really weren't words to describe what had gone on between us or how to apologize for acting out of my mind.

"What the fuck?" I heard Raine's distressed voice and grabbed the gun from the back of my jeans. "I said let go of me," she snarled. I rounded the corner to see her pushed up against the soda machine by some guy wearing a dark hoodie. I couldn't see his face, but I didn't need to. I knew what he wanted from her. Money or sex, and sometimes both—it was always the same.

My lip lifted in a snarl. No one hurt Raine. No one but me, anyway.

She was quick and broke the jerk's hold before rounding on him with a hard punch to the face. I smiled as she braced herself against the machine and kicked out with both feet. The guy grunted and stumbled back, almost landing on his ass. Raine glared at the guy, no one paying attention to the threat coming from the side.

"Bitch!"

"What the hell is wrong with the fucking male population?" She struck out and landed a couple more solid hits as he attempted to get close again. My heart soared with pride as the guy grabbed at his gut and narrowly missed the shot to his dick. That's my Tink. Feisty to the core. "Can't a girl just get a fucking drink without being harassed?"

"You fucking bitch!" The guy lunged at her, slamming her into the machine. She winced with the impact but snarled as she scratched at his face and kicked him in the gut.

"Fucking cunt," the guy yelled as Rained continued to strike at him like a feral cat. This was really fucking hot, and there was no denying it as I adjusted myself that it turned me on. I wanted to see her kick his ass, but hoodie guy wrapped his hand around her throat and lifted his fist to strike her.

I growled like a dog as I stepped up beside him and shoved the gun into the side of his head hard enough that he tilted it to the side and froze. "No one touches what's mine, but hit her and see what happens," I said, keeping my voice low and threatening.

Raine's eyes snapped to mine. Those beautiful blues looked worried—as worried as the guy at the end of my gun must look— but under that was shock.

"Let go of her now," I ordered. His hand dropped, and he slowly lifted them both up. "If I didn't already have an engagement tonight, I'd blow your fucking hand right off for touching her, so consider this your lucky night. Now turn toward the breezeway and run. Run like your ass is on fire before I change my mind and kill you anyway," I said, shoving the guy's head with the gun.

There was no hesitation as he turned toward the back of the motel and took off in a sprint through the gap separating the buildings, disappearing into the darkness. Dropping my gaze to Raine, her nostrils flared, and her eyes narrowed as she stared at me. She was pissed, and I was so here for it. God, I wanted her right there— looking at me just like that—up against the machine.

"What the hell are you doing here," Raine asked and then hit the button on the vending machine. She'd obviously already paid, or they liked giving away free beverages, as the bottle tumbled before it was spat out the bottom. Whenever I saw a soda machine work, all I could think of was The Matrix. I was forever ruined.

"I thought it would be pretty obvious that I came to see you. I don't make it a habit to wander around the seedy parts of Atlanta," I said.

"Why not? I'm sure you skulk around other seedy places," she quipped back as she bent over to grab her bottle.

"Ouch, you wound me," I drawled, and she glared over her shoulder as she fought with the machine. I never understood why they made the slot so awkward to get your hand in. Raine's ass was right in front of me, her hoodie riding up and showing off the string of her thong. Before I could stop myself, I reached out and grabbed her hip. My finger brushed against her bare skin, and all I could picture was ripping those jeans off her and fucking her just like that.

Spinning around, Raine smacked my hand, but all it did was encourage the fantasy playing out in my mind.

"Don't touch me." She glared, and I smiled.

Before I could get into more trouble, I stuffed the gun under my jacket to conceal it once more as Raine walked away.

"How the hell did you find me anyway," she asked as I fell in step beside her.

Lifting a shoulder, I let it drop. "I have my ways."

Banter should not make me this hot, but with each step she took, the harder I got.

"Go away, Kai, Snake, or whoever the hell you are tonight. I don't want to speak to you. I just want to be left alone. It's really not too much to ask."

"I need to speak to you," I said.

Right now, I wished everything was solved as easily as fucking it away. I knew it wasn't possible, but shit, she was tempting. Like a top-shelf scotch, she had my mouth watering.

We reached the corner room, and she pulled out the key from her pocket and unlocked the door. Stepping inside, she quickly turned and tried to push the door closed. I knew she would try and slam the door in my face, so I got my boot in the way. She made a little snarling noise at me, her nose scrunching up as she stared down at the boot.

"Fuck! Why are you so fucking annoying? Can't you just leave me alone?" She yelled and let go of the door, giving up. That was the question. Why couldn't I leave her to live her life, whatever that entailed?

Stepping into the small room, I closed and locked the door behind me. The fuzzy television was on low, showing some old sitcom. Raine opened the soda and took a swig like it was something much stronger. My lip curled up, figuring she wished it was.

"I told you we need to talk," I said.

She spun around, slammed the bottle down, and her hands balled into fists. "About what? How you decided to ruin my life? How I gave up the one piece of happiness that I'd finally managed to carve out for myself because you can't stand to see me happy?"

"It's not like that." She glared at me, her head twisting slightly as one of her eyebrows raised. It was her you're a fucking liar look. I'd seen it so many times when we were younger, but I didn't remember it being so damn sexy. I was having trouble concentrating, and my emotions couldn't keep up with the storm swiftly brewing inside of me. "I swear to you it's not. I mean, it was, but it's not anymore."

I ran my hand through my hair as she stomped in my direction, and my muscles tensed. The closer she got, the more charged the room became between us. By the time she was standing in front of me, I was breathing hard as I tried my best to keep my hands to myself.

Raine pushed on my chest, and my back hit the door.

"Oh really? Then tell me what the hell it's like, 'cause the guy that busted into my bubble of happiness last night didn't seem too concerned about what damage he caused. I'd say you got exactly what you wanted. Me on the run, scared to death of you all over again. Stripping me of all the hard work that I did to put myself back together again. I hate you, Kai." Her voice held so much venom that the poison seeped into my body.

"Don't say that. You don't mean that," I said, her words stopping my heart.

"I do. I hate you!" She swung for my face, and I grabbed her arm out of the air. But she was quick and landed a hard blow with her left fist that knocked my head to the side. Fuck she had a hook.

I saw her gearing up for another strike and snatched her wrist. Spinning us around, I pushed her back up against the door.

"Stop looking at me like that." She struggled in my hold and wouldn't look me in the eyes.

"Like what, Tink?"

"Please, this is me begging you to go away," she said, her voice breaking.

"No, tell me what you see." I felt the anger shifting to another level like a geyser getting ready to blow. Her body trembled, but it wasn't from fear. It was the same powerful connection I'd always felt between us.

"Stop looking at me like I actually mean something to you." Her eyes were as angry as I'd ever seen them and filled with tears.

All the layers of hurt, love, and memories piled onto me all at once, and my body mirrored hers, trembling while I held her. She pushed against my hold and growled, but that only made me want to lay her on the bed.

There was a good chance she was gonna bite my tongue off, but I didn't care and dropped my lips to hers before she could spew any more hate.

Her lips were firm and wouldn't grant me access. So I nipped at her bottom lip and sucked it into my mouth as I held her hands above her head. Even as she tried to twist her head away, I followed the movement.

"Please, Kai..." She got out, and I took advantage and deepened the kiss. The building energy in the room soared off the charts as she opened her mouth further to let me kiss her properly. It was our first real kiss since that fateful night years ago. Her lips were warm and so soft, but her mouth was hot, and I could taste the lingering sweetness of the soda. She felt perfect and exactly like I dreamed she would.

She stopped trying to fight me, and I let go of her hands to grip her hips. She was mine. She was made for me in every way, including our broken and damaged souls, which were twined together.

"I don't hate you, Tink. I wanted to so badly, but I don't hate you," I mumbled against her lips and then attacked her mouth again as she touched my chest. I felt each of her fingers as they fanned out like she was tentative to touch me, but couldn't resist.

She moaned as I explored what I'd wanted for so long. Years I'd craved and wanted her just like this, and then I ended up behind bars. I spent more years thinking she wanted to hurt me. In all that time, not once did I think she'd actually suffered. Why hadn't I thought more about it? I'd assumed so much because it was the easy answer. I was no better than her. If I'd known someone had hurt her...I shuddered with the thought. I would've found and killed them before they had the chance to lock me up, and I never would've signed off on a plea deal.

The raw pain of what she'd experienced was in her eyes last night. I saw the same trauma I shared shining back at me. She was willing to die at my hand to end the agony we'd caused one another. I loved her more now than I ever thought was humanly possible. I was obsessed. There was no other way to put it. Raine Eastman had always been the one consuming thought in my mind, but now she'd taken over my soul.

Cupping her ass, I pulled her up my body. She didn't fight me, wrapping her legs around my waist and her arms around my neck as she kissed me harder. "I'm sorry, Tink." I shook my head. "I...I don't know how to make up for what I did, but I want you. I've always wanted you."

"I don't know, Kai," she said.

"Yes, you do. You've always been mine. From the first day, we met, I knew we were meant to be together."

Breaking the kiss, she pulled back, and even though her eyes were still hostile, the edge was gone. Raine's eyes searched my face, and I wished I knew what she was looking for.

"You have a terrible way of showing it," she finally said, and I smiled. It felt like it had been forever since I smiled for real. "But, I'm not yours, at least not only yours," she said, and my smile turned into a snarl. "Be pissed all you want, but I had a life before you decided to blow it up."

"You can't mean those two assholes?" Her eyebrow lifted as she quietly sassed me. I let go of her ass, and her feet dropped to the floor. "You're serious? You want them?"

I backed away from her, needing to put space between us. I couldn't think straight when she was close to me. Reaching the furthest part of the small room, I turned to face Raine.

"But you said you loved me." I knew I sounded pitiful and was happy that none of the guys at the clubhouse could hear me. "In the letter you left for Avro. You said you still love me."

Her eyes got big and then narrowed as she crossed her arms. "How exactly did you end up reading a letter I left for Avro? You better not have fucking hurt him."

I rolled my eyes. "No, of course not, and I didn't raid your house if that's what you're thinking. The guy came to me and ordered me to find you. It was really stupid of him. But pretty brave. I'll give him that." Raine rubbed her face and sighed.

"Of course he did," Raine mumbled.

"How can you say you love me but want them and whatever you had going on?" I reached for my smokes and remembered I had already smoked the last one. Fuck, of all the times to be out.

"First, I know it's a stretch for you, but don't be an asshole,"

Raine sniped, making my lip curl up. Her face went bright red as she continued to fume. "And don't try to tell me that you haven't had more than one girl at a time before, or am I reading you all wrong?"

I swallowed hard as images of group sex with sweetbutts flashed behind my eyes. I stuffed my hands into my pockets.

"That's different."

"Oh, I see," Raine growled, and fuck, my body flushed hot. I could see the spark of anger and jealousy in her eyes, and my heart pounded hard for it. Why did she have this power over me? "Then please, by all means, explain to me how it's different. I'm really fucking curious to hear that answer."

I felt a trap coming. Licking my lips, I tried to find a way to back out of the pile of shit I was stepping in. Hopefully, there wasn't one of Wilder's landmines under it. "Cause...."

"Cause? Wow, I'm impressed with the overwhelming argument you pose. Good thing you didn't decide to be a lawyer. Your clients would be fucked."

My eyes narrowed into a glare, my neck cracking as I tilted it to the side. All I wanted to do was stomp across the room and force Raine to see I was the only one she wanted. Fuck those other two guys.

"Gimmie a second. I'm thinking how to word this."

"Well, you're doing a bang-up job so far. Go on. I'm waiting with bated breath."

"Damn, you still have that fucking sass. You make me want to fuck you stupid, Tink. Watch that mouth. I'm hanging by a thread here," I growled out, but it only made her angrier as her hands balled into fists. I didn't know what the fuck had happened on her trip to Atlanta, but this was not the same Raine that left Miami. Maybe it was the air, but I had a feeling it had to do with me pushing her over her breaking point last night. No longer fearing death changed a person.

Before I did exactly what I wanted to do and didn't get anything solved, I tried again.

"Fuck. It's just different, okay. The sweetbutts or any other girl don't mean anything to me. I fuck them and move on to the next. Doesn't matter if it's one or ten because there is nothing between us. They are there to be used, and that's what I do. Fuck 'em, use 'em, leave 'em, done."

It was like the air was sucked out of the room as the glacial glare she gave me somehow turned more lethal. She looked so badass, and all I could think about was ripping her clothes off. My head was fucked.

Raine whipped the door open, and I stared out at the poorly lit parking lot. The scent of stale air, loneliness, and regret wafted in at me. If I stepped through that door, that was it. I knew in my heart that as surely as the door would close behind me, so would the opportunity to make this right. I couldn't let that happen.

A mix of panic and rage burned in my gut. I didn't even know who the rage was pointed toward anymore, which added to the internal confusion. The only thing I was clear on was that I couldn't step one foot outside that door if I wanted Raine.

"You said you love him. How can you say you love him and me too? I don't get it. At least tell me that. Tell me why these other guys are so important when we can finally be together. As fucked up of a situation as it is, Tink, I want you. I've never stopped wanting you," I blurted out.

She slowly closed the door, and my heart rate slowed, but when she turned her head and looked at me, the pain in her eyes gripped my throat as surely as a hand would.

"You don't get it, do you," Raine asked, her voice soft. She let go of the handle, and I swallowed hard as she stepped toward me. "I've always loved you."

She gripped her shirt in her hand over her heart, and I swear I felt it as if she was squeezing the pounding organ in my chest. "Even when I thought you hurt me in the worst way possible, I never stopped loving you and mourning you like you'd died because, to me, that's what it was like. I'd stare at your photo and cry for hours, wondering why you did what you did, and I hated myself. I loathed every part of my being because I couldn't stop loving the guy who looked at me like I meant something. You made me feel like I was worth seeing, and then...." She snapped her fingers. "Just like that, you tore me down."

I opened my mouth, and she held up her hands to stop me. "I know it wasn't you, but I didn't know that then. I'd already lost so much, and at that moment, I became nothing." She walked closer, and my chest constricted a little more with each step. "I didn't want to live, I didn't want to wake up in the morning, and every day I fought to fix this." She tapped the side of her head. "You may have been locked away in a concrete cell, but my mind became my prison, and there was no escaping the torture it would inflict again and again."

Tears trailed down her cheeks, and for the first time since I found her, I truly understood that we'd both been caged that night. Our souls were tossed into a different hell of darkness, but both were just as lethal. The emotion was so raw on her face that when she reached me and smacked her hands off my chest, it felt like she'd hit me with a car and drove the air from my chest.

"Do I feel bad that you went to prison for something you didn't do...fuck, of course I do. I didn't think I could hate myself anymore, but I do. I sent the one person I loved and trusted in this world to prison, I...."

Her hands gripped my leather jacket into her fists. "You joke about having however many people a night and had the nerve to ask me where my pussy had been." I licked my lips as my throat went dry. "No one Kai. No one until Avro touched me. Eleven years I've had no contact with another living soul. Not to shake their hand or give them a hug."

The leather complained as her fists tightened. "It took Avro years to earn my trust. He was my only friend. I have no family. They were all dead, and the Collinses sent me packing the day I was released from the hospital. There were no nameless faces and wild orgies, no sweetbutts, as you put it, to satisfy bodily desires." She jerked on my jacket, and my stomach gripped in a tight ball. "I was terrified. Do you get that? My only experience was extreme pain that landed me with two operations and no idea if I can ever have children, and all that time, I thought you did that to me. I still see your face in my mind sneering at me. I couldn't see their faces, but it didn't matter. My mind conjured you. How you'd hold me down...."

Raine let go of my jacket and walked to the dresser. Her shoulders shook as she covered her mouth and cried, but I didn't move. I wasn't even sure what to say at this point. We had so much pain between us. So many memories and misinformation.

She choked back a sob and turned to face me again. I hated to see that pain. I thought for so long that it was all I wanted. I loved her pissed off and fired up, but this...I didn't want this anymore between us. It was toxic and destroying us both.

"So, to answer your question. Yes, after eleven years of knowing nothing but fear and loneliness, I finally let someone in. Someone that is wholly good and saw the scars on my soul and my damaged heart and didn't run. For the first time, I could breathe again because I realized I could trust. It was freeing to finally not see everyone as a hooded figure looking to hurt me, and I took it."

Her face fell. And I wanted to wrap her up in my arms. I had no idea that she'd lived like that. It made my rage toward Dave, Frank, and the now rotting-in-hell Jim burn that much brighter. I wanted to tell her about Jim and that I planned on making sure they all paid. But now I didn't know if it was worse for her to know that two different people she trusted did this. I didn't know, but I wasn't willing to set any progress back further.

"And then you come along, and just like that, you crush me and the sliver of happiness I was building," she growled and stomped the few steps to me and pushed my chest hard enough that I stumbled back and hit the wall. "You almost killed me, Kai, and then you almost killed them after you said you never wanted to see me again. I'm the problem? What the fuck?" She growled at me.

"And now what? You hunt me down. Say you want me and that I'm yours. Like you own me." She shook her head. "What's next? You planning on giving me a cut that says your property? Then the cycle will be complete. You can officially own my body and do whatever you want with whoever you want. That is how it works in an MC, right?" She shrugged, and I still couldn't figure out what to say.

"The old ladies...." Raine lifted her hands and made finger quotes in the air. "First off, a sign of respect or not, if you ever call me an old lady, I will rip your fucking balls right off your body."

I licked my lips, torn between impressed, a little terrified by the look in her eyes, and turned on so bad that I thought I might fucking cum in my jeans.

"But that is what they do, isn't it? They have to shut up and support their man, right? Let their man fuck who they choose and never cause drama, all for the privilege of sitting on the back of your fancy bike." Raine laughed and backed away. "No, I don't want to live like that. I've felt like I had a sign saying I was owned by you for far too long. You already took my body, have my heart and mind—hell, you fucking have my soul. I have nothing left to give you, Kai, and I don't want to be controlled by anyone, including my fear, any longer. I'm not that same girl you knew." She looked down at the ground and then squared her shoulders as she looked up and her eyes found mine. "That girl died." Turning around, Raine walked to the door. "I'm going to ask you again to please, just leave."

"It's not always like that." Her brow furrowed in confusion. "With the old...the wives, I mean. It's different for everyone. A lot of the guys are loyal to their other half." Her hand gripped the door handle but didn't turn it. "I'm here, Tink. I came because I want you, so tell me what you want?" I lifted my shoulders in a shrug. "I will listen."

Raine crossed her arms and leaned against the door as she stared at me.

"Just say what you want, Tink."

She smiled, but it was a sad smile as she wiped at the dampness on her cheeks. "I want to be selfish for the first time ever. I want it all. Call me greedy, or a slut, or whatever you want, but I want all of you, and no, that doesn't mean you can fuck whoever you want." It was my turn to cross my arms.

"You want all three of us exclusive to you and at the same time?" Rubbing my eyes, I ground my teeth together.

The thought of the bartender or rock star touching her had all the dark and dangerous parts of me coming to life. I needed to try and stay calm, or I would tear apart this room and then drive back to Miami and shoot those two fuckers in the head.

I knew she'd run, and I could let her. It would solve the issue. If she wasn't around, then maybe I could finally move on too. The small voice in the back of my head laughed hysterically. I'd been locked up for ten years and hadn't seen her a single day, and I wanted her more now than the day I was put away. It didn't seem like her leaving town would stop me from wanting her.

"I don't mean we all have to have sex together," she said, and a low growl rumbled in my chest. "I mean, if you all could and not kill each other, I'd be open to the idea," she said, and my eyes snapped up to hers. "That would be really fucking hot, actually," she mumbled and tapped her chin.

The murderous side of me wanted to rip them apart. Even

though, by all accounts, it sounded like they were decent enough, I just couldn't wrap the possessive part of myself around the idea.

"Not fucking likely. Just thinking about them touching you makes me want to cut off their cocks and shove them down their throats."

"Well, you asked what I wanted. There it is. I want all of you." Raine laughed. "I don't want to deny myself anymore."

I looked up to the ceiling like, by some fucking miracle, I was going to find the answers written there. "Do you love them?"

"Avro, yes, but Jace is still new to me. They have been together along time so Jace is part of the package with Avro."

I shook my head, trying to wrap my head around this disaster. "So, you're in love with Avro, but not Jace, but Jace and Avro are together, so to have Avro, you need to fuck Jace?"

Raine's eyes turned murderous again as she glared at me from across the room. "Don't be an asshole Kai. You're the one that chased me down. You're the one standing in my motel room, and you're the one that just asked me what I want. You don't see me standing at your door, do you?"

I leaned against the wall and crossed my arms. "Fine, just explain to me why it is that I can't have you, Avro have Jace, and we go our merry fucking separate ways?"

"Because what I wanted for my life before you stormed back in and started pounding your chest was vastly different than becoming your leather-wearing, bike-riding side hustle."

"Fuck Raine! I don't want anyone else. I don't ever want to fuck anyone else again." I yelled, my body shaking as I tried to contain the rage that wanted blood. "You've been tattooed on my heart from the day we met." The admission had me sucking in a deep breath. She was the only good thing I'd ever had. Even when shit went sideways, it was still her face I dreamed about. It had always been her.

I ran my hand through my hair. "Now you're asking me to be

okay with you sleeping with other guys, while we're together? I've never been okay with other guys around you. Fuck you must remember that. Tink, you're it for me."

She looked down at her boots, her arms crossed. The minutes ticked on, and I glanced at the clock. Sweat broke out on my brow when the number clicked over to exactly five minutes. It was the only thing moving in the room.

"I can't explain this any better to you, Kai," she finally said, her voice a whisper, yet I heard every word. "I have actively tried to push you from my mind and heart since the night I was attacked." Her eyes slowly lifted, and I knew she wouldn't give in. I felt the anger and panic building.

The one person, the one thing I wanted more than anything else in this world, was her. A family with her, and I couldn't find a way to make her see that we belonged together. I couldn't force her emotions away, couldn't buy them away, and couldn't scare them away. Raine would rather accept being alone or dead. I saw it behind the shimmering blue of her eyes. My heart pounded frantically, trying to figure out how to make this work and make her see things my way.

I'd always been able to sway Raine, always had the power to make her smile and talk her into whatever I wanted. I slumped against the wall as her words sank into the deep recesses of my brain. I wasn't the boy she swooned over anymore, who she dreamed of and would sneak into his room. I was who she saw when she was attacked, the embodiment of her worst nightmare.

I was the creature that lived under the bed, that made her run screaming or die trying. My body shook with the harsh reality of what Irene, Dave, and his friends had cost us. They stole my happy ending. Our happy ending.

"Kai, this is only going to work one of two ways. You can leave, and I will continue on my way, and none of you get me. Because I know you couldn't handle seeing me around town or know where I'm living with them without you having another meltdown like last night. I won't put them or myself at risk or even risk the possibility of you going back to jail."

"And the second option?"

"You can concede that I want Avro in my life, and with that comes Jace. This is your choice, but there is no third option. The one thing I'm not doing, is going half-measure on what I want. You asked. There is your answer."

"And I assume killing them is off the table?" I snickered as Raine gave me her best 'Are you fucking stupid look.' It was the same look she gave me when we were kids, and I'd say something to get under her skin. It made me smile.

"I don't know if I can do that and not kill them." I lifted my hands and let them drop. "I'm being honest. I don't want anyone else, so being faithful to you isn't the issue." I left out that I'd tried to get a blowjob, but my dick had been annoyingly uncooperative since I found her. "But adding two guys...Tink, you're like the blood in my veins. Sharing that, sharing you is...." I held my hands out as I thought of the right word.

"The reality is, Kai, that my heart shattered into a million little pieces the day those men took my innocence. I've spent the rest of my time slowly gluing the little shards back together. It finally started to beat again, but I'm changed," she said, her voice firm in her conviction.

Raine gripped the bottom of the hoodie she was wearing, and my throat stopped functioning as she peeled it off, leaving her in a black lace bra. "I'm no longer that innocent teen. I'm a woman exploring what I want and who I want, and I want it all. Please don't try to deny me that or control my heart with an iron fist and fear."

She tossed the sweatshirt aside, and my eyes roamed over her body. The bruises I'd left were green and yellow, and I hated seeing them. It was a visual confirmation that I'd tried to kill her and almost succeeded. That I had done what she feared the most. I really was the monster.

"Am I not worth trying for," Raine asked, her voice soft and silky. The sound made me shudder. She bent over and pulled the laces on her shitkickers, kicking them off along with her socks. Her toenails were painted black with one pink one, which made me smile—a tiny bit of the girl she had been wrapped up in this badass woman.

My cock strained under my pants as she bit her lip. I groaned as her hands unbuttoned the top of her jeans, and I heard each link of the zipper as she pulled it down.

"Am I not worth the effort?" Her voice sounded somehow both sad and alluring. "For us to still find a happy ending to the pain we were put through?"

"You're not playing fair," I said as her hands worked at pushing down the tight denim, her hips wiggling from side to side and making me groan as she stepped out of them. She was left in a mismatched set of lacey underwear, and I smirked at the look. The black bra and pink bottoms just did something to me. I was practically panting like a dog by the time she was within arms reach. All my muscles strained to remain still.

"Fuck me, Tink. It has nothing to do with your worth, I...I'm just not great at sharing anything, and you are the most prized piece of my heart. To share that...." Her cheeks pinked with a blush, but she didn't retract her request.

Her delicate hand reached out, and I watched it, knowing that she would seal my fate like her touch was magical, and yet I couldn't move away. I closed my eyes as her hand made contact with my chest and slid up to wrap around my neck. Her other devious hand slipped under the leather jacket and gripped my shoulder. I could feel the pulse pounding in my neck as I tried to draw a deep breath.

"You can have me, Kai," she whispered like a siren, and I shuddered. "You can have me whenever you want. However, you want." She stepped in close until her body was brushing against mine. Even through the T-shirt, I could feel the warmth of her body and wanted to blanket myself with her touch. "I'll try whatever you want and wherever you want. You want to put me on display, if you want to fuck me on your bike, then I'll do it, but Avro and Jace are my only condition. I'm worth the effort, or I'm not."

I stared down into her blue eyes that had always drawn me in like a whirlpool and threatened to whisk me away right now. She had power over me. Something I couldn't understand and never explained to anyone, but it had always been there. If she wanted the stars plucked from the sky, I would've found a way to make them hers. If she wanted me to kill someone, I wouldn't stop to ask why. She was my it, my forever, my all.

My hands had a mind of their own, and I sighed as I gripped her waist, finally touching her soft skin. She took that as a sign and pressed her body up tight against mine, and whatever brain power I had left to argue flew out of my head. Slipping my fingers under the lace, I gripped her ass, and a deep growl rumbled from my chest as her muscles flexed under my touch.

"You still love me," I asked.

"Yes, I always have. Not a day has gone by that I have stopped loving you," she said as her nails softly scraped along my neck, making me shiver. "And I will always love you. No matter what you decide, a piece of my heart will always be yours. No matter what has transpired between us, I would never change that."

"And this is the only way?" I licked my lips as she raised up on her toes and laid a soft kiss on the side of my mouth.

She nodded, and as her body pressed into mine, she could've asked me to do anything, and I would've agreed.

"Fuck me," I growled and dropped my head to her neck, breathing in her scent. She smelt sweet, like flowers and candy. I wanted to devour her. I opened my mouth again and knew that I'd at least try. If that meant I needed to do this, then that was what I'd do. Her leaving and never seeing her again wasn't an option.

Because fuck me, Raine was mine, and I needed her like I needed the fucking air to breathe.

Chapter 5

R^{aine}

"Fine, I'll fucking try, but I can't make any promises that this is going to work." Kai's voice was hoarse and gravelly, like he'd drunk an entire bottle of whiskey and swallowed a sandpaper chaser.

I could taste the remnants of a cigarette and spearmint as he gave in and dropped his head to kiss me. I had no idea what I was thinking. Kai keeping his shit together and not killing Avro and Jace was laughable in my own head. But him not getting me at all was the only card I had if I wanted to have the life I hoped to build. If I didn't lay down my terms before I gave over my heart and let him have my body, the battle would be lost.

Kai said he loved me, and I was his, but I wasn't sure Kai knew how to love. Maybe at one time, but now...I wasn't so sure. We were so volatile that it felt like the earth beneath our feet could shift and swallow us whole. It was exciting, but it could also end with all of us dragged under.

Even if Kai held it together, it still might all blow up in my face. Avro would agree, but Jace accepting this was almost as laughable as Kai. I was walking a tightrope with no safety net, and each step made me feel less sure about my decisions. All I knew was that I wouldn't be forced to choose one over the other, not by Jace or Kai.

"Fuck," Kai swore against my lips, allowing me a moment to catch my breath.

I thought Jace's kisses were demanding, but I wasn't prepared for the ravenous and overwhelming kiss from Kai. He broke contact only long enough to peel off his leather jacket and toss it on the chair in the corner before he attacked my mouth again. His hands gripped my ass tighter, pulling me hard into him as he bowed my body back with his ferocity. Heat bloomed like my body was being licked by flames as it spread like wildfire.

"Fuck Tink, what are you doing to me," Kai asked, leaving me lightheaded and with swollen lips. He released his hold, his fingertips trailing gently over my skin, and everywhere he touched, goosebumps rose. My eyes fluttered open, and I couldn't look away from his blue eyes, so intense that they stole the air from my chest.

I gasped in a breath, my heart racing as hard as it ever had as he ran his thumb over the marks he'd made on my neck. They were fading now, but traces of his fingerprints were still visible without makeup. I didn't move as he stared at the imprints. His face was dark and so unreadable that he could've been thinking about fucking me hard or questioning why he hadn't already killed me.

"I was planning on killing you, you know," he said, and I shivered, my feet instinctively taking a step back, but his hands locked onto my shoulders, and I was once more trapped. "I meant that night. I'd dreamed about it for so long, but I couldn't."

His voice sounded wistful, like he craved to go back in time and finish what he had started. I swallowed the massive lump in my throat as my pulse pounded harder through my veins.

"Do you regret not killing me," I asked, and his eyes snapped from my neck to my eyes.

"No." Nothing sweet followed the single word, yet it held as much weight as if he'd gotten down and begged my forgiveness. "Stand on the bed," Kai ordered.

I shivered from the chill as I stepped away from the warmth of his body. Doing as he asked, I turned to face him just as he laid his cut down on the dresser. Unlike the jacket, he placed it as carefully as one would a child. I didn't know why his doing that touched me, but it did, and I felt tears prick the back of my eyes.

Under the gruff 'I don't care' exterior was the teen I knew, who wanted a family and to be accepted. It didn't surprise me that Kai had ended up in an MC. The little I knew of clubs was that even when at odds, they had one another's backs, and deep down, I knew that was something he always craved.

I was that person for him at one time, the person he could turn to and trust, and I destroyed that. I glanced at the club's name on the cut and then at Kai as he pulled his T-shirt off over his head.

"The name is fitting," I said. "We are definitely lost souls."

"Were," Kai said and kicked off his boots. He stomped toward me. Anyone else would think he was angry, but it was the desire in his eyes that drove him, not anger. Everything he did was with purpose and demand. "We were lost, but not anymore."

My lip curled up. "Speak for yourself. I don't know if I will ever be found," I said, letting him in on the fear that always gripped my heart.

His features darkened, and I sucked in a startled breath as he grabbed my waist and pulled me in close to him. "You are now. I see you, Tink. I've always seen you."

I stared into his eyes, tears threatening to spill once more, shuddering as his tongue flicked out and traced the first of six thin white scars. By the time he'd traced them all—never taking his eyes from mine—I was a mess and could barely see him through the blurriness.

"I will kill them for what they did to you. For what they did to us." His hands tightened on my waist. "That's a promise."

I knew he would and should be terrified, but I felt safer at that moment than I had at any time in my life. Unable to form words, I simply nodded.

Kai nipped at the lacey material of my underwear, and the feel of his teeth made me whimper in his hold. Drawing a line with his tongue down, he stopped on my clit, swirling and sucking until the material molded to my skin, making me moan.

"Fuck I want to devour you," Kai said, and my head fell back as he attacked my pussy with the same voraciousness as he had my mouth.

"Oh god, Kai,"

He yanked the lace aside and drove his tongue into me. My hands gripped his hair, pulling him harder into my body. The lingering doubts about whether this was a good idea were firmly pushed aside with each passing second.

"Cum in my mouth," he growled. I shook in his hold as he pushed my body toward the edge of a cliff with a drop that would have my body soaring. "Look at this fucking sexy pussy." His finger slipped inside of me as he continued his dirty talk. "I'm going to fuck this sweet hole all night, and you're going to scream my name until you can't scream at all."

"Oh god, yes," I moaned as another finger was added. My legs trembled and wanted to give out as he resumed sucking on my sensitive clit, but Kai held my hips up and pressed his face harder into pussy, making me yell.

"Don't stop. Please don't stop," I begged and pinched my nipples. The rough material of the bra only enhanced the sensation.

"Yeah, that's it, cum for me, cum all over my tongue Tink." Hearing my nickname on his lips seemed so dirty, and I loved it. All the time that had passed between us, all the hurt we'd caused one another disappeared, even if only for this moment in this small motel room with the squeaky bed.

"Oh fuck, Kai," My eyes closed as the climax hit and rocked my body. He made a sound that was more animal than man, and it vibrated through me. My fingers dug into his hair and held him tighter as I rode out the sensations.

"Fuck you taste like sweet sin," Kai said as the shuddering slowed. I couldn't stop the cheeky smile that pulled up the corner of my mouth as he licked the inside of my thighs. I was sure this was a kink, and if it was, I was into it. The way he slowly dragged his tongue up my leg like I was his meal with that feral look in his eyes was everything.

Hooking his fingers in the waistband of my thong, he pulled the little piece of material down.

"Turn around and get on your knees," Kai ordered as I stepped out of the underwear. Turning my back on Kai made me shiver. It was like turning your back on Satan himself, and yet I slowly turned around and lowered myself to my knees. He unclipped my bra, and I'd only gotten the material off my one arm when his hands slid around my body and cupped my breasts.

"Fuck, you're going to kill me with need. You're my poison and the antidote all wrapped into one. I can't not have you, and yet...." His teeth nipped almost painfully at my neck as his fingers tweaked my nipples until I cried out. "The idea of another cock but mine inside of you makes me see only red. Do you know what you're asking of me?" He growled into the side of my neck.

"To tame the devil," I whispered and panted out a breath as he pulled me back against his chest. He was so hot that it felt like maybe he had stepped out from hell itself, and yet all I wanted was for him to do what he wanted with my body.

He sucked my earlobe into his mouth, and even that was done as if he was going to bite it off. I realized then that the line between the man I knew and the man he'd become in prison was as narrow as the tightrope I felt like I'd been walking.

"That's right, Tink, and some things just can't be tamed," he said and wrapped his hand around my throat. The pressure of his fingers made my pulse spike, and a tremor of fear spread throughout my body.

"So, I want to make myself clear." Stepping back, he bowed my body with his movements until I had to put my hands on my ankles to keep from falling off the bed. I was left staring up at him, my chest heavy and pressing my sensitive nipples higher into the air. Kai's blue eyes seemed so dark as he leaned over me, his hand still around my throat as his lips hovered over mine. "I said that I will try, and I'm a man of my word, but I'm going to take all my aggression and anger about it out on your body. You will take the punishment for making me concede to this, do you understand?"

I knew that there was something different about me. Whether from birth or due to my trauma, no matter the reason, Kai's words only made me want him more. My pussy was wet and already aching, and the fear racing through my body heightened my senses. It all screamed the same thing. I wanted Kai, and if that meant he did things that others would call me crazy for allowing, I didn't care. I'd welcome every depraved thing he could think of.

"I understand," I whispered through his tight grip. My arms were starting to shake, and still, I held the position until a wicked smile curled up the corner of his mouth. It was the kind of look that told me just how much trouble I was in.

"I don't think you do, Tink, but you will. You were right. The devil does live under my skin, and you're the angel he wants to consume."

I expected his kiss to be as demanding as the first time, but he surprised me by kissing me sweetly as his fingers tortured my nipples. He rolled them around between his fingers and alternated which nipple he teased until I was trying to attack his mouth.

"What's the matter, Tink," he asked, breaking the kiss and running a soft line from my lips to my ear. "You seem pent up." I glared at him. He damn well knew exactly what he was doing to me. "Are you wanting my cock?" His voice was a whisper, yet I could still hear the taunting tone underneath.

I was tempted to be a smart ass but decided I should wait to push that button. "Yes," I said and nipped at his lip as he brought it close to my mouth again.

"Sit up," he ordered and let go of my neck. My muscles complained as I pulled myself up to kneel once more. "Now get on all fours."

My hands touched the bed, and I cried out and jumped forward as his hand cracked down on my ass. Kai gripped my hips and yanked me back. I could still feel the sting of his palm and wanted to jump away again as I looked over my shoulder and saw his hand raised again.

I closed my eyes and tensed for what I knew was coming, but I couldn't stop my body's reaction and leaped forward on the bed as that sharp slap hit my bare ass.

"Fuck," I yelled. "That fucking hurts." I rolled over to glare at Kai, welcoming the cool feel of the comforter against my heated cheeks.

"Oh, there she is," Kai said, a smile spreading across his face. "I was wondering when the angry sass would show up. That didn't take long." My eyes narrowed further as he undid the wide leather belt on his jeans and slowly pulled it out of the loops.

"Don't you dare," I said, backing up on the bed.

"Oh, I dare. Have I told you how much I love it when you look at me like that? How hard it makes me," he said, his voice strained, and my eyes immediately went to the large bulge that had formed behind his zipper. I licked my lips and squeezed my thighs tighter as the aching intensified. "Like what you see, Tink?"

I jerked my eyes away from his jeans and the outline of his cock, up to his face.

"I told you that you would be punished, and I meant it. So if this is really what you want and those two guys mean that much to you, you'll crawl over here and lay on my lap while I punish you."

I snarled at him, which only made him smirk. "It's your choice, Tink." He folded over the leather and smacked it off the palm of his hand, the sound loud in the otherwise quiet room. "I mean, if you can't handle this...." He lifted his shoulder. The look on his face made my blood boil but my pussy wetter. It was a potent combination.

"Oh, I can take it," I said, rolling over to crawl to him.

"Are you sure? Cause I'm going to make your ass good and sore," Kai said, his eyes glittering with dark desire.

"I'm fucking sure," I bit out, wanting to punch him and ride his body to the ground at the same time.

He sat down on the edge of the bed and patted his lap. "Then lay on my lap facing that way." He pointed toward the front of the bed, and I crawled around his body, making sure my eyes said 'asshole' as I positioned myself over his lap. I could feel his cock pressing into me through the rough denim and wanted to feel him against my skin, but I figured this was all by design. He wanted to torture me for asking him to bend his own possessive code. A sliver of doubt tried to worm into my brain, but I stomped on it. I could do this. I wanted to do this, and he could go fuck himself if he thought that I was going to back down.

"Yeah, that's it. Keep looking at me just like that," he said, laying the cool leather against my still-warm ass. His finger stroked between my thighs, and I shuddered as he rubbed my pussy lips. "Look at how wet you are, Tink. You're going to leave a big wet spot on my leg by the time I'm through with you."

He wiggled his finger, and I bit my lower lip to keep from moaning. "You're wrong. I don't like it," I said, and he laughed. The movement jostled me on his lap and pressed his stiff cock into the softness of my belly.

"Oh, you're a sexy little liar." He dipped his finger inside my pussy, and my body writhed with the feel. "I bet you won't just cum all over me. You'll be gushing and embarrassed as your cum soaks my jeans." I turned my head to glare at him. "Just like the other night when you coated my cock."

I remembered clearly how hard I came for him despite the fear racing through my body and how the sheets were soaked from the mess I had made. As if to prove his point, his finger fucked me a little faster, and I clenched my teeth against the pleasurable sensation thrumming through my body.

"That's it, Tink, try and fight it. It just makes you all the sweeter to break."

I opened my mouth to swear at him when the leather smacked down on my ass. The sound was almost worse than the bite, but I cried out nonetheless. I jerked on his lap, and he groaned and shuddered under me.

"I hope you cum in your fucking jeans," I growled at him, and he laughed again as the leather found a fresh spot to hit.

"Not likely, Tink," he said.

"Ah," I yelled out and couldn't stop the moan that followed. He fucked me with his finger and only stopped to play with my clit. I could feel just how wet I was and hated that he was right. My body rocked against his hand, wanting more and purposely rubbing against the cock under me.

"That's it, fuck my hand," Kai said, and his voice was strained.

Two more hard cracks of his belt hit my ass, and tears stung my eyes with the sharp bite. I yelled out, my hands gripping the comforter. This time as his finger slipped inside me, my legs opened, giving him better access. "Such a naughty girl liking to be punished."

Pushing back hard into his hand, I didn't even care who was winning the battle of wills. All I wanted was to cum. I could feel it building and was so close to the edge that the walls could have crumbled down around us, and I wouldn't have cared.

"Fuck, you're so hot." I picked a steady rhythm and rocked my hips down so my clit brushed his jeans with every little movement. "I can't wait to bury my cock into this wet pussy. Maybe I should stop this now and take what I want."

"No," I cried out, not wanting him to stop.

"You don't want me to stop," he asked and removed his finger to squeeze my ass. He pressed his fingers into the soft skin like he was massaging my tender cheeks.

"No, don't stop," I panted out, thrusting my ass up higher into the air to entice him to keep going.

"Whatever you say, Tink. Just remember I'm going to fuck you after this." I shuddered and moaned loud as his fingers pressed into me once again. "Oh, and talk dirty to me. I want to hear that sweet mouth of yours begging for it."

I looked at him, and as his eyes met mine, I knew he was serious. He'd leave me like this all night to prove his point. I licked my lips, and his eyes tracked the movement making me squirm.

"Well, Tink, I'm waiting."

"Yes, oh god, yes Kai, fuck," I said, giving in. "Yes, yes, fuck me with your fingers, make me cum."

"I love your dirty mouth. Say it again," he ordered, his fingers working faster and making my head spin.

"Make me cum. Make me cum all over you," I cried out and yelled his name as he shoved me over the edge, and the orgasm stormed through me. I could feel my body soaking his lap like he said I would, and I didn't care.

"Oh fuck, you're so fucking sexy. You almost made me cum in my jeans, Tink," Kai said as I collapsed onto his lap, panting hard. "I need to be in you. Now." Kai stood, and I was too relaxed to care that he took me with him and then laid me on my back in the center of the bed.

My head lulled to the side, and I smiled as I stared at the dark wet mark on his jeans that only accentuated the outline of his hard cock.

"Fuck me," Kai growled out as he undid his zipper, and his large cock sprang free from the confines of the denim. The head of his cock was shiny, and I didn't know if that was from me or his own precum, but I licked my lips, wanting a taste. "Sorry Tink, maybe later. Right now, I need in that pussy of yours."

Kai ripped his jeans off and tossed them across the room. "Get up," he ordered.

As I did, he grabbed the blankets from the foot of the bed, yanking on them like he was pissed off, and untucked them. He walked toward me, and the energy around us grew until it felt like electricity racing over my skin.

"Get in," he ordered, lifting the blankets so I could slip in. Confused as to why he'd bother. "I plan on fucking you until we pass out, but I'm going to stay buried inside of you where I belong, and every time I get hard, I'm going to fuck you all over again."

I shuddered as he answered the question in my mind and crawled between my legs. "Lift your hands over your head."

I lifted my hands and couldn't help jerking a little as he licked up my stomach to my nipple, stopping long enough to suck each one into a stiff peak and making me squirm from the overstimulation. As he settled between my legs, I could feel his cock pressing up against my opening.

Slipping a hand between our bodies, he lined up his cock, and I moaned as the thick head pressed into me. It didn't matter that I was soaking wet. He was thick enough that my body needed to adjust to his size, a luxury I wasn't given the first time we did this. I firmly slammed the door on that thought. If we were moving forward, I couldn't keep thinking about that night.

He sucked in a deep breath, pushed in a little further, and ran his hands along my arms until he could hold mine. This time as our lips met, it was with a tenderness I didn't know he was capable of until this moment. The kiss didn't command anything from me, and it didn't promise pain. Instead, the kiss spoke of deeper things, and my heart swelled as a tear fell from my eye.

"You're perfect," Kai whispered against my lips as he slid deeper into my body until he was fully inside me. "I plan on cumming in you all night. Are you on the pill?" I shook my head. There hadn't been the need until recently. "Good. If there is even a one percent chance that you can get pregnant, then I want the kid to be mine."

Tears clouded my eyes as he stared down at me, leaning in to kiss me again. I didn't think he could've said anything more endearing or that screamed how much he loved me. He began to move, but there was no urgency to his movements. It was like he was taking the time to enjoy what we'd missed all these years. We were quiet and let our bodies speak for us as he slowly picked up the pace. Our lips continued to touch, the kiss deepening as slowly as the way he was making love to me.

He'd said he loved me, but I didn't truly believe it until now. His eyes held all the emotions he'd been hiding underneath the rage. There was no anger or fury, and the walls that had been firmly in place were gone.

I wrapped my legs around his waist, and he sank deeper. He groaned as I moaned, but we both shuddered as he bottomed out. My heart, which had calmed from the intense orgasms, was once more pounding hard for him. I could feel the thump in his chest as easily as my own as he held me tighter.

"I've wanted this for so long," Kai said and broke the kiss to stare into my eyes. "I'd lay in my cell and dream of this moment, of what it would be like to be held by you. To no longer hate you. To go back in time and fix whatever I'd broken." Tears spilled over, blurring his image. "I'm sorry. I'm sorry I never gave it a single thought that you were actually attacked. That will haunt me for the rest of my life.

"I'm sorry too. I can never say sorry enough for not being stronger and listening to the voice that kept saying it couldn't be you. Maybe if I had...." My lower lip trembled as the complex emotions continued to rise. Kai dropped his head and stole the next apology from my mouth.

"I know," he said and laid his forehead against mine as his cock continued to slowly coax my body into reaching for a third orgasm. "I just wanted you to know that nothing I could ever have imagined compares to you. I love you, Raine, I always have."

My heart swelled and felt like it would burst right out of my chest. "I want to hold you," I said. There was no hesitation as Kai let go of my hands, and I wrapped my arms around his neck. He couldn't be close enough, and I held onto him like he would disappear as our breathing increased.

"Fuck, I can't hold back any longer," Kai said, breaking the kiss and burying his head into the crook of my neck. "Cum for me," he whispered in my ear, sending a shiver down my spine. "Fuck, you drive me crazy," he said and thrust into me harder with each word. His teeth nipped at the sensitive skin on my neck, and I turned my head to give him better access.

"Yes, Kai. Right there, please keep going," I begged as I reached the top and felt close to tumbling over the other side.

"You like it like that," he asked as he thrust into me hard.

"Yes. Don't stop, oh god Kai, I'm so close."

"Fuck." Kai reared up onto his arms, and all his muscles strained as he pounded into me hard, making the bed bang against the wall. "Cum for me, Tink, right now," he growled as he closed his eyes, his face tense as he tried to hold off for me.

"I'm. All. Most...ahh. Yes, Kai, I'm cumming," I screamed, my body arching off the bed as the most powerful orgasm gripped me in its hold. My nails dug into Kai's shoulders, and his rhythm picked up to a furious pace. I was still riding the high of my climax when Kai roared. His face contorted as he came. I could feel him filling me with each thrust. "Fuck me, Tink."

Kai collapsed on my body, both of us damp with sweat and panting to catch our breath.

"I love you," I whispered into his ear, and his arms tightened around me. I had to find a way to make this work because I never wanted to let him go again.

FOURTEEN HOURS EARLIER

A vro

Although I never wanted to take up stalking as a career, I had to admit I was pretty fucking good at it. Racing home, I grabbed my baby. I only took her out for special occasions. The fancy Mustang was my pride and joy, but only Jace knew I had it. I was going to show Camille off to Raine when the moment was right to introduce them, but Camille was the jealous type, so these things had to be handled delicately.

The only issue with a sexy ass muscle car was that it drew a shit load more attention than the sedan I normally drove.

I doubted Raine would head deeper into Florida. If I were going to run, I would find the furthest point I could get to and call that home, and since we were almost always on the same wavelength, I chose that as the most likely option. She didn't drive or have a car, so that left planes, buses, or hitchhiking. The last option I eliminated immediately.

Raine might be braver, but there was no way she was walking down the side of an interstate with her thumb sticking out. So here I was, sitting in the dark shadows of the overpass and the closest interstate on-ramp to where Kai and the Lost Souls were located. If he was heading out of town as fast as possible, this is where he would come.

Hopefully he didn't decide to go to Walmart for socks or some shit. That would screw up my perfectly thought-out plan. Luckily, I didn't have to wait very long to find out. The loud rumbling of the Indian motorcycle roared passed my hiding spot and shook my car as it went. I'd positioned myself perfectly and caught a glimpse of him as he rode by with the Lost Souls emblem on his back. I could admit that the motorcycle held a certain appeal. The shiny black paint job and glittering chrome looked sick.

"How did I fucking know you'd find a way?" I tried tracking her with all my tricks, but anything I had was no good when she left her phone behind.

Revving the Mustang, I pulled out as the motorcycle started up the ramp. I followed and spotted the red taillight of the motorcycle gaining distance. I didn't bring Camille out just so Kai wouldn't recognize me. She had a whole fuck ton more get up and go.

The car roared like a lion as I shifted into fifth, making me smile wide. "I know, girl, it's been a while since I opened you up, but don't worry, we have a bit of ground to cover." I wanted to ask her if I could make out with Raine in here one day, but I didn't need her having a fit and stranding me on the side of the road. Camille could be a petty bitch.

We flew down the outside lane, and once I was a comfortable

distance away, I pulled in behind another car to follow. It was way too bright out to get close

I knew what Kai's plan would be. He didn't give a shit about Jace or me, so as soon as he found Raine, he'd try and convince her to only be with him. Kai didn't exactly strike me as the sharing type, but I had something that the other two guys involved didn't have, and that was faith.

I'd seen and felt Raine's heart, and I truly believed she wouldn't let Kai storm into her orbit and steal her away. She left for a reason, and it wasn't because she didn't love me. It also meant I needed to be smart. Kai would still try to talk her into only being with him, and if by some miracle she talked him into sharing, he would have demands. I needed them to work out whatever that was before I stormed the castle. If Jace were here, he'd say, 'Fuck that shit,' and bust the door down to get to Raine.

Of course, when we argued last night, his solution was to announce to the world that she was his girlfriend. He also suggested flying off and making some other place our home, like Venice, Paris, or maybe Ireland. It was great in theory if Raine wanted to do it, but I doubted it. That would only last so long if Kai saw Jace and Raine on the television. Then he would only become more obsessed and enraged. I knew my personality types, which was why I handled the talking and Jace did the stomping.

I smirked at the thought and picked up my phone, staring at the missed calls from Jace. I couldn't listen to these messages or answer them right now. If I did and told him what I was up to, he would have a meltdown of epic proportions. I loved him, but sometimes that overprotective side was a bit much.

We had been on the road for three hours when Kai pulled off for fuel. This was the tricky part. I should top off too, but the question was how to do it without being noticed. I pulled up to the furthest pump from Kai and lifted the hood on my sweatshirt to cover my face.

I looked over my shoulder and spotted the little sign on the pump, covering the credit card slot that said I had to pre-pay inside. Well, wasn't that just fucking perfect? I watched Kai go inside the store and head to the men's room. This was my opportunity. Jumping out, I made my way inside. The guy behind the counter gave me a once-over. I realized I must look like I was about to rob him with my hands stuffed inside the pocket.

"Hey, I need fifty on pump six, and I'll take these," I said, grabbing a handful of different candy packages. "Oh, and a bottle of water."

"Which one," the guy asked.

"Which one what?"

"Bottle of water?"

"I don't know your biggest, I guess." The guy looked at me like I had two heads. I tapped my foot, nervous about being found in here if Kai came back out. "I'll grab one," I said calmly while inside, I felt like screaming.

Marching over to the fridge, I opened the door and grabbed a large water. Of course, that was when I heard the men's room door's hinge squeaking open. Oh fuck, please let him have already paid, was all I could think as I walked back to the counter to pay. Of course, I didn't have that kind of luck and could hear his heavy boots on the cheap tile floor coming up behind me. The hair stood on the back of my neck, warning me of the danger.

It felt like the guy working the counter was moving as slowly as possible as he put my stuff in a bag and handed it over. I stepped sideways, pretending to look around, and then escaped to the bathroom and locked the door.

"Oh fuck. What am I doing," I asked my reflection. "I'm going to get myself killed." I gave myself a stern look. "No, I've got this."

Shaking off the building anxiety, I quickly took a piss and washed my hands, horrified that I would have to touch the handle.

The bike was still in the same spot when I got outside, but there was no sign of Kai. I was so busy staring at the black bike that I didn't notice him until I rounded the far pump and froze in my tracks. He was leaning up against my driver's side door, smoking a cigarette and looking as casual as could be, but as his eyes met mine, I knew he was contemplating murder.

"Hello, Avro," Kai said and took a drag off his smoke.

"You really shouldn't do that," I said, and he cocked an eyebrow at me. "Smoking at a gas station. There's a reason they have all those, do not smoke here, signs up."

Smirking, he took another pull and then dropped the cigarette to the ground stomping it out with his shitkicker. I was pretty sure he was going to try and shove the boot up my ass.

"Why are you following me?"

"Who says I was? Maybe I was just out for a nice drive in my sexy car."

Kai smiled. "She is a sexy car, I'll give you that, but the rest is bullshit. I spotted you an hour ago. So, I'll ask you again, why are you following me?"

Giving up the lie since I sucked at it anyway, I lifted my shoulder. "Well, I thought that would be obvious," I said, and Kai rolled his eyes and then rubbed at them as he swore something about a Wilder answer. I had no idea what that was supposed to mean.

"Look, if you know where Raine is, then I'm going to follow you. I know you don't like me, but I love her, so if that means you're going to shoot me for it, then so be it. I'm not letting her disappear."

Kai turned sideways and leaned against Camille, his eyes roaming over the shiny paint job. Internally I screamed don't scratch my baby, but managed not to say anything and give him the ammunition. I imagined him dragging the large silver rings on his hand along her side just to make me faint.

On a bright day like today, it was blue, but as soon as the shadow hit, it would look purple, then black at night. I spent a fortune for it to be done, but it was worth it. She was a beast and deserved the best.

"You played me." He smirked, but it wasn't a friendly look. "You figured I'd find a way to track her down, didn't you?" I shrugged, not agreeing or disagreeing. "You're braver than I thought, Avro. Stupid, maybe, but definitely braver. Go home. I'm not hunting down Raine. If she wants to take off and never come back, then so be it."

"Ha!" I barked out before I could stop myself. "Now, who's the terrible liar?" I dug around in my plastic bag and pulled out a couple of packages of candy. I tossed one at Kai, and he caught it. "Don't ever play poker. You'll lose."

"What's this for," he asked, staring at the gummies.

"People tend to eat them," I said, smiling as Kai glared. "I'm not sure what the wildlife does with them."

Kai made a snorting sound like he almost found my joking insult amusing. "And you have a sense of humor, good to know. One that is going to get you killed, but it makes me like you a little bit more," he said and tore open the package.

I glanced at the large window and the guy behind the cash register staring at us as if expecting things to turn into a shoot-out.

"Well, we seem to be at a stalemate because I'm not continuing with you following me," Kai said.

"Another asshole move. I shouldn't be surprised after you stormed my home, attacked Jace and me, destroyed my sitting room, and almost shot us all. For no reason, I might add."

"I had my reasons, just not ones you'd agree with," he said, and fuck, he sounded way too much like Jace. I just couldn't picture either of them sharing Raine with one another, but that was a problem for another day. One problem at a time.

"Fine. I'll make you a deal," I offered.

"I'm not really sure you're in a position to make deals," Kai said.

"Maybe not, but I will sit here and watch you like a fucking annoying ass fly and stick to you like glue until you either shoot me or lead me to Raine. So I'd take the deal."

Kai glared, and I was sure it scared a great many people, but this was Raine we were talking about, and I wasn't about to back down. He could fucking forget about it.

"I wouldn't tempt me with shooting you," he said and dumped the last of the candy in his mouth.

"I'm sure it is tempting for someone used to simply taking whatever they want. The thing is, I don't think that's the real you. At least not the you before prison, but what do I know?" I rubbed at my chin as I analyzed his glare. "Maybe you really are the type that if you want something, you just take it. You don't like someone. You shoot them in the face." Wisely or unwisely, I took a step toward Kai. "I honestly don't give a fuck what you do to me, but I've never done anything to you, and you're the one that will have to live with my death on your conscience." I took another step so that I was standing at the trunk of my car. "And if Raine ever finds out what you've done...well, you don't need to be a rocket scientist to know how well that will go over."

"Okay, it's official. You're fucking annoying me." Kai pushed away from my car and stood with his hands on his hips.

I shook my head and sighed. "I'm right, and you know it, Kai. From what Raine has told me about you, one thing was made very clear. She said that you had a good heart. She said that you stood up against bullies and that it was breaking her heart to see how much you've changed. How much she no longer recognized you. How much who you'd become scared her."

It was like I punched him in the stomach. All the anger fell from his face to be replaced with uncertainty. I had a feeling that people didn't call Kai out much. They probably weren't brave enough or didn't care.

"Raine still sees the good in you, and I think I see it too, but this...." I pointed my finger up and down his body. "This attitude and the threatening to kill me because I was Raine's friend and dared to look out for her when no one else did. Because I fell in love with her and her beautiful soul that was broken when we met. Because I would lay my life down for her. None of those are reasons." He licked his lips, and I could see him warring with his inner demons, whatever those were.

Kai cracked his neck and sucked in a deep breath. "What's this fucking deal?"

"Pull out your phone," I said, and he slowly reached inside his leather jacket. "Now go to text messages and send whatever message you want to this number." I held up my phone with my number glowing across the face. A moment later, *fuck off*, came in, and I smirked. "Perfect, now I will know it's you."

"What are you talking about?"

"I'm going to turn around and go home like you want. You want this time with Raine alone. You want to try and convince her to just be with you. Go for it. I won't stop you. What I want is to know she's alive and well. So as soon as you find her and know she's okay, you'll text me and let me know she's alright."

"And? What's the catch?"

"No catch. You try and convince her to come home and be with you or whatever you want, as long as you don't hurt her again. Then you will piss me off, and I may not look it, Kai, but I'm a lot smarter and more resourceful than you're giving me credit for." I smiled wide. "Just make sure she is doing well and stays that way and text me that she is, and I'll call it fair."

"I don't understand."

I smirked. "You wouldn't."

"What's that supposed to mean?" Kai growled, his hands immediately balling into fists. Okay, he was like Jace if he was on steroids. I wanted to shake my head but watched a few cars driving by, minding their own business, before I answered.

"It means that what you fail to realize is that at the end of the day, what happens from this moment onward has nothing to do with you, me, or Jace." I paused, and Kai cocked his head as he stared at me. "The decision is Raine's." I shrugged. "If you truly love her the way you seem to, then you'll eventually see that, and you'll have a choice to make."

I stepped up to Kai, and at first, he didn't back away from my door as I reached for the handle, but I waited patiently until he finally stepped away. Opening it halfway, I stopped before I got behind the wheel and looked at Kai.

"For the record. I don't see a monster when I look at you. I see who Jace and I would've become if we hadn't had each other. There's time to heal Kai if you let yourself. You just have to give yourself the space and stop telling yourself you're no longer worth the effort." I slipped behind the wheel, and Kai remained standing in the same spot as if I'd frozen him in place.

I went to start the car and then remembered I had prepaid for gas and never put any in Camille. Fuck. So much for a grand dramatic exit.

"Son of a bitch," I swore under my breath as I got back out.

Chapter 7

LOST
1% MC
SOULS

Kaivan

I hated Avro more now than ever before. That knowing look on his face when he'd spoken to me. He fucking knew what Raine would demand. Him and his stupid amber eyes had silently mocked me. Who the fuck had amber eyes anyway?

For all I knew, they set this up together, but I didn't think so. The emotions they'd shown were authentic, and Raine wasn't great at lying. She'd never been the type to keep what she was thinking off of her face.

I looked down at her sleeping form and couldn't remember feeling like this ever. It was a potent combination. Raine's arms wrapped around me, holding me as if I would disappear. Her head was on my heart, her leg stretched over my legs, and her hand on my chest.

I'd never spent the night with anyone unless I counted when we were younger, and she snuck into my bed because she had a nightmare. Fuck, it had been way too difficult not to hold her or touch her, and I had ended up taking her out back and sitting in the large swing. She fell asleep with her head on my shoulder, but I had to tell her never to do it again.

My resolve where she was concerned was always on life support. Even back then, everything inside me screamed that Raine was mine. Guys would look at her, and I wanted to punch them in the face. The boys at school would try to flirt with her, but I knew what they were thinking and put a stop to that. No one touched her or went near her without my permission. If you had a dick attached to your body, your intentions better be pure.

She was so fucking innocent and sweet. A bright light in my dark world that made me smile just by looking my way. I didn't know what to do with the emotions then, and eleven years, three months, three weeks, and two days hadn't made it any easier to navigate.

Having sex with women was easy, but with Raine...she pulled me all over the place. One moment I was happy, then scared, horny as hell, pissed off, and finally confused. My head had been a mess for a long time, but this emotional shit had it all scrambled up like someone came along and swiped everything off my already disorganized desk into a heap on the floor.

I traced my finger along Raine's bare shoulder. She shivered and snuggled closer, right on cue, making me smile. Grabbing the blanket, I pulled it up to cover her. She sighed, and I knew I was seriously fucked. I couldn't picture my life without her. I didn't do fluffy shit, yet words like soulmate bounced around inside my skull. She made me crazy. That was all there was to it. Raine had stolen the heart from my chest and refused to give it back.

Her fingers twitched on my chest, and a glint caught my eye. I hadn't noticed the ring before but stared at it now. Without even trying, she had me wanting to cry and fuck her into oblivion all over again.

The thin silver band was a gift I bought and gave to her the day before our worlds exploded. I had wanted to tell her it was a promise ring, but instead, I said it was an early birthday gift since we always celebrated our birthdays together. I loved that she was two years, two weeks, and two days younger. The little unity symbol on the top had felt so right to buy for her, and she'd smiled wider than I'd ever seen. She had practically jumped into my arms to hug me as she said thank you over and over again.

Sliding my hand under hers, I lifted her fingers enough to see the ring clearly, running my thumb over the symbol. She kept it. All this time, and she still wore it. My silent promise to her that I would forever be hers, and she was mine.

The anger that consumed me for so long was still there. I was annoyed as shit that what Raine wanted went against every one of my base instincts.

But I was more pissed off at those that manipulated a traumatized teen into thinking I'd hurt her and put us in this position in the first place out of spite. She told me more about what Dave had said to her. How the police caught me down near the fights, and my hoodie had her blood on it, how I'd admitted to being obsessed with her.

That last part was true, but no one knew that. I hadn't admitted it to myself, let alone a bunch of cops. Irene had put on quite the show. She cried and told her that I was so angry when I thought she went downtown to see another guy that I lost it and attacked her, and that was how she got the black eye. I'd bet money it was Dave that put it there when he found out about her fucking around on him with me.

Raine said she didn't have a reason to think they'd lie to her and didn't ask to see any of the evidence. She was in the hospital facing a second surgery, scared out of her mind. Every noise made her heart monitor leap, and they put a security guard at the door for a week so that she could get some sleep.

What hurt my heart the most was how she wished she had died. That last part killed me more than anything else. They almost succeeded and took any hope from my life with a single act. I don't know what I would've done if she had.

I shivered and wrapped my arms around Raine, linking my fingers together. She said that so many times during the investigation, she had doubts, but the response was always the same. She was making excuses for my actions because of her feelings for me.

Raine suddenly jerked, a whimper escaping her mouth. "Shh, it's okay, Tink, I've got you. I've always got you," I whispered, kissing the top of her head. "I'll never let anyone hurt you again."

Her body twitched a few more times before she settled again. "I love you," she slurred out in her dream state.

"I love you too," I said.

Yeah, there was no letting her go. But she was clear about what she wanted, including two other men. My nostrils flared with the thought of them touching her. I had to figure out a way to live with this if I wanted her in my life. Without her being chained to my fucking wall like a prisoner. Wilder came to mind, and I couldn't help wondering who he was keeping prisoner and what he was doing to them. Nope, don't wonder. You don't want to know. Plausible deniability was what I was going for. Hell, it wasn't like I was going to be turning his crazy ass in, so better off not to know.

Maybe I could talk Raine into hitting the road with me for a few weeks or months. Everyone else seemed to be able to take off whenever they wanted. Why the fuck shouldn't I have the opportunity?

Raine bolted upright from my hold, her hand clutching her chest as her wide eyes searched the room before finding my face.

"You okay," I asked, trying to pull her back into my arms, but she shook her head.

"I will be. I just need a few moments alone. I'm going to go shower." Leaning down, she gave me a quick kiss, but I saw the shadows in her eyes. She didn't have to say it, I knew what haunted her dreams, and here she was, lying in the arms of the man she thought had hurt her. I guess there was going to be an adjustment for both of us.

"You sure you don't want me to join?"

Raine gave me a small smile as she stood from the bed. Fuck me. My eager cock stirred at her naked body and the faint outline of my handprint on her ass as she dug around in her small backpack.

"Thanks, but I just...." Raine ran her hand through her short hair as she clutched a T-shirt to her chest. "I just need a few minutes to...." She closed her eyes and covered her mouth. I watched her battle back the emotion like it was her enemy. "Just give me ten minutes and then join me," she said, walking into the bathroom as the first tears started to fall.

Murderous thoughts bounced around my mind as I pictured Dave's smug face. Swinging my legs out of bed, I stood and hunted for my jeans as a knock sounded at the door. I looked at the time as the clock clicked over to five-o-one in the morning. I grabbed the T-shirt and pulled it on as the knock came again.

"Hang on to yourself," I yelled, yanking my legs into my jeans but didn't bother doing them up. I grabbed my gun and stood to the side of the door. "Who the fuck is there?" I called out. "Answer me, or I shoot through the door and then find out who's on the other side."

"It's me."

Fucking Avro. I yanked open the door, my hand shaking on the gun as I stared at his calm face.

"What the fuck are you doing here?"

"You said you'd text when you found Raine." He held up his phone. "Oh, look at that, no text."

"So I lied. Sue me. You said you were heading home," I growled.

"So I lied, sue me," he mocked.

"I want to knock your teeth down your throat," I said, and he smirked. "I swear to god, wipe that look off your face before I do." Avro stopped smiling and crossed his arms over his chest.

"Are you going to let me in?"

"I'd prefer to punch you in the face." He glanced down at my shaking hand, gripping the gun.

"So we're back to you wanting to kill me?" Sighing, he leaned against the open archway of the door.

"Technically, I don't think I ever stopped," I said. His face was bruised with a cut along his jaw and tape on his nose. He still looked like a fucking model and far too perfect. That alone was enough to make me want to shoot him. Guys like him running around ruined shit for the rest of us.

"Well, I'm not leaving," he said. I chanted in my head that Raine would never speak to me again if I killed him. It was the only thing keeping me from snatching him by the neck, dragging him into the room, and putting my gun in his mouth.

"Avro?" I groaned at the sound of Raine's voice. No hiding the body now.

"Yeah, it's me." He leaned around me to look at Raine, smiling wide before pushing my arm out of the way and walking in.

"Come on in, why don't you? We weren't having a private moment or anything," I muttered under my breath. Closing the door, I turned and watched as Raine's face shifted. In a blink, she looked relaxed, like the guy had some superpower to make her feel okay. Yeah, I was gonna kill him.

"Did Kai call you?"

Like I'd actually call Avro. But the hopeful look in her eyes made me feel guilty that I hadn't. Fuck, fuck, fuck.

"No, but he was about to," Avro lied smoothly, and I raised an eyebrow.

Raine smiled and hugged Avro, her eyes closing. What the hell was it with this fucknut? I found him...creepy. He was too perfect. Just look at his hair and teeth and his bone structure. No one had that perfect of a jaw. Then there was the supernatural ability to soothe Raine. That really annoyed me. I needed to mess his pretty face up some more. He was unnatural.

"If Kai didn't call, what are you doing here?" Raine asked.

"I asked him the same question," I said and put the gun down. I didn't trust myself not to shoot him just because he was in the room. Raine only had the bath towel wrapped around her body, and I ground my teeth together as Avro's hand lingered on her shoulder.

Marching past them, I grabbed my jacket and swore for the second time. I still hadn't gotten more smokes. I sat down in the chair and played with my lighter instead. All I could think about was whether I should kill him or not. Maybe I should bring him to a field and pull the petals off a daisy to decide his fate.

"I came to make sure you're okay. I waited as long as I could, but it was terrible sleeping in a sports car. I don't recommend it," Avro said, and Raine's face scrunched up in confusion. "I need to use the bathroom. I'll be back."

Raine watched him disappear into the bathroom, and then her eyes found mine. She silently asked me if I was alright, but I didn't have an answer for her. Standing, I stuffed my arms into my jacket and pulled on my boots.

"Where are you going, Kai?"

"I need smokes, or I will shoot him." I looked up as I finished tying my laces, and Raine's lips pulled down in a frown. "Look, I said I'd try. I didn't fucking say I'd like it or that I would spend time with him in the same motel room. All I really want to do right now is shoot him in the head, so space is required." She crossed her arms and looked away. "And please have some clothes on when I return. I might not be so angry with him touching you if you weren't practically naked."

Raine sighed and pinched the bridge of her nose. "Are you coming back?"

Cupping her face, I kissed her hard, loving the fresh minty flavor of her mouth. Her hands went to my waist, and she gripped me tight. My lips lingered on hers, not wanting to leave her alone with Avro but knowing I needed to. Avro stepped out of the bathroom but stayed near the door.

"I'll be back," I said.

Grabbing the rest of my crap on the way, I stomped to the door. Flinging it open, I stopped dead as I almost ran into a raised fist about to knock. Jace lowered his arm as I glared.

"You have got to be fucking kidding me!" I growled at the sight of him. My body trembled with the burst of adrenaline. It took all my resolve not to tackle him out the door and continue what we started at the house. The dark glare in his eyes said he was thinking the same thing.

"Funny, I was just thinking the same thing," he said. My eyes flicked down to his hand. I thought he was holding a gun but realized it was a Taser and smirked.

"You brought a Taser with you?" My respect for him notched up slightly.

"You can never be too careful these days. Don't know what sort of asshole you'll run into anymore. I'm really hoping you try to hit me again, though, just so I have an excuse to use it. I've been dying to see what this can do when turned on high."

My eyes narrowed. "I'm flattered that you think you need that toy."

"Unlike you, who would jump straight to murder, I'd prefer to stop you, then throw you back into the cage where you belong. The one you never should've left," Jace said, and the curl of his lip had my fist clenching. I reminded myself that he was pushing me on purpose. He wanted me to make the first move.

"Jace? What are you doing here," Avro asked.

"Seems to be the question of the day," I muttered, stepping out of the way for Jace to enter. Why the fuck not at this point? My plan to whisk her away for a few days was officially ruined.

"If you bothered to check your messages and call me back, then I wouldn't have to track you down," Jace growled as he stepped inside but kept his eyes trained on me. The tension grew with his proximity. Our eyes locked on one another.

"I didn't want to worry you," Avro said.

"You didn't think that leaving me a message that you're going to go speak to him...." Jace pointed a thumb in my direction. "And then go radio silent, wasn't going to worry me?"

"He does have a point. I've thought about killing you multiple times already," I said, and all three sets of eyes turned in my direction. "What? I'm being honest. Jace has a valid point."

"See," Jace said, glaring at Avro.

"Don't get like that with me. You're the one that decided you were going to leave before anything was resolved," Avro shot back. My brow lifted as Jace's face went dark, his lip pulling up in a snarl. He would've held his own in lock up. I might've liked him if he didn't want to put his cock in my girl.

"Enough!" Raine shook her head. "Not that I'm not happy to see all of you, but I don't understand. Did I leave a fucking breadcrumb trail for you all to follow? And if you two are only here to fight with me about Kai, then don't bother."

I couldn't stop the smile that lifted the corner of my mouth. At least she was just as firm with them as with me. Good to know.

Jace crossed his arms over his chest. "I haven't decided why I'm here other than to make sure the two of you were alive. Obviously, that was a waste of time since Avro was actively dodging me."

"I was not," Avro said and stepped toward Jace.

"Don't fucking lie to me. You knew I didn't trust him and knew I'd worry when I couldn't reach you. Yet, you set out to see him alone and then disappeared. What the fuck was I going to think? I pictured you floating in some swamp as alligator bait."

"What, no love for me?" I drawled out and earned a glare. "I hate to admit it, but I do have alligators and have thought about it." It was fairly close to what I'd debated doing.

"Why do you have alligators," Raine asked, and I smirked.

"Would you believe me if I said they make great pets?" Before they could drag me into any more of this argument, I grabbed the door handle. "I'm out of here so you all can have your lovers quarrel," I said mockingly.

I slammed the door behind me. Closing my eyes, I took a slow deep breath. My heart was pounding hard while the anger tried to consume me. I sucked in the cool, early morning air and spotted Avro's car tucked in the corner of the lot. Was the asshole here all night? The fact that he kept an eye on the room was unnerving, but that also meant he let Raine and I have that time together. It was confusing. I wouldn't have been able to stay in the parking lot knowing that they were having sex inside.

The thought of the three of them alone had my blood pressure rising. My hand twitched as I mapped out all the areas I could dispose of their bodies. I needed to step away, or I really would lose control It wasn't just words. I felt myself stepping close to the line that always took over when I was sent to teach opposing club members a lesson.

Walking away from the room, I made it three doors down when a guy stepped out, lighting a smoke. Fucker.

"Hey buddy, do you have a smoke I can bum off ya?"

The guy turned his bloodshot eyes in my direction and snorted like I'd said something funny. The anger I was trying hard to control slipped a little more. I hated that look. I'd been stared at like I was worthless most of my life.

Before he even answered, I knew what words would come out of his mouth and pulled my gun.

"Go fuck yourself," he said and spat at my feet.

The gun was up and pressed into his forehead before my mind registered what my hand was doing. I glared into his terrified eyes that suddenly didn't look so smug.

"Do I look like someone you want to fuck with?" My voice dropped low as I growled the words. He shook his head slightly. The cigarette, long forgotten, was now dangling from his lips. "So, I'm going to ask you again, and I expect a different answer. Hey buddy, do you have a smoke I can bum?"

His hand shook as he pulled out the pack from inside his jacket, and I plucked it from his fingers. "Wow, thanks man. You're too nice," I drawled as I put the pack in my back pocket. Snatching the one from his mouth, I tossed it on the ground and stepped on it, crushing it so I didn't do the same to his face.

The guy's chest heaved as I lowered the gun, and he took a deep breath. "So generous of you to give me your whole pack," I drawled as I tapped the gun against my leg. His eyes followed the movement like a scared rat. "It's a nice day for a walk, you say? You want to get more smokes? What a fabulous fucking idea. Run along then," I said and watched as he slowly turned and walked away so fast he looked like he was in one of those weird walking races. He had decent form with his straight back and tight ass. Okay, it was official. I'd completely lost my mind.

Pulling out the pack of smokes, I lit one up and took the first sweet pull. Did Raine still hate that I smoke? Why the fuck did I care?

Was this my new reality? Wondering what Raine liked and didn't like every time I did something. Who was I kidding? It was always my reality. I just couldn't admit it until now.

Shaking my head, I wandered back to the room and leaned against the wall outside, clearly able to hear them through the shitty door.

"No fucking way! I'm laying the law down right now. We are not getting into a relationship with that psychopath," Jace yelled. "The pair of you have lost your fucking minds."

"He's actually not a psychopath because he has emotions, and a lot of them, including regret," Avro said and the room went silent. I smirked as I pictured the look on Jace's face. Okay, I was man enough to admit this was entertaining shit. At least it wasn't just my nerves that Avro got on. I could picture him swinging off Jace's last nerve right now.

"I don't need you to be the Webster dictionary to know that man is unstable as fuck. By his own admission, he has thought about killing you and feeding you to alligators. He could decide today he is okay with this and tomorrow that he wants the two of us dead and do it." Again very accurate of Jace. Apparently, there was more to him than singing.

"He won't," Raine piped in.

"Oh yeah, and how can you be so sure about that? Let's not forget he's attacked you, raped you, and almost shot you the other night. Not exactly an outstanding track record," Jace growled.

I sucked in another drag of the smoke and hated Jace a little more for calling out all the shit I'd done to Raine in a very short time. I rubbed my eyes. He wasn't wrong. I was angry and had never stopped to think that she might actually believe I was the guy.

"I know because he made me a promise," Raine said, surprisingly calm. I loved the sound of her voice. She used to hum all the time, and I would sneak closer to whatever room she was in to listen. From the first moment we met, she calmed the storm of toxic waste that was my soul.

"A promise? That doesn't sound like much of a reassurance, no offense."

"Jace, I know you hardly know me, and the only thing you know of Kai is the anger and violence, but...he is to me who Avro is to you. I know Kai inside out. I never should let myself think for even a moment that it was Kai that hurt me all those years ago." Her voice was getting louder and I knew she was close to the door. "We have a complicated and sordid past that binds us in a way I can't explain, but I know his heart. Any doubt I had left about my attack is gone. I love him." I rubbed at the spot that had ached for Raine for so long. Hearing her talk about me like I was worth something made me warm all over. I didn't deserve it. I didn't deserve her, but I couldn't walk away.

"Fuck, Raine. I get that. I do, but...shit, this is so dangerous."

"Maybe, and I'm not going to force the two of you to be in a relationship with Kai if you don't want to be. It's what I've asked for from him and now from the two of you, and I will hold true to my choice. It's either all of you, or it's none of you. I'm not going back to live a half-life, and I'm not going to be forced to choose between one side of my heart an the other."

I wasn't sure what was worse at this point. Jace not agreeing and Raine taking off again, never seeing her again, or was it worse for him to agree? Forcing me to try and accept them. I felt physically torn, but I shocked myself when I realized I was rooting for him to say yes.

"You know what happened to my family," he said, his voice softer, and I perked up. For some reason, I suddenly wanted to know what had happened to his family. I pulled out my phone and began an internet search for his name.

"I know, and what happened to them was tragic, but Kai is not your stepfather. His heart is battered and bruised, but under that, he is still the man I remember, and his word is as solid as any contract." My lip curled up. "I can assure you that if Kai makes a promise, he will never break it unless you force him to. Despite what he did to me, he has honor in his soul."

Fuck, why did she have to make me sound like I was a decent human? I wasn't, not anymore. The part of me that had been decent died in prison, yet the emotion she evoked clogged my throat. I flicked the forgotten smoke down on the ground.

"Avro, what do you want," Jace asked, his voice sounding exasperated.

"You know that I want you and Raine in my life. I love you both, and if Raine loves Kai and wants him in her life, then I trust her judgment."

I heard a loud sigh and almost felt the frustration coming through the door. "Fuck! Fine, I'll try if he will, but I want it to be known right now that I don't like it. I don't trust him." Jace bit out, and I chuckled at the disdain in his tone.

You and me both, Jace Everly.

Chapter 8

K aivan

Just when I thought my life couldn't get any stranger, I ended up in a three-way argument over who would drive Raine home. Yup, in one night, I'd entered pathetic whipped boyfriend status. The three of us didn't even notice when Raine left the room. She grabbed her shit and walked across the street for breakfast at the waffle place while we waved our cocks around in a metaphorical fight.

We all looked pretty fucking stupid as we searched the room and the parking lot like she was a kidnapped child. Not my finest moment.

The argument ended when Raine said she could sleep in Jace's limo. The one thing we all agreed on was that when the limo stopped, we all stopped. Did I like the idea of her in the back of a limo alone with Jace? Fuck no, but this was my new reality. So here I was, following the limo with the tinted windows, trying to see any movement. All I could picture was Raine giving him a hot blow job as she knelt on the floor between his legs. I didn't know what pissed me off more, that he might be getting one or that I wanted one. The image played over and over in my mind, and I didn't know who was growling louder, my motorcycle or me.

We were nearing the exit to head to my house, and I would have to leave Raine and the black car. It was so tempting to follow it. I hated to leave her. No, hated wasn't a strong enough word. I despised it. I wanted her with me, barricaded behind the fucking door, but Roach had been blowing up my phone, and I refused to call him back. The fucker and his quest to stalk Lane could wait.

My hands ached, gripping the handlebars like I was trying to choke them to death as I forced myself to peel away from tailing the car. As soon as it was out of sight, my heart rate skyrocketed. This was insane. They were only going twenty minutes away, not taking off forever. Although I wouldn't put it passed Jace to drive to the airport and fucking take off. If I had a private jet, that's exactly what I'd be doing. I think I was going to need a few more trackers.

I rolled into the Lost Souls parking lot, and the gate rattled closed behind me. I glanced around for Wilder like he'd poke his head out of the grate or some shit but didn't see him in the bright afternoon sunshine.

"Snake," Mannix called out. I looked to the front door of the clubhouse as I dismounted the bike. "Where the fuck have you been?"

I ground my teeth together, annoyed with the interrogation. "Busy. What the fuck is up?"

"Roach has been trying to reach you. We're having an emergency meeting. Let's go." Mannix disappeared inside and I swore under my breath.

"Fuck, of course the one time I don't answer is the one time it's actually important," I grumbled, stomping to the door.

I yanked it open, letting it bang against the wall, and treated the stairs like they were my next victim. A few sweetbutts wandered around the lounge, which was odd for this time of day, as I made my way to the meeting room.

"Hey Snake, did you want me to help you get rid of that frown later?" I looked over at Dee. She smiled, but I didn't say anything. Dee was one of my regulars or had been. Not that I felt the urge to fuck her, but I didn't have time for sweetbutt shit right now.

I closed the door and pushed the thought out of my mind as the room bustled with activity. The secret door hidden behind a panel in the wall was open, and men were pulling out an assortment of guns and ammunition.

"What the hell is going on," I asked Roach as I stepped up beside him.

"Desert Vipers are on the move. May or may not be heading our way, but they are armed, and none of the old ladies are riding with them. Not a good sign."

"Fuck me. I knew this was going to happen sooner or later." I looked around the room at the men pulling on bulletproof vests and covering them with their T-shirts and leather jackets. This was bullshit. "How many of them are on the move?"

Roach slowly turned his head a looked at me, calm but worried. An emotion I didn't see on his face often. "All of them."

I shook my head and wanted to wrap my hands around Chase Mathers' throat and squeeze. I would say my piece if I lived. The satisfaction of punching Chase in the face was too tempting not to live. Stepping up to the open compartment, I grabbed a vest, and the noise slowly disappeared into the background.

"You love me?"

"I've always loved you."

The conversation with Raine played again in my mind.

"Hey man, you okay?" Roach gripped my shoulder, and I nodded, not bothering to say anything. What did you say when you realized that you actually gave a crap if you lived.

Quickly getting ready, I loaded my guns and made sure they were working well when an idea came to me.

"Be right back," I said to Roach and jogged out of the room.

"Is everything okay," Dee asked as I went through. All the girl's heads turned my way.

"I'd get a gun and a safe spot to hide. Kill anyone that is not one of us," I said and left them as they scattered. Jogging down the stairs, I pushed open the door and ran around the side of the large building. "Wilder? Hey man, are you here? Wilder?"

It would be my luck that the one time I actually wanted the guy to be stalking my ass, he wouldn't be anywhere in sight. A flash of light caught my eye, and I looked up toward the top platform of an old rollercoaster. I couldn't see anyone, but the reflection caught my eye again and it was too rhythmical to be anything but Morse code. I wasn't up on my code, so I lifted my hands in confusion, hoping Wilder understood I couldn't understand him. I got my answer as my phone rang a second later with an unknown number.

"Wilder?"

"Hey man, you should really get in a better spot than that if you're going to be fighting. You're out in the open."

I bit my lip. "Thanks for the tip," I drawled. "I take it you already know and are planning on helping?"

"Why else would I be on the top of a rollercoaster," he asked, and I'd never wanted to punch myself in the face so hard in my life.

"Okay, great." I pulled the phone away from my ear, but Wilder called my name. If it weren't for the fact I was pretty sure he had binoculars trained on me, I would've just hung up on him. "Yeah man?"

"I was thinking of getting her a friend to play with," he said. I waited to see if there was more to the random statement.

"I'm assuming you mean the girl you're interested in?"

"Who else would I be talking about." I turned away from him and bit my fist before I said what I really wanted to say. I needed his insane ass right now.

"Not sure, just felt it was best to clarify," I said.

"Good idea. It is always best to have a full understanding of any situation. Yes, the girl that fascinates me seems lonely."

Again with the veiled comments that had me picturing a girl trapped in a cell while he poked at her with a stick like she was an exhibit.

"So you want to get her a friend?"

"Yes, someone for her to play with and talk to," Wilder said.

"You sound like you're talking about a dog," I said.

"No, she is human."

Oh, for fucks sake, give me strength. "I assumed she was human, but it sounds like you're talking about a dog. Never mind. What do you mean by get her a friend? I'm pretty sure you can't just pick one of those up at the store unless you plan on choosing another of the sorority girls?"

"Hmm, I wish I could go to the store. That would make things easier."

"I have to head inside and finish getting ready for the fight, but if she seems lonely, then getting her a pet would be my suggestion. I'm not sure a random person will have the desired effect."

"A pet, now that is an interesting idea. What if I got her a friend that could also be her pet? That would serve two purposes in one." My hand stilled on the door to the front entrance of the club.

I really wanted to ask if he planned on dressing a person up like a dog or cat and telling them to pretend to be her pet. That was some kinky shit that I did not want to picture Wilder doing. Raine wearing a catsuit. Now that had fucking possibilities.

"You getting her a collar, too," I asked sarcastically.

"You think she'd like that?"

I smiled wide, the asshole in me needing this at the moment.

"Oh yes, I really do. Especially one that you can't get off and maybe some gemstones to make it look pretty," I said and chuckled to myself.

"See, this is why I keep coming to you for ideas. She is screaming less lately, and I owe that to you. Don't worry Snake, I have your back," Wilder said and then hung up.

I snorted and shook my head as I pictured what he was going to do to this poor girl, whoever she was. Why I didn't turn this into a game sooner was beyond me, but this was too good to pass up. Wilder never ceased to amaze and surprise me with his ability to confuse the fuck out of me and creep me out. Yet it was comforting to know that the crazy ass that was once a Green Beret would be watching my back.

Beast was coming down the stairs as I walked inside. "What's the latest," I asked.

"Nothing good. They divided into four groups and are coming at us from all different sides. I'm sending six guys to watch the back and the families, but...." He stopped, and I knew what he didn't want to say. It was what I'd been saying all along. Chase left us with our fucking pants down and no one to help.

"Doesn't matter now. What's the plan?"

Beast sighed, and for the first time, the mask he had worn for so long as the leader of this club slipped. Worry danced in his eyes.

"I think it's best to stay in here. This is our home, and we know all the hiding spots."

I rubbed my chin. "That's true. Are the cops staying away?"

Beast laughed. "Yeah. I heard from my friend at the department that they are telling their officers to let us fight it out and to stay out of the line of fire."

"Helpful," I said, rolling my eyes. "Of course, when we actually want the cops to come around, they are going to ghost."

Beast shrugged, his big shoulders dropping dramatically. "Makes it easier for us. At least this way, they're not on our doorstep, and we won't have to worry about them searching the premises."

I opened my mouth to answer when the sound of motorcycles could be heard a moment before the warning alarm went off. The red light and piercing siren sounded in the building.

"Inside it is," Beast said and ran up the stairs. "You coming," he asked when I didn't follow.

I shook my head no. "Can't have them trapping us and starting a fire," I yelled over the alarm. "I'm staying on this level."

"Fuck, why did you put that thought in my head," Beast said and took off as the roar of the motorcycles got louder until the entire building was shaking. The guards pulled open the doors a moment later, their eyes wide with fear.

"Head up to the roof with the M4s and stay low," I said, and they took off. I locked the door and brought the thick security bar down into place. It would hold for now. There were a few windows on this level that we never used, but if they got past those on the roof and couldn't get in the front door, this was their next point of entry.

I'd already walked the building a million times and found all the weak spots. It didn't matter if the rest of the club was here or not. We always ran the risk of being attacked. With them gone, I'd been extra diligent.

Marching into the back room we used for storage, I slipped

through the piles of boxes and shelving units until I reached the three windows but stopped short when I felt a draft. Staring along the aisle, I spotted the open window and reached back for my gun. Movement caught the corner of my eye a moment before I was jumped.

The air was driven from my lungs as we collided with the unforgiving wall.

"Fuck," I growled and drove my knee up and my elbow down at the same time. The guy grunted as my knee connected with his stomach and yelled as I drove my elbow into his back three more times before he stumbled away. He came at me again, and we sailed past the first window and landed hard on the ground. I was really sick of being tackled. It had happened more than once in prison, then Jace, and now this guy.

I was all for ending up on my back, but not with this guy and not like this. There was no room to maneuver, but I managed to connect with the side of his face and ear before he could land a blow.

"Ah fuck," the guy yelled, and I recognized the voice as he rolled off, holding the side of his head.

"Sparky, what the fuck? Are you lost? I'm not a fucking intruder," I growled out and stood up, letting Sparky get to his feet.

Sparky was here when I got out of prison. He fixed all the bikes and did other mechanical work. I'd always known him as a fun, easygoing guy and one of the most loyal assholes in the group.

"Seriously, what the fuck?" I dabbed at the back of my head, but there was no blood.

"You should've left when you had the chance Snake," he said and held the side of his face as he stood up. I'd never seen him look so serious. If you wanted to laugh, you went to Sparky. "I actually liked you, but you should've just gone. I thought you had when you didn't come back last night."

"Leave the club? Why would I leave the club," I asked.

"You said it yourself. It was only a matter of time before another club knocked on our door to kill us, and here they are." He held his hand out toward the front of the building and the sound of gunfire. "I'm not dying like that. I know a losing side when I see one."

My eyebrows shot up, and you could've knocked me over with a feather. I was so shocked. Of all the members, he was the last I would've ever thought to go turncoat. "So, you planned to sneak out a window and slink to the other side like a fucking traitorous piece of shit?"

"No, not quite." Sparky pulled a gun and fired before I had time to flinch. The bullet hit center mass, and at this range, I flew off my feet and landed on the ground with a loud crash as I slammed into stacks of boxes. The contents went flying and littered the floor. My back arched up, and I gasped for air as I pulled at the front of my shirt. I couldn't get a grip on the vest to relieve some of the weight that felt like it was crushing me. I now knew what it felt like to be hit by a sledgehammer.

Sparky walked closer as I rolled onto my side and managed to take a wheezing breath. I knew this was it. I'd already used my nine lives, and it was time to pay up for all the shit I'd done.

"I really didn't want to kill anyone, and I liked you, Snake. I truly did."

I watched the arm holding the gun raise and stared down the barrel. "Don't do this, man." I coughed and managed to drag in another breath that felt like knives piercing my chest. "You're not a killer. It changes you," I managed to get out.

"You're leaving me no choice. I can't let you live. I'm sorry, Snake."

Taking a shuddering breath, I closed my eyes and pictured Raine's face. The way her eyes crinkled at the corners when she smiled and how her cheeks would pink slightly just from looking at me. I could feel her in my arms, and I couldn't get enough of the weight of her head lying on my chest as she held me tight. I wanted to take everything about her with me when my heart stopped beating. She was the only person I ever loved, and my only regret was that I wouldn't get more time with her.

"Fuck, I'm sorry, Snake."

Bang.

Snake

Chapter 9

K aivan
My heart stopped, and my whole body jerked with the sound of shattering glass. I rolled and covered my head as shards rained down. Something fell on top of me, and I turned to stare into Sparky's wide and unblinking eyes, while his arm draped over my body.

His sightless eyes looked confused, but I knew what had happened. The perfectly placed hole at his temple was all the answer I needed to know that Wilder had been watching. It was only then that I could once more feel the beating of my own heart. Grabbing the gun from his hand, I winced and pulled myself out from under his arm.

No matter what crazy fucking Wilder needed from me, I owed

him my life and would return the favor. That was how this place worked. Prison was a favor for a favor, and like a chip to be played, once it was used up, it was gone until you earned another.

One thing that the MC had given me was a place where favors didn't come with an expiration date. I yanked my other leg out from under Sparky and got to my knees to pull at the Velcro sides of the bulletproof vest. Air was still hard to get in without the feeling of someone pressing on my chest, and I needed to take a moment to rest and assess the damage. The Desert Vipers had other ideas. Shadows could be seen passing the furthest window. I stayed low and crawled to the wall.

I couldn't hear any gunshots, but the yelling told me Wilder was picking guys off. The third window shattered with what sounded like an explosion, and I pulled up on my leather jacket to protect myself from the raining debris.

Guns were firing, and bullets were randomly sailing through the window, hitting boxes. Pieces of history and memories from members long past were torn apart with the rain of bullets.

A Viper jumped through the middle window. He landed and rolled before looking my way, and I sneered as I glared at my enemy. My hand moved fast, experience and instinct putting two bullets in the Viper before he got his gun up. Another member tried to jump through the window, but he wasn't as graceful. He screamed as he landed on the bottom portion of the shattered window piercing his stomach as he hung half in and half out. He fell back out a moment later, leaving a trail of blood sliding down the wall.

I knew they would keep trying to get in. This was the only decent access point, and we were so low on men that they would easily overwhelm us.

If I ever wanted to know what being on The Walking Dead was like, I'd just gotten my wish as more men tried to pile through the windows. Their moans and yells were loud as bullets hit them. The floor and the boxes were now coated in blood.

Sparky had planned on giving them an easy in, but I'd fucked with that. What started as five guys turned into ten. I fired as men yanked the dead out of the way and leaped through the frames to find me on the other side. My guns clipped empty, and I quickly reloaded one, but I didn't have the right size clip for Sparky's gun and dropped it to the ground. I fired faster than I could keep up with the sheer number of men crawling over one another to get into the windows. The pile of dead, dying, or groaning people on the floor was building up like a wall.

"What the fuck zombie movie did I wake up in?" I grumbled as one of the guys I shot pulled himself across the floor, leaving a blood trail in his wake. I quickly put a bullet in his head as he reached his hand out for me.

"Get the fuck in the window. We need to get in there." A loud voice boomed as my gun clicked empty for the second time. *Shit.* I reached for another clip, but it was missing. *Fuck.* It must have fallen out when Sparky shot me.

Dropping to my knees, I crawled to one of the dead Vipers. Each movement felt like being stabbed in my side. Grabbing the gun, I pried it out of his hands and checked the clip.

"Full, thank fuck."

The gunfire outside was getting louder. I wasn't surprised. We'd been sitting with a bleeding limb in a frenzy of sharks and no boat to save us.

Sliding across the floor to my vantage point, I caught my breath. I really needed to get this fucking vest off. Leaning against the wall, I managed to pull myself upright when the sound of heavy boots coming down the hall drew my attention. Gripping the gun tight, I shifted positions slightly to see who it was. The cool metal felt heavy in my hand, my finger rubbing over the trigger. Was this going to be it? I figured I would die like this at some point, but I didn't think today would be the day.

If it wasn't my guys, I would have a hell of a fight on my hands, but as the shadows stepped into the light, I sighed and slumped against the wall. It was fucking Tanner leading the charge. I'd never been so fucking happy to see his face.

"What the fuck took you so long?" I barked out as Tanner jogged the rest of the way to me and then shot a guy that stuck his head through the window.

"Traffic was a bitch. What the hell are you doing starting the festivities without me? You know I like to party."

I snorted. "Have at 'em," I said.

"You heard him. Let's have some fun! Yippie ki-yay mother fuckers!" Tanner did his Bruce Willis impression. I shook my head as he hooted and hollered, firing at the living and the already dead. More men piled through the door, and soon anyone outside the windows was retreating.

You needed to be careful when it came to Tanner. He had a knack for taking a shit storm and somehow turning it into a shit hurricane and not in your favor.

I let my leather jacket drop so I could peel my vest off and winced, reaching around to grab the velcro.

"Snake, fuck," Roach said as he joined the room now filled with Lost Souls members. "Shit, you okay." His worried eyes scanned me as I leaned, panting against the wall.

"I need help getting the vest off," I said. Roach grabbed the Velcro sides, pulled hard, and lifted it off over my head. He dropped it to the floor with a thud. Without the weight of the thirty-pound vest, I took a shuddering breath.

"I have no idea how cops wear those all the time, fuck, they're terrible," I said.

"Lift your shirt." My hands shook from the boost of adrenaline still coursing through my body, but I got the T-shirt lifted enough to show Roach.

"We need to have you looked at," Roach said, ignoring my cop joke. My eyes flicked to his as he pulled out his phone, and I knew he was calling the doc we always used for the club.

Reaching out, I squeezed his forearm as he spoke into the phone. His eyes found mine as he relayed the information and location. Roach said nothing as we stared at one another, but I knew what he was thinking. I was fucking lucky. We may not have been blood brothers or even childhood friends, but we had a friendship that had seen the worst and lived to tell the tale.

"Thanks," I said, as he hung up the phone.

That one word held so much weight for me. I didn't thank or rely on people, but Wilder had just saved my life, and I knew Roach would've jumped in the way of that bullet if given the chance. I was grateful for their friendship, something I hadn't fully realized until now.

Looking down, there was a black bruise already forming. I gently touched the spot and knew I had at least one cracked rib. I knew the feeling all too well, having had more than my fair share in life.

I was fucking lucky, though. If the bullet had been a couple of inches higher, it would've been a direct blow to my heart. From such a short distance, it could've stopped it for good.

I placed my hand over the beating organ. "I love you, Raine," I whispered as the gunfire dwindled and stopped.

"Fuck, they're retreating. Bunch of fucking dicks. I was having fun," Tanner said and ran out of the room.

"Let me help you get upstairs," Roach offered when everyone was gone.

"Naw, I need a moment alone." He nodded, turned, and disappeared down the hall.

Emotions locked up tight were set loose, and I covered my face and let a tear fall. I almost died the same way my mother had. Choking on blood with no one to help, and all I could think about was that I would never see Raine again.

The next breath I sucked into my lungs had never felt so sweet.

Jace

Chapter 10

Jace

I sat in the back of the limo, watching Raine as she slept. She was out cold, curled on her side, her hood pulled up, and her head on her backpack. One of the blankets I kept in here covered her body. She looked adorable.

That was a word I never thought I'd use for a woman I was getting involved with, but it was the only word that came to mind. Unable to keep to myself anymore, I crouched low and moved to the other seat sitting down by her head. It was second nature to be sweet with Avro after so many years together, but I fumbled for what to do and settled on placing my hand on her side.

Raine lifted her head and looked at me. That tug in my chest pulled me closer. She was dangerous to my heart. I hated feeling unsure about moving forward with this relationship. I was falling fo

Raine, and Avro was all in, but...there was Kai or Snake or whatever other name he wanted to be called. The fact that I felt it necessary to take a Taser to that motel said it all, yet here I was, staring into her eyes and allowing myself to be dragged into this relationship much faster than I wanted.

"Can you hold me? I'm cold," she said sleepily.

"Sure, come sit in my lap," I offered. The thought of her sitting in my lap and having her all to myself was fucking enticing. As Raine sat up, I slid to the center of the seat and smirked as she crawled into my lap like a cat before sitting down and cuddling into my chest.

Fuck all that shit about it not being right to want to protect your girl. There was nothing that felt as good as this. Raine needed me, and it wasn't for something fancy or expensive or because I was Jace Everly. I was desired on a primal level that until you had it, you couldn't explain it, but we all craved it. Every person out there wanted to be needed like this. To feel vital to someone's existence.

I spent too much time warding myself against those who wanted to use me for something. It came with the territory, and some of it I genuinely didn't mind. Like helping a new and talented musician get started. But there was a lot of bad that came with the good. Those who just wanted my money or to be seen with me to enhance their careers. It made it tough to know who was legit and who wasn't.

Grabbing the edges of my jacket, I wrapped the bomber around her body and linked my fingers together. She sighed and wiggled closer, pressing right on my cock.

"Jace?"

"Yeah Peaches."

"Are you angry with me for wanting Kai to be part of us," she asked, and my immediate response was fuck yes. But that wasn't the whole truth.

I sighed, settling deeper into the seat, wishing I could see her face. "No, I'm not angry. I'm scared for all of us, and when I'm scared,

I'm an even larger ornery asshole than normal." She chuckled, her body vibrating. I bit my lip to keep myself in check as her ass rubbed against me. "The problem is Peaches that you see who you want Kai to be, which is the person you knew. I see who he's become. I see him as clearly as I understand myself, and the dangerous edge is never far from the surface. He would snap my neck if given the opportunity, and right now, the only thing keeping him from doing that is the fear of losing you."

Raine turned her head, and for just a moment, I considered having the driver take us to the private jet and forcing her to get on. It was irrational, I didn't really want to kidnap her, but old fears that I'd managed to tame over the years were gripping me by the throat.

"You may be right for now, but Kai is as loyal as they come. If you two find common ground, it won't just be me that holds things together."

I rubbed my eyes. "I need to be careful, Peaches. I'm always in the spotlight. If I'm found hanging around with an MC member who is most likely a killer, it will make headlines worldwide, career-ending headlines. That doesn't just put me at risk. That puts all of us, including Kai, at risk. He will never be able to go anywhere without people filming him, and forget wiping his record if they start digging into what he's been doing for the club since he got out...."

"Oh shit," she said, sitting a little straighter in my arms. "I hadn't even thought about that. I mean, I knew you were always being watched, but it didn't dawn on me the implications with Kai." She paused, and her brow furrowed. "Do you really think he's killed people?"

"More than one, and I'm not saying that to scare you. I'm simply stating a fact. He's an enforcer. That's what they do. They ensure other groups don't want to mess with their club and teach a lesson to those that have. Besides, he has a look in his eye that tells me he's far more comfortable with death than most people."

Raine pulled down the hood on her sweatshirt and stared at me. "How would you know that?"

I swallowed and looked away from her. "Killing someone changes you. I mean, those in the military will tell you that, and police officers as well. He has that closed-off dead look," I said, covering up the real reason. I wasn't sure I was ready to share that particular secret with anyone. Some secrets were better left in the past and never spoken about again.

Raine looked around the car and then back up at me. "Why are you being so understanding and nice? Are we being recorded or something?"

I laughed and gripped her face with one hand, squeezing her cheeks enough that her lips puckered. "Do you like me being the asshole, Peaches?" She swallowed, the sound loud in the quiet car. "You want me to bring up that overnight you've turned into a cock slut?"

Raine's face flamed bright red, and she narrowed her eyes at me. "Nowhere to run off to in here," I said as she shifted like she was going to move away. I nipped at her bottom lip, which was begging to be kissed. "I'm always the asshole," I whispered in her ear. Raine rolled her eyes at me, making me smile, but I felt the slight wiggle of her ass on my cock.

"Tell me, Jace. Is this the real you, or is the sweet guy that wanted to keep me warm the real you?"

"Why can't they both be me? I'm not one-dimensional, but I do love getting you all fired up. I bet if I checked, you're already wet and ready for me."

She crossed her arms. "Don't you wish."

I chuckled again. "Should I check?"

"Okay, can I have nice Jace back? Is there like an off switch to this one or something?" I laughed hard, something that I didn't often do, and as hard as she tried to hold it back, Raine ended up laughing as well.

Sobering, I smirked at her. "Good luck. Avro has tried for years and still hasn't found one."

"How does he put up with you," Raine asked, yet the question hit close to things I didn't want to look at. I'd been lucky to call Avro my friend, and I won the lottery when it turned out his feelings for me were as strong as mine for him. How I'd managed to hang onto him this long was a mystery.

"I was joking," Raine said, her hand landing on my chest over my heart like she sensed the fear and sadness that filled me.

A smile tugged at the corner of my mouth as I traced my thumb across her lower lip. I wanted to lose myself in her. "I know, Peaches." An idea struck. "I have an awards show I need to attend coming up, and I want you to go with me."

Raine's mouth fell open before she started to laugh all over again. "You can't be serious?"

"Why not?" I shrugged. "I have to take someone. I've already been told that I can't attend alone. Which means I will end up at the mercy of Allen and what and who he decides. He wants drama, so lord knows what he has cooking."

"You're serious," she asked.

Picking her up, Raine wrapped her hands around my neck as she straddled my lap. I groaned as her ass settled into place. Sliding my hands under her hoodie, I sighed as my fingers came into contact with her smooth, warm skin.

"I'm very serious," I said as I unclipped her bra with one hand, the material springing apart. My cock thickened as she moaned under my touch. "I don't invite people to go with me, Peaches. I've always been assigned someone that will make me look good or start a conversation. You know what they say, 'No headline is a bad headline.' But, I'd like to have someone that I want by my side for once."

"I'm not sure I'm red carpet material," Raine said, her voice breathy as I pushed the sweatshirt up over her tits. Pulling her closer, I sucked the first nipple into my mouth and loved how it hardened as she squirmed in my lap.

"You're more red carpet material than I am," I said, then switched nipples to give the other one equal treatment. "Fuck you taste good." My tongue licked over the sensitive tip, and Raine moaned loudly. Nails seductively scraped the back of my neck as I teased her.

"Take off your hoodie and T-shirt," I ordered, my mouth finding her soft skin as soon as the material was out of the way.

"Oh fuck," Raine moaned. "I don't know if I'm ready for such a huge public event like that," she said.

"You never are." It was an honest answer. I'd thought I knew what I was getting into, but I had no idea. "I almost threw up when I stepped out of the limo, and all the lights started flashing."

"Not a selling point," Raine teased, and even though I couldn't see her face, I could picture the look she was giving me. I gently nipped at her nipple, and she yelped but wiggled closer.

"That's it. Keep wiggling on my cock like a good girl," I said, and let my tongue trail a line from her nipple all the way up to her collarbone. Gripping the back of her neck, I pulled her closer and growled against the soft skin under her ear. "Do you really want me to go with some random girl?"

She stiffened, and I smiled. "We'll have to hold hands and kiss for the cameras. I'll have to stare longingly into her eyes and answer questions like we're hot for each other." My breath fanned her skin, and goosebumps rose, making her shiver. "Maybe get caught coming out of one of the private areas with our hair a mess and cleaning lipstick off my face to get the rumors flying."

Raine made a little sound in her throat like she was growling. Fuck, that turned me on. I'd always played it off like Avro's jealousy was too much and over the top, but I secretly loved it, and it made me so hot for him. When I could, I would make a special trip home to surprise him after the event. It was always the same each time I had to go to one. Avro would text me every fifteen minutes, sending me dirty photos and videos that made it hard to focus on a single conversation, and insisted on having phone sex when I got back to the hotel. He may have said he was fine with our lifestyle, but he didn't like it splashed on television, especially when I needed to pretend to be in love with someone else.

Raine had the same jealous streak, she may not fully realize it yet, but I knew she would lose her mind if she saw girls hanging on me. The anger was vibrating off her now, making me so fucking hard.

"Is that what you want, Peaches? For me to pretend to be fucking another woman for all the cameras. Maybe have to pretend to live together for a while before it all falls apart?"

"I don't fucking care," she said, but her clenched jaw and tight, annoyed tone told an entirely different story.

"Okay then, I'll call Allen and set someone up. Maybe two this time," I said and pulled away from her neck as I reached for my cell. She grabbed my forearm, and her eyes were fierce as she stared into mine. "Something wrong? I thought you said you didn't care?"

"I thought you said you wouldn't be with anyone else?"

"Peaches, this is not cheating. This is part of my job. Just like a hooker offers sexual favors for money, this is something I must also do." It was a stretch, but the sparks of rage in her eyes were too much for me not to toy with a little longer.

"You're comparing yourself to a hooker," she asked, and I had to bite the inside of my cheek not to smirk.

"Like I said, just part of the job. Would be nice to have someone there that isn't just grabbing my ass and cock for the cameras," I said, pouring it on thick. I tried to move my arm, but she held it firm.

"I'll go," she said.

"Are you sure? You don't seem that interested. I really can just call Allen," I said. "I mean, Avro is used to it, and I don't want to force you to go if you'll be that uncomfortable?"

"Fuck you, Jace. I'm going," she growled.

"If you say so." Dropping my cell, I cupped her face. "You're so fucking hot, and I bet you'll look like a damn queen in a designer dress. Avro will be drooling back here."

"Why don't we take him too?"

"To the awards?" I bit my lip at the possible backlash and wondered if I really cared. I didn't. But as open and all-inclusive as things had become, that might create more of a stir than even Allen was ready for. I would do it in a heartbeat, but Avro hated the spotlight. Crazy considering what he'd planned on doing for a career before his knee surgeries. He kept telling me that was different. I didn't see the difference.

"No, he can stay at the hotel. I'm sure you're going to have a room, right?" She lifted a shoulder and let it drop. "He can be waiting for us there."

"I like that idea a lot." Gripping her ass harder, I pulled her tight against my body and stared up into her blue eyes. "You know what other idea I really like the thought of?" A coy smile played along her lips, but she devilishly shook her head. "Having you all to myself."

Raine's eyes held a mischievous glint, and as she opened her mouth, I wrapped my hand around her throat. "Don't bother lying to me, Peaches. I know your pussy is fucking wet for me." I gave her throat a little squeeze, and her hands tightened on my shoulders. "You want to wiggle right now. Rub yourself along my cock," I growled. "You can barely contain yourself."

She shuddered, her pulse jumping under my fingers. "Not a chance," she whispered.

The devil would've been impressed with the smile I gave her. "Then prove it, take your jeans off, and let's find out."

"I don't need to prove anything to you," she quipped.

"No, but you will."

"And why is that?"

"Because if you don't take them off," I said, pulling her close enough to attack her lips and leave her gasping for her next breath as I tasted every inch of her sweet mouth. "I'll rip them off your body and fuck you on the floor with the partition to my driver down, rather than here on the seat, without an audience. Your choice," I said and smirked. "Go ahead and call my bluff and find out if I care about being seen fucking you."

I released her body and let her decide. "What if I said I didn't want you at all?"

"You could. I'm not going to pull a Kai on you," I smirked, but her eyes flickered with the jab.

"Asshole," she said. Her tone was angry, but her eyes were sad, and even though I knew I may have pushed the line too far, I also didn't regret it. Why did Kai get a hall pass? She needed to treat us all the same if she was serious about us all being one.

"Yes, I am, but it only bothers you because I poke at things you don't want to look at. Go ahead and deny it, but I'd call you a liar."

I could see her wanting to argue. Her eyes said it all—if looks could kill, I'd already be dead—and that was the sexiest look ever. Raine's body tensed, and her hands balled into fists which made me smile wider. Her nostrils flared as she sucked in a deep breath.

"Do it, hit me. It won't change the fact you want to fuck me, and it won't stop me from being an asshole." Raising my hips as we went over a bump, Raine lost her balance. She gripped my shoulders, which put her nipple right in front of my mouth. Taking advantage of the angle, I flicked it with my tongue. "In fact, hitting me will only have the opposite effect. I like you all fired up."

"You and Kai both," she said, and I was sure that the comment was supposed to sting.

"Means he has good taste in at least one thing," I said. "Besides, if he wants to challenge me in the bedroom, he can come at me. I'd love nothing more than to play who can last longer and make you scream louder." Raine's eyes widened, and she swallowed hard. "Now, are you taking your jeans off, or am I taking them off for you?"

Her hands went to the button.

"Good choice, Peaches."

I shouldn't push her the way I did, it was bound to blow up in my face at some point, but I couldn't help it. There was something about Raine that made me want to push her to her limits. See just how much she would take before she snapped.

Slipping off my lap, she finished undoing her jeans, glaring at me the entire time she pulled them down her legs and set them aside.

"Come here," I ordered. My cock throbbed as I stared at her naked body and the wet patch on the hot as fuck, boy shorts she was wearing. There was something entirely too sexy about this look. My muscles tensed as she maneuvered so she was on her knees on the seat beside me, her tits swaying hypnotically with the movement of the car.

"Now mine," I said.

"I'm making a mental note never to ask about asshole Jace again," she said. Her blue eyes were full of the same fire as earlier. I wanted to shove her naughty mouth down on my cock until she was choking. My hand itched to teach her sexy ass a lesson. I wanted to leave bright pink handprints all over it but held myself in check.

"I bet you are," I drawled as she undid my belt and the buttons on my jeans. I liked the button-down style, less chance of zipping my cock or my piercings in the little metal teeth after I've had a few drinks. Been there and never want to do it again.

Lifting my ass up, Raine pulled down on my jeans, and my overly eager cock sprang from the confines. The silver ring was already shiny from my excitement. Raine's eyes tracked the movement of my cock, hypnotized by the sight.

"Don't worry, Peaches, I plan on having my cock down your throat soon enough, but I want you now, so those fun games will have to wait." Raine opened her mouth, a scowl drawing her eyebrows together. Reaching out, I put my finger on her lips. "Don't bother with the attitude." I wiped at the corner of her mouth and the imaginary drool. "I can already see how much you want my cock."

I stuck my thumb in my mouth and sucked as Raine's eyebrow arched up. Removing it, I held it out to her. She glared and opened her mouth. I hooked it over her bottom teeth, and she growled at me seductively as I pulled her closer like she was on the end of my line.

I forced her onto my lap so she was settled in place and resting on my hard cock that remembered all too well what it felt like to be inside her tight pussy.

"Suck it," I ordered, and groaned as she sucked my thumb and swirled her tongue around the tip. "Now raise your hips," I said and then flicked my gaze up to hers. "Did I say you could stop sucking?"

She bit down slightly, and I smirked, shifting under her. Using my free thumb, I rubbed at her clit as she moaned and shuddered for me.

"That's it, Peaches, give in to what you want. There is nothing wrong with wanting to be my slut. I will treat you like fucking gold, but I have some unusual tastes. Fucking you in public, for example, or chasing you down as you run away, both of which you already found out at the cemetery." Raine moved her hips back and forth, making me wet with each twitch of her sexy ass.

"What else?"

I groaned and watched my cock sliding between her legs. "I like to watch and to be in charge. Put them all together, and it's a potent cocktail I'll always be down for. Does that make you nervous?"

She shocked me when she shook her head no. "Good. Now lift your hips."

She didn't hesitate this time and braced herself on my shoulders as she lifted enough that I could straighten my cock and find that sweet entrance. As soon as I was in place, she sucked in a sexy ragged breath and slid all the way down as she threw her head back and moaned.

Fuck she was stunning. I clenched my jaw tight with her heat soaking into my cock, making it want to explode.

"You feel so fucking good, Peaches," I growled out and gripped her tits to fondle as I feasted on them. The little whimpers of pleasure were like the sweetest song to my ears. I could listen to her all day and never tire.

Taking me by surprise, she kissed me hard, her tongue slipping into my mouth, seeking out my tongue piercing like it was her toy.

"Fuck me, Peaches. Ride my cock," I managed to get out as she broke the kiss. Grabbing her ass tight, Raine rose up and back down. As she picked up the pace, I encouraged her faster, my fingers pressing into the soft skin.

"God, Jace," Raine moaned, then sucked my bottom lip into her mouth. Her hands ran all over my chest, slipping under the material to tweak my nipples and play with my piercings. "I love these," she said.

"Fuck," I groaned, with her endless exploring. She bounced faster and nipped at the side of my neck. The girl was making me wild. I was coming undone in the back of my limo, a completely new experience. Despite what the entertainment magazines thought, I had never held orgies in the back of this thing. In reality, it was my office away from my office. I never let anyone travel with me unless it was a scheduled appearance, and we would hardly speak, let alone fuck.

"You going to cum for me? You going to cum all over my cock?"

"Yes."

"You have no idea how badly I want to put down the windows so everyone can see me fucking you." I smirked. "But I won't, at least not today," I added as her mouth fell open. "Come on, Peaches. You want to let go. Do it. I want your cum. Give it to me. Soak my cock." I slapped her ass, and she moaned louder as she feverishly picked up the pace. My hips thrust up fast and hard as I drove into her at a blinding pace. "You're thinking about two cocks in you, aren't you, Peaches? Two of us filling your holes as we use you, and you want it. You want it so bad, don't you?"

"God, yes," Raine cried out as she wrapped her arms around my neck and hung on tight as the orgasm hit her body. She bit down hard on my neck and screamed. The sound muffled as I continued to hammer into her. I groaned at the feel of her marking me. It spoke to the monster that I kept buried deep inside of me. The monster that wanted to feel her struggle beneath me while she was unsure if she was screaming for me to stop or fuck her harder. I could feel the waves of her release coating me as the walls of her pussy clamped down around my cock.

"Peaches, you're so good, fuck you're amazing. I'm almost there." The sound of slapping skin was loud as my cock drilled deeper into her with each thrust and had Raine whimpering all over again. "Fuck yes, right there. Rub yourself, keep cumming for me." Her hand slipped between our bodies and rubbed her clit as she moaned out my name over and over, feeding my soul.

A thought came to me, and I stopped moving. I gripped Raine's chin hard and savored the worried look in her eyes. "Did he cum in you?"

Raine bit her lip. "I'll take that as a yes."

"Yes," she said, her voice wispy as she wiggled, trying to get me to continue.

"Well then, Peaches, I guess it's a race to see who can get you pregnant first." She opened her mouth, and I didn't wait to see if she would argue, fucking her harder than before.

"Ah! Jace!" Raine screamed, her head thrown back as the climax she was riding gripped her again. The sound of my name coming from her mouth like that was all I could handle. My back arched, and Raine hung on to me tighter as I came, the release so powerful that I felt frozen in place as she continued to bounce and drain my cock of all I had.

Panting, Raine draped herself over me, and I held her close. "So many fucking positions I want to fuck you in, Peaches.

"Is that so?"

"Yeah, and I can't wait to get back and gloat that I've had you twice to myself," I said and smiled as she leaned back and hit me with her patented glare.

"You really are an ass."

Cupping her face, I kissed her long and slow, allowing myself the luxury of her soft pillowy lips. "You'll fall in love with it. I can promise you that."

"Always so sure of yourself."

"I'm sure of you," I said, grabbing her discarded hoodie and wrapping it around her shoulders. "What you crave deep down is what I can give you. What I'm willing to give you. What I want to give you."

"And what exactly is it that you think I want?" Her voice was soft as she cuddled into me, seeking my warmth.

"You want to let yourself go and feel safe." Raine didn't say anything. "You're safe with me. I will protect you, Peaches. However I can, and I won't stop." She kissed my neck softly. "And you want to experience everything you've denied yourself for years. You want the three of us to give it to you. I don't like Kai, and I certainly don't trust him, but I get the appeal. I said I'd try with him, and that means I'm in until he gives me a reason not to be." She made a little sound, and

I wasn't sure if she was crying, but she held me tighter. "And you love to be praised. I've figured out another one of your kinks, and I'm going to keep finding them, and I'm going to fuck you in all the ways you crave."

"You confuse me, Jace," she said softly, and I chuckled.

"I confuse myself, so we're even."

"I'll move." She went to get up, but I held her tight.

"Oh no, you don't. We have another hour left in this ride. That gives me lots of time to have you again, and this time, I'm going to tan your ass every time you disobey me."

I smiled as she shivered.

Oh yeah, I was falling for her, fast and hard, like I was jumping off the tall diving board. This was why I didn't stay. I knew myself too well. Avro and now Raine were filling up my heart. If Kai came at us again in any way, I'd be prepared, but I prayed that it never came to that.

Raine's body relaxed, and her breathing deepened as she napped. I really did have a thing for being needed and kissed the top of her head.

I grabbed my phone and found the latest text from Allen, who was still freaking out over me turning the plane around and missing the interview he'd set up. I was purposely ignoring my bandmates, who were just as pissed off. They were used to me going rogue, but even I didn't miss concerts or interviews. That was money out of our pockets and looked terrible without a good excuse. I had a great excuse, but they wouldn't see it that way. I did have an idea, though.

J: You said you wanted a good story to sell before the awards show. I have one for you.

A: I'm not speaking to you.

I smirked at his response. I could easily picture him pouting somewhere, half wasted, looking like he'd been drug in from a back alley by a tom cat.

J: I'll make the last concert on the list. Reschedule the interview with my apologies that it was an emergency, and I have a date for the awards.

A: Please tell me it's Taylor Swift

I glared at my phone.

J: I've told you a million times we're just friends.

A: I can keep hoping. Fine, who is it, and don't say some cousin of yours. I can't spin that, no matter how hard I try.

My face screwed up as I stared at the message.

J: No, she's not a family member. What kind of fucked up question is that anyway? How much have you been drinking?

A: Lots, I deal with you daily. You're giving me a fucking ulcer Jace.

J: Her name is Raine Eastman, and she is not rich or famous or a princess, before you fucking ask.

A: You mean the manager from the bar? What good is she?

I ground my teeth together as I stared at the question. I couldn't tell if he was purposely trying to be a dick, but the implied tone was pissing me off.

> J: What do you mean?"

> A: I mean, if she has no pull, clout, or workable drama, then what good is she?

I squeezed my phone tight as I glared at the screen even though Allen couldn't see me. This was what I hated. I loved the music, I loved writing and recording and even singing for the fans, but this bullshit was what I was sick of. My fingers hovered over the keypad as I thought of what to say. How did I explain Raine to him and not mention Avro or Kai?

> J: She's the girl that I love.

Did I love her? I didn't know yet, but it felt like that was where we were heading and what I needed to say to shut Allen up. There was no immediate response. The little dots appeared and disappeared multiple times. I couldn't believe that I had just typed that to Allen. I couldn't believe I typed it at all. Raine sighed, and I could feel her breathing even out as she slept in my arms.

> A: I don't know what to say. I don't know how this happened, and I don't know if this is a good thing or not. I mean, I thought the show you did there was the first time you met.

> J: Of course, it's a fucking good thing. Raine is coming with me to the awards show, and I don't need to explain myself.

A: Not to be a downer here, but you better have some answers prepared because there will be a ton of questions, and they won't just be coming for you. They'll go after her if they sense she's the weak link in the story.

Allen wasn't wrong about that. It meant I needed to prep Raine before she spoke to any reporter or interviewers without me by her side.

J: I'll make sure she is prepared. I want the penthouse booked at the same hotel I stayed at last time. Put the room under Mr. Beck.

Allen knew that I liked to fuck Avro, but he didn't know just how close we were or what his last name was. This way, Avro could book in and get all the keys, and we'd never even have to put my name on a room.

A: Who the hell is that? Do you suddenly have an alter ego?

J: Just do it.

A: Fine.

J: Oh, and Allen. If you dig up shit on Raine and try to exploit it, I will fire you. Not even a moment of hesitation, I mean it.

I really wanted to say that I'd destroy him, and they'd never find his body, but you just didn't put shit like that in a text. At least not if you were smart.

A: Why are you always making my life difficult, Jace?

J: It's just my nature.

I quickly left the chat with Allen and found the group chat with the band that had completely blown up. Sighing, I started answering questions. Glancing down at Raine in my arms, I knew I'd do it all over again.

Snake

Chapter 11

LOST

1% MC

SOULS

K aivan

Holding my side, I stomped around the far corner of the clubhouse.

"What the fuck do you mean it's just you guys? Where the hell is Chase?" I looked around at the added fifty-two people and ground my teeth together. We were up to a whopping eighty-two since Sparky was now gator bait with the rest of the trash.

Tanner bit off another piece of the banana he was eating, and I was fucking tempted to jam the thing down his throat when he winked at one of the sweetbutts and shoved the entire thing in his mouth. Of course, now the guy chewed like a fucking cow with a mouthful of cud and gave me a view of the yellow mush moving around his open gob. He was giving me flashbacks to prison and making me want to vomit. If I did, I was aiming it at him.

"Just what I said, he didn't come back with us. Shit is pretty much wrapped up, but he still had some crap to sort out with Keenan." Tanner lifted his shoulders and let them drop.

"Hey sweetheart," Tanner yelled and pointed at the couch with every one of the sweetbutts occupying a lap. Both Mannix and I rolled our eyes when they all pointed at themselves. "Yeah, sure, any of you. Someone get me more food, and I want a bottle of whiskey. Oh! And one of you better be ready to fuck me soon."

My hand clenched as I fantasized about knocking this guy the fuck out. Had I been this annoying at twenty-two? Naw, I was already four years into my sentence and a hardened, miserable prick by twenty-two.

"Can we focus," I asked, glaring at Tanner's smiling face. He'd already chugged a few drinks and was more annoying and immature than ever.

"I am. On my stomach. Next will be my cock, 'cause it's hungry too," Tanner said. He took a swig of the latest beer before letting out a loud belch that sounded like his name before pointing at one of the girls.

Luckily Mannix stepped in before I decided that a couple of cracked ribs were no big deal and beat the shit out of Tanner.

Mannix grabbed Tanner by the arm.

"Hey, what are you doing man?" Tanner whined as Mannix marched him off to the meeting room and away from the other guys. Roach and I followed.

I kept looking out of the corner of my eye to see if anyone was more interested than they should be, but I didn't see anything unusual. Didn't mean shit, as I found out, but I felt like I needed to interrogate all those left here while Chase was away. I bitched about Chase, fuck, I didn't even like the guy, but it took next-level scum to switch clubs and do what Sparky had planned. If I left, it would be to lay my pale white ass on a beach somewhere for the rest of my breathing days.

Once inside the meeting room reserved for church sessions, I closed the door so no one else could eavesdrop.

"Where the fuck is Beast? He wouldn't let you treat me like this," Tanner complained as Mannix released his arm.

"Beast had other things to take care of, and my guess would be that he didn't think you'd act like a newbie and force me to drag you in here," Mannix drawled, crossing his arms over his chest. I bit my tongue to keep from laughing. Being called a newbie or a bootlicker was a huge insult to anyone in the club once you'd been here for over a year.

Tanner had been a breath of fresh air after being in prison for ten years, but I quickly learned that the immature and fun side got old when that was all he ever did. He was always looking for trouble or getting drunk and doing shit that would normally get him punched in the face or a bullet between the eyes. Chase was the only reason the other members held back.

I was shocked that Chase hadn't given Tanner his one percenter patch regardless of how he acted. It gave me hope for our Prez.

Beast had gone home for the night. I couldn't blame him. All the dead lying around was bound to stir up memories of his wife. As tough as he showed himself to be, I knew he was still hurting. Raine had only been back in my life a short time, and I couldn't imagine losing her. After years of marriage and the kind of love Beast and Jaz had...the guy was lucky he could put a foot in front of the other.

Didn't mean I went any easier on him. Beast would've found that disrespectful, and someone needed to make decisions with Chase gone. Beast had volunteered himself, and that came with assholes like me pointing out shit, such as we were vulnerable. If I didn't point out the crap, people died. We got lucky tonight. I'd gotten lucky, but I didn't like luck. It tended to shit in your face and then drink your beer.

"Did I piss in your fucking beer, Mannix?"

"Tanner cut the attitude. There is no one in here for you to show off for. I need you to focus on the questions. What is the ETA for Chase and the rest of the crew? We now have multiple bodies to clean up, cops to keep away, and more than ever, we need to build an alliance with a local club. We have a huge target painted on our backs. So, tell me what you know," Mannix said, his voice as calm and firm as ever.

"Look, I don't know why you're all in such a twist. I'm back, and so are some of the men. Chase will be back soon enough," Tanner said, crossing his arms. "It's not like he gave me an itinerary."

"Tanner, for fucks sake. We're still breathing because you took them by surprise when you came back, and they thought the entire crew was home. The Vipers have ninety-seven members more than us at the best of times," I said.

"A few less now," Tanner mocked and sat down laughing.

"Do you ever take anything seriously?" I growled. I lifted my T-shirt to show off the bandages. "I almost fucking died. Does that not register with you?"

"Fuck Snake, you can remove that stick from your ass any time," Tanner said. "Maybe we need to get you laid."

I looked at Mannix. "I'm going to kill him." I reached for my gun, but Roach grabbed my arm.

"You could, but we all know I'm Chase's favorite. He'd send the whole club after you." Tanner smiled and reminded me way too much of the jerks I used to beat the shit out of in school. I was tempted to do it again now. Ribs be damned.

"The only reason you're his favorite is cause he sees you as a charity case. You're the piece of shit he pulled out of the garbage. Ever wonder why you need a babysitter Tanner? Why you never get sent on important jobs alone? Why do you think you don't have your patch yet?" I growled out. "Even the man you follow around like a pathetic dog knows you're not worthy."

"Fuck you, man!" Tanner burst from the seat like he'd been ejected and was in my face a moment later. Our noses touched as he tried to intimidate me.

Ten years in prison had done many things to me, but one thing it had done right was to teach me to shut off my humanity. That place and those that thought they could control me taught me how to kill without remorse. A deadly calm washed over my body, and I needed to get away from Tanner, or there was no telling what I'd do. It would certainly be something I couldn't come back from with Chase, even if the rest of the club would cheer. Roach touched my shoulder, and I remembered I had something else to live for. Someone else, and I took a deep breath.

"Both of you knock it off and sit down," Mannix ordered.

Tanner backed off first with Mannix's meaty hand firmly on his arm. "You too, Snake. Sit the fuck down."

"Sitting hurts," I said and wandered over to the wall to give myself space from Tanner. I didn't normally give a shit about whatever crazy antics he got up to, but this shit was getting annoying fast.

"Do you live in the real world, Tanner," I asked, and he crossed his arms and glared at me.

"What the fuck is that supposed to mean?"

"You lack the ability to understand what is real life and what is one of your video games. We lost people tonight. People that someone loved, people that Beast is planning a service for, and you're acting like this is all a big fucking party." I pointed out toward the clubhouse. "You're more worried about getting fucked."

"It's how we deal with shit. All those guys out there are acting the same way. I'm not doing anything different."

"But we're not out there. We are in here asking you a few simple questions, and you're being evasive." I shook my head. He just didn't get it. Then again, anyone that would light a Molotov cocktail and toss it in a room full of chemicals while we were all in there was a case in point that he couldn't see past the end of his nose. We were all fucking lucky he didn't kill us that day, and the fucker only laughed like we'd regenerate.

"I'm telling you, Snake, you're too tense. Just have a drink and relax."

"Don't bother wasting your breath," Roach whispered. He was right. There was no point trying to explain something to someone that had no interest in seeing the bigger picture.

Tanner was shrugging off the very real possibility of another attack and us losing more people, all while grabbing his cock and saying bring it on. It was a sure way to get us all killed. I did dangerous shit all the time, but this was different. I'd never been this cavalier with my attitude. I spent ten years in prison looking over my shoulder and protecting those that would protect me. I had looked out for Raine before that, and now I looked out for those in this MC. I would've thought that a kid that came from a shit start—like me— would have more respect for the home he'd found. It was obvious that he'd been spoiled, and I had no intention of feeding into that. I almost died tonight, and with that came clarity.

"Everyone take a fucking breath. We're all on the same side," Mannix said.

"Are we though," Roach asked, shocking me. He stood by my side, his arms crossed and his stare fixed on the two men. "Snake was almost killed by one of our own. Someone we thought we could trust." He pointed toward the door, the sound of music and laughter getting louder.

"We have no way of knowing how many more men were pulled into other clubs. Snake is right. We need order. We need our men and our prez back. We have no idea how many are sitting out there right now waiting like sleeper agents to be activated. What's next? Slit our throats in the night?"

Tanner rubbed at his chin, and I could tell by the smile on his face he was still thinking about the shootout and the fun he had killing the Vipers. Or the girls he was getting later. Tanner rolled his eyes and made a scoffing sound like Roach was overreacting.

"Give it up, Roach. No one wants to slit your useless throat," Tanner said. "And so what if we lost some people, we always do. It's just the way it is."

If I weren't leaning against the wall, I would've fallen over when Mannix punched Tanner so hard he flew off the chair he was sitting on and crashed to the floor in a heap.

"What the fuck? Why the hell did you do that?" Tanner growled as he rubbed his face.

"Do not disrespect our fallen members, not ever. They were part of this family, and they deserve to be remembered with honor." Mannix roared. I'd never seen the man so angry, and his presence filled the room as his stare stayed firmly on Tanner.

"Inside this room is all business Tanner and we are meeting about real issues. If you can't handle that or the responsibility that comes with your potential position in this club, I'll speak to Chase when he gets back about removing you for good." Mannix placed his hands on his hips. "I will not put up with any more of this crap from you," Mannix said.

"Chase wouldn't do that. We're family," Tanner argued. "And I've done things to help. I've done lots of things."

"Don't kid yourself, Tanner. You're no longer in Ashen Springs, fucking all the lonely, married housewives. The members of this club hardly know you, and they will vote you out if you keep this attitude up. Chase's hand will be forced, and I'll be the first to nominate you to leave." Mannix growled. He was fucking scary when angry. The fact we rarely ever saw him that way made it more impressive. "Are you listening now? If not, I'll happily knock your fucking teeth out of your head one at a time until you do."

"Fuck, you're all wound way too tight. I just wanted to party off this energy, and we could've talked tomorrow or something," Tanner grumbled.

"But I'm asking you now, and that's what matters. So, answer the question, or my next move will be to call Chase and settle this once and for all."

Words I never thought I'd hear.

"Fine, Chase said he'd be three to four days tops. Some of the men were wounded, and we lost a few. Chase is making arrangements to have their bodies brought home. Happy now," Tanner asked as he picked himself up off the floor. "And don't fucking hit me like that."

Mannix puffed out his chest, and his hands balled into fists as large and destructive as any sledgehammer. "Then stop acting like I need to tune you in. You might be the youngest member at twenty-two, but you're not a kid anymore. It's also not just you and Chase in Richie Rich world, where you can play all day without any cares. You might know Chase better than I do, but I've been helping run this club since before you were cum shot from your father's body. So don't think because Chase likes you that, you have an unlimited shield of protection." Mannix stepped up to Tanner and stared down at him. "This is a motorcycle club with real business and real family. This is not your personal playground. Do you hear me?"

I almost heard the balloon pop as his attitude fizzled. He stuffed his hands in his pockets and looked his age. "Yeah, fine, I get it. Can I get on with my night now? My ass is sore from the long ride, and I'm hungry," Tanner said, his voice missing all the earlier cockiness.

I still had a million questions, but Mannix nodded and stepped out of the way for Tanner to head to the door. He stopped with his hand on the handle and turned to look at the three of us.

"I am sorry you got shot, Snake, and if anyone is playing two sides, I'll find them," he said, walking out.

"I swear that guy makes me want to kill him some days," Mannix grumbled.

"Get in line," I said.

"At least we have an answer," Roach said, lighting a smoke. "The question is, can we keep shit together until the rest of the men are back."

"I'm just happy that at least the two of you see why I've been so fucking angry." I shook my head and went to cross my arms and thought better of it. "I'm heading home unless you need me for anything else?"

"Naw, whatever is going to happen isn't happening tonight," Mannix said and made his way to the door. Roach and I followed. I expected Roach to veer off and hang out with the group, but he stayed with me instead.

"What's going on," I asked as we reached the bottom stair.

"I may need you to help me check on Lane tonight. I haven't seen her in a couple of days and need to make sure she's okay. I think she found ways to avoid me following her around." Roach looked genuinely concerned, but it was never too early or too late to fuck with your best friend.

"Oh, I saw her," I said.

"You did?"

"Yeah, she was giving some frat guy a spit polish. She had good form too," I lied, keeping my face straight as Roach's eyes narrowed, his lip pulling up in a snarl.

"You better be fucking joking."

"Sorry man, wish I was. She was down by the beach where Raine's club is. You know, the one you forced me to go to? Anyway, I suspect she's back at the sorority now." I grabbed his shoulder. "You may need to consider that cage after all. She looked really into it. Not sure what she got up to after that, but...."

Roach yanked his shoulder away and swore as he stomped out the door. "I'm going to find this guy and kill him."

I smiled as I watched him get on his bike and ride away. And that was how you fucked with your best friend, who was totally in love and seemed completely oblivious. I could admit it was a little sadistic.

What I needed was a shower, a bite to eat, a pack of ice for my side, and...fuck. Raine was with Avro and Jace, but I wanted her with me. I ground my teeth together, already fucking hating this.

Raine

Chapter 12

Raine

I was wrapped in warmth and didn't want to open my eyes. I technically didn't have a job to go to, but I should call my boss, Chris, and let him know that my family emergency was...not an emergency? I had no idea what to say to him. I'd made up this whole thing about my aunt being deathly ill in another state and how I was going to look after her. I didn't even have an aunt, let alone one that was sick, and saying she died seemed morbid. This was what happened when you lied. You always got caught with your foot in the pile of shit.

The room was bright. Blinking and rubbing my eyes, I found myself staring at Jace's sleeping face. He looked so sweet like this. Not the ass that he could be. His long lashes fanned his cheeks, and the messy hair that was almost hanging in his eyes looked like he'd gone to bed with it styled.

Avro's arm was wrapped snuggly around me. His body pressed tight like he wanted to make sure that I didn't run off. Glancing over my shoulder, I saw he was still very much asleep, and I desperately needed to use the bathroom. It took some wiggling, but I got myself out from underneath Avro's arm and down to the end of the bed.

Grabbing the closest T-shirt I could find, I pulled it on. It was a mini dress on me. Laundry was suddenly a necessity. I didn't have many clothes to begin with and hadn't done a wash in a few days. Quietly padding over to Avro's long dresser, I pulled open the drawer I'd seen him pull boxers out of and found a pair with yellow minions all over them. Smiling, I stole those and my phone from my bag before heading into the bathroom.

It looked like I had a million messages from Kai. Unlocking my phone, I started going through them.

> K: I hate this

> K: I want you

> K: Can I come get you?

> K: Tink, poke. Poke. Poke. Poke. You can't be asleep already. Actually, you better be asleep. I don't want to think about you fucking those two.

> K: Why did I type that? Now that image is stuck in my head. Fuck.

I shook my head as I scrolled through the messages that were basically Kai arguing with himself. It was stalker-level obsessive, and yet, I was smiling into the mirror like I was the one that needed help.

> R: Hey

The response took a few minutes, but soon the little bubbles appeared.

> K: Finally! I've been lying in bed thinking about you.

I bit my lip, and even though he wasn't in the room, I could feel my face going bright red. Glancing in the mirror confirmed my suspicions.

> R: Oh yeah? What exactly were you thinking about?

> K: How about I show you instead?

A video arrived before I could ask what he meant. Tapping play, the short clip caused my legs to rub together. I pressed play again when the clip ended and watched his hand travel up and down his hard cock. A second video came in, and I hit the play button immediately. This one had sound. He groaned as he worked his hand faster, and I had to lean against the counter.

> K: Do you want the ending?

> R: Is that a real question?

> K: Lmfao. Then you need to come see me. Today.

> R: Oh, that's just mean.

> K: Mean is my MO. Today, and I'll show you the ending you deserve, or…I can just finish now. Here. All alone. Fuck I'm hard.

R: Okay, I'll come see you, but I have to go to work and sort some stuff out first, and there are errands I need to run. I'll have Avro drop me off after that.

K: ...Way to ruin my mood by mentioning his name.

I shook my head at the phone like Kai could see. My lip curled up, and a nervous energy washed over me as an idea came to me. Hitting the little camera, I lifted the T-shirt and struck a sexy pose. This felt ridiculous, but I gave him my best pout while my fingers splayed over my nipple like I'd been playing with them. Snapping the photo, I stared at my image and could admit it looked hot. I still felt silly, but before I lost my nerve, I pushed send.

K: Oh fuck! Hello! Okay, I want those fucking sexy lips of yours wrapped around my cock.

R: Will that hold you over until I get there?

K: What? You're leaving me like this. You're terrible.

R: Gotta keep you coming back somehow. LOL!

K: I will take a dirty photo from you anytime, but Tink, I'll always come back to you, sexy photos or not. TTYL

R: LV U

K: LVU2

I had to blink back tears as I read those four little letters that gripped my throat. I couldn't stop staring at them. I felt each word like they were branded on my soul.

I turned on the taps and splashed cool water on my heated face before I finished up in the bathroom and tackled my main obstacle for the day. How do I get my job back and not sound like a flake or an asshole?

Opening the door, I screamed as Jace picked me up and sat me on the counter. "Geez us Jace, you scared the shit out of me," I said as he smiled and stood between my legs. "And get the smile off your face. I can't right now. I have things I need to do today."

"Yeah, like me," he said, kissing the side of my neck.

I glared at him as Avro laughed from somewhere in the bedroom. I peered around Jace to see Avro making the bed. I wish I had his affinity for neatness. Jace pressed forward, and no matter how hard I tried, I couldn't stop myself from looking down at the large tent in his boxers. My hands went to his waist, and he groaned. The sound made me squirm. It wasn't fair that they were so tempting. I mean, it wasn't really a hardship to stay in bed and fuck them all day.

"Fuck you smell good, and I love you in Avro's boxers." I laughed.

"Yes, super stylish of me," I said.

"I got them as a gift for him, but they look better on you."

"I heard that," Avro called out.

"I swear he has superhero hearing," Jace whispered, making me giggle as he tickled my ear with his breath.

"I need to get my job back before he hires another manager," I said.

"Too late," Avro said and came to stand in the doorway. Jace waved his hand in his direction.

"Go away. I'm trying to convince her to come back to bed," Jace said. I hadn't seen this lighthearted teasing much from Jace, and I really liked it. He was a very complex personality, but puzzles were something I always enjoyed playing with.

"Who did Chris hire?" Avro cocked an eyebrow. "Shit, I totally forgot that I told him to hire you. Sorry, I should've remembered that."

"Yes, and you have an interview for your new position today. I might even let you in my new office." Avro smiled as I swore under my breath.

"See, lots of time to come back to bed," Jace said. "Would it make a difference if I told you that I have to fly out tomorrow for a few days?"

"Ohhh laying it on thick with the guilt, are we?" I leaned back on the counter and braced myself on my hands.

"Fuck look at this," he said and slid his hands up the shorts. I smacked at his hands, but he continued until he could grip my hips, his thumbs tracing the inside of my thighs.

"Stop it you. Is he always like this," I asked Avro, who was smirking.

"Worse, actually. I kinda enjoy his trips for work, or I'd be stuck in bed all day with a sore ass."

Jace laughed and looked over his shoulder. "True story, but you love it."

"Also true," Avro said. "I have an idea. Why don't you go with Jace?"

"What?" Jace and I said together.

"I'm serious. You said you want to take Raine to the awards show, so why not start laying the groundwork now? It will be more believable if you're seen together sooner. You can catch the two concerts you need to do and fly back. It's what? Three days?"

"Oh, I don't know if that's a good idea." I nibbled my lip as I thought about Kai's reaction. Who was I fooling? He was going to lose his mind.

Jace turned his steely gaze on me. "Let me guess...Kai?" He shook his head. "Are you always going to walk on eggshells where he is concerned?" He stepped back and crossed his arms. I looked between him and Avro and wanted to be pissed off, yet I couldn't think of a good comeback. "I mean, if you start now, then he'll dictate everything you do. You realize that, right? Don't fool yourself, Kai may have agreed to, try, as you put it, but he's already formulating a plan to pry you away from us."

I narrowed my gaze at him. "And how can you be so sure?"

"Because it's what I would do if I were him." Walking over to the shower, he ran the water and turned around to face me. "I'd make sure that I was always in your face. Texts, phone calls, surprise visits. Then it would be jealousy. Have you see me with other women and make sure that you were good and pissed before I fucked you so good that you wouldn't be able to walk right for a week. Then I'd make you feel guilty for thinking that I'd actually ever fuck those girls. Then I'd mark you, something like a tattoo or fancy jewelry that screams you're mine and that the other guys can't compare. Last is undermine the other guys and find a way to make them look bad."

"Wow, you've put some thought into this," I said, glaring at him, yet I couldn't stop thinking about the text messages waiting for me.

"I don't need to think about it. It's classic alpha behavior." He held up a finger. "One treat you like a goddess." He lifted another. "Two make you jealous." He held up a third. "Three make you doubt yourself and your feelings." He lifted a fourth finger. "Mark you somehow so you feel labeled and owned." He held up his whole hand. "Lastly, separate you from the pack."

"But Kai is not like that," I said and realized as Avro and Jace laughed that either I was naive or they were right, and I didn't like either option.

"Oh yes, he is. Every man is capable of it, even if they don't mean to do it. Kai may not set out to complete the steps consciously, but unconsciously, his whole goal is still to make you solely his. He has no interest in sharing you with anyone. You wait and see."

"And that's not your goal. Right now, putting doubts in my head?"

"Wrong, I'm educating you. I'm used to having multiple people in a relationship and navigating the waters with different personalities that have their own agendas. Can you say the same for Kai?" Jace lifted his shoulders and let them drop. I wasn't sure what to believe. On the one hand, he had a point, but on the other, I saw Kai as more of a stomping around, beating his chest type rather than using mental manipulation. "Look, all I'm saying is stay watchful until things find a good groove. Just because you want this to happen doesn't mean it's magically going to be okay."

Jace pushed down the boxers he was wearing and smiled as my eyes fixed on his still, very hard cock, the argument I was about to make crashed into a wall.

"I'm going to shower. Anyone care to join," Jace asked.

"I'm in," Avro pushed his boxers down, and I was left staring at the two of them completely naked. I licked my lips as my eyes roamed over their bodies. They stepped in the shower but kept the door open. As their lips met and hands roamed over each other's bodies, I felt myself wanting to cave. What the hell had I done to myself?

Avro broke the heated kiss and turned his head my way. Water dripped off his chin and slid down his body in thin streams.

"Are you coming, or am I getting Jace all to myself?" He smiled at me, and my heart fluttered.

I had no idea what had gotten into me, but no one could say no to that eye candy.

Snake

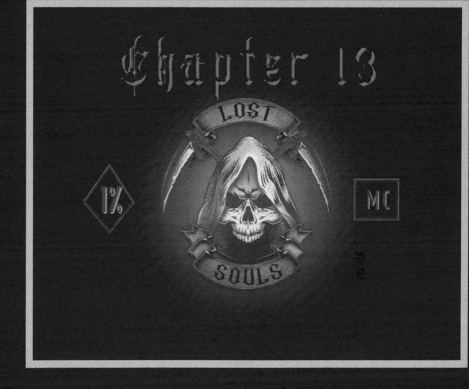

Chapter 13

Kaivan

Raine was late. She said that she was busy shopping with Avro. So, instead of sitting around the house like a sap, I came to the clubhouse for a drink. Now, I wasn't sure that sitting with the obnoxiously loud group of people was helping my state of mind.

My fingers tapped off the top of the bar while I stared at the television tuned to the latest horse race. I wasn't much for betting, I preferred certainties, but I could appreciate the rush of watching the powerful animals speed around the oval at a breakneck pace.

"Come on, Fartindawind," Brick yelled at the television. "Yes, that's it, Fartindawind, you can do it! Come on, girl. Push, push, push."

I snickered as I swallowed down the last of my drink. Did Brick even know that he was yelling?

"Yes!" Brick yelled, and I watched in the mirror behind the bar as Brick jumped up with a yell and brought the sweetbutt that was sitting on his lap with him. "Fuck yeah, what a fucking rush. The next round is on me!"

"Big talk since the drinks are free," Ink drawled.

"Shut the fuck up, man. It's the thought that counts."

As the two began to argue, I turned my attention back to my drink. I swirled the liquid around and watched it swirl up one side and then the other as if mirroring my own messed-up emotions.

"Hey there, Snake," Dee said and ran her arm over my shoulders. "Do you want to spend a little time relieving your stress," she asked, laying her other hand on my leg.

"We could make it a party," Crystal said as she pressed against my other side. She was so close that I would only have to turn my head, and her tit would be in my mouth. The small piece of leather she wore would easily pull off and leave her ready. Could I appreciate that both women were talented? Yes, I could, but shit was a lot more complicated now.

"I wouldn't touch me," I drawled. The two women must have thought I was joking, as they only laughed. "I have a girl," I said.

"Yeah, we know. Us," Crystal said next to my ear. The girls were hyped up with the extra guys and the excitement from yesterday, but I was shocked that they were approaching me. They normally flirted from across the room until I called them over, so I wasn't sure what was up. Did I have a new allure now that I was taken? Could they sniff that shit out like bloodhounds?

"I have to say. This is entertaining." Roach laughed. He was the only one I told about my new relationship, and even with him, I hadn't mentioned Avro or Jace. The guys here wouldn't get it, and as much as I didn't really give a shit what they thought, I wasn't in the mood to explain it either.

My eyes met Roach's in the mirror, and I shook my head in disbelief as he made a kissing face and then shook his finger at me like we were teens. At this point, I didn't think the guy would ever grow up.

"You could help here," I said to him.

Dee's hand slid up my leg, trying to palm my cock. Grabbing her wrist, I stopped her from reaching her goal. "I said I have a girl, and I wouldn't touch me." I turned my head to stare at Dee, her lips set in a pout as her eyes blinked back with confusion.

"You mean like a real girl?"

"What other kind is there," I asked, my brow furrowing.

She shrugged. "I don't know. It's you. Didn't really think that was a you thing," Dee said. "You don't have relationships with anyone, barely even the guys." She wasn't saying it to be mean. In fact, her tone was soft and unsure, but it felt like a smack all the same. I purposely distanced myself, which came with bonuses and the reality that I was isolated as much as Raine.

"I'd listen to him, ladies," Roach said. He was turned on his stool so that he was leaning against the bar but made no effort to peel Crystal off of me as she rubbed up on me like a cat in heat. "She's on her way, and she's going to be pissed if she sees this," Roach said.

An image of what that might look like crossed my mind, and my lip lifted. Would she be jealous? Would she get angry? I actually loved the idea, and my cock stirred with the fantasy playing out in my mind. I was so distracted by the sexy images of Raine fuming mad and fucking her hard that I didn't notice Crystal lift her leg to straddle me.

"We need to repay you." She rubbed her tits against my arm and giggled. Blinking and pulling myself out of the fog, I let go of Dee's wrist and looked up at Crystal.

"Whoa, Crystal, you need to get off of me," I said.

I felt the pull of Raine's arrival like she had some sort of magic. My eyes snapped up to Raine's reflection in the mirror behind the bar, and I sucked in a sharp breath. It felt like the oxygen was sucked out of the room as our eyes locked. If I thought I'd seen her angry before, I knew nothing as her face darkened. My cock jumped along with my heart, going from flaccid to hard in an instant. I licked at my suddenly dry lips. Fuck she was beautiful.

"Oh holy crap," Roach said the words that I was thinking. Raine marched across the floor, her eyes never leaving mine in the mirror. "Come on, Crystal. Get off, Snake," Roach said, trying to take control of the situation since I couldn't seem to move while locked in her stare.

"Now that's better," Crystal cooed as she gripped my hard cock through the jeans.

Oh, this was bad, like really bad. I could feel Raine's wrath the closer she got, the tension filling the room and making everyone look at the newcomer. I grabbed Crystal's hand to stop her. I'm dead was all I could think as Raine's lip pulled up in a snarl which only made me harder. I shuddered.

No one moved as they watched her, and I didn't blame them. The only one that was stupid enough to jump in the middle of a relationship issue was Tanner, and right now, I had money down on Raine to win. Besides, if anyone tried to touch her, I'd cut off their hand. Every bit of her jealous fury was mine. She was mine, but I couldn't seem to make my brain function properly to stop this from turning into a bloodbath.

"I'd intervene, but even I'm not that stupid," Roach said, sitting his drink on the bar and moving away.

Raine's eyes broke the stare first, and it felt like I'd been caught in a tractor beam from Star Trek. I hated the show, but Raine loved it. I'd lost count of how many nights we sat and watched a marathon of them.

"You need to get off me now," I said, grabbing Crystal's wrists. A sound rippled from Raine's mouth that was more animal than human.

Raine moved much faster than I thought she would ever be able to as she grabbed Crystal's arm and wrenched her off my lap in a single tug. Crystal's confused scream was short-lived as she landed on her ass with a crash.

The dark glare Raine gave me sent cold racing down my spine. She was blackout mad, I'd seen that look in my own eyes a time or two, and you did things you normally wouldn't when that happened.

"Raine, no."

I reached for her, but my mouth fell open as Crystal jumped up, and Raine went full MMA on Crystal's ass. Raine looked small next to Crystal, but that wasn't slowing her down. Crystal backed up and tried to block the hits as Raine advanced on her.

I should really stop this, but fuck, it was hot. Crystal yelled once before Raine's fist caught her across the jaw and sent her stumbling backward. Crystal hit a chair and flipped over it with a groan as she landed on the floor. Raine gripped the edge of the small card table and, with no effort at all, flipped it out of the way. It crashed near Roach's feet and rolled.

"Oh fuck, you're a dead man," Roach said, stepping further away. Fucking coward.

"Now, do you believe me?" I said to Dee, still standing very close with her mouth hanging open. Swiveling around on the stool, I jumped up as Crystal rolled over onto her back and screamed as another fist cracked down hard on her face. Raine's form was good, like she'd been professionally trained, as she knocked Crystal out cold with one shot.

Before she could think about doing more damage or attacking

anyone else, I gripped her around the waist and picked her up. I backed away from Crystal as she flailed her arms and legs.

"Don't any of you ever fucking touch him again," Raine snarled and clawed at the air. Fuck she was making me hard, like bust a nut hard, as she thrashed in my hold. "I'll kill you." I shuddered at her words. Damn, I loved this side of her so much. It was always there, but she kept a tight hold on her emotions. She was the understanding one, the sympathetic one, but apparently, even Raine had a limit.

"Oh fuck," I growled as Raine's elbow caught me across the jaw hard enough to rattle the teeth in my head. I dropped her to her feet and rubbed at my jaw with one hand while I kept hold of her with my other.

She twisted out of my hold, leaving me holding a leather jacket. Spinning around, I managed to get a hold of her as she stomped toward the group of sweetbutts gathered together as they watched.

"You too, don't think I don't see all of you. If you fucking touch him...I will claw your fucking eyes out," Raine yelled, her body fighting mine as she wriggled in my hold. Holy fuck, I didn't think I could love this girl any harder, and she goes all Rhonda Rousey with jealousy. I mean, a guy could hope, but I never thought she'd actually do it.

"Tink, calm down."

"Don't you dare fucking tell me to calm down," she roared and caught me in the gut on the same side as my bruised ribs with her hard elbow.

"Ugh, fuck." My grip loosened, and I thought she was coming for me next as she turned to face me. Instead, she yanked the leather jacket I was still holding out of my hands and marched for the exit. "Fuck you, Kai."

My long strides ate up the ground, and I caught her before she could get out the door.

"Tink, stop," I said, gripping her shoulder, but when my hand touched her, she whipped around and caught me with another wild fist that knocked me back a step. Fuck, she could really hit when she wanted to. This was not the same scared kitten I found in her home. She was another animal altogether. This was the girl that was locked away, but she was free now, and I loved her so damn much it hurt.

"You can't even go a single day, and you have the nerve to talk about me," Raine said, her voice dripping with anger and jealousy. Raine's hands slammed into my chest with a hard shove. "Fuck you. I never want to see you again. We're done."

"Fucking hell we are," I growled, my temper flaring.

That was so not happening.

TWENTY MINUTES EARLIER

Raine

It was later than I had planned when Avro dropped me off at Kai's house, but I'd never traveled except for my bus ride to Atlanta. So I needed luggage, and I had very little clothing to my name. So after the rigorous yet enjoyable shower with Avro and Jace, I had a nap and some food, then went shopping with Avro.

It was official the man could shop. He knew all these great stores I'd never been to that had amazing clothes with even better deals. We were both loaded down like pack mules by the time we were done.

"Thanks for dropping me off. I guess one of these days I should learn to drive and get my license," I said.

"Well, if you want me to teach you, just say the word. I know many empty parking lots where you can't hit anything." He smiled.

"Such a vote of confidence." I looked down at the new leather jacket I wore, running my hands over the material, and couldn't stop wondering if Kai would like it. My stomach was all butterflies which was crazy considering what we'd already done, but I couldn't seem to get the jitters under control.

"Are you going to give me a kiss," Avro asked as my hand went to the door. Jace was right. I was worried about what Kai would think and how he would feel. I needed to stop that if this was going to be my reality from now on. Either he was in and okay with them in my life, or he wasn't, and we would have to part ways. I couldn't let his anger dictate what I did.

Leaning across the seat, I grabbed Avro's face and kissed him as if I didn't care if the whole world saw. "I love you," Avro said.

"I love you too." I opened the car door and stepped out, then leaned in and looked at him. "By the way, how did you find me and Kai?" He smiled wide and winked.

"A story for another night."

"I'm not going to forget if that's what you're hoping?"

"I'd never dream of such a thing," he said, laughing as I closed the door. Backpack in hand, I waved as he turned around and left. I waited until he was gone before I walked up the steps to the porch, knocking on the door to Kai's home.

Avro said Kai's motorcycle was an Indian, so he drove to the dealership and helped me buy a plain black jacket with the small emblem on the sleeve. It was so soft and way too hot, but I never wanted to take it off. There was something about slipping it on that made my heart pound hard. I thought about what it would be like to sit on the back of Kai's bike and hold him tight. It was a hot image that had me blushing.

"Why are you doing this," I asked Avro as we got back in the car from our last stop of the afternoon.

"Because I love you, and I want to see us all happy, and that's not going to happen unless Jace and Kai get on board. Don't kid yourself. They said they would try, but they're both making plans. Regardless of Jace's speech this morning about Kai, he is no better. He wants to cocoon us for himself," Avro said.

"And you don't?"

Avro lifted a shoulder and let it drop. "First, you must know by now how much you have me wrapped around your finger," he said, smiling as he linked our fingers together. He effortlessly set me at ease and made me smile. I squeezed his hand. "Second, I'm more pragmatic than either of them. I'm also more open with what I'm okay with in a relationship...the majority of the time."

I laughed at that statement. Based on what Jace said, you'd think that Avro was a raving jealous lover, but it seemed that Avro was good at playing up what Jace wanted. I smirked and leaned back to look his face over.

"What? Why are you staring at me like that," Avro asked.

"I'm just realizing for the first time what a chess player you are." His eyes darted away from mine, but I saw the truth before he looked away. "You manipulate Jace. Are you manipulating me too?"

"Whoa, manipulation is a strong word. I simply know what he likes and needs and mold myself, not because I have to, but because I like to."

"And you're doing the same with me and Kai?"

He lifted a shoulder and let it drop. "Again, I'm in love with you. If the only way to have you is with Kai, then I work within the parameters given to make things happen."

I wasn't sure what to make of that and then froze, my mouth falling open. "You really did ignore Jace's calls on purpose, didn't you?"

He laughed as he started the car. "Yeah, I definitely did that. I wanted him to turn around, and trust me, there is one thing that will always override his fears, and that is if he feels he needs to protect."

I couldn't help but laugh, it was wrong, yet I laughed. "And here I thought you were the nice one."

"Pfft, I am the nice one. Could you imagine those two lunatics left alone in a room together?"

"So me going with Jace to the concerts for three days? Let me guess. This is to solidify his feelings for me." Avro's eyes glittered with mischief. "Okay, you're a devil," I teased, but I felt like I'd just gained an ally as we pulled out onto the main street.

"Kai, I'm here." I knocked on the door again, louder this time. The sun was just starting to set, making it hard to see into the home, but I covered my eyes and peered through the small triangle piece of glass and didn't see or hear any movement. "Kai?"

"Are you looking for Snake?"

Screaming, I whipped around and then screamed again as I jumped back and slammed into the door. My gaze flicked up and down the man dressed up like a bush. He reminded me of those army guys in movies that would lay out in the open, and you'd never see them cause they dressed like a tumbleweed or a scraggly bush. His face was painted the same but with stripes, and he held what might actually be a sniper rifle in his hands.

"You're Raine, right? You're looking for Snake?"

I licked my lips. "Yeah, I am. Who are you?"

"I can't tell you that," he said.

"Oh...okay. Is it like you'd have to kill me sort of thing," I asked teasingly.

"Yes."

My face fell. I looked around for any sign of any other person, but no one was even walking along the sidewalk.

"You're a girl," he said before I could excuse myself and get the hell out of there.

"Last I checked."

He narrowed his eyes as he shifted his weight like he was intrigued. "Do you have to check often? Is this normal? Is it possible to wake up not being a girl?"

What the fuck? "Um, no. It's just a saying. It means yes, I am."

"Then why not just say, yes, I am?"

"Why are there sayings if we're not going to use them," I asked.

"Huh. That is a good point. Tell me, what is your favorite position to be fucked," Bush man asked.

I cleared my throat after I picked my jaw up off the porch. Did he really just ask me that? "I'm not sure."

He pulled a small book out of somewhere inside the bush garb and flipped open to a blank page. "Why don't you know?"

"I think I should go," I said and stepped to the side to try and get around the man, but he stepped in my way.

"Snake always answers my questions," he said. His voice didn't change, but there was a daring edge to the statement. Like if I walked away, I wasn't as good as Kai.

I crossed my arms over my chest. "Okay then. I don't know because I don't have a lot of experience to know. I don't have much experience because of something that happened to me when I was fifteen. No, I don't want to share what happened, but I can tell you that every girl is different, and what I like doesn't mean that the girl driving by would be the same. Does that help?"

He tapped the pen off his chin. "So how do I find out what a girl wants when she refuses to tell me?"

I wasn't sure I should answer this question, but I did anyway. "Why doesn't she want to tell you?"

"I have her locked up. I must think on this some more," he said, like he hadn't just admitted to kidnapping and possibly being a serial killer or something. "Snake is at the clubhouse. He usually goes there to fuck the sweetbutts. Have a good day." Bush man jogged down the stairs and then stopped. "Oh, by the way, Snake's favorite position is the reverse cowgirl."

Smiling, he jogged off around the corner of the house. It was official I was going to kill Snake. The initial shock of the strange encounter was quickly wiped away as his parting words registered in my brain. My fists clenched as I marched down the stairs and walked around to the clubhouse.

The gates were closed, but a guy was sitting in a small metal booth that looked like it had been shot at more than once. Not very comforting.

"Yes," he said.

"I'm here to see Snake. He was expecting me. I'm Raine," I said and planned on punching him in the face when he walked out thinking he was going to tell me to go away, but instead, the guy looked at a sheet and opened the gate for me to walk in.

"Front door and then up the stairs," the guard said and left me to find my own way.

Walking past the long line of motorcycles was intimidating as hell. It was the visual confirmation that Kai really was a badass in a motorcycle club. I mean, I knew it, but it was different knowing it and understanding it. Pulling open the door, I could hear the music and the sound of television as well as the yell of someone who was overly excited.

The smell of stale smoke wafted down at me, and I suddenly wasn't so sure I wanted to walk up those stairs and find out what he was doing. If I saw him with someone, it would break my heart. Nibbling my lip, I put one hand on the railing and closed my eyes for a moment to gather my courage. I needed to know. I couldn't leave without knowing, and I'd be pissed off with myself for not finding out the truth.

With each step, my blood pressure rose a little higher. Just as I got to the top step, I saw Kai sitting at a bar where two girls were openly flirting and touching him. He didn't push them away, he didn't stand up and yell I'm taken and my bottom lip trembled as I turned to walk away.

As I looked down the stairs, my body shook with a crippling sadness that quickly morphed into a wild rage. I'd never been this angry, but when I thought about all the pretty words and promises. The lies he said so easily in the motel and how he tried to convince me to just be with him. How he said how much he loved me. A fire erupted in my chest.

A fury stormed up from the depths where I kept all my pain and loss stored. I wasn't turning away again. My body shook as I turned around to step up the final few stairs into the clubhouse.

Kai's eyes locked with mine, and I wanted to destroy the world. I wanted to rip it apart with my bare hands. I was done being hurt.

Done.

Raine

Chapter 14

Raine

"Let go of me!" I yelled as Kai's hand gripped my bicep. "I hate you and your stupid lying mouth." I yanked hard on my arm—it felt like it was in a vice grip—but Kai's hand was unyielding.

"It wasn't what it looked like," Kai said, and I pointedly looked down at his belt, partially hanging open.

"Is that so? And just how stupid do you think I am?" I could feel all the eyes in the room silently watching us like we were the best soap opera in town. Some had glasses halfway to their mouths, while others sat wide-eyed like they were scared to move or breathe, but I didn't care. I didn't care if they saw me kick his ass, either.

"Okay, I know this looks bad, but I swear I wasn't going to fuck her. I was just telling her to get off me."

I shook my head.

"Excuse me if I don't believe you. Now let go of my fucking arm and stay away from me. I should've known this would never work, but I was stupid and fell for all the crap you spewed."

"Tink if you'd calm down for a second so I can explain," Kai said. I could tell he was getting angry, and a part of me wanted him to be as angry as he made me.

"Why so you can feed me more lies? I never should've trusted you. Jace said you'd pull some shit like this." Kai's lip pulled up in a snarl at the mention of Jace's name, and a thrill shot through my body as he jerked me close to him. "I guess I should've believed him instead of defending you." Part of me knew that I was poking at a bear, and yet...I couldn't stop myself.

"Fuck this," Kai said, his voice rough. He let go of my arm, and my heart stupidly sank, but it was short-lived as he grabbed me around the waist and tossed me over his shoulder.

As if on cue, people started taking bets on who would win. Money was passed around while odds were shouted. This was crazy.

"Let go of me, you asshole," I yelled and smacked his ass.

"We're done when I say we're done," he said. "All of you get the fuck out of my way," he growled. I couldn't see who he was talking to but knew it was whoever was on the couch as he unceremoniously dropped me on my back.

I should jump up and run for it, but instead, I stared up at him as he towered over me. My mind and body fought over what I wanted. Kai glared at all those watching the show. "Spread the word. If anyone ever touches Raine Eastman, I'll cut your fucking hands off. She is mine. If anyone ever touches me again, you'll have to deal with her, and next time I won't stop her. Understood?"

There was mumbling and nodding and a few cheers I didn't understand. This all seemed crazy. I should've just left and never looked back. The problem was that Kai was part of me. We were forever tied together, no matter how angry or hurt we got, and it felt like those wild and very turbulent emotions bound us tighter. Now he'd just claimed me, and my stupid heart swelled with a toxic joy.

"You think threatening people will make this all go away?"

Kai gripped the front of my shirt, and I sucked in a deep breath as he brought us nose-to-nose. "No, it's because I fucking love you, and I don't care who knows. You're mine, Tink, and I'm only letting go if I'm in a body bag."

My heart hammered fast inside my chest with his words. Why that turned me on and made me want him more was beyond me. My body was heating up for a totally different reason as the anger subsided a notch.

Kai's stare made it hard to draw a breath, but as he grabbed the jacket from my hold and tossed it on the table, I stopped breathing altogether.

"Take your shirt off," he ordered.

"No. Why?" I looked around at the dozens of eyes and wanted to sink into the couch and disappear.

"Because I'm going to fuck you right now, in front of them." He pointed to the crowd that hadn't dwindled at all. In fact, it seemed like more people were staring.

"Have you lost your mind?" I whispered harshly.

Kai leaned down and gripped my jaw in his hand, and I gasped in a sharp breath as he got right in my face. Our noses softly touched, and all I could feel was my pulse pounding in my neck.

"By your own words, I can have you anyplace, anytime, and any way that I want. Were you lying?"

I licked my lips. "No, but...."

"No buts. No one in here will touch me ever again, and now it's your turn to prove you meant what you said."

I'd said it, and I'd meant it, but I never thought in a million years he would want to fuck me in front of his club in the middle of the clubhouse. I turned my head and looked to the side, but Kai used his finger to turn my eyes back to his.

"You only look at me. I'm the only one that matters," he ordered, and I nodded. "Good. We have something to take care of first, though. Take your T-shirt and jeans off," he stood and looked around. "Leech, go get your kit," he said.

I wasn't sure what the hell he was up to, but my shaking hands went to the button on my jeans. Was I really going to do this? I'd never even kissed a guy in public until Avro.

"I said take them off, don't make me rip them off you. You know I'll do it," Kai commanded, and I glanced at the exit for just a moment as I contemplated bolting for the door and then wondered how far I'd get before he caught me.

Pushing the jeans down my legs, I balled them up on my lap, trying for a semblance of modesty. A man who reminded me of an old wizard dressed in biker gear pushed through the crowd so deep that I couldn't see the far side of the room. I spotted the girl I hadn't gotten a chance to hit standing in the inner ring of people, and the memory of the other girl on Kai's lap crossed my mind.

A steely resolve formed in my chest, along with the earlier burning jealousy. No, if Kai wanted to make a statement, I'd let him. I'd rip her hair out one handful at a time if she ever touched Kai again, and if this would stop that from happening, then I would do whatever he wanted.

"Stand up," Kai said. Pushing myself to my feet, I dropped the jeans on top of the jacket and peeled off my shirt. Kai groaned, and I looked up to see him staring at my body. He held out his arm and tapped on a tattoo that said, Lost Souls. "I want this font, and I want you to put her name right here."

Kai pulled his T-shirt up and over his head. My hands covered my mouth as I saw the bruising that lined the left side of his ribs. "Kai, what the hell happened?"

"We were attacked yesterday by another MC, and I got shot."

I thought I was going to faint, and grabbed his arm, my nails digging in.

"I don't understand."

"I'll explain later." He tossed the T-shirt on top of the growing pile of clothes. "Right here over my heart." The older guy opened what looked like a small toolbox and got everything set up.

"You want a tattoo of my name," I asked softly.

Kai didn't bother answering with words. He grabbed the back of my neck and dropped his mouth to mine. Any lingering voices of doubt were wiped away. He didn't stop kissing me as the buzzing of the tattoo artist's gun started up. Even the kiss was a demonstration or a message, maybe. He didn't let go of my neck or release me from the kiss until Leech finished his work. It looked amazing, and I felt myself getting all emotional and quickly reined it in.

"Now it's your turn. I want my name right here," Kai said, tapping the front of my leg right at the very top. This was just another thing I shouldn't want with all the uncertainty swirling around us, but I did. "Make it look sexy." Leech sat down on the low coffee table and was now right in front of me with his head at the same height as my pussy. My tiny thong was the only barrier between myself and this stranger.

Leech placed his hand on my leg, and Kai growled. "Leech, if you touch her more than you need to or in any way I don't like, I will cut your fingers off one at a time with a bolt cutter. And I'll make it nice and slow, so you feel it compressing the bone before it snaps."

My mouth fell open as I stared at the dark glare Kai gave the man in front of me. He was visibly shaking, and I didn't blame him.

"Kai," I whispered, and his eyes flicked to mine. "I really don't want a shaky tattoo. Maybe try not to glare at him like you're going to eat him."

A smirk pulled up the corner of his mouth. "Good point. I don't want it to look like Keven or something."

The buzz of the machine started up again, and I sucked in a sharp breath as the needle came into contact with my leg. I nibbled my lip and decided to ask the question that wouldn't stop nagging at the back of my mind.

"Were you going to push her away?"

"What do you mean?"

"When I came up the stairs, I saw that woman hanging on you, and you didn't push her away. What would've happened if I hadn't walked in when I did?"

Kai's hand was quick as he gripped me by the throat, instantly making it hard to breathe. I tried not to move, but as his lips grazed my ear, I couldn't help but shiver.

"Don't move, Tink," he said and nipped my earlobe. His hand squeezed a little tighter, and instinct had me gripping his forearm.

"Do you feel that? Do you feel how you're struggling to take a breath?" I could only stare into his commanding eyes as a trickle of fear traveled down my spine, and I wheezed out the air in my lungs. "How every little gasping breath burns like acid in your lungs as you dream of death while you fight to survive? That's how I've lived every day without you. Never question my love for you again." Kai released my throat, and I sucked in a deep breath, my mind reeling from what he'd just said. "Of course, I told them to fuck off. I made you a promise." He picked up my hand and ran his finger over the silver ring I'd never taken off. I hadn't known if he recognized it until this moment. I couldn't tear my eyes away from his penetrating stare that seemed to reach into my body and grip my soul.

"I'm done," Leech said, wiping my leg with something cool.

Gripping Kai's face, I kissed him hard, no longer caring who the hell was standing around. If they wanted to watch, they could watch. Kai groaned. Cupping my ass, he pulled me up against his body.

"I hear your favorite position is the reverse cowgirl." I smirked as his brow furrowed.

"Fucking Wilder," he mumbled. "I'll try and explain about him another time. Yes, I do enjoy it."

I undid the button and zipper on his jeans and was rewarded with a growl as I slipped my hand inside the open flaps to pull him free. His face contorted with a dark desire as I stroked his very hard cock.

"Then sit down," I ordered and gently pushed his chest.

Kai smiled, and the noise around us faded into the background. As soon as he was sitting, I went to push my thong down. He grabbed my hand and shook his head no.

"They get to have a show, but not that much of a show. Just pull it aside. As it is, I may have to rip all their eyes out of their heads for doing this," Kai said, his voice lethal, making me shiver.

Leaning over, I braced my hands on the couch on either side of his head. "We could just go to your house." I sucked his lower lip into my mouth.

"No." His hand slid around the back of my neck, and I captured his lips as his fingers tightened. He didn't say anymore, and I didn't push. If this was what he wanted, then I wanted it too. "Get on your knees, Tink and suck my cock," he ordered and ran his hand through my short hair. He managed to grip a handful and pull my head back, bowing my body away from his. I whimpered as his lips attacked the sensitive skin at the base of my neck and sucked.

"Now," he said as he let go of my hair. Kneeling, I slipped between his open legs. Wrapping my hand around his cock I opened my mouth, and Kai gripped my chin between his thumb and finger, forcing me to look up at him. "No hands, Tink. Put them behind your back. I want to see if you can take it all."

My mouth fell open as I stared at the long cock and then up at Kai's eyes. Did he think I was a fucking superhero? I was lucky it fit in my pussy let alone down my throat. My lips wrapped around the tip of his cock, and any tentativeness I had subsided when he groaned and shuddered as my mouth slid down. There was no greater aphrodisiac. Sucking hard, I bobbed my head, and it didn't take long for Kai's hands to grip my hair again.

"Fuck Tink, you've been holding out on me. Damn, that feels so fucking good," Kai said, his praise going through my body and ending between my legs. The desire that had been a steady roar since he picked me up was now throbbing steadily between my legs. Moaning, I bobbed faster, loving the feel of him sliding in and out of my mouth and the sounds of pleasure he made. The room had become a roar of sounds, but in the chaos, there was only an intense calm between us.

Kai groaned and pulled my hair harder. Before he could force my head down, I closed my eyes and sucked in a deep breath as I managed to swallow his cock down. The panic was there, but I fought it as Kai swore, his fingers tightened painfully, adding to the moment.

"Fuck Tink, shit," Kai said and pulled my head off his cock. I gasped in a breath, my lips swollen. I licked at the moisture around my mouth and savored the taste of him. "Where did you learn that," he asked, his face dark with threads of anger.

I cocked a brow and smirked. "Jace is a good teacher."

The words had the exact reaction I expected as he snarled like an animal and hauled me off the floor. "Is he now?"

"Apparently. You liked it," I said softly, purposely poking at him. It was like a matador waving something red in front of a bull. His eyes took on that murderous glare, a growl ripped from his chest, and I melted at the sound.

"You think you're being cute, Tink?" He turned me around and yanked my thong out of the way. "I'm going to fuck his name right out of your mouth." Kai's voice was rough, and I could feel the anger rolling off of him. But where it scared me the first night he crashed back into my life, now I craved it. I wanted his love as much as his anger and jealousy. I hated to admit that Jace was right. He'd seen my dark desires, but I hadn't been ready to admit it to myself.

Now I fully understood what I wanted, and the crazier Kai became, the more I wanted him. It was toxic and completely unhealthy—a psychiatrist would have a field day with me—but I stopped caring somewhere between that first night and this moment. There were no sweet and kind words of love as he thrust into me, and the hands gripping my hips forced me down to meet him.

"Ahh," I screamed with intense pleasure and intoxicating pain. "Fuck, Kai," I yelled and fell back against his body as he pistoned in and out of me. I tried to help, but his pace was too quick, and the orgasm that was building now soared toward the cliff's edge.

I screamed loud as sharp teeth bit into the soft skin at the base of my neck. I gripped his legs as Kai slipped his hands around the front of my body and cupped my breasts. A whimper was forced from my mouth as he thrust into me and pinched my nipples hard. My eyes snapped open, and my mind registered a massive group of people, many half-naked and fucking or jerking off to our show.

The once sane part of my brain was in shock, but the rest of me only wanted more. More of him and more of this.

"Kai," I moaned as I was pushed over that edge and came hard in a rush, but he never let up or slowed down. If anything, he seemed more frantic.

"Get up," he growled, releasing my neck from his bite. I stood on wobbly legs. Kai grabbed my hand and dragged me around to the back of the couch. "Bend over," he ordered, pointing.

I was almost bent in half over the back, and I groaned as he slammed home in a single thrust. My hands clawed at the leather as his hips punished me.

"You're so fucking naughty, Tink," Kai said, his hand hitting my ass hard. "Play with your clit like the bad girl you are." My hand slipped between my legs, and I could feel him pushing into me. He felt so fucking good. There were no coherent words to describe the waves of pleasure washing over my body.

"I see you, Tink. Trying to make me jealous." Another smack. "Make me angry." The third smack had me teetering at the top of the climax peak all over again. "Make me want to hurt you."

"Yes, please Kai, hurt me," I cried out as he smacked my ass for the fourth time, this one the hardest of them all. The sharp sting made me jerk, and I rubbed furiously at my clit as desire shot between my legs.

"Such a naughty fucking girl, and I love you more for it," he said and then groaned as he slammed into me hard. The force of the thrust pushed me over the edge for the second time, but the orgasm was drawn out as Kai came. "Fuck, yes," he hollered. I could feel the powerful release that came with each stroke until he went still, buried deep in my body.

Slumping over on top of me, we were breathing hard and sweaty, but I still welcomed the heat of his skin pressing into my back.

Wrapping his hand around my throat, he pulled me up from the bent position until my head rested against his shoulder.

Kai's lips brushed my ear, and I trembled. "I love you, never doubt it." All I could do was nod. "Good, now get dressed. I want to take you home and fuck you again."

Chapter 15

LOST

1% MC

SOULS

R aine
                    The world hadn't been kind to me.
                    That was an understatement, yet I felt like I should be
on the highest peak yelling at the top of my lungs that I was the luck-
iest woman alive. Kai, Avro, and Jace each filled a part of me. We
were a mass of fucked up situations, toxic and painful, all coming
together and melding into a picture that worked. At least, that was
how it felt to me. There was a long ass road ahead to keep things
stable, but last night was a huge step toward Kai being truly on
board. I understood him better than I ever have.

        I was in the glorious, floaty, still might-be-dreaming phase of
waking up when the bed shifted. Someone was getting on the bed in
front of me, and I smiled. Then the groggy wheels in my brain

screeched to a halt as I remembered I was at Kai's. I felt back with my hand, and yes, Kai was still there, pressed up behind me.

"Good, you're awake. Did you like the reverse cowgirl," the male voice whispered, and my eyes snapped open. I stared into the hazel eyes of a man I didn't recognize but could only be "Bush Man."

Screaming, I jumped and rolled backward wildly and smacked my head off Kai's as he was woken by my scream. We rolled off the bed together in a heap, with him blanketing me.

"There's a man in your bed," I yelled, pointing frantically. Kai hung his head and seemed totally unaffected.

"Wilder! Learn boundaries, man, get the fuck out," Kai yelled as he pulled the sheet to cover me more.

"But I wanted to ask a few questions of your female interest."

"I don't fucking care. Get out. Now." Kai glared at the man that came into view and walked to the door. All I could do was stare up at Wilder dressed in military fatigues. Once again, he looked like he'd just walked out of a movie. What the hell was this guy's problem? My heart, which had nearly jumped right out of my chest, was slowly calming to a normal pace.

"But...."

"Now." Kai bellowed so loud it felt like the floor shook.

Wilder walked out the door and closed it. Kai slumped before kissing my forehead, where we'd collided. "Sorry about that."

"Who the hell is this guy? Yesterday he scared the shit out of me on your porch. He was dressed up like part of the bushes and was carrying a sniper rifle. Is he sane?"

Kai snickered. "Well, that's debatable. Come on. We better get up. I can almost guarantee he's waiting downstairs." Kai groaned and gripped his side as he moved. I didn't like the look of the bruising, and after he told me how he got it, I wanted to bring this Sparky back to life so I could kill him all over again.

"Was he in the clubhouse watching us?"

"Knowing Wilder, it's a very distinct possibility. You don't want to know everything he knows about...well, probably everyone. I don't banish him because he's relatively harmless in his stalking and helped the club out. He also saved my life. He's the sniper who shot and killed the guy about to kill me. He's quirky as fuck, though, and has zero boundaries."

"Well then, it doesn't matter what weird stuff he does. I'll need to kiss him instead." Kai stopped moving as he pushed himself up and stared at me.

"I didn't mean actually kiss him. Relax. Are you sure you're okay," I asked as he grimaced. "You look like you're in a lot of pain."

"Yeah I'm fine. I've had worse, but I'll have it looked at later to be safe. The doc is coming by to check in on everyone that was injured." Kai untangled me from the blankets. I jumped to my feet and darted to my clothes. "What are you doing, Wilder won't come back up now, or at least I don't think he will."

"I know, but I think we should get you some ice and new bandages. I'm such an asshole. I never even thought about your ribs with...well, you know, all that we did," I said, clipping my bra into place. I pulled on my top but didn't get any further when Kai laid his hands on my shoulders.

"Stop and breathe," he said softly. Everyone liked to tell me that lately. Kai's lips made me shiver as he placed a soft kiss on the side of my neck. "Everything we did yesterday is worth every bit of pain today." He ran his hand over the bruise from his bite mark.

I turned in his arms, my eyes flicking to the clear bandage over the tattoo of my name, and I smiled as happiness bubbled inside me. He seemed so different when we were alone like this. He was gentle and quiet, reflective. I'd never say it, but Avro was right. Kai and Jace seemed to have a lot in common. It was like they were completely different, yet cut from the same cloth.

"I love it when you look at me like that," Kai said, his lips soft as they touched mine.

"You may not say that when I tell you what I agreed to do tonight, and no, I'm not asking," I said. Kai froze, but his eyebrow arched up in question. And just like that, he went from sweet to intimidating with a single look. "Jace has two concerts over the next three days, and he invited me to go. Well, actually, Avro suggested that I go because I'm supposed to be going to some red carpet awards show, and going to the concerts will help sell us being a couple." I rambled out and then shifted back and forth as Kai continued to stare and not say anything. "In hindsight, I probably should have told you about the coming out as a couple part, but I was just so excited. How many people get to say that they walked the red carpet? I really want to go to this and stop staring at me like that."

I was getting ready for the explosion, planning my argument as to why I should go, and ready to race to the door and block it before he stomped out to find and kill Jace.

"Okay," Kai said.

I stared after him as he stood up straight and wandered over to his closet. He said nothing as he pulled on a black T-shirt, and I couldn't take it anymore.

"Okay? That's all you have to say?" I crossed my arms over my chest as I analyzed his body language. He didn't seem angry, but he could be faking it and waiting for me to let my guard down.

"Yeah, what else did you want me to say? You already made up your mind anyway, so what would it matter if I said no?" He slipped his leg into his jeans, and I still couldn't decide if he was masking a meltdown or was really okay with this.

I shook my head. "Something is not adding up here."

"What do you mean," he asked.

"I don't know, but...wait." I tapped my chin as I ran through all the possible scenarios in my mind. "What do you already have planned that you don't want me to know about?" I knew that look. His eyes shimmered with the truth. "That's it, isn't it? You have something going on and either didn't want me around or weren't going to have the time for me, and this helps you out?"

"You know, Tink, you always were the smartest in the room." He smiled as he did up the belt on his jeans. "First, yes, I have a few things that I need to take care of for the club, and I wasn't going to be around anyway, so yes, this helps me out." Kai walked toward me, and I couldn't decide if I should be happy that he was this calm and accepting or annoyed and worried. "Not that I don't want you around," he said, wrapping his arms around my waist. "But you'd be a sexy distraction, especially when you seem to like standing around half-naked." His eyes lingered on my lips. "I do get you wanting to attend a red carpet event. I mean, I'm not a heathen."

"Yeah...okay, I don't trust this attitude. I don't know if I should go."

Kai laughed and then grabbed his side. "Don't make me laugh. It hurts."

"I'm serious. You can't stand Jace. The fact that you're this calm has me worried about what you're planning on doing. I expected rage and a mantrum at the very least."

His face sobered, and he cupped my cheeks. "I promise I'm not doing anything that will hurt me, and no, I cannot tell you, so please don't ask." I nibbled on my bottom lip, the worry settling into my gut regardless of what he said. "Look as far as Jace and Avro go." Kai sighed. "Avro is okay. Jace...I don't like at all, but I don't have much of a choice and need to figure out how to deal. So this way, I'm busy, and if you're out of town, it makes it hard for me to just kick in a door and wave a gun around." Kai smiled.

"Not funny." I crossed my arms. "But I get your logic. You promise me that you're not going to get hurt."

"I can't promise I'll never get hurt. It's the nature of who I am, my club, and what I do, but I'll always be as safe as I can."

"This feels exactly like when you used to go to the fights. I'd worry and pace my room until I heard you come home and knew you were alive. It made me sick to my stomach to see you all bruised up. You have no idea how many times I was tempted to try and lock you in your room."

"You paced your room?"

My cheeks warmed. "Yeah. I told you, I've always loved you."

Kai dropped his lips to mine and kissed me softly, making my head feel light. Breaking the kiss, he leaned his forehead against mine and linked our fingers together.

"No matter what, our souls are forever twined," he whispered, melting my heart as he kissed me again.

Snake

K aivan
I decided what really annoyed me about Avro was that there was no way to get under his skin. At least, that's what it felt like. I kissed Raine like I was going to eat her alive when he came to pick her up and the entire time, he just leaned against the car, sipping his drink. He acted like he was out there catching the sun for a modeling shoot as he leaned against his Shelby Mustang, which I had to admit I was jealous of. Even Avro's fucking eyes seemed to be smiling, which of course, made me want to snarl at him. How was he so cool with all of this?

Despite my calm demeanor about Jace and Raine being alone together for three goddamn days, on the inside, I was a volcano ready to explode. Of course, the rich rock star would want to whisk her away on a fancy private jet and pamper the crap out of her with five-star meals. I had visions of her giggling and fanning herself as she sat backstage at his concert. I sipped my coffee and contemplated throwing it against the wall.

If it weren't for the fact that I really did have shit I needed to take care of, calm wouldn't have been my first response. I rolled my eyes to Wilder and wondered if this was a good idea. Asking Wilder for help with anything seemed like it could turn into a movie. I was already running through possible titles like *Wilder and Me*, *Fifty Shades of Wilder*, and my personal favorite, *Throw Wilder From The Train*.

"You sure you're good with Roach meeting you?" I looked out the window to see the man in question pulling into the driveway.

"Of course I am. You act like I'm paranoid." I wanted to yell you are paranoid as Wilder clamped a hand down on my shoulder. "A road trip with my friend and his friend. This will be fun."

"You do know this is not a road trip, right?"

"We will be in a vehicle and on the road. By definition alone, that is a road trip."

Shaking my head, I decided this was a terrible idea, but I couldn't back out of it now. The Wilder wheels were in motion, and that truck planned on rolling until it crashed. Grabbing my leather jacket off the hook, we walked to the door and stepped outside as Roach honked the horn.

"What the fuck, man? Are we in high school? You picking me up for a date?" I yelled at Roach's open window.

"Only if you plan on sucking my cock," Roach yelled. Roach's eyes darted to the man practically skipping beside me like a fucking golden retriever out for a walk.

"What are you doing?" I stared at Wilder in his black fatigues with a massive bag slung over his shoulder that I knew was loaded with every gun man had created. He smiled wide, the look so fake that it seemed painted on his face. He was only missing the clown nose and little car to ride in to complete the picture.

"I'm happy. Isn't this what people do when they are happy?"

"Sure, when you're five or if they've had too much LSD," I said.

"Oh. How do I show my enthusiasm properly?"

I stopped walking before we reached the truck. Taking a deep breath, I asked the question I'd been dying to ask since the first moment he decided I would be his ask-it-doll. "Wilder, you were in the military, so I need to fucking ask you. How the hell did you get by without being kicked out?"

"Because I was good at my job."

"I don't doubt that, but how do you have so little life experience to know what is proper? You were around other soldiers all the time and must have had to go to school and had parents." His face remained blank, like he didn't understand the question. I pinched the bridge of my nose and decided never to do this again. Dealing with robot Wilder was like a computer that kept putting up an error box without reason. "Dude, why are you so awkward? Emotions or not, you're older than me. How is it possible no one has taught you about emotions or proper reactions? Have you never asked these questions of anyone?"

"Are you two getting in or are you going to grab each other and make out?"

"Gimmie a minute," I chirped back at Roach.

"No, I did not ask these questions of anyone," Wilder answered, his voice softer like he might be able to experience sadness.

"Why?"

"I had no one to ask that I wanted to ask. My parents didn't want me after I stabbed a kid." My eyes went wide. And people thought I was the bad apple. "But the guy had it coming. I was placed in military school and excelled in the field, but the others avoided me until I became a Green Beret. I did ask some questions and learned to pleasure my body." Okay, that was a visual I never needed swimming around in my head.

"You've never dated, never had a friend?"

"My unit were my brothers, so you could call them friends, but we did not speak much, and when we did, it was about the missions we were assigned."

"And they are the ones that died?"

"Yes, they were all killed on a mission, and now you are my friend."

I wasn't sure how to feel about what he'd just told me. "Yes, I'm your friend, and I'll answer your question. We would give each other a fist bump, maybe smile a little more, and offer to buy a round of beers if we needed to stop. There is definitely no fucking skipping."

"I wasn't skipping. That was my happy walk."

"That's how you walk? Okay, never mind, whatever it was, don't do it." I grabbed his arm before he could skip off to the truck. "And Wilder, we need some fucking boundaries because that shit this morning was not right, and it can never happen again."

"You had a problem with your shit?"

My brow furrowed. "No, I mean with Raine."

"You had a problem with Raine's shit?"

"I swear to god...." I started and caught the slight lift of the corner of his mouth. "You're screwing with me right now, aren't you?"

"Yes, I like to pay attention to your jokes. I'm confident that soon I will be able to say sarcastic things and be funny, too," he smiled. "You're a really good teacher, and I enjoy watching you." Smiling, he walked away and left me staring after him. He always managed to answer a question and leave you wanting to ask a million more.

Wilder opened Roach's backdoor, tossed in the massive bag, and then proceeded to get into the front passenger seat, leaving me standing outside.

"Hey Roach, I'm Wilder," I heard him say as he closed the door.

What the fuck? Watching me? What the hell did that mean? And now I was going to wonder if he was playing me or if he was truly that fucking awkward. The possibility of him messing with me this entire time was terrifying, and now I didn't know which version of Wilder worried me more. Who the fuck was I kidding? They both scared the fuck out of me, and he just took my fucking seat. Asshole.

Roach looked back at me as I climbed into the back and smirked. "Shut the fuck up. I don't want to hear it," I grumbled as I crossed my arms.

"Are you okay back there, sweetheart?" I glared daggers at Roach in the rearview mirror. This was humiliating.

Wilder turned in the seat to look at me. "Do you like being called sweetheart?"

"No."

"Yes."

Roach and I answered together, and Roach laughed as I glared. I shouldn't have warned him about Wilder. That gave him too much time to prepare for this moment.

"Where are we heading first?" Roach put the truck into gear and pulled out of the driveway.

"The gas station where we saw Dave. I'm hoping Wilder here has some tricks in his bag to help us get the outside camera footage from that day. I want to see if Dave got into a car."

"You think that will help?" Roach asked.

"It's a start. Jim's phone had nothing. It was like he'd already wiped it clean or got a new one before I got to him, and the moment I answered that call, Dave disconnected his phone. Smarter than he looks."

"Your girl is obsessed with bunny slippers," Wilder interjected, and Roach and I both looked at him.

"Who, Raine?" I hadn't seen any in her room.

"No, his girl. She has them in every color." I bit back my laugh at the horrified and then enraged look on Roach's face.

"How the fuck do you know what slippers she likes?" Roach's voice was threatening, but the glare he gave Wilder was worse. Before Wilder could say something else that would end up with Roach crashing the truck, I interjected.

"Chase asked him to keep watch over the sorority house and all those that live there to keep them safe," I said, and Roach's shoulders relaxed.

"Yes, I watch them sleep at night. She tends to wear zoo animal pants and a cutoff top to bed or sometimes no top."

Roach's head whipped around again, the corner of his lip pulling up in a snarl as I pinched the bridge of my nose. This was going to be a long fucking day, and one of us may end up buried yet.

Chapter 17

Jace

Raine looked more nervous than I had been for my first concert.

The flight to Nashville was only two and a half hours. Raine was fine flying and amazed by all the features of the jet. Her enthusiasm reminded me why I loved doing this for a living and what a gift it was to sing.

The nervousness started when we passed the lines of people outside the stadium waiting to get in. They screamed and jumped around when the limo passed. Waving, they held up signs of love and marriage. I was used to the fanfare, but Raine looked like she was ready to jump out of the car and say forget it as a more rambunctious group broke the line of guards running over to the limo as we parked. They banged on the glass and tried to peer inside.

Raine jumped in my lap as she stared wide-eyed at the overly eager faces.

Since then, she'd been nothing but a ball of nervous energy threatening to make me the same way.

"Peaches?" Raine spun around to face me as Sherry, the hair-dresser, put the final touches on my hair. "Sit the fuck down, or I'm going to find something to tie you down with."

"You wouldn't dare."

My eyes locked with hers in the mirror. The bright blue color looked fiery as she narrowed them to glare at me.

"Try me." My voice was husky, and I licked my lip, letting her see just how much I hoped she tried to test my patience.

Sherry stepped back like she expected me to leap up from the seat at any moment.

"I have a stress ball," Sherry said, her voice soft. She was always the same, sweet and helpful. The rest of the band thought I'd fucked her a million times, but we'd never touched. Other than for her to do my hair, of course. Just because the rest of them couldn't keep it in their pants, they thought I fucked everyone that walked into my dressing room. Idiots.

Raine was the first to break the staring contest, her eyes going to Sherry. "Good, I can hit him with it."

"Oh, I didn't mean...um...I'm done, so I'm going to go. If you change your mind, hunt me down," Sherry said. She gathered her array of sprays and muds, combs and brushes, and stuffed them all in her bag before making her mad escape.

I leaned forward to inspect the job that Lori, my makeup artist, had done. Other than the slight swelling around my left eye—that no amount of ice was getting rid of until it was good and ready—the rest of the bruising from the fight with Kai was covered.

"I can't believe you just said that in front of someone that works with you."

Turning in my chair to face Raine, I gave her a hard stare. "Yeah, 'cause that is the worst public embarrassment you've had in the last twenty-four hours," I said.

The moment I saw the bite mark—hidden by the sexy outfit Raine was wearing—and the tattoo of Kai's name, I almost lost my mind. He moved fast. I didn't think he would work so quickly to try and tear us apart, but I'd underestimated him and would use these three days to my advantage. Fuck Kai and his marking. If he could do it, then so could I.

Raine's face became a vibrant shade of red as she blinked and looked away.

"Fair enough."

"So, we are going somewhere after the concert, and I don't want any arguments."

Standing, I stretched and peeled off the T-shirt I wore to put on the one chosen for tonight.

"You're really fucking bossy. Has anyone ever told you that?" Raine crossed her arms over her chest, pushing her sexy tits up in the low-cut top.

I sauntered across the room, and the closer I got, the more she looked around like she was trying to find an exit. She was fucking adorable.

"I'm very bossy, but you also like it." Stopping in front of her, I glanced down at her cleavage. It was making my mouth water. "I'm going to enjoy getting you out of this later."

Raine pulled down on the short skirt that would've shown off her ass if it hadn't been for the leggings she was wearing underneath. I was tempted to cut the leggings off her body, but I figured I'd kill one of my bandmates for staring at her ass if I did that. They wouldn't be able to resist. Marcus was the worst. He had a sex drive like I'd never seen. While performing a concert in the Bahamas, I walked in on him fucking an entire watermelon. The guy had it on his makeup table going to town while red juice sprayed everywhere.

He didn't bat an eye as he looked over and said he still preferred coconuts. That was the last time I walked into his dressing room without knocking and asking if he was decent. That was also key since he really didn't care if the world knew the crazy shit he did. It was also why I never questioned the exorbitant cleaning bills that always came from his room. I never wanted to fucking know.

Draping my arms over Raine's shoulders, I leaned on her. She scowled, but under the annoyed façade, she was already picturing me stripping her later. I could see it in her eyes.

"Don't you trust me to make it worth your while?" I stuck out my bottom lip, purposely wetting it with my tongue.

"The last time you said that, I ended up being chased through a cemetery," she said, making me smirk.

"Yes, and if I remember correctly, you came multiple times." Dipping my head to hers, I nipped at her bottom lip until she opened her mouth so I could kiss her. Our tongues lashed as the kiss went from sweet to intense and all-consuming. It was tempting me to say fuck it to the concert, so I broke away. I looked down into her face, loving the hooded eyes and swollen lips. I moved closer to her ear.

"You screamed my name so loud they heard you cumming in the next town." Raine shivered, and my cock rose. I pictured being inside her and planned on bending her over every piece of furniture in the hotel room.

I sucked in a deep breath before I was late for my own concert. It wouldn't be the first time, but it would be when I was already on site and because I was fucking someone.

Bang, bang, bang

Raine let out a yip at the loud knock. "Yo man! It's time," Damon called out.

"That's my cue. You ready?" Raine smiled and nodded even

though I could see her shaking. "You'll be fine. You get the best seat in the house."

Linking my hand with hers, we walked for the door. The guys all wore the same creepy stare as I swung the door open. They didn't even blink as they looked Raine—in her sexy outfit—up and down. Even used to them, I found it annoying after the first five seconds.

"You can stop staring now. Yes, you know her, yes, it's serious, and no, you can't fuck her."

"Dammit," Marcus said, unsurprisingly.

"Peaches, this is the band. You saw them in passing, but let's make this official. This smiling asshat is Marcus, the walking hardon." I pointed at my drummer.

"Hey! Okay yeah, that's fair," he said, making Raine laugh.

"Damon, my bass guitarist. Stone is all over the electric and steel guitar, and lastly, Owen plays the piano, keyboard, and really anything else we need. He's like a freaking wizard." I pointed out the guys one at a time.

"Owen is just an overachiever," Damon teased.

"You're just jealous that all the girls want me instead," Owen shot back.

"Eat shit," Damon said, punching Owen in the arm.

Stone didn't say anything. He was also the only one who wouldn't shake Raine's hand when she offered it. I glared at him, then he at least nodded and said hi. Raine looked up at me as the group moved on, and I knew she was confused by his reaction to her.

Turning for the stage, I held Raine back, walking slower until the guys were out of earshot. "Don't mind, Stone. He takes time to warm up to anyone new. We've had our share of crazy ass groupies that attach themselves to the guys. He's making sure we stick before he bothers getting to know you."

"Oh, okay. I get that, but he seemed angry." Raine hesitated, and

I watched her while she stared through the slim crack in the stage wall.

"No, just an ass. He's like that with pretty much everyone other than the band."

The roar of the crowd was extra loud tonight inside the football stadium. These were my favorite venues. They always got my heart racing and the adrenaline pumping. Raine's eyes were wide, and her mouth was hanging open.

"That's a lot of people. Like a lot, a lot. It's one thing to see it on television...."

"But a totally different experience in person." I smiled wide and glanced through the crack. "Yeah, sometimes I can't believe this is actually my life. Even after three years, it blows my mind that this is real." I gave her hand a gentle tug. "Come on. The announcer is getting everyone hyped for us to go on."

After squeezing her hand and giving her a quick kiss, I ran out in front of the insane crowd. The stage vibrated with the stomping of feet and screaming fans. I glanced over to where I'd left Raine at stage left and winked. This was the first time someone that meant something to me was at my concert. Avro never wanted to take the chance on his identity being discovered, so he had never come. I didn't like admitting it, but it hurt.

He would be devastated to know he hurt me, which was why I never said anything. I knew he thought he was doing something to help us, but seeing Raine smiling off to the side of the stage made me warm all over, and for the first time in a really long time, my stomach flipped.

Raine

This was incredible. It took a few songs to stop being nervous about the thousands of people singing, screaming, and waving their hands in the air, but once I did, I fell in love with the entire experience. The energy in the building made it impossible not to fall in love with every second.

I never saw this happening. I wasn't the kid that dreamed about being famous or meeting someone famous. I had dreamed about my parents being alive or playing a school sport. Making a team without worrying about moving to a different school cause I was shipped to a new home.

I'd listened to Jace's songs many times. He really did have an amazing voice with smooth, sultry tones that broke at just the right times to make you want to wiggle in your seat in all the best ways. He was in his element, the cockiness and arrogance coming off as captivating on stage. I still couldn't wrap my head around how this all happened, but I wasn't going to let go now. I was all in on this entirely new me.

"Are you enjoying the show?" I yelped and jumped as Allen yelled in my ear. "Sorry, didn't mean to scare you," he said.

He reminded me of an accountant who, at one time, was a bad-boy rocker himself. His hands and forearms were covered in tattoos, but he wore a tidy suit with glasses, and his hair was styled messy. He had a clipboard in hand, a pen behind his ear, and rings on every finger. It didn't feel put together like some people pulled off. It was almost as if he couldn't make up his mind who he wanted to be. It was the same when he was at Eclipse, but I noticed it more now, not in business mode.

"Yeah, the show is amazing." I had to yell for him to hear.

"This thing with you and Jace, is this for real," Allen asked out of nowhere. His eyes searched my face, and I didn't like it. It felt like he was analyzing or maybe judging me. It was hard to tell.

"Yes."

"How?"

"What do you mean?" I crossed my arms over my chest.

"I'm just trying to figure out when this sudden love of his life situation started. I mean, I'd never heard your name until I had to make arrangements for the band at the bar. When have you been spending time together? Did you sit out in the audience at other concerts? How did you sneak into the hotels without me knowing? When exactly did the two of you fall in love?" He yelled, and I swallowed.

I looked around at those behind the scenes working, and a few sets of eyes flicked my way. My brain raced, and then it hit what he'd said about Jace being in love with me.

"Fall in love?"

"Yeah, that was what Jace said, is that not how you feel?"

My gut told me not to give him any ammunition. He could simply be looking out for Jace since he was his manager and agent, but I had an uneasy feeling in my stomach. Had Jace really told him that he loved me? Do I confirm it?

The song Jace was singing ended, and both Allen and I clapped. Putting two fingers in my mouth, I blew hard, making a loud shrill whistle. Jace turned, looking at me, and I smiled. He was infectious. Avro's description of him was very accurate. Butterflies took flight in my stomach as my body warmed, and it had nothing to do with the huge crowd.

Jace had a way of penetrating your senses. His touch lingered long after he let you go. If I didn't know better, I would think the man was a walking morning glory flower. Jace and all of this felt like an illusion.

"So, do you have an answer," Allen said, and I wanted to punch him in the face.

Even though I didn't want to, I smiled.

"Honestly, I'm just surprised he told you at all. We were keeping the news quiet, but I guess taking me to the awards show derailed any plans you were making, and it forced his hand," I said, as if I had a hell of a lot more knowledge than I did.

I lifted a shoulder and let it drop casually. "As for how that's not really any of your business unless Jace wants to tell you." I looked away from his expression, which was darkening by the second. "Since it's obvious you don't know, it's not my place to say."

I could feel him ready to explode beside me. He was like a volcano about to erupt, and I felt tremors. My hands twitched in my lap as my heart rate spiked. Jace was well into the next song when Allen spoke again.

"I will find out if you're just here to use Jace to climb out of that shithole bar." He bent over so his face was near mine. "Even if it means digging up everything in your life to do it. There will be nothing that is not out there for public consumption."

The pounding of my heart got worse as I pictured my childhood, my parents, the assault, the depression I suffered, and the anxiety meds I took. Then finally, my involvement with Kai splashed over every social media site. My painful and sordid story would be out there for anyone to read and judge. I could picture the twisted tales now.

Abused drug addict using Jace Everly to climb the social ladder while she continues to have relations with a known criminal and MC enforcer. The same man was charged with her assault. Does this girl just like trouble? What are her real intentions with Jace Everly?

Allen's glare told me he was going to do just that. He would have someone look into me and leak it, regardless of what Jace wanted. That thought made my throat close up.

"Do we have a problem here?" Jace's voice made me jump, and I jerked away from Allen.

"No, of course not," Allen interjected. "I was just getting to know the love of your life a little better. Considering you never mentioned her until the other day, I was curious about her." Allen smiled like a snake oil salesman and clapped Jace on the shoulder. "Great concert as always."

The crowd was cheering for an encore, but Jace didn't budge as he stared Allen down. Without batting an eye, Allen turned and walked away. I watched Jace as his eyes tracked Allen.

"What did he really want," Jace asked his voice on the verge of seething. I looked over my shoulder to where Allen was now talking to one of the crew. If I said what happened, I knew Jace would do something that neither of us could come back from. Visions of Jace punching Allen in the face flooded my mind, so I decided to keep my mouth shut, at least for now.

"He seems overly concerned and confused as to where our relationship began. He was asking some questions about how we met." I shrugged. "You know, he's the person that looks out for you. If I were him, I'd have questions too."

Jace's silver eyes were drilling holes into mine, making me so hot that I wanted to rip my clothes off. He was acting more intense than normal, so I slipped off the stool and stood not to feel quite so small as he towered over me.

"So he didn't threaten you?" He glared, his jaw twitching as his eyes flicked to Allen and back to me. "Cause if he threatened you...so help me god..." Jace growled, and a shiver raced down my spine. This was exactly what I was worried about, and quickly shook my head. Wrapping my arms around his waist, I rose up on my toes and kissed him.

"All is well. Now come on, you need a shower. I thought only athletes got this sweaty." I stepped back and held my arms out as if disgusted, making Jace laugh.

I squealed as he picked me up, and I was forced to wrap my arm around his neck. "Jace, put me down."

"Nope, I intend on making it so that you have to shower with me." Smirking, he kissed me hard and wiggled his chest against me.

"That's disgusting," I said, laughing.

"Maybe, but I plan on having you sweaty very soon." Jace had a way of deepening his voice at just the right moments that made you shiver, and I did now, which only pulled up the corner of his mouth in an arrogant smirk. "Three whole nights of me, all alone. You think you can handle it?" We turned the corner to the dressing rooms.

"Can you," I asked as he walked to his room and closed the door with a kick.

Jace buried his head in my neck, his lips brushing against my skin. "Oh Peaches, the little bit I've done with you is only the tip of the iceberg. You'll scream until you pass out. That's a promise."

Jace's voice was husky, and there was not a doubt in my mind that he wouldn't follow through on his promise or threat, depending on how you looked at it. The old me would've jumped out of his arms and ran screaming. But that girl, scared of new emotions and experiences, had packed her bags and disappeared. I never wanted to see her face again.

Jace walked us right into the shower with all our clothes on and hit the water, making me squeal with the sudden burst of cold. We laughed hard until our lips met again, and Jace pulled my shirt off over my head.

I was a whole new me. I was going to live life and experience what it had to offer, and right now, that was Jace Everly, the rock star with a commanding personality. Life was way too short to do anything else.

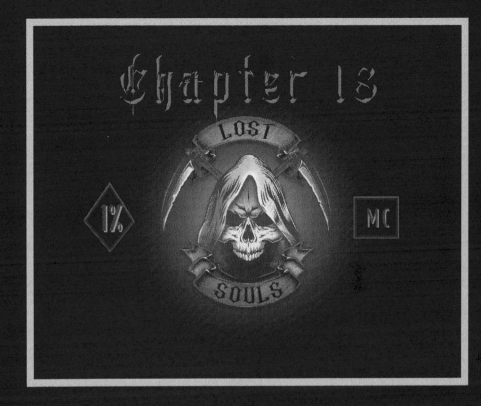

Chapter 18

A^{vro}

This didn't seem like a smart idea.

Being summoned by Kai for anything felt wrong, but it screamed slasher flick when it was almost midnight. My headlights bounced over the rough driveway, the beams shining on the old farmhouse, and I shivered. It was straight out of a horror movie. Amityville or something could totally be made here. What made it fucking creepier was the fact there wasn't a single light on, and yet when the lights flashed over the large bay window, I could clearly see Kai standing behind the glass, staring at me like a fucking mannequin.

Drumming my fingers on the steering wheel, I was tempted to turn the fuck around, but the porch light turned on, and Kai stepped outside.

"Shit, shit, shit."

> A: Hey, I'm having a weird beer with Kai. If I disappear, you'll know who to look at first.

> J: Like he wouldn't have already been my first choice. Why are you having a beer with him?

> A: That is a good fucking question. I'll keep you posted.

> J: Don't get yourself fucking killed.

> A: Thanks, I'll try not to.

Stuffing the phone in my pocket, I got out, and Kai smirked at me as he leaned against the support beam. Not walking any closer, I leaned against my car and crossed my arms.

"Making sure someone knows where you are?"

"You know what they say. Someone should know where you are at all times." My eyes darted to the darkness beyond the pathetic glow of the lone light. "Especially when visiting a gang member in the middle of the night."

"I'm not sure I'm the most dangerous thing out here, but I do like that you're smart and think ahead. You do that a lot, don't you, Avro?"

Kai lit up a smoke, the little flame of the lighter glowing brighter than anything else. I didn't bother to say anything and watched him calmly as I thought about the baseball bat in the back seat and how I left the keys in the ignition for a quick escape. I might love Raine enough to accept this situation, but I was no one's fool, and trusting Kai blindly was a sure way to get myself killed.

"You not planning to answer?"

"Didn't know I needed to. You seem to have me figured out," I said.

Kai snorted, and I couldn't tell if he was amused or annoyed, but he sat down on the top step of the porch and opened the small cooler waiting for him. It was as if he knew I wouldn't go inside the house alone and had anticipated that. He pulled out a beer and tossed the can for me to catch. When he said, 'Have a beer,' this was not what I had in mind, but it worked. Holding the can away from my body, I opened it and let the fizz bubble out onto the ground before taking a sip.

"Decent. At least you have good taste in more than a particular woman," I said. It was a brand I'd never seen before.

"It's from Canada, just had a shipment arrive."

"Huh."

"So tell me, Avro, how do you see all this ending?"

"Is this a serious question?"

"Yes."

I took another sip of the beer as I thought about the question and the best way to answer it. "Well, I see this ending in one of two ways. You and Jace find common ground, or everything explodes, and we all lose Raine."

Kai took another drag on the cigarette, the light scent of it floating in my direction. He leaned back on the wooden porch reminding me of one of the deadly snakes that liked to lounge in the shade. They were fine as long as you didn't disturb them, but watch out if you did.

"What if I told you that I thought it would be in your best interest to make sure Jace doesn't try anything stupid."

I narrowed my eyes. "What exactly does that mean?"

"Don't act stupid, Avro. You know as well as I do that Jace would love to persuade the two of you to fly off into the sunset with him. I can picture him convincing Raine that she wants to be his traveling groupie and forget all about me."

I tilted my head and snorted. "Pot, I'd like you to meet kettle," I said, holding out my hands. Kai just laughed. "Well, if you think that Jace has that kind of power, then you're not giving Raine very much credit. Are you that insecure?"

"I love your mind, Avro. This is exactly what I'm talking about. You see all the pieces and how they are moving and what you should say and do next. It took me a bit to figure you out, but it hit me when you showed up at the motel and said exactly what each of us needed, wanted, or expected to hear. Well, that and you're really good at hiding secrets. Secrets I'm sure you don't want the world to know."

My heart jumped in my chest, but I forced myself to keep the surprise off my face. "I will admit that I'm strategic, but not to be harmful. I know what Raine wants, and that is all three of us. I'm simply trying to make sure that happens."

"Come now, Avro. You're being modest," Kai said, and I gulped down the rest of the beer as I thought about what Kai might be referring to.

"What the hell is that supposed to mean?"

Kai stood and slowly walked down the stairs. There was something far more lethal about the stroll than if he ran at me. Stuffing his hands in his pockets, he stopped a few feet away. My body tensed as I readied myself for a physical or verbal attack.

"I have to say, Alex, I'm impressed. I didn't think you had it in you to kill someone, let alone cover it up and get away with it for this long," Kai said, his voice low, yet I sucked in a breath like he'd punched me in the gut. He knew my real name, and how he found out about something that Jace and I refused to speak about to anyone was beyond me, but the pounding in my ears made it hard to hear his next words.

"You and Jace did a great job covering your tracks. Don't worry, your secret is safe with me, or it will be if you can make sure that Jace doesn't play dirty," Kai said, his eyes filled with dark humor that only he found amusing. "You'd get bonus points if you walked away and took Jace with you, but I'm not going to push that button...yet."

"So you're threatening me?" I shook my head and glared at Kai.

"I wouldn't say I'm threatening. I'd say I'm being strategic," Kai said.

"You're an asshole." I didn't care if he hit me. Let him attack me at this point. He was digging at the wound I'd tried to heal from for most of my life. "Do you even know what happened or why?"

Kai smiled, and there in his eyes was the man that had attacked us at my house. The man that wanted to rip me in two and would happily do it if it wasn't for Raine. A cold shiver raced down my spine as I stared into his cold, blue eyes.

"I don't care about the why—the exact how is also lost on me. I just know that your uncle is dead and that you and Jace are the prime suspects. It was so long ago, and you were both minors, that it has gotten swept under the rug. But I'm sure some poking around would cause a new stir, especially with your other uncle being a general. How long do you think it would remain buried what the two of you did? How do you think that would affect Jace's singing career? You might even do jail time since you're now adults."

"Why are you doing this to me? I've done nothing to you, Kai. I'm the one trying to make sure we all get along for Raine's sake."

Kai stepped forward, but I didn't flinch. At this point, I'd rather him kill me than force me to relive what happened in a court, or worse, drag Jace down for his part.

"I'm doing this for that exact reason, Avro or Alex, whatever you want to call yourself. You are the lynchpin to this fucked up relationship. Raine loves you, although I'm still baffled as to why. You obviously love her, or you would be helping Jace undermine me, but I don't see you doing that. At least, I don't unless Jace wants you to, and I'm stopping it before it ever happens. I will keep your secret, but in return, you keep your rock star boy toy in line. I need you to understand that Raine was mine. If it hadn't been for a tragic situation that drove us apart, we'd be living our life without the two of you. I need her and will do whatever is necessary to keep her."

I could feel the anger radiating off his body. "If Jace tries to sweep her off her feet and whisk her away, then I'll make sure you're the collateral damage. Before you ask, I don't care about what happens to you. You and Jace are not in my bubble of give-a-shit, but Raine is my heart. If you or Jace try to rip it out of my chest, I will take you down with me. Do I make myself clear?"

Swallowing, I nodded. "Crystal."

"Excellent. I'm so happy we had this little chat to clear the air between us." The sarcasm was obvious and dripped off every word.

Kai stepped back, and I pushed away from the car to walk around to the other side. Opening the driver's door, I stopped and glared at Kai.

"You know, I didn't need to be threatened to keep Raine happy, but thank you for showing me your true nature. It's eye-opening to what a fucking piece of shit you really are. Too bad Raine didn't see this side of you, maybe she'd think twice, and it would have nothing to do with Jace or me if she ran in the other direction. Sleep well, Kai."

His face darkened, and his hands clenched into fists, but nothing was worse than what he'd already threatened.

Slipping into the car, I quickly started it and drove out of the driveway, caught between fuming mad and terrified. My hands squeezed the steering wheel, and it complained with a squeak.

"Fuck," I swore and slammed my hand off the top of the wheel as if that would somehow help.

· · ·

"Dude, for fucks sake, what the hell happened," Jace asked as he gripped my arm and yanked me into an empty classroom.

I jerked my arm away. "Nothing is wrong."

"Yeah, not buying it. You've been weird ever since you got home from that camping trip. You won't look me in the eye, you refuse to hangout, and you're dodging my texts and calls. Now you refuse to turn around when I call your name in the hall? What the fuck?"

"Nothing happened. I'm fine. You're just imagining it." I went to walk around Jace and out the door, but he grabbed my arm again, and this time when I tried to jerk away, he wouldn't let go.

"Let go."

"No." He closed the door and leaned against it before letting go of my arm.

"Fuck off, Jace, just let me leave. This has nothing to do with you," I said, anger and fear bubbling to the surface. I couldn't sleep, and I had to have the lights on all the time. The sound of light rain sent me into a panic attack that I couldn't explain to my mother, and the last thing I needed was to share what had happened with Jace.

"Alex, you're my best friend. You know you mean more to me than that." His voice softened. "If you met someone else and you know...don't wanna...hangout anymore, then just tell me."

Hangout was code for us. It was simple, mundane, and all the other kids used it, but for us, it meant exploring our interest in one another.

"It's not that." I ran my hand through my hair and turned my back on him. I jumped and yelped as his hand touched my shoulder. When I turned to look at him, I lost it, and tears broke free—tears I'd refused to cry for almost two weeks. My lip trembled, and Jace stared at my face, worry evident in his eyes.

The door opened, and Jace looked over his shoulder at the math teacher about to walk in. No words were exchanged, but Mr. Mattacini backed out and closed the door.

"Great, now we're in trouble," I groaned.

"No, we're not. I caught him and the new art teacher doing it in the storage room, and I made sure they both knew it," Jace said and lifted his shoulders, which didn't help him look more innocent.

"Caught as in by accident or followed them?"

"Does it really matter? Knowing is knowing, and with that comes power. He won't say shit to us, and I'm no longer failing math." He smiled, and I shook my head. "What? It's not my fault he decided to fuck someone at work. He's a cheating dick, and as far as I'm concerned, he's getting what he deserves. He's just lucky I don't leave a note for his wife."

I wiped away the wetness on my face, annoyed that I was crying at all. "Whatever. Can I go now?"

"Fuck no. Not until you tell me what happened," Jace said.

"I don't want to talk about it here." I crossed my arms and looked down at my new sneakers. "After basketball practice."

"Fine, but I will find out, and I want you to be the one to tell me. Don't force me to go all undercover P.I. on you."

True to his word, as soon as practice was over and everyone had left, Jace called his mom and asked if I could stay the night to work on a school project. He amazed me with how easily he could lie.

I was never that good. It was why I tried so hard never to give my parents any reason to question my sexuality. It was safer to pretend everything was fine, and I'd gone along with it since I started to see Jace as more than my friend. I figured if they didn't ask if I liked guys, I wouldn't have to answer, and they wouldn't be faced with kicking me out. They'd both made it very clear that no son of theirs would fuck another guy.

I guess my uncle didn't get that memo.

My mom only agreed to the sleepover when I said it was for school. I thought I heard relief in her voice. They hadn't said much to me since the camping trip. It was what Courtney said and had nothing to do with my Uncle Martin. I didn't think they knew what he did. If they did and were protecting him...no, I couldn't think about that.

"Okay, we're alone. I even double-checked the locker rooms and got rid *of Matt and Lacey making out under the bleachers,"* Jace said as he dropped down beside me. *In his very Jace way, he sprawled out on the bleachers. The giant Gator logo stared at us from across the gym.* "Spill, what's going on?"

I ran my backpack straps through my fingers, my body shaking as I thought about what had happened. Jace moved, and although I knew he'd touch me, I still couldn't stop myself from jumping as his arm wrapped around my shoulders. Instead of pulling away, he gripped me tighter, hugging me.

"Alex, what the hell is going on?"

"Jace...I don't want to say it out loud. It feels like it will make it worse somehow, or I don't know, but...." I stammered out quickly, my chest heaving. I wiped my hands on my jeans over and over like that would wipe away the stain of what had happened.

"Okay, slow your roll. You're gonna make yourself pass out," Jace mumbled as he held me tighter. "Whatever happened has happened, and nothing you say will make it worse."

"I know, but I can't help feeling like this."

"No, but it's true." Jace pulled back, and I didn't want him to let me go. For those few short seconds, I felt safe. Jace always made me feel safe. "And no matter what you tell me, I'm here. You know that."

"You may not be. You may decide to fuck off," I said, and Jace's brow furrowed, his eyebrows pressing so close together that they almost touched. I knew what was coming before he opened his mouth.

"Are you fucking stupid?"

I smiled, but the happiness faded as I blurted it out. "My uncle hurt me, Jace. After I texted you and fell asleep, he snuck into my tent."

"Hurt you? You mean like hit you? For what?"

I shook my head no. I wished he'd hit me. I'd take a thousand punches over what he'd done to me.

"Did he say mean shit?"

It was my turn to stare at Jace. He just wasn't clued in, and I didn't want to say it. His eyes remained confused a moment longer and then went wide. "He...he hurt you like...touched you...like not hitting?" I nodded, and once more, the fucking tears filled my eyes. "Like just hand or more?"

"More," I choked out. "Like everything."

Jace grew really still and quiet, and I dared to look up. He seemed frozen. My stomach dropped as his eyes went wide. Was this the moment he was going to shove me away? Panic gripped my heart, and a moment later, it tried to jump out of my chest as Jace leaped to his feet.

"I'm going to fucking kill him," Jace growled. He turned and stomped down the bleachers.

I believed him. I could picture Jace running to my Uncle's house to do it, and then he'd be in jail.

My brain registered what was about to happen, and I jumped up, chasing Jace down before he could leave the gym. His lip pulled up in a snarl when I got in his way. He looked terrifying with his fists balled and muscles flexing. We might have only been thirteen, but we were both almost six feet, which was part of the reason we were so good at basketball. Jace had been working out hard since he turned twelve, and he looked it.

"Stop, Jace. Please, you can't make this worse."

"Worse? Alex, he not only hurt you, but he is family. I watched that prick sit in the stands and cheer our team on last night and act like he's not a fucking piece of shit. I wondered why your shots were so terrible. I just thought you were having an off night." Jace tried to walk around me, and I fisted his T-shirt.

"Please, Jace. I'm begging you. I can't deal with whatever happens if my parents find out. At least not yet. I'm not ready. Besides, I can't lose you."

"Oh, for fucks sake." I let go of his shirt as he began to pace. "Aren't you supposed to go there next week, with your parents going on that second honeymoon cruise or some shit?" I nodded, already terrified to go. I'd been dreading it since the moment we got back.

"So, you have to stay with your uncle for a week and don't want me to do anything?" I nodded. "Not happening. You can stay with me."

"I already thought of that. I asked my mom, and she said it was too much to ask of your mom with the two young kids. She's made the arrangements. If I push, they'll start to ask questions."

"Fuck that," he yelled, his voice echoing in the empty gym. I jumped.

"Jace...."

"No, Alex. He doesn't get away with this. Give me a couple of days to come up with an idea that doesn't let your family know what happened and ensures he won't touch you again. Okay?"

I sucked in a deep breath, knowing I could scream from the top of my lungs that I didn't want him to get involved, but it wouldn't matter. Nothing stood in Jace's way when it came to what he wanted.

Jace

Chapter 19

J ace

I was startled awake as my phone buzzed again. Unwrapping myself from around Raine, I rolled over and grabbed it off the nightstand. Avro was calling at three in the morning. He never called this late unless he knew I was awake. Hitting talk, I slipped out of bed and padded out to the sitting area of the large suite.

"Good to see you're still alive," I said, yawning. "But it would've been nice if you called in, say, three hours," I teased, but there was only silence on the other end of the line. "Avro?" I heard him breathing, but he still didn't say anything. Fear shot through me and settled like a weight in the pit of my stomach. "What the fuck is wrong?"

"He knows," Avro said, his words slurred like he'd been drinking.

Avro rarely ever got drunk, and the fact that he'd clearly had more than normal worried me.

"Who knows what?" I walked over to the large window and stared out at the city and the lights of cars moving steadily along the interstate.

"Kai. He knows about us."

My brain whirred, but Avro wasn't making sense. Of course, Kai knew about us. He fucking came over to our house with a gun. Just how much had Avro drunk?

"Dude, you okay? Of course, he knows we're together. Did you hit your head tonight?"

"For fucks sake!" Avro swore, and I had to move the phone away from my ear.

"Geez us, Avro. What the fuck is up with you? Just spit it out," I grumbled, annoyed now.

"He knows about us at thirteen. He knows about things we swore we'd never talk about again," he said, and I stopped breathing.

"What?" I growled into the phone as my mind caught up. "How? And what the fuck does he plan on doing with the information?"

"How? I don't know. I mean, he has connections with some seedy people, so who the fuck knows, but as of right now, he doesn't plan on doing anything with it." My hand tightened on the phone while I ran the other through my hair.

"I don't believe that," I said, the initial shock turning into anger. Hadn't this guy done enough already? He had to go and dig up dirt on us?

"Well, he did have one request," Avro said, and a low growl left my mouth.

"I'm not giving Peaches up 'cause he's threatening us. I won't be scared off Avro. That's an asshole move, and if he wants to play that way, so can I. I'm pretty sure I can find a long list of dead in his wake."

"Stop! Just listen, for once, please just listen to me before you react."

My teeth ground together, but I sucked in the rage and tried to push it down. "Fine, what is his demand?"

"That you don't try to tear him and Raine apart," Avro said.

"I hadn't planned on it, but now he makes me want to fucking try. Fucking dick. Have I told you I don't trust him? And I really don't like him."

Avro groaned on the other end of the line, which turned into a mumbled litany of swear words.

"Jace, you know I love you, but let's be real for just a moment. The two of you don't like each other cause you're cut from the same fucking cloth. He knows you'd try, just like you knew he would. I'm telling you right now, Raine will split and tell us all to fuck off if we start playing that game."

Even though he couldn't see it, I tossed my hand in the air in frustration. "Dude, I'm not the one that started this."

"I know, but you're always the one to end it, and I'm asking you, no...I'm begging you and calling in every favor I have. Do not do whatever you have cooking up in your head," Avro said, his voice pleading with me through the phone.

Fuck I hated not having the upper hand. I needed something on Kai. Even if I didn't use it, I needed to have the shield to block his attack. No matter what Avro said or thought, Kai would push later on. I knew it cause Avro was right about one thing, the two of us thought alike, and I would use it when needed. Maybe even when I didn't if I thought I could get away with it.

"Fine, I won't do anything, but if he makes even one move to release or leak anything he knows, someone better be watching out for his soul because I will take him down with us."

I could picture Avro's face on the other end of the line as he rolled his eyes at me. "I worried you might say that."

"I promise to be good as long as he does. There is that better?"

"Jace?" I turned at the sound of Raine's voice. She looked adorable in my band T-shirt that stopped mid-thigh. Oh, I was sending her home with a fucking case of those. Petty? Most definitely, but it made me smirk as I pictured the look on Kai's face when she wore one for him.

"Hey Peaches, you okay?"

"Yeah, I just woke up, and you were gone." She padded across the floor, her footfalls quiet on the fancy tile.

"Just talking to Avro. Do you want to say hi?"

Raine shivered and tucked herself under my arm. Why was it that girls were always so much cooler to the touch? I handed her the phone and went back to staring out the window as my mind traveled back in time.

"I'm telling you Alex, this will work. We just need to get him on film, and he'll never want the video released. He'd never dare touch you again," I said, laying my hands on Alex's shoulders. He still looked unsure as he chewed on his lip.

"But it means I have to get him in the car, and I'll be alone with him until we get to the park. What if he decides to stop somewhere else, and you're not there, and I'm stuck in the car with him?"

They were valid concerns, and I didn't have an answer for any of them, but I knew he could pull this off. It was the only reasonable plan, and there was no way I was letting Alex stay even a single night without blackmail.

"You've got this. Nothing is going to go wrong. Just think about how well you did when auditioning for the school play. Pretend you're doing that again," I said.

"Fine, I'll do it, but you better be there," Alex said.

"Well duh. The whole thing hinges on me being there. I've got you."

When it got dark outside—and my mom and Lyle were watching a movie—I told my mom I was heading to bed early since I had practice the next day. She kissed me on the cheek and wished me a good sleep. I felt bad lying to her, but it needed to be done. No one else could know about this.

I stuffed the small video camera in my backpack, put all the pillows under my blanket, and turned off the light. We were screwed if she came in to check on me, but it was worth the risk.

Climbing out the window, I closed it softly behind me, moved to the end of the low eaves, and jumped. It wasn't far, ten feet at most. I wondered what Alex would say to lure his uncle out of the house. Would he tell him that he wanted to be alone with him or that he wanted to talk? I didn't know, but the longer I thought about Avro alone with Martin, the more worried I got.

Hopping on my mountain bike, I peddled hard and soon traveled almost as fast as the cars on the main street. I weaved through the subdivisions and then onto the road that led to the state park. It was where I'd told Alex to lure Martin. There was a huge parking lot, no cameras, and lots of places to hide so I could film.

Wheeling my bike into the entrance, I kept an eye out for gators. Not that they wandered away from the water too much, but I really didn't feel like getting bit or worse.

I'd come prepared and pulled a flashlight from the pack. Something glinted in the distance when the light hit it, and I pushed the bike in that direction. It was a spade shovel left behind by the maintenance crew, but it was a perfect weapon, just in case.

Hiding my bike behind the map of walking trails, I got the camera ready and crouched down to wait. The wind picked up, bringing with it the smell of rain. You could feel the moisture in the air and hear the rumbling of thunder in the distance.

My watch said it was almost eleven-thirty. I flipped open my phone to see if Alex had texted me, but there was no new message, and I didn't dare text, just in case. I was just stuffing the phone into my pocket when bright lights turned into the long driveway and closed in on the parking lot. I stayed completely hidden as the car parked.

"Come on, Alex, get out of the car," I whispered as I stared at the side of Alex's face through the passenger side window. I could hear the muffled yelling from my hiding spot, which made me antsy. I was about to stand up when Alex's door swung open, and he jumped out.

"Get the hell back here," Martin yelled.

I turned the camera on and set the small camcorder on the large rock near the sign. I could see the car and everything clearly now. Alex marched away from the car, straightened his spine, and turned to wait for Martin as he got out of the driver's side.

"No, I wanted you to know I'm never letting you touch me again," Alex yelled, the shadows from the parking lot light making him look fierce. He was so hot.

Martin stomped around the car, looking like a bear. Alex's entire family was tall, but it wasn't his height that made him look big. It was his college football build. He was still all muscle with his large hands balled into fists.

"Is this a joke? You got me to come all the way out here for this?"

"It's not a chat we could have at the house, but I wanted you to know that if you touch me again, I'm going to go to the cops, and I'm going to tell my parents," Alex said.

"Oh no you won't."

Martin stepped closer to Alex until he was towering over him. I could see him beginning to shake, and his fear had my blood boiling. I hated bullies and especially hated someone picking on Alex. I'd bloodied more than one guy who thought they could say mean shit.

My hand tightened around the handle of the shovel as Martin reached out and snatched Alex by the front of his shirt. "I will. I'll tell them what you did on the camping trip, and I'll tell them about tonight. The police will drag you off to jail."

"For what? You wanted it."

"Let go of me," Alex said, grabbing Martin's forearm.

"You're an ungrateful shit. How do you think your parents can afford to keep you in the fancy basketball academy to train? They don't have that kind of money. I pay for it. You owe me, and you're lucky I waited this long to collect."

My mouth dropped open at the same time Alex's did. This man was crazy. Donations for us came in from the entire neighborhood. Did he think we were supposed to fuck everyone as payment?

"I said get off of me," Alex said. I could hear the wavering in his voice and knew he was close to losing it.

"And I say get on your knees," Martin growled. His hand went to the belt on his pants, and Alex swung at his face. His fist connected hard, and Martin looked rattled as he shook his head but didn't let go of Alex. If anything, his fist twisted tighter in the material.

"No. Get the fuck off of me, you perv."

Martin hit Alex hard in the stomach, and he doubled over, coughing. A growl ripped from my chest, but Martin didn't hear it or see me stand as he dragged Alex toward the car. His back was to me, and all I saw was red.

"You dare threaten me. I'll ruin you. You can kiss any chance at basketball in high school or college goodbye. No one will want to take you after they hear what I have to say. You're nothing." I squeezed the shovel and gripped it like a baseball bat. "You'll regret ever messing with me."

Martin pulled his arm back to punch Alex again, and I swung. I didn't care how hard I hit him. I didn't bother to aim or think about the angle of the shovel. All that mattered was that he let Alex go. That he never hurt him again. No one hurt Alex, not ever.

I heard him yell, and a thrill traveled through my body. I swung again, and this time Alex screamed. I froze mid-swing. I wasn't sure what happened until Martin fell to his knees at my feet with his hands covering a massive wound on the side of his neck. Blood poured through his fingers and down his arm, and I stepped back, eyes wide.

I expected to be horrified, but instead, I watched him choke as his eyes *flicked up to mine, and his mouth moved as he begged for help. Alex whipped off his T-shirt and pushed it against Martin's neck.*

"Jace, you were only supposed to scare him," Alex said, his hands shaking. "I need to call for help. Do you have your phone?" I shook my head no, even though it was a lie. Martin gripped Alex's arm, fear glittering in the depths, and all I could think was it was time he met his end.

"No, no, no," Alex said. He continued to press on the wound as Martin tipped over sideways and landed on the ground. His mouth opened and closed, and I stood there silently watching. I was the monster tonight. I'd swung my weapon and taken the life that needed to be sent to hell. Not an ounce of guilt filled me.

"Jace do something. Why are you just standing there?"

"Because he deserves to die."

"No, he was supposed to go to prison," Alex said, his body shaking as he looked up at me from his knees. The blood seeped into the ground around Martin, and it felt right that this was how he died.

Then it was over as quickly as it started, and Martin lay staring at nothing. I'd never seen someone die, and I wasn't sure what I was expecting, but the quiet nothing that followed hadn't been what my mind conjured. I wasn't struck down by lightning, and there were no sirens as if the police would know what I'd just done.

I waited a few more moments, my eyes trained on Martin's lax face and blank stare, my heart pounding hard. Was I going to feel anything more than happiness? Maybe, but I didn't right now. The one thing that was there was relief. I didn't have to worry about him hurting Alex again.

Alex stood, his arms covered in blood, shaking. "Oh my god, oh my god, he's dead. Jace, he's really dead. What the hell are we going to do?" He was a wreck, sweat dripping off his forehead and mingling with the wetness already on his face. I didn't know if it was sweat or tears.

"We need to call the cops. We can explain that it was self-defense," Alex said, his voice shaking as much as his body.

I stabbed the shovel into the ground and gripped Alex's shoulders. "Look at me." His eyes found mine. "No cops. He got what he deserved."

"Jace...."

"No. He was never going to stop. Watching Martin with you, I'm surprised he didn't attack you before the camping trip. He was sick, Alex. He needed to die."

Alex pulled away and stepped around Martin's body. He paced in front of the car and jumped at the sound of a semi's engine brake. I sighed and knelt down to stare into Martin's eyes. Shaking my head, I decided what we needed to do.

"Alex, come here and help me." Pulling the shirt away from his neck, I left it on the ground and picked up one of his arms.

"What are you doing?"

"I'm fixing the problem. From this moment on, we will never speak of this again. Now pick up his other arm and help me drag him to the water."

"What? I can't do that. Jace, please, we need to call the cops. We're only thirteen, they'll let us go, but if they find out we hid a body, we could go to jail for the rest of our lives," Alex begged.

"The cops aren't going to believe us. Look, I know you're scared, but this is what we need to do. I have your back, always." My adrenaline was pumping hard. I wasn't as sure about this plan as I made it seem, but it was our best shot. I had a bad feeling about calling the police.

Alex sighed. "This doesn't feel right. My Aunt Tilly and Courtney will be worried about him." He held his hand out toward Martin.

"He's dead, Alex, not sick. They can worry all they want. He's never coming back. Now are you going to help me or not?"

"Fine." As Alex bent over, I thought he would lose his nerve, but he grabbed Martin's arm, and one slow step at a time, we dragged his body to the calm, black water. Daring to wade in up to my knees, I pulled Martin into the water, then pushed his body away from the shore. Pulling off my T-shirt, I looked at Alex, whose eyes were trained on the floating man.

"Quickly before a gator thinks we're fair game. Soak your arms." I snapped my fingers in front of his face. "Alex, do it now."

He blinked as if I'd just appeared in front of him and then did as I asked. Forcing him to step away from the water's edge, I used my T-shirt to wipe off the remaining blood, grabbed his arm, and marched us back to the car.

"Stand here." I opened the car door and found the gym bag I'd seen Martin toss in here a few times. Unzipping the top, I found a couple of rolled white T-shirts. I tossed the bag back on the floor and closed the door. "Here put this on."

"You want me to wear my dead uncle's shirt?"

"He's dead. It's the least of his worries at this point." We both turned at the sound of splashing, and I looked over to see a tail flick above the shimmering water bathed in moonlight.

"I think I'm gonna be sick." Alex closed his eyes, his hand covering his mouth again.

"No, you can't. Look at me. He deserved what he got, now focus."

I ran over to the camera and stopped the recording. It felt like it took forever for the cassette to release. Picking up the bloody T-shirts on the way, I went to the garbage can and tossed everything in.

"What are you doing?"

"Destroying the evidence, do you not watch any crime shows? We can't just leave it like this."

"Shouldn't we do that somewhere else," Alex asked.

"No time." Running back to the car, I pushed in the lighter and waited for it to pop before jogging back to the can. It didn't take long for the shirts and other garbage to ignite, and soon the barrel was engulfed in flames.

"Bring me the shovel."

Alex handed me the shovel, and I threw it in handle first.

"Okay, now for the car," I mumbled.

"What are we doing here, Jace? Alligators just ate my uncle."

"Again, he's beyond caring. Now you need to care about yourself. So *stop worrying about him and worry about us." I stared at Alex's face and wondered if we would be okay after this. I couldn't think about that right now. "This is what we're going to do."*

"Jace?" I jerked and sucked in a deep breath. "Are you okay? You were shaking," Raine said.

My heart warmed, looking down at her bright blue eyes. "Yeah, I'm good. I think I was dozing, and I'm chilled. Let's go back to bed."

Nodding, Raine wrapped her arm around my waist. One thing was very fucking clear. If Kai wanted to play games, I would play and win. He wasn't stealing anything from Avro or me. Not now, not ever.

Chapter 20

K aivan

    I glared at the television, the beer bottle touching my lips, but I had yet to take a sip. Raine had been gone two nights. She texted and called, sent photographs, and...she looked fucking happy. Not just happy, she was practically glowing in the selfies she sent. Even the cute little kissy faces and suggestive lip bites couldn't do anything to cool down the steadily building unrest flowing through my body.

    Of course, because this world fucking hated me, the news—usually filled with shit like war and people dying—tossed up glimpses of Jace's concert like a fucking entertainment show. I didn't see Raine on the stage or in the audience with the quick pan, but it didn't matter. I knew she was there.

    "You plan on drinking that or kissing it all night," Roach asked.

I side-eyed him as he put his glass down. "Why are you in such a bad mood anyway? I mean, some of the guys are back, all is quiet with the other clubs, and you have a fucking hot ass old lady that anyone here would die to have."

Sitting the beer down, I contemplated telling him the situation, but with Roach, there was a fifty-fifty chance he would be understanding or stand up and yell out that he had just heard the funniest shit ever. I wasn't taking that chance. The last thing I needed or wanted was for every fucking asshole in here to know I let my woman fuck other men, but I needed to stay faithful.

"I just have a lot on my mind. Consider this my resting bitch face."

"Oh, it's hard to tell since your 'I sucked on a whole lemon while I killed your dog' look you have going seems to be the norm lately."

"Fuck off," I grumbled. I wasn't upset about not fucking anyone else. I wasn't even sure I was pissed off at her fucking Avro and Jace...no, that bothered me. But that wasn't what turned my stomach.

The more time she spent around them, the more she would realize I was nothing but a worthless piece of shit criminal. I was a killer and couldn't say I didn't enjoy it. I did my share of drinking, fucking, and drugs and watched more people die than I could remember. I'd become the monster she thought I was.

If she saw me, really saw me for what I was, why wouldn't Raine feel she was better off with just Avro and Jace and fucking disappear into the night. Avro had cut a sore spot open. I'd called him over to get the upper hand, and now it felt like he had it instead. Would he dare tell her? What would she do? Shit.

I rubbed my chest and tried to focus on anything other than Jace as he was interviewed on television. His smiling face practically yelled 'Fuck you, Kai,' through the television screen.

"Can we turn to something else? There's got to be something

other than fucking news on," I barked. One of the newer sweetbutts jumped and ran for the remote.

I glanced around the room, and my eyes stopped on the couch. Not very long ago, I had Raine bent over right there. The thought made my cock stir.

"Okay, fine, don't tell me. Do you think the shit that Wilder guy knew about what Lane sleeps in was true?"

I smirked. It had taken longer than I suspected before he asked, but it was the burning question in Roach's mind. Had someone else seen Lane's tits before him.

"With Wilder, anything is possible. He takes his job seriously," I said. Roach's face darkened as he polished off his drink.

"If he does anything to her, I'm going to kill him...."

"He won't," I said.

"How can you be so sure?"

Whatever pile of bullshit I was about to hand, Roach was squashed at the sound of the main door opening. Chase's voice boomed up the stairwell as he laughed while Beast talked. All the anger I'd contained curdled in my gut, and a growl ripped from my throat.

Then like some grand magician making his entrance Chase stepped into the clubhouse smiling.

"Hey!" Cheers went up as the men sitting around spotted the prez, returned from his Canadian tour. He was back earlier than Tanner said, which made me wonder if the asshole was lying to us all along.

I slipped off the bar stool and walked across the floor, fully intending to welcome Chase home. But as he shook hands with those he couldn't care less about, my fury rose to new heights.

"Fuck, it is good to be back! Someone grab me a celebratory drink," Chase called out.

"I have your drink right here," I said. Chase turned in my direction, and a moment before my fist connected with his jaw, I saw the confusion in his eyes.

"Fuck," Chase said, holding his jaw as he stumbled backward. I was impressed he didn't end up on his ass.

Before I could land another hit, someone grabbed me from behind. I knew it was Beast without having to look. Only two people would dare grab me like this, and Mannix wasn't here tonight, leaving one person.

"Get the fuck off me," I snarled over my shoulder.

"No fucking way. You need to calm your ass down," Beast said.

Like fuck I did.

"Let him go, Beast. If Snake has an issue with me, we'll sort it out between the two of us."

"Are you sure?"

"Yes, I'm sure. Let him go," Chase said, dabbing at the blood on the corner of his mouth. Beast's python-like arms released me, and I was tempted to lunge for Chase again but kept myself rooted to the floor. "I take it you'd like to have a meeting?"

"I'd rather continue punching you."

Chase smirked. "I deserve that," he said, the anger diffusing, which pissed me off more than if he had yelled back. I wanted him to fight me, and all he did was fucking agree? Fuck him!

Beast stayed close like a looming giant as I stomped up the metal steps behind Chase to his office.

"It's fine, Beast. Go back downstairs, I think Snake and I need a moment."

"I don't think that's a good idea," Beast said like I wasn't standing two feet away.

"Fuck you," I growled at Beast, but he ignored me. What was it with everyone? Had I lost my touch?

"Yeah, I'm sure. I don't need a bodyguard." Chase pulled a bottle of whiskey and a pair of glasses from the bottom drawer of his desk.

"Whatever, but if he tries to kill you, don't say I didn't warn you." Beast slammed the door to the office on his way out. The Harley picture on the wall rattled and tipped sideways. I stared at it until I couldn't take it any longer and straightened the frame.

"Here." Chase held out the full glass of whiskey, and I grudgingly took it from his hand.

"You can't placate me with alcohol," I said. Taking a sip and flopping into the leather chair as Chase sat down on the couch. I wondered how often that couch had been slept on over the years. How many times had Beast slept there trying to hold this place together?

"I know I can't. I like you, Snake. You're loyal but not afraid to speak your mind. Too many yes men in this place." Chase rubbed at his jaw, a bruise forming already.

"You calling Beast a 'yes man?'"

A deep chuckle filled the room as Chase shook his head no. "Beast speaks his mind, just not openly. Look, the point is I owe you and the club an apology. I haven't been the prez you all deserved."

I glanced around the office. "Is this a joke? Am I being punked?"

Chase smiled and then took a sip of his drink. "No. I know it may seem like I'm an oblivious asshole—"

"No, just an asshole," I said, cutting Chase off.

He laughed and nodded. "Fair enough." Chase leaned forward so the drink dangled from his fingers between his knees. His eyes were fixed on the floor for a long time, and I wondered if that was the end of the conversation.

Music and laughter could be heard through the two-way window as the other members were welcomed home. I wouldn't be participating in the festivities tonight. I had a lead on Dave and planned on looking into it before the slippery slug could vanish into another hole.

"Look, I'm gonna be straight with you, Snake," Chase said, and I jerked out of my fantasies of killing Dave. "We don't know each other well, but I never wanted to run an MC. I'm sure that's not a surprise to you. This place was my father's legacy, my grandfather's, and so on. I always thought my brother would get the gig. He was older, and it made logical sense."

Chase shrugged as if he still couldn't believe that this had happened. This wasn't news. He was given the MC before I was sent to prison and had hidden, pretending to be dead the entire time I was locked up.

"When my father handed the Lost Souls to me instead and started the war between my brother and me...." Chase's eyes turned to look out the window. It was like he was watching a movie play out on the glass that only he could see. The sound of a crash was followed by loud laughter from the clubhouse below.

"Let's just say that if I could go back, there are a lot of things I would've done differently, but that's the fucked up thing about time. It only travels in one direction, and all we can do is move forward." He held up his finger as I opened my mouth. "Fuck time zones and the clocks moving an hour," he said. I smirked. "Stupid forward, backward shit. You know what I mean."

"Yeah, I do," I said, tapping my finger on the glass. I wanted to hate Chase, maybe pick him up and toss him through the glass, or I thought I did. Seeing him as a decent man wasn't something I wanted, but he made it very fucking difficult.

"Don't kill him, but Mannix filled me in on your old man a while back," Chase said, and my eyes snapped to his. Just the thought of my father made me want to put my fist through the wall. "I knew him or knew of him. Jackson McMillan, otherwise known as Razor, was an enforcer for the Wild Dogs. Not many of them around anymore."

My hand tightened on the glass as I glared at Chase. The anger that had simmered was beginning to rise. Why the hell was he telling me this?

"Oh yeah, I wouldn't know. After he got my mother killed and I watched her bleed out on my living room floor, he got himself tossed in prison for life. That was about when I stopped giving a shit."

Chase rubbed at his eyes. "Listen, man, I'm no shrink, and I wouldn't even profess to be highly intelligent most days, but I've done some shit that has paralleled your past."

"What the fuck are you trying to say that I think of you as my Daddy? That's why you being an asshole burns my ass so much? Cause I can tell you right now, I'm never fucking calling you Daddy Chase."

Chase laughed hard, the sound coming out like a bark as he started to cough. He sat the drink down and continued to laugh hysterically. Fucking idiot. I smirked and then chuckled. Okay, it was kind of funny.

"Oh shit, please, for the love of God, never say that around Tanner. He'll fucking start calling me that out of spite," Chase said, and I sobered with the mention of Tanner.

"We need to talk about him," I said. "The guy has no loyalty to the club. To you, yes. The club, he would watch burn for all he cared. I don't really feel like having to kill one of our own again anytime soon, so could you talk to him or beat the shit out of him? I'm not picky as long as he stops acting like he's a fucking eighteen-year-old punk."

"I fucked up with Tanner. He had his run of Ashen Springs. He fucked every housewife there, partied hard, and was never locked up for any of the shit he did. I made him untouchable, and now he's...."

"A fucking immature punk. Despite his eagerness to help kill, he's a wildcard in any situation which will get someone killed. His open lack of respect is rubbing more than just me the wrong way, and that is not doing him any favors." I sighed. "Look, I like the kid, but he needs to grow the fuck up. Chase, he will get kicked out or a bullet between his eyes. If you want to stay in control, then take my advice, don't give him the one percenter until he proves he won't abuse the power that comes with it."

He grated on my nerves and used this place, the people, and his friendship with Chase like a get-out-of-jail-free card. If I had to kill him, I would, but I didn't want to. Chase nodded but didn't say any more on the subject, and I was done talking about Tanner.

"I'm sorry for what happened with your mother," Chase blurted, dumping cold water on my head all over again.

I gulped down the whiskey, loving the burn on the way down. That sensation told me I was still alive. The only other time I felt that way was holding Raine. She made me feel grounded and worth something. "Let's not talk about my mother, okay?"

"Fine, but I need to tell you something because I owe you. It's the least I can do for everything you've done to hold this place together and keeping my ass from being tossed in jail for the shit I did." He rubbed his forehead and gulped his drink. Chase looked me in the eyes, and I knew I wouldn't like what he said.

"It was my father that ordered the hit on your mother," Chase said, and it was like the air was sucked out of my chest. I didn't move or blink. There was only the pounding of my heart loud in my ears.

"What the fuck did you just say?" My voice was low and lethal as my muscles shook.

"Snake, you know how this shit goes. People on both sides make decisions for their clubs, and there is always collateral damage. From what I know The Wild Dogs sent your father to kill my brother, but he wasn't killed, and my father retaliated. The Lost Souls enforcer at the time did the job, and my brother rode shotgun on the back of the bike."

"You fucking knew this MC killed my mother, and you let me join?" I burst from my seat, and my hands clenched as I pictured slitting Chase's throat. "You let me stay for a year and never opened your fucking mouth," I yelled. "I must really look like a sucker to you." I held my hand out toward the desk. "Did you sit up here laughing at me as you sent me to clean up your fucking mess?"

Every part of me was ready to kill, all I saw was red, and it was taking every bit of self-control I had not to jump on Chase.

"Whoa. Whoa, no. It wasn't like that. Let me explain before you try to kill me." Chase held up his hands. "And before you ask, no one else knows. Not Beast, Mannix, Roach, or anyone else." Chase glanced at my hand, and I realized that I'd pulled my knife. I was still tempted to use it but eased myself down into the chair. I wanted answers before I decided if I was going to kill him. His eyes told me he wasn't lying, which was why I hadn't already slit his throat.

"I only started to look into your family history after I learned they were MC legacy. I asked Mannix a few questions about you, and he told me what happened with your mother, but it didn't click right away." He rubbed the back of his neck. "This all fell in my lap just before I left for Canada, and I've warred with telling you the entire time I was gone. Some shit is better off being left buried."

"Then why the fuck are you telling me now? Why take that chance?" I growled.

"Because I thought you deserved to know. This way, at least you got to see my brother killed. It's a small thing, but in life, the little moments help us move forward," Chase said calmly.

"What did you smoke a bunch of that strong Canadian weed while you were up there? What's up with the introspective, laid-back act? Where the fuck is the Chase that was snorting coke like it was going out of style, burning the world down, and leaving me to clean up your mess?"

The corner of Chase's lip curled up before he polished off his drink. "All I can say is I have a second chance at life. The baby coming helped me pull my head out of my ass. That version of me is not who I want my child to have as a father."

"I'm not sure I'm buying this act. It's easy enough to say you want to do better, but it's a whole other thing to keep it together long-term. What assurance do we have that you won't disappear again at the first sign of trouble? Spend another ten years hiding in a small town or go on a drug-induced rampage?"

"There is nothing I can say to convince you. I can only show you with time. And, for the record, I'm not saying me or your father are saints, but he tried to do right by your mother when it came to revenge. He stormed our clubhouse and shot it up good, killed three members before he ran for it and got caught by the cops."

"I'm confused now. Are you saying you're going to do better by the club or running?" I smirked as I sat back in the worn chair. At one time, I would've wished it swallowed me whole, but not anymore. Raine coming back into my life changed all of that.

"Always the sarcastic jackass, but I guess I deserve it. I'm going to prove myself to you and the rest of the club. I need to earn respect. I fucked up. I ran off and haven't been the Prez or the leader I need to be. I'm just asking you to give me the opportunity to make good on my word."

I stared at the man that sadly did remind me of my father. Until Chase said the words, I hadn't seen the similarities, but I couldn't unsee it now.

"I should still kill you," I said.

"Normally, I'd expect you to try."

Our eyes locked, and I couldn't do it. It would be like someone trying to kill me for the shit my father did. I had no control over that any more than Chase had control over what happened with my mother. He could've easily kept it bottled up, and I would never have known the truth.

"Before I can agree to let this drop between us, I need to know one thing. What happened to the old enforcer? Did he die?"

"I don't know. He was with my brother at the docks but disappeared during the fighting. His body was never recovered, so I don't know if he's dead, caught by the cops, or...." Chase shrugged.

"Or out there living his best life," I finished. "You gonna try and stop me if I decide to find him?"

Chase smiled. "You'd be doing me a fucking favor. Skin him alive for all I care. He goes by Happy Harris, which is ironic cause he was the most miserable fucker you'd ever meet."

"Well, I can drink to skinning him alive," I said. Chase smiled and stood when the door banged open, making us both jump. The knife I'd never put away sliced the arm of the leather chair as I stood and spun around.

"You fucking get home after weeks away, and this is the first place you go? Do you even know what I've had to deal with?" Naomi seethed. She didn't look much better than the last time I saw her. She'd tried to put her hair up in a bun, but it looked more like a bird's nest. Her makeup—which at one time was always perfect—ran in streaks down her face along with the tears.

"I had to come and...."

Naomi pointed her finger at Chase, and I strategically moved out of the line of fire. "Look at me! I'm a horse! No, I'm a fucking walrus! This kid is ruining my perfect body. I have stretch marks, you asshole," Naomi cried, then broke down into hysterical sobbing.

I glanced at Chase's horrified face, his eyes pleading with me not to leave him alone, but this was sweet payback. Mouthing good luck, I snuck past Naomi, who began to shriek a long line of profanities, and closed the door.

Raine

Chapter 21

Raine

"Did you get everything that you need," Jace asked as I got back into the limo. The lawyer was very helpful, and I now had a copy of the papers I filed to have Kai's charges removed. Jace had been surprisingly on board when I told him I wanted Kai's record expunged. He said it was better for all of us if that happened, and although I agreed with him, I couldn't help wondering what else was going on. As with Kai, I worried there was an ulterior motive for their actions.

The plane landed much earlier than expected, so he had the driver bring us straight to the lawyer's office. How he got an appointment for me so quickly was another Jace mystery.

"Yeah, they printed off all the paperwork and had me sign it but said it could take some time to get through the system and that I might need to speak to a Judge, but the ball is rolling."

Settling beside him in the back of the limo, he tapped on the divider, and we pulled away. Jace wrapped an arm around my shoulders but kept typing on his phone.

"Thanks for bringing me here and helping when I know you're not Kai's biggest fan."

"What gave it away?" He teased. "But you're welcome. I've dealt with a few lawyers over the last few years. You get to know the good ones." His eyes lifted to mine and then went back to his screen.

His jaw was tight, and he was glaring at his screen. "Everything okay?"

"Just typical disagreement stuff with Allen, our tour dates and locations. I only agreed to do certain countries and dates, but now he wants us to go to Southeast Asia for six months. I'm not doing that. I strategically planned everything so I could come home at least a couple of days a month."

"What do the other guys want to do?"

"They don't care and will follow my lead on this," Jace said.

"Then stick to what you have. He can't change it if you don't agree. Offer to do three weeks and no more."

"Yeah, I think this is going to be a phone call argument," he said, turning off his phone as more conversation bubbles popped up. "Now he can't annoy me for a few minutes."

Jace laid his head back on the seat, and I cuddled into his side. The short trip had been a whirlwind of excitement, and I was still processing all that had happened.

"Is it normal for the two of you to fight this much? It seems to be all you do." I asked, my voice soft. Something was off about him, but I couldn't put my finger on what it was that bothered me. Allen had well-laid plans for Jace's career, and he always found a way to let me know I was messing with them when no one else could see or hear him.

"Things have changed. I can't even explain it. I don't know if it's cause we made such a quick rise to the top or if it's something else, but he's been strange recently," Jace said.

"Could it be that he senses you're not as happy as you were before and is worried you'll quit?"

"I guess anything is possible."

Jace fell silent, and I chose not to press anymore. He seemed stressed enough. I pulled out my phone and brought up a group text, smirking as I pictured Avro and Kai's faces when they received the message and saw who was in the chat. They had to get along at some point, and Jace's phone was off, so I knew it wouldn't bother him right now.

> R: Hey guys, we're back and about an hour away from the house.

K: Which house?

A: Mine and Jace's house, obviously.

K: What the hell are you doing in here?

A: That's a dumb question. Raine sent out a group text.

> R: I did. It's much easier to let you both know where I am.

K: I don't like it.

A: Of course you don't. Why would you like anything that makes Raine's life easy?

K: I swear you make me want to kill you a little more each day.

I rolled my eyes at that. Well, if nothing else, this provided an outlet to bitch at one another. Did everyone with multiple partners have this issue? I really wanted to know because I often felt like hitting them all.

> A: I'm shocked. Your threats are getting old, Kai. Maybe try something really shocking and be nice. That will confuse everyone.

> R: Okay, that's enough from both of you. I just wanted you to know that I'm back safely. Isn't that what's most important?

I felt like I was wrangling children and not men.

> A: Yes, you're right, it is. I'm happy you're back safely.

> K: Suck up.

> R: Kai!

> K: Yes, of course I'm happy you're back. Now I don't have to hunt Jace and his fancy jet down.

I smirked but wanted to hit my forehead at the same time. Kai was impossible, yet I couldn't help the butterflies fluttering around at the thought of him moving heaven and earth to find me.

> R: See you soon.

Shifting on the seat, I curled into Jace's warm body and closed my eyes. I had to admit that a private jet was pretty badass. I mean, I wasn't one to be wowed by the glitz, but we had the entire thing to ourselves for the short flight, and Jace made the most of the alone time. I was officially a member of the mile-high club.

My lip curled up as I replayed how voracious he could be and how much I enjoyed myself. For the first time, my heart felt full, and my body relaxed. I didn't have to talk to myself to stay calm and didn't jerk at someone brushing by me.

The jumpiness over loud sounds was still there, but I no longer searched every shadow and craved to learn and experience more. I wanted to ride on the back of Kai's motorcycle and have Avro teach me how to surf.

I couldn't help wondering what my parents would've thought of my choices if they'd lived. Then again, I probably wouldn't have met Kai if they had, and the thought of that hurt more than their loss. It was a sad truth, but I'd technically spent more time with him than with them. He was my rock and my shoulder to cry on and so much more. The time apart had done nothing to lessen the feelings he stirred.

I heard the lyrics of Jace's songs in a whole new way while away. Sitting at the side of the stage, humming along while tapping my foot, it felt like the words were written for me. Now I found myself singing all his songs in my head, the words on a loop and each one cutting or healing my soul.

My heart won't stop bleeding
The final curtain is calling
I have hurt you, and you have hurt me
Gripping your heart and my four-leaf clover
I'm only human, my heart won't stop bleeding
Can't you feel my pain?
I can feel yours, but you break my heart in two
Yet, I still love you
I'm only human, my heart won't stop bleeding
The bite of the wind hits my face
The rain drenches me to the bone

I can't give up on you
I can't give up on you, so don't you dare walk away
I'm only human, my heart won't stop bleeding
You promised you'd never leave me
That we'd be together til the bitter end
You promised not to let me fall
I'm only human, my heart won't stop bleeding
Don't leave
Don't leave
Don't Leave Me
You promised not to leave
I can't stop the memories
Times of better days
Baby, please, don't you want to stay
But final curtain is calling, your hands barely keep you from falling
I'll be damned if I don't fight
Until I take the final flight
I will never change, but you're always my light
I'm only human, my heart won't stop bleeding
I'm only human, my heart won't stop bleeding

Why I'd never seen the pain in the words before, I couldn't say. I loved the song as much as the next person, but it was more personal now. It gave me insight into the man. For all of Jace's bravado, I could feel so much of him locked away, and I wanted to find the key.

Closing my eyes, I snuggled closer, loving when he kissed the top of my head before I fell asleep.

Raine

Chapter 22

R aine

"Are you fucking kidding me?" I jerked at the sound of Jace's angry voice. Confusion set in as I blinked and realized I was no longer in the car. How long was I out for, and where was I?

"Are you going to let me in or what?" That was Kai.

If my reflection in the gas fireplace was anything to go by, I was a mess. Quickly combing my fingers through my hair, I tried to get it to lie down with little success.

"Try not to trash the place this time," Avro said.

I pushed myself to my feet as the three men walked into the living room, and it was as if all the windows had been thrown open to let in the midday heat. They stared at me like they were waiting for orders, and my brain flat-lined.

"Why are you all staring at me?" I looked down and smoothed out the Grimhead Crew sweatshirt I was wearing.

"What the hell are you wearing?" Kai crossed his arms. If he thought the band hoodie was bad, he would freak out when he saw the extra tattoos I got with Jace and Avro's names.

"It's my band hoodie, and it looks fucking amazing on her," Jace said.

Kai glared, and the tension in the room tripled. I couldn't deny I loved it. There was something far too sexy about the three of them in the same room together. The problem was I wasn't sure how to approach this. Who did I go to first? Did it matter? Should it matter?

Kai made the decision for me when he stomped around the coffee table. My heart hammered hard as I stared into his blue eyes. A deep rumble rippled from his throat when he growled and wrapped his arms around my waist, dropping his lips to mine.

Our tongues battled as the burn in my stomach erupted into an inferno. Kissing Kai felt like drinking a sweet poison. So potent it could kill you, yet you could never get enough.

"Yeah, yeah, you made your point," Jace drawled, and my cheeks flushed as I remembered we were being watched. This was more awkward than I thought it would be. Kai broke the kiss but kept his hand on my waist like I would try and run. "Don't need to eat her alive."

"Jealous rock star?"

Jace scoffed and crossed his arms over his chest. "After that plane ride home, not likely." I felt Kai tense. "Nice tattoo, by the way. Such a great idea. So great I couldn't resist adding my name. I took the prime spot between her legs too."

Avro pinched the bridge of his nose as he swore under his breath, and I felt like doing the same as Kai made a deep primal noise.

"You think you're smart, do you?" Kai let go of my waist and got in Jace's face.

"Smart enough to have had cameras installed in all the rooms of the house, so if you're planning on pulling a gun again, I'd think twice, asshole," Jace said, his lip pulled up in a smirk. "Unless, of course, you liked prison enough to want to go back there for life."

I didn't know if Jace was telling the truth, this was news to me, but I looked around the room the same way Kai did.

"I really don't like you," Kai said.

"Aw, my heart is breaking," Jace made a sniffling noise. I knew he was purposely trying to get under Kai's skin now. That glimmer he got when he was enjoying himself way too much was back in his eye, and all I wanted to do was knock their heads together. "And here I thought we were going to be besties and braid each other's hair."

"I'm going to knock your teeth out of your fucking head," Kai growled.

"I'd like to see you try," Jace said, stepping closer to Kai.

"Can you two not have a single, civil conversation," I asked, and they both looked at me.

"No," they said in unison.

"Wow, the first thing you can agree on. At least it's a start." I wandered to the bar and grabbed two bottles of wine from the selection and a pair of glasses. Holding up my hands, I motioned to Avro while the other two just stared. "Avro, why don't we go upstairs and let these two work out their differences?" Avro smiled wide.

"I won't say no to that. Less chance I get a fist in the face too," he said, and stepped around Jace and Kai to meet me.

"You're really going to leave us alone," Kai asked.

"Why not? You're both adults. At least, I think you are. You need to work this shit out so we can get on with an actual relationship. I don't want to tippy-toe around the two of you. So say what you need to say to one another and be done with it already." Avro took the wine from my hand and linked our arms together. "At least one of you thinks with more than the little head between your legs."

"My cock is not little," they said in unison again and then glared at one another.

Shaking my head, I did the only thing I could think of and left them alone. They could both end up dead, but they were grown-ass men, and I didn't feel like playing ref for the rest of my life.

"Are we really leaving them alone?" Avro whispered as we walked up the stairs.

"Yup. Want to have a shower?"

"You never need to ask me that. The answer is always yes." Avro chuckled.

They would tear the entire house apart as they tried to kill one another, or they'd figure shit out—either way, I wasn't giving them more fuel by being in the same room. I refused to be the flag they fought over in their tug-o-war match.

Jace

"I can't believe she actually left us alone together," I said. "But I'm happy she did."

I cracked my neck and rolled my shoulders as Kai smirked, his eyes going from cold to lethal. I should be scared, I knew he was a great fighter, but there was something open about his aggression. He didn't keep it hidden like Lyle did. There was no doubt in my mind he'd kill me if given the opportunity and motive, but he'd make sure I saw it coming. There was no hidden agenda, sneak attacks, or shooting me in my sleep.

My hand clenched as the memory of my family's murder flashed behind my eyes. The pain gripped my chest as it had that day. It never stopped aching, and the what-ifs never stopped flowing, but I hid it well because no one really wanted to hear about your pain. They asked how you were but only wanted an 'I'm fine.' The moment you started to open up, their eyes got squirrely, and they shifted in their seat, uncomfortable with the sudden heavy reality. So I kept my crap locked up tight.

Except with Avro and now Raine. Avro lived it all with me, and Raine held onto every word I shared. After the wild night in the cemetery, she'd hugged me tight and whispered how sorry she was. They mattered. No one else did.

"Oh yeah, and why is that? If you're thinking of going round two, I'm more than happy."

I snapped back to the present as we glared at each other.

I felt the same rage in me rolling off of Kai and knew we were too similar for my liking. Avro and I were balanced. It wasn't that Avro didn't get a say— he usually made all the decisions—but I made the final call when it came to certain shit. Kai was just as demanding, and I saw him wanting to yank that away from me. There wouldn't be any sharing or negotiating with Kai unless we had an understanding.

"I don't like being threatened," I said, and as I suspected, Kai's lips curled up, obviously pleased with himself. I was about to wipe that smile away. "You think I don't have resources just because I'm in a rock band, didn't go to prison or spend my time with shady people?"

"I'm surprised that Avro told you. I really thought he'd keep that to himself."

"Then you don't understand what we share because we don't hide anything from one another. Then again, I'm not sure you'd ever understand the concept of real trust, not with how you live and what you do," I said, picking at the wounds I knew we shared.

"It's unwise to trust that much, then the other person holds the cards," Kai said.

I smiled wide, a low chuckle escaping my mouth. "And that's why you'll never really have all of Raine, because you won't give all of yourself."

"You don't know anything about us," Kai snarled as I hit the right chords. His hands gripped the front of my shirt, and I cocked a brow at him but didn't move to further the fight. If he hit me, it was on camera, and I warned him, so he couldn't say I tricked him.

"I know enough, and I know your type. You'll fuck up, and this will all fall down around you because you can't hold your shit together." I glanced down at the fists holding my shirt. "Case in point," I said, my voice as cool as a spring rain. "Do it, Snake," I growled low, accentuating his name. "Hit me. I dare you."

One finger at a time, his fists uncurled like he had to order his hands to let go of me. I smoothed out the wrinkles, just to be annoying as fuck before continuing.

"I know what you're trying to do, and you're not fucking worth it," Kai said, his hands going to his side.

"Calling Avro out in the middle of the night to threaten him...." I shook my head. "Not a smart move. It's a good thing you don't play poker. All you did was piss me off, and when I'm pissed, I stop playing nice. The things that I found about you...."

"I don't give a fuck what you have. I have no problem making a few calls and ruining you if you ever try to run off with Raine and think you can cut me out." Kai stepped in close again so our noses were almost touching. "I will do anything to keep her. Do you understand that? She is mine."

"Ours," I growled back, and his body shook with the building tension. "There are three of us now, in case you didn't learn to count past one."

"I swear I'm going to kill you. One of these days, you're going to push me too far. I can already see it."

I smiled wide but knew that my eyes held as much hatred as the blue ones staring back at me.

"You don't scare me, Kai, which is what I know really bites your ass. You're used to intimidating everyone wherever you go and it almost worked when you came here waving your gun the first time. But, I see you now. I see you for who you really are. I'll never let you intimidate me again, and you're already toeing my give a fuck limit." He took a deep breath, and we were so close his chest pressed into mine. "I've been blackmailed by much worse than you. And, here is the funny thing about blackmailers, they always have shit in their past that they don't want anyone knowing about." I narrowed my eyes at Kai. I'd only scratched the surface and found more dead bodies than he would ever want to be shared.

"Isn't that right, Kaivan McMillan? Son of Jackson and April McMillan. It's incredible what you can find when digging through the graves of someone else's life."

Kai's nostrils flared, and the excitement grew in my body, making my heart pound as uncertainty flashed behind those cold, blue eyes.

"What the fuck do you think you know?"

"I know enough. And as we speak, I have more being dug up on you. Not just one, but four private investigators I use regularly have all been sent to dig up everything on you they can find."

Kai stepped back, his eyes searching my face. I assumed to see if I was joking. "Does the name Keith Moore mean anything to you? You would've called him Red. Don't bother answering. I already know you do. He was the first man you killed and got away with it. Or you have up until now, that is. It's amazing what can be pried away from a prison guard for the right price." The cocky expression on Kai's face fell, but I had to give him credit. He didn't back down.

"I know you stood over his dying body with a bloody shank in your hand. I also know a guard covered it up because he owed you a favor and because of what Red did to you first. I bet the warden and the parole board don't know that, though, do they? A new murder charge on your list of offenses, and I'm certain that by the time my investigators are through, I'll have a deep pile of bones to shake from your tree. More than enough to bury you forever and send you away for life this time."

Purposely turning my back on him, I wandered over to the bar, readying for any move he made. Pulling out the bottle of rum and a coke, I poured two drinks and sat down with mine.

"For you, if you want it," I pointed to the glass and sipped my drink.

Kai made his way to the bar but kept his eyes on me the entire time. He picked up the drink and sat in the seat across the way. As soon as he was settled, I continued.

"I'm also sure that all those you call friends would be at risk. That Roach guy, and how about your friend Hollywood who's still in prison? Then there is a Mannix...."

"This better not be recorded." Kai looked around the room.

"I'm not that stupid. There's no sound," I said.

He glanced around the room again before his eyes settled on me. "You think your expensive shit and piles of money will keep you safe?"

Kai might not have realized it, but he just told me how he saw me. I was a walking moneybag of annoyance. Someone or multiple someones with money had done him dirty, and I tucked that knowledge away for another time.

"I'd spend every last cent I have to keep those I care about safe. So yeah, in this case, I do."

"Your money won't stop me from putting a bullet through your eyes," Kai said.

"Not much is going to stop that if you don't care about hurting

Raine, or going back to prison, but I don't think you want either of those things."

His eyes narrowed into slits. "What the fuck do you want," Kai asked.

I tapped my finger on the top of my glass. "The same fucking thing you do, for you to fuck off and never come back, but I also know that's not what Raine wants, and unlike you, I plan to respect that. So all I want is for you to stop digging, and so will I. What you learned is burned, and I'll do the same."

As his glare darkened, my muscles tensed, hoping he'd jump across the space and attack me, but I knew he wouldn't. We were at an impasse, and the next move could tilt the entire board, and everyone would lose. Kai wasn't stupid and didn't want that to happen anymore than I did.

But he was unpredictable, so it was better to be safe. I was sure of one thing...how much he cared for Raine. It was in everything he did and said, and even if he didn't admit it to himself, he was scared. Kai didn't strike me as the kind of person to handle fear well. I also knew what that was like. Some ran when they were scared, but with Kai and I, the monster that lived inside of us came out, and we were more dangerous backed into a corner than ever before.

"But I want to make myself really fucking clear. If you threaten Avro and me again, I'll burn you to the ground."

Kai shocked me when he smiled and rubbed at his bottom lip. "You have balls Jace. I didn't think you had it in you." I didn't say anything and just waited for him to speak. "Fine, it seems we're at a stalemate, but if I catch wind you're trying anything stupid, then all bets are off, and I won't use money to solve my problems."

"Same goes for you," I said. We stared at one another for a long time, like two animals in the same cage sizing one another up. "I'm going to take a chance and tell you something."

"You going to admit that you killed someone," Kai asked.

I smiled, sipped my drink, and let the fizz and alcohol soothe my nerves.

"You're funny, Kai. I won't confirm or deny any such thing, but I will tell you this as a show of good faith. The man that Avro and I allegedly had something to do with his disappearance and untimely demise pulled a Red on him when he was thirteen. I'm sure you can understand why something may or may not have been done."

I watched Kai's face closely, and other than the subtle tick of the muscle in his jaw, no other emotions showed, but the hard lines of his scowl lessened.

"I just thought you should know that, and I'd do it all over again if given the chance," I said, lifting my glass and tipping it in his direction like I was offering a toast. Kai surprisingly did the same.

"Then I guess it's a good thing we're determined to keep both situations buried," he said and downed the rest of his drink. "Do you really think they are having sex without us?"

I burst out laughing. "Oh guaran-fuckin-teed. Avro wouldn't waste an opportunity like that." I could hear his teeth grinding, and right on cue, the sounds of wild sex echoed down the stairs. Kai shot to his feet, gripping the glass so tight he could crush it.

His leather jacket was squeaking as his body vibrated with pent-up rage. "Did you want to join?"

Kai's eyes narrowed as he glared at me. "Fuck no."

"Sure, I believe that." I stood and stretched.

"Get that smug fucking look off your face," Kai growled as the sounds got louder. He took a step in the direction of the stairs and stopped as if he couldn't help himself. Kai slammed the glass down on the table before balling his hands into fists. It was easy to tell it was taking everything in him not to get involved. Trying to kill Avro was also possible.

"Sorry, no can do. I've been told that I have a resting asshole face." Kai crossed his arms over his chest but didn't move further for the door or the stairs. "I guess make yourself at home. You can sit here and listen, leave, or join, I don't care, but I'm not missing out," I said.

"Oh, like hell you are leaving me down here alone," he growled as he stomped along like an elephant behind me. I wasn't sure if he was making sure they knew we were coming, but the stairs shook with each step. If Avro saw that, he'd lose his mind, but I didn't think this was the best time to mention it. Score one for me on not being a total asshole.

As soon as we rounded the corner to the bedroom, I knew we were the butt of a joke. They were jumping around and making noises as they tossed pillows at one another.

Raine stopped first. "Yes, I win. Pay up," she said, laughing.

"What the fuck is happening right now?" Kai tentatively stepped over the threshold like it might swallow him whole.

"They're jerks, is what's happening. Got me all hard for nothing." Leaning against the door frame, I couldn't be angry even if I wanted to.

"Who said it was for nothing," Avro asked.

His amber eyes practically glowed with the sun's rays pouring through the window. He whipped off his T-shirt and threw it at me. I caught it a second before Avro pushed me against the wall and captured my lips. Whatever else was happening was forgotten as his body pressed into mine.

I had no idea if this would ever work, but a part of me felt that Kai and I had at least come to a truce. Don't fuck with me, and I won't fuck with you. It was simple, and yet I could only hope it held. I didn't give a fuck about me, but the idea of Avro behind bars for something I did, lanced my heart. I'd never let that happen. I'd kill Kai first or die trying.

Chapter 23

Kaivan

What the hell was going on? Avro marched across the room and threw his shirt at Jace before attacking him. I'd never been into guys, and if Roach kissed me like that, I'd kick his fucking ass, but I had to admit there was something hot about the two of them together.

My body jerked like I'd been electrocuted as Raine's hands slipped around my waist. She pulled at the bottom of my T-shirt and slid her hands across my abs. I sighed and felt like growling at the same time as she drew her nails along my skin. Fuck, that alone had me hard.

Grabbing her arm, I pulled her around so she was in front of me. "Not very nice to trick me." I loved the devious glint that was staring back at me.

The girl I knew was still in there. She'd been buried and hidden, but the more time we spent together, the more of her I saw. She didn't bother to cover the faint bruise where I'd bit her days before. My thumb rubbed over the mark, and she shivered under my touch, biting her bottom lip.

"We had to get the two of you up here somehow," Raine whispered, and my heart pounded so hard that I needed to take a moment just to admire her.

"I fucking missed you." I needed to taste her and wasn't waiting a second longer. Dropping my lips to hers, I kissed her hard. She gripped the front of my jacket and moaned as I bent her body backward. Our tongues fought a battle that neither of us backed down from.

"Oh fuck," Jace yelled. Breaking the kiss, my hand went to my gun, but as my eyes found him, he was definitely not in any position to attack me. He leaned against the dresser with his jeans around his ankles while Avro went to town on his cock.

"Never mind them right now. Just keep looking at me." Raine's voice was soft as a whisper, her breath fanning my neck just before she pressed her lips against my skin. "This is no different than the clubhouse," she said, but it was different.

I'd made a statement, a proclamation to everyone there that she was mine and I was hers. This felt very different. Even if Raine and Avro hadn't been up here having sex, they'd been together and would be again. The rage that stirred was dangerous and explosive, and it scared me how much I wanted to kill them and fuck Raine between their dead bodies.

"Please, Kai." I looked down and met Raine's pleading look. Her eyes were the only thing pulling me back from the edge of insanity. She pushed the leather jacket off my shoulders, and it fell with a thud to the floor. "This is for us. Don't think about the time we've lost, but what we can have. You know I love you." Raising up on her toes, she nipped at my ear, and my hands gripped her ass, pulling her flush against my body. "Are you really going to let Jace and Avro have all the fun? Are you going to let them show us up?"

"I know what you're doing, Tink, and you're not playing fair." She knew I loved a challenge. The harder, the better. I'd always been that way, and she was poking at me, but it worked. My cock was hard and begging to be buried inside her. To make her scream where they could see it and know that no matter how many times they fucked her, her heart was mine first.

"Maybe, but it's the truth. I missed you too."

Tilting Raine's head up with my finger under her chin, I stared into the eyes that had gripped my heart like barbed wire and never let go. "Did he really tattoo you?"

Raine's face flushed a bright red, and she licked her lips. "Yes."

"I swear to fuck, I'm going to bury his body somewhere no one is going to find it," I growled, my head snapping back to the two men that had changed positions. Jace didn't glance my way, yet it still felt like he was laughing at me.

"Kai, I let him, he didn't force me, but you'll always be on the front where everyone will see it first. It was only fair. There are three of you, and I can't play favorites as much as each of you would like that."

"I don't like this fair crap. I don't like any of this," I said and grabbed her hand, pulling her over to the large seat in the corner of the room. "Take your jeans off. I need to see this."

Her hands went to the top of her jeans and unfastened them in record time. I smirked as she wiggled them down her body. Standing straight, she stretched her leg to show off her new ink. I glared at the signature on the inside of her thigh. Then she turned to show me the outside of her leg and Avro's name. I should've fucking had a ring of my name done all the way around, but the prick would've just picked another spot. Tattooing her whole body with my name suddenly didn't sound crazy.

"Now mine."

Raine tilted her head and smiled as her eyes snapped like she was telling me to fuck off. There wasn't a world in which I'd be okay walking away from her, no matter the dangers to my soul.

Reaching out, I gripped her face and forced her to step forward. "Take. My. Jeans. Off. Now," I groaned, needing her.

She actually fluttered her eyes at me—which was fucking sexy as hell—before smirking as best she could in my grip.

"No."

"Fuck you make me so hot," I said, holding her face tighter. "And you know it too, don't you?" She made to nip at my hand, but it was a playful, half-hearted effort, and I wanted her spitting mad. When she was that angry, she couldn't see straight, and fuck, that got me so hard I didn't care who was around. Maybe that was her goal, or maybe this was just us. Either way, I wanted her on my lap and her ass tanned red.

I stared at the band T-shirt and the rock logo splashed across the front with team Jace in the corner. This guy knew how to get under my skin, and it pissed me the fuck off. He was worse than Roach. At least Roach was an asshole that didn't want to steal my girl.

Growling, I grabbed the material by the front and pulled hard. Raine squealed, and the loud tearing sound was sweet music to my ears. Fucking Jace and his fucking band. I didn't have any Lost Souls T-shirts, but I suddenly wanted a box of them made up just for her to wear instead.

Of course, she wasn't wearing a bra.

I swear she walked around like this on purpose, so I'd always have a permanent hard-on thinking about her tits brushing against the material. How it made her nipples hard, and all I had to do was slip my hand under whatever she was wearing to get a feel.

Yanking her close, I buried my head in the crook of her neck and breathed deeply. The sweet scent of her body wash calmed the darker side of me that wanted to toss her over my shoulder and take her from the house like a fucking caveman while I shot the other two men in the head. With each breath, her hard nipples rubbed against my chest, driving me insane, yet I never wanted to release her from this position.

"I can't decide if I want to eat or fuck you." Raine shivered in my hold but pressed her body closer, and my mind snapped like a brittle stick. The remnants of her shirt and mine disappeared in a flurry. I set my gun on the table as Raine pulled at the button on my jeans. When the material was pulled down to my knees, she caught me off guard and pushed me.

The jeans locked my legs together, making me stumble back, and my ass landed hard on the large chair behind me.

"Oops." The sexiest curve of her lips pulled up as she pretended to be sorry. I fucking loved everything about her. The sweet and sexy side, the innocent and timid parts that warmed my heart, the wild fury and jealousy that made my cock rock hard, and even the mischievous games she liked to play. I was all in on all of it.

"Oh fuck." My voice strained as she bent over before me and grabbed her ankles. Inches away were her soft, lush ass and her already glistening pussy. Torn, I gave in to both desires, cracking my hand down hard on her soft skin, then burying my tongue into her delicate folds.

The yell that accompanied the smack ended with a moan as my tongue swirled over her sensitive clit. Clamping my lips around the little ball of nerves, I sucked hard as my hand cracked down hard enough to sting my palm.

"Ah! Fuck, yes," Raine cried, and I growled. The vibrations had her pushing back harder into my mouth. As much as I wanted to continue punishing her, I gripped her hips instead, pulling her back so my tongue could get as deep as possible. She tasted so fucking good, I was addicted, and the whimpering noises were like ringing a dinner bell. My cock ached and begged to be buried deep inside her, the agony building as the delicious flavor of Raine coated my tongue.

"Keep your legs straight," I ordered as they shook in my hold.

"Oh god," she moaned.

"There is no God in this room. You only say my name when I'm touching you ." I looked down to where she was peering around her leg and waited until she nodded. Her short blonde hair waving from the upside-down position she was in. "Are you going to cum on my tongue?"

"Yes."

"Are you sure?" I teased and swirled my tongue around, not staying on any one area too long. Raine moaned, desperate, and stepped back until the back of her legs touched the edge of the chair, forcing her to stop. I moved my head back so the contact never got any deeper.

"Yes," she panted out.

"Say it louder."

"Yes," she yelled.

"Yes, who?" I sucked on her clit hard, and her legs trembled, the small panting breaths going straight to the tip of my cock and making my racing heart pound faster.

"Yes, Kai," she yelled.

It still needed some work, but my needs clouded my judgment, and I wanted her to cum in my mouth before anything else. Spreading her cheeks further, I got as deep as I could and licked from her clit to her adorable little rosebud before doing it again and again. Raine was leaning most of her weight into my hands as her panting became more insistent.

"Fuck Jace, yes, fuck, fuck, fuck." Avro's scream was jarring and pulled me back from the edge for just a moment. I glanced over

Raine's ass to see Jace on his knees and Avro sitting on the bed. I knew what a man's face looked like as they came, and Avro was doing so now. Why it pissed me off that Jace was able to get Avro off before I could get Raine to cum was not something that I could logically explain, but as soon as I started to suck again, I did so with urgency.

"Yes, right there," Raine moaned a moment before she came on a yell that made me proud. I sucked harder, forcing little whimpers from her, and drank down every last drop she gave. There wasn't a spot my tongue didn't lick, and as I drew lines over the tempting globe of her ass cheek, I couldn't resist and nipped at her.

With the most adorable fucking sound, she leaped forward and went to her knees. The dark glare she gave me over her shoulder was so sexy that my throat went dry, and I couldn't think of a single word to say.

"Not cool, Kai," Raine purred as she turned around to face me. "Maybe I should return the favor and bite you." I was paralyzed as she crawled the short distance to me and settled between my legs.

"Do it. Bite me. I want your teeth marks on me forever." The words tumbled out, but my cock kicked hard, and my heart hammered at the thought of her marking me.

A wicked grin pulled at the corner of her mouth as she leaned in close enough that her warm breath fanned my cock. I was so turned on that the precum looked like my cock was drooling as it dribbled down the side.

"I have a better idea, and before you say anything, hear me out." Oh god, if she said anything to do with Jace, then I was going to have to grab my gun and shoot him. Raine placed a finger over my lips like she knew I would protest, but it brought me back to her and her tits brushing against my cock. "Why don't we tattoo your cock with my name? You already have one over your heart, but this would make a real statement."

Not what I thought she was going to say, but as her tongue swirled along the top of my cock and her eyes stared at me with that much lust, I would agree to any fucking thing she wanted.

"You want a little property of Tink on my cock?" I sucked in a sharp breath as she sucked the tip into her hot mouth. "Fuck me," I groaned.

"I think it's only fair. You did start the tattoo idea, and this way, if another girl decides to try and take liberties...it's my name staring back at her if she gets it out of your jeans."

Grabbing her wrists, I pinned them to the arms of the chair, and her eyes locked with mine. "I will tattoo my cock with whatever you want, it is yours forever, but no one will ever touch me again. If they're stupid enough to try, I meant what I said at the club. I'll cut every finger off their hand." Raine's eyes were wide, but she licked her lips like she wasn't sure if she was horrified or turned on.

"I shouldn't, but I love that," she said, her voice soft and soothing and not at all like she was instantly condemning anyone who ever touched me. I would do it and wear the fingers as a necklace for her. My hands locked her wrists to the chair like iron shackles.

"You've always been my forever." Her cheeks flushed a bright red. "Now, before I cause a fight by tackling you to the floor, suck my fucking cock."

Raine's eyes flared with dark passion. She loved the dirty talk, and I smirked as she once more sucked my cock into her mouth. I shuddered, the pleasure so close to pain as she hollowed out her cheeks.

"Yeah, that's it bitch. Keep sucking just like that." Raine's body stilled, her eyes rolling up to mine. "No bitch?" She cocked a brow, and even though she didn't say a word, I knew she was daring me to say it again. Then I would really find out what it was like to have her teeth leave marks. I was tempted, fuck, I was so tempted as her blue eyes glared daggers at me. Any sane man wouldn't want to piss off the person with his cock in their mouth, but the angrier she got, the harder I got. I was fucked. "Okay, I won't say it again unless you want me to."

Appeased, she bobbed her head with renewed vigor, and my hands gripped her wrists and the chair harder as my body soaked up the intense pleasure. Fuck she was good.

"Ah fuck," I cried out as she licked down my shaft and sucked on my ready-to-explode balls, taking me by surprise. Every muscle strained, and my back arched away from the seat as her mouth and tongue worked magic, leaving me gasping for my next breath. Like a master, she divided her time. I tried to hold back the urge, not wanting to release yet, but as she slid her mouth over my cock and I felt her swallow me down her throat, I lost all control.

"Fuck. I'm going to cum. Oh fuck me!" I roared, but Raine removed her mouth at the last second, and the release landed all over my chest in long lines. "Fuck!" I released her hands with the full intention of jerking the last bit out, wanting so badly to be touched. But Raine had other ideas, and this time she grabbed my wrists and pinned them down.

She stood and leaned over me, my eyes fixed on her like a wild animal as my cock continued to kick, my body begging for more. I'd never seen a more beautiful sight as the wicked grin that played across her lips a moment before she dropped her head and began to clean my chest.

"Oh dear god," I grumbled as she lifted her mouth and showed me my cum on her tongue before swallowing it down.

"There is no god in here, remember?" She quipped before licking another line off.

"Tink, you are fucking incredible," I said, smiling as she finished her work and stood straight, licking her lips. She reminded me of a cat that had just lapped up a bowl of milk, and I wanted to see her do it all over again. I'd be her fucking bowl any damn day of the week.

"Shit," Jace said, drawing our attention. He was in a similar position to me, and the look on his smug ass face—this time, he lasted longer—pissed me off to the core of my dark heart.

"Hey, Peaches, you want more?"

Before I could snatch Raine's wrist, she was out of reach.

Jumping from the chair was a lesson in always removing your boots and jeans. I fell to the floor and landed in a push-up position. Oh, this was not happening.

I glanced up at the sound of Raine giggling, her eyes filled with humor that I wanted to tan her ass for.

"You think this is funny?"

"Do I get spanked again if I say yes," she asked.

"I'm going to fucking spank you no matter what, but you're going to get extra for laughing at me," I growled.

"Then what do I get if I do this?" Bending over, she kept her eyes locked with mine but joined Avro in cleaning Jace's chest. A snarl rippled from my throat, but she didn't stop.

Rolling over, I grabbed at the laces of my one boot and fought with the knot. Jace groaned, and I looked over to see Raine running her tongue along his cock and then playing with the cock ring on the tip. Of course, he had a cock ring. Why wouldn't he have something that cool? I didn't think I could hate Jace more than I already did, yet he somehow found a way to make me want to throw him out the window.

"Fuck that feels good," he said, and I ground my teeth together, but I couldn't peel my eyes away from her mouth.

"Are you going to join or just stare all night," Jace asked.

"I'm going to rip your fucking balls off," I said.

"You can try, but you'd have to get your other boot off first. That seems to be a real battle you have going on." Jace smirked, and two things hit me. I wasn't sure which was more unsettling. The first was that Jace's antics were similar to Roach and the banter I enjoyed. The second was that watching Raine lick his cock was turning me on. Neither sat well.

Focusing on my stupid boot, I got the second one off and my jeans. I'd never live it down if Roach ever heard about this. Pushing myself to my feet, I marched for the bed and froze, almost tripping again. Raine knelt on the floor in front of Jace and Avro. Her hands were wrapped around their cocks as her mouth swapped back and forth between the two.

There were no words to describe the sexiness of the image and the rage that overcame me in a single shuddering breath.

"He looks like he's going to cum and blow a gasket at the same time," Jace said.

My eyes flicked up to his, and my hands clenched. There was a good chance I would've jumped over Raine and tackled him if she hadn't picked that exact moment to stand up in front of me in all her naked glory.

"Come here," she said, and my feet moved as if she held a remote to my body. My hands wrapped around her waist, and my body tingled with the feel of her skin. "Wanna play a game?"

"What kind of game?" The sound was rough as my body continued to tremble. Raine bit her lip, and some of the control I'd managed to lock into place slipped. My body sang with the silky soft feel of her skin as I slid my hand up between her tits. I couldn't explain what she was doing to me even if I wanted to.

Wrapping my hand around her throat, I glanced over her shoulder to see Avro and Jace watching but not moving. There was an ethereal quality about Raine that had always been there for me. She'd called to my senses when we were young and made them sing now, but my heart had grown so dark that everything was twisted like a patch of thorns.

"Jace said it would be fun to see who could last longer. Him with Avro, of course," she whispered, and I shivered. Raine squeaked like a terrified mouse as I turned her and forced her to walk backward until the wall stopped us. My hand tightened ever so slightly around her throat, and I could feel her pulse jumping under my fingertips.

"Did he now," I asked so only she could hear.

"Yes." She trembled under my hold, and her hands went to my arm. I could see her fighting her instincts. Everything in her was telling her to fight. The flash of fear, anger, and dark desire, was conflicting. I brushed my cheek against hers, and she sucked in a sharp breath, her pulse pounding harder with each passing second.

"You make me want to do dark things, Tink. You make me want to watch the light fade in your eyes just so they can never touch you again." She swallowed hard as goosebumps rose on her body. "You see it, don't you? You see the edge of insanity in my eyes. It's you that makes me this way. It's always been you."

I sucked her delicate little earlobe into my mouth and bit down enough to make her gasp and whimper. My cock throbbed at the sound, and I took a moment to close my eyes and breathe in her scent as the fantasy of either her or them dying played out behind my eyes.

"Are you going to hurt me," she asked, her voice far too sweet for the moment.

Leaning back, I once more stared into the pools of blue that swallowed my soul and refused to give it back.

"No, Tink. But you need to understand that you're fully in the driver's seat of every dark and depraved desire I have. I want their blood to run red as we fuck between their cold bodies. I want to throw us off a tall bridge and die clutching your hand in mine. Images of blood and pain are like a vivid painting in my mind, and you are the muse in all of them."

Releasing her neck, she sucked in a deep breath, and even that made me shudder with a need that coursed through my body. I ran my thumb over her bottom lip and wanted to bite that soft skin until she screamed.

"I said I'd try this Tink, but be very careful what buttons you push. The trapdoor to my sanity is hidden under one of them." She nodded, her eyes never leaving mine. "Yes, I will accept Jace's challenge, but I doubt he's going to win," I said, loud enough for him to hear, and smirked when he scoffed.

"I wasn't even trying earlier, and I beat you," Jace said. Over my shoulder, I looked at the cocky grin. So he was paying attention. That told me he was a good actor and wasn't as secure as he liked to let on. That thought simmered the wild static in my mind.

"Who says that I was," I said.

"Well then, by all means, let's see what you've got." Jace held his hand out toward the bed.

Was I really going to do this? Like Raine said, was it that much different than the clubhouse? I was about to find out.

"I have a feeling my ass is going to get punished, and I wasn't even a jerk tonight," Avro said, crawling onto the bed.

"You tricked us into coming up here together. That's worth at least one blackout fucking," Jace said, and as hard as I tried, I couldn't stop the corner of my mouth from pulling up. So the gauntlet was tossed down. Fuck them until they blacked out.

Now that was a challenge I could get behind.

Raine

Chapter 24

R aine

       Why I thought Kai would take it easy on me the first round, I didn't know. I screamed as he thrust himself into me, his cock filling me and shooting intense pleasure and pain throughout my body.

He growled something at Jace that I didn't catch over Avro's yell and knew he wasn't getting it any easier. What was I thinking when I decided it was a good idea to have not just one but three men and then have them all in the same room?

Kai's hands gripped my hips hard as he stayed pressed fully inside me, allowing me to catch my breath and adjust.

"Go," I heard Jace say, and a shiver raced down my spine. Were they actually going to race? My question was answered a moment later when Kai pulled out and slammed into my body so hard that my hand shifted on the bed, and another scream lodged in my throat.

"Fuck Tink, why are you so fucking tight? You're making me want to cum already."

I dared to glance over my shoulder. The stereo sound of groaning and slapping skin was intense from both Kai and Jace. A dark passion masked their faces. They didn't look at Avro or me but shot menacing daggers at one another. Apparently, staring at each other proved something I couldn't understand.

Sweat dripped off my forehead, and with each powerful thrust, my nipples ached as the breeze brushed against the sensitive tips. I bit my lip hard, my arms burning from the strain of remaining on all fours and meeting his strokes with an even pace.

I felt the orgasm building, the steady pleasure hitting all the right places, and I lost my ability to focus on anything else.

"Oh," I moaned and closed my eyes as I reached the amazing cliff. "Yes, Kai, please," I begged, not wanting him to stop.

"Touch yourself, Tink. Cum for me, cum all over me," Kai growled, his fingers pressing harder into my hips.

"I...yes, I can't," I breathed out with a gasp.

I shuddered, unable to stop myself, as Kai slipped his fingers around my throat and pulled me up until my back was against his chest. Somehow his pace remained the same. His arm snaked around my waist as the other tightened on my neck. As he whispered into my ear, the dark edge of his voice had my body trembling.

"Do it now. Cum now."

My hand slipped between my legs, and it didn't take long with all the buildup and teasing. I screamed as I came, so hard that my legs quaked, and my body arched and froze in his hold. Kai was relentless. He never slowed or allowed me to catch my breath. The iron-like grip around my waist only loosened so he could pinch one of my hypersensitive nipples.

"Oh fuck," I yelped.

"I'm going to fuck you until you pass out or Jace gives up." The words should've seemed sexy, but they were slightly terrifying. How long could he go? How long would I last before my body was too worn out to go any longer?

Avro yelled, and I watched him as his hands gripped the bed hard, balling the sheets into his fists.

"Please, Jace let me touch myself," he begged. It was easy to tell he was on edge and just needed a little push.

"Are you aching yet?"

"Yes."

"Is your cock brushing against the bed and driving you crazy?"

"Fuck, yes," Avro groaned.

The loud crack of a hand meeting skin had me lurching forward in Kai's hold, even though I knew it wasn't me that received the smack.

"Jace, fuck. Please."

"Only because you begged. Go ahead," Jace said, and within seconds Avro was yelling as he came.

"You like that," Kai asked against my neck. His hot tongue drew little designs, driving me wild. "You like watching them? I can feel you squeezing my cock tighter, and your breathing gets faster." I licked my lips. This felt like a trap. "Do you?" He asked firmer this time and then nipped at my neck.

"Yes," I breathed out and expected his hand to tighten around my throat, but instead, he picked me up with his cock still deep inside me. I had to wrap my legs around him and didn't know my back could bend back that far. I gasped with the added pressure from the unusual position. Walking around the bed, he placed me down, and I unlocked my legs.

"Roll onto your side, but you better make sure I don't fall out," Kai ordered, and I gripped him as I made the turn to make sure.

"Good, now lift your leg onto my shoulder." He tapped my left leg, and I put it straight up in the air, leaning it against him like he told me to.

"Oh fuck!" I slapped a hand over my mouth as he thrust harder than before. He was getting so much deeper as he hammered into me. The volatile mix of pleasure and pain made black dots dance across my vision. My eyes rolled to look at Avro's face, and he wasn't in any better shape. His face was contorted like he was trying to scream but instead groaned with pleasure.

"You going to cum for me, Tink?" I could barely think straight, let alone answer, and that was before his thumb started furiously rubbing my clit in circles. Just when I thought I couldn't take anymore, he slipped his thumb in with his cock.

"Fuck that feels good," Kai groaned, his body shuddering.

My hands reached out, nails clawing at the blanket when my fingers linked with Avro. I knew Kai noticed, his rhythm changing ever so slightly, but that was all the indication I got other than the furious pounding my body took as he pushed me at full speed toward the next climax.

As if we'd timed it, Avro and I yelled at the same time. Our hands tightened, lending each other support.

"Oh fuck, no, not again. I can't yet. I'm tapping out," Avro moaned.

"What? How am I supposed to finish the challenge?" Jace complained.

"I don't know, but I need a cold shower and a few minutes to recoup." Avro looked at me. "Sorry."

He rolled off the bed, and even though Jace had acted annoyed, he stopped and kissed him tenderly, asking if he was okay. Avro spoke so quietly you couldn't hear him, but I knew what he said. Working at Eclipse helped with lip reading.

"I'm good. I just need some ice and painkillers. I'm done for the night. Sorry." Avro said as he limped to the bathroom.

"Don't be sorry. I'll come with you." Turning to us, Jace said, "I'm out, Kai. You win."

"No, you stay."

"No, don't argue with me," Jace ordered.

Kai stopped moving, and I looked up at him, silently wondering what was happening, but he wasn't looking at me. I held perfectly still and allowed my body to rest up.

"You'd hand over victory just like that," Kai asked. "Did you cum? Is that what's going on here?"

Jace crossed his arms, and I nibbled on my cheek to stop laughing as he gave Kai the 'Don't be stupid' look.

"Does it look like I came?" He pointed to his cock, which was still standing perfectly upright. "I do anything for those I love, and beating you is not as important as making sure Avro's knee is okay. I'm done. Take the win," Jace said and turned to head into the bathroom to join Avro.

"Hold up. I don't do winning by default," Kai growled. "You got me to agree to this. You can't just back out now."

"I'm not sure what you expect me to do. I won't force Avro to be in pain for us to play a game," Jace said.

Kai's eyes narrowed, and with a creepy slowness, he turned his head and looked down at me.

"What?" I couldn't help but ask, my already racing heart tripling in time with the dark look. He didn't say anything for what felt like an eternity.

"I don't know what you're doing, but you two have fun," Jace said, getting a few strides away when Kai growled.

"Stop. Fuck, what the hell am I thinking?" He roared and pulled out of my body. I moaned and slumped on the bed, my body tingled, and all my limbs felt heavy. "Fuck, fuck, fuck," Kai growled and turned in a circle. Jace seemed just as confused as me and cautiously watched Kai and his strange outburst.

I stared wide-eyed as he cracked his neck, his muscles flexing like he was getting ready for a fight, before he took a deep breath and locked eyes with me once more.

"Could you do a third round?"

"Yeah, I'm okay," I said. I knew I'd ache all over, but it was worth it.

"Fine, let's do this. I can't believe what you have me doing, Tink. I swear to God or the Devil, whoever reigns over my soul...." I had no idea what he was going on about as he sat down beside me with his legs over the edge. "You want both of us?"

My eyes went wide, and my mouth dropped open. "Like at the same time?" Kai nodded. "I mean, it's something I've thought about trying, but I never thought you'd be interested...."

"Good, then it's settled. Get on me, and you better hold my wrists over my head."

"Are you serious?" Jace asked the question that was on the tip of my tongue.

"Yes, don't ask any more fucking questions. Let's just do this," Kai growled, turning to look at Jace.

"Alright, give me a minute to clean up and get more lube," he said and marched to the bathroom.

I turned my attention to Kai as I pushed myself off the bed and straddled him. I sucked in a breath as I slid down on his cock, my body already telling me off.

"You feel so fucking good," Kai groaned. Leaning down. I kissed him slowly, pouring everything I was feeling into the kiss. He moaned softly, his arms wrapping around my body, and I pressed myself into his warmth.

"Thank you." My voice was breathy and filled with hope. My lips brushed against his as I took advantage of this sweeter moment between us. "You don't know what this means to me," I said, and his arms tightened.

"I love you, Tink. One thing Jace and I have in common is that I will also do anything for those I love, and that is you." Smiling, I used my fingers to turn Kai's head to the side. "What are you doing?"

"I'm marking what's mine," I said and loved how Kai shivered as my lips touched his neck and I began to suck. I was so engrossed in what I was doing that I didn't know Jace was back until a cool liquid was poured onto my ass. I moaned as Jace used one of his fingers and slipped it into my ass.

I couldn't believe I was attempting this. My first time wasn't exactly pleasant, but nothing about my reunion with Kai had been. I'd grown so much since that moment, and Jace's finger was magic. I found myself wiggling and moving as I moaned into Kai's mouth.

"Hold my wrists, Tink."

"I have leather cuffs," Jace said. I looked over my shoulder at him. "What? They're fun."

"Yes, get me those. Where are your hooks," Kai asked. Was it wrong that I thought Kai tied up with leather was sexy as hell?

"Head of the bed, you'll have to move if you want the tie-downs."

"Sure," Kai answered. I didn't know what they meant, but I got the picture as Jace wandered back with leather cuffs and a black rope. I couldn't help but laugh as Kai pushed his body up, keeping me firmly with him as he repositioned and laid his arms once more above his head.

Jace tossed the cuffs by my hand, and I smiled. "You don't have to look so happy about this," Kai said, but there was no anger in his voice.

"Oh, but I do. I really, really do." Teasing Kai was fun, and I was nearing giddy as I buckled the first cuff and then the second around his wrists.

Jace was bent down beside the bed and stood holding the rope.

"I'm making this simple with a quick-release knot, so if you want to, all you have to do is roll off the bed and pull the second line," Jace said as he slipped the rope through the rings on the cuffs and then squatted down once more. "I won't bother with the other side."

"Do you really want it to be that easy for me to get up and untie myself," Kai asked. "Not scared that I'm going to kill you?"

Jace chuckled as he stood. "Try the tension," Jace said. Kai tugged and couldn't move his arms. "I'd be stupid if I thought there was no chance of you trying to kill me. But the fact that you initiated this and want something to keep you from killing me tells me it's not what you want. You're worried about your snapping point. Consider this a trust exercise given the circumstances."

I grabbed Kai's face as Jace got on the bed behind me and resumed his playing, prepping, or whatever it was he was doing.

"Just kiss me and look at me," I murmured against Kai's lips.

"I'll go slow," Jace said.

I tried to keep a straight face for Kai, but fuck, the feel of Jace stretching me was intense on its own, let alone with Kai already inside of me.

"Oh shit, oh wow," I moaned with each inch he pushed deeper. I could feel them filling me up to levels I didn't think possible, and the pleasure stole the air from my lungs. My mouth opened to scream, but nothing came out. It was too much, and my heart was beating so fast that I thought I would pass out. At least they wouldn't have to worry about sharing for long.

"Bite my chest," Kai growled low against my cheek. "Breathe, Tink. The tension will make it worse."

"I'm trying," I gasped, tears forming as the pain and pleasure brought back memories. I blinked, trying to force them away as the sounds and smells of that night and those men flooded my senses. As if sensing things were at a breaking point, Jace stopped moving altogether.

"Look at me," Kai whispered. "You're not there." I nodded as a tear escaped and dripped onto his chin.

"I know," I breathed out but couldn't look him in the eyes. The embarrassment over what happened and the guilt of what I did to Kai...what I did to us, bounced around inside my brain. It couldn't have picked a worse time to race to the front of my mind.

"We can stop Peaches. This doesn't need to happen if it's too much too soon," Jace said, his voice smooth. Them both being so nice was freaking me out more. That wasn't like either of them.

"Do you still want to do this," Kai asked.

I was tempted to say no, that I couldn't handle it. But if I stopped now, I'd hate myself later for being weak and letting the past sneak up and grip me. This might be the only time Kai and Jace let this happen. And I walked away? No, I couldn't stop now.

"Yeah, I do." I took a deep breath and ordered my body to relax, not that it did much good. So much for the yoga classes. They don't prepare you for two cocks inside of you.

"Okay, then bite my chest as hard as you want. I fucking love the pain when it comes from you. Give me all you've got, Tink. I want your mark on me forever."

I bushed my lips against his chin, and his eyes softened briefly. These glimpses of Kai under the mask of an MC enforcer gave me hope for us...for all of us. I licked at the area I was going to bite down on and reminded myself he wanted this. My teeth just touched his skin when Jace thrust the rest of the way in, his body hitting mine.

"Ah!" I screamed as I bit down hard. Kai growled and arched up into my mouth.

"Fuck yes! Harder!" Kai said, mixing with my screams.

Jace held off moving to let me adjust, but once he started, there was no holding back. He was as voracious as ever, and then Kai thrust his hips, mirroring Jace.

"Damn, Peaches, you have a sweet, tight little hole. You're making me want to cum already," he said, his pace quickening.

I unlocked my jaw and released Kai's chest as the sharp, burning pain shifted into passion. Desire erupted in my stomach. No logical thoughts or words would've come from my mouth as I closed my eyes and let my body soak all this in. Kai's muscular chest beneath my fingers, and the dueling cocks determined to tear me apart with pleasure.

"Holy fuck Tink, you're so tight," Kai said through clenched teeth.

"Please don't stop," I mumbled as the tremors started in my body. Kai sucked my lower lip into his mouth. "Right there, oh fuck." The thrusting increased, yet they managed to stay in rhythm while I was reduced to a drooling mess and laid my head on Kai's chest.

Their primal grunting and groans were sensory overload to my system, and I screamed their names as I came. The orgasm was so powerful that the black dots once more formed behind my eyes, and still, they pumped on.

"You want me to cum, Peaches? You want me to cum in your tight little ass?" I didn't answer, and he smacked my ass hard.

"Ah!" I screamed, but the sting only drew out the climax that my body was riding.

"Answer me, or you get another one," he said.

"Yes, yes, I want you to cum," I wailed.

"What about me, Tink? You don't want me to cum," Kai asked, and I felt like hitting him for asking such a stupid question.

"Yes, I want you to cum too."

"Then say it like you mean it. That was weak," Kai bucked up harder, and I cried out as my body revolted against the possibility of cumming again, and yet I could feel it in the distance like a slow-moving train that was picking up steam.

"Fuck, Kai! Yes, I want you to cum in me, cum for me."

"Where do you want me to cum?"

"In my pussy. Please, please," I begged, my muscles losing the ability to hold myself any longer.

"Here I come," Jace groaned, his body slamming into me hard and holding still.

"Fuck! Yes, Tink!" Kai growled. He pushed up and froze.

I could feel them both filling me, and I fucking loved it. It was the last thing I remembered before I passed out, my head over Kai's pounding heart.

Chapter 25

K aivan
　　Things I never thought I'd be doing, spooning Raine in a California king bed with her sound asleep while I stared into Jace's eyes. More like glared, but it was close enough. He was in the same position holding Avro, and we were left wide awake, making sure the other didn't move or try anything.

"You can go to sleep, you know," I said quietly.

"Like I'm going to close my eyes with you in the house," Jace countered.

"What the hell do you think I'm going to do? Slit your throat or something?"

Jace's eyebrow arched, and I smirked. "See, I wasn't thinking that, but then you go and put that thought in my head, and I'm definitely not closing my eyes now. So you go right ahead."

"Not a fucking chance," I said.

We were quiet for a long time, and I could just make out the digital clock glowing behind Jace. It was two-twenty-three and counting.

"Aren't you getting sleepy," Jace asked.

I snorted. "You trying to hypnotize me now?" Raine mumbled something and wiggled closer in my hold. I would've been tempted to slip between her legs again. Toss her leg over mine and fuck her while she slept until she woke up, but I knew she was tender. So I adjusted myself, my cock already thickening with the image and feel of her body pressed up against mine.

Lifting my arm off Raine, I eased out from under the covers. I hated to admit it, but the stupid bed was comfortable, and I loved holding Raine. I'd missed her way too much the three days she was gone, and she was leaving again for a night. I didn't like this at all.

"Where are you going?"

"Drink. You want anything," I asked, being nice instead of being my usual sarcastic self. It felt weird not instantly wanting to go another round of who could sling the better pile of shit.

"Bottle of water. Thanks."

"You better not switch spots while I'm gone. I'm not cuddling Avro," I said, and Jace chuckled.

"No promises. Peaches has a nicer ass to cuddle."

I glared, and he laughed a little harder.

"Too soon?"

"Fuck you," I mumbled and padded out into the hall and down the stairs. I wanted to tour the rest of this house. I always liked to know every inch of any place I stayed for more than a single night. Even in a shitty motel room, I checked under the bed, the windows, door locks, and the best place to store my weapon. Fun little habits you pick up locked away.

"What the fuck? Who the hell is this organized?" The impeccable organization that I found when I opened the fridge was intense. It looked like a showroom model fridge with fake and perfectly aligned food. Reaching in, I grabbed two waters from the stocked door.

I was just about to close it when a small container caught my attention. The label read: homemade lasagna, single piece, made Sunday at 6:00 pm. This had to be Avro. I couldn't see Jace labeling anything like this. I grabbed the container, my stomach growling as I lifted the lid and took a sniff. Fuck that smelled good.

"Fuck it." I tossed the container in the microwave and fumbled through the drawers to find a fork. "Holy shit," I mumbled as I stared at the built-in trays and the technically redundant labels. I liked it. No one I knew appreciated organization. I didn't do it with my cutlery: dessert forks, salad forks, dinner forks, butter knives, and steak knives, soup spoon and so on. I mean, could he not see what the items were? This was next level, leaving me wondering why go to all the trouble. If I wanted to get all introspective, I would say it made him feel like he had control, something leftover from whatever trauma he suffered at the hands of his uncle.

I did kinda hate that I threatened him with that information. If I'd known what happened and hadn't been so focused on getting at Jace, I wouldn't have done it. I still would've held onto it for insurance. I wasn't an idiot, but calling him out could've been avoided. The look of terror in his eyes...shit, it didn't feel right. Fuck I was going soft.

The microwave dinged, and I grabbed a *dinner fork* before re-closing the drawer and claiming my meal. Leaning against the counter, I peeled off the lid and had to admit it smelt a little like heaven. The first bite told me all I needed to know. Whoever made it could really cook. It was rich and bold with flavor and had the perfect combination of meat, sauce, noodles, and cheese. I had no idea when I became a food connoisseur. Move over, Gordon Ramsay.

I put my dish in the sink, disappointed that there wasn't an entire pan to eat 'cause I would've been all over that. Grabbing the two bottles of water, I cracked my lid and was taking a big gulp when I stepped out of the kitchen. Something caught my peripheral vision, and I stopped moving, my eyes searching the darkness. The hair stood on the back of my neck, letting me know someone was there. I'd learned the hard way to always trust my senses. Of course, I didn't have a weapon on me.

A car drove by. the bright lights flashing in the living room, and —even though I should be used to the unusual visits by now—I jumped at the sight of Wilder. My open water bottle squirted from the top and landed all over my chest.

"Geez us, fuck!" I hissed and glared at the man who was worse than a flea on a dog's ass. "Wilder, what the hell are you doing here?"

Stepping into the room, I hit the light switch closest to me. It turned on four small ceiling lights around the room to show Wilder casually stretched out with his hands resting behind his head. He looked like he didn't have a care in the world with his boots on the new coffee table. All I could think was Avro would faint at the sight.

"Sitting," Wilder said in his standard monotone way that told me nothing and only confused me more.

"Fuck. I mean, why are you sitting in this house? Why are you here at all, and how the hell did you get in?" I took a step back, just enough to glance at the door with the security panel. It still had a bright red light announcing it was armed.

"Because it was late, and you weren't home. I was concerned, so I decided to ensure you were alright," he said. Stuffing his hand into his pocket, he pulled out a handful of almonds and tossed a few into his mouth. "I tracked you down here."

"I didn't realize I needed a curfew at twenty-nine years, seven months, and thirteen days old, but heck, why not start now?" Wilder's eyes found mine, and his head turned slightly as he fixed me with a stare right out of *The Exorcist*.

"I like that you do that. Why do you do that?"

"Do what," I asked, exasperated.

"Count time so specifically. I do that."

Great, something we had in common. I shrugged and drank some water, glaring at what was still trailing down my chest.

"I don't know why. I just do. So, are you still concerned for me, or are we good, and you're going home?" When had Wilder stepped things up from the odd, weird questions to a personal stalker?

"No, I'm no longer concerned. You seem to be in perfect health. Your stamina while fucking is very impressive. You would do well with the *Art of Kamasutra*. At least that's what I've been told." Wilder said and casually closed his eyes.

"First, why the hell were you spying on me having sex...again? Second, why are you still here if you see I'm alright?" I leaned against the wall. I was pretty certain that I would need the support after whatever 'What the fuck' answer he gave me next.

"I always take notes of everything. It's much easier to refer to my books when I want to look something up." He pulled a little black book out of someplace and held it up for me to see. "And I'm still here because this couch is comfortable."

Great so he was making notes of me fucking. I pinched the bridge of my nose. I shouldn't have asked. This man was going to drive me to drink. Well drink more than I already did.

He wiggled a little deeper and sighed. Such a strange combination of personalities, this guy was. I had visions of the egg he was made from trying to swim away from the sperm like it knew they weren't a great match, but the sperm tied the egg up until it submitted. I was fucking tired. That was the only reason for that random thought

"Don't you have a bed?"

"I have a cot, and most of it is taken up with the object of my affection. She steals the blankets and wraps them around her like a cocoon. Is this a girl trait? I find it much harder to fuck her like that. We usually have a rumble session over the blankets first. She's very possessive of them."

"You don't say," I drawled out and covered my eyes as I pictured what he was putting this girl through.

Wilder sat up and produced a pen from thin air like he performed a magic trick. I felt like asking what was next, a rabbit? My luck, that would be exactly what Wilder pulled out of his cargo pants. That, of course, would lead to more questions I didn't want to know the answers to. Like, 'Why the fuck is there a rabbit in your pants?'

"I don't know if it's a girl trait. The only girl that has stayed the night with me is Raine, and she didn't steal them, but she may now, after waking up to a strange man in our bed."

"I'm not a stranger," he said, his brow knitting together.

"To her, you were. She doesn't know you, Wilder. You scared the shit out of her. Not literal shit, I don't mean she shit the bed, although I'm sure she felt like it." The fact I had to explain this boggled my mind.

"Hmm." Wilder rubbed at his chin. "I see."

"I'm going to bed. Do you need me to let you out?" I asked and then realized I didn't have the alarm code.

"No, I have a key." Of course, you do. "And I have the code, so no worries, the place will be secure once more." Except from you, was all I could think.

Creepy fucker.

When Wilder continued to sit and stare at me, I gave up and hit the light switch, plunging us into darkness as I turned to leave.

"Snake?"

I was so close to escaping, so, so close. He saved my life. I repeated that in my head as I turned to face him once more.

"Yes, Wilder," I said, hoping my voice didn't sound as annoyed as I felt.

"Why do you choose to sleep with your enemy?"

There was a movie title in there somewhere. "I'm not. They're not my enemy." I really hated that—of all people—it was fucking Wilder that made me say that out loud.

"Avro did sucker punch you in the face. You don't consider that an enemy?"

Of course, he saw that humiliating moment, the guy sees everything. "No, it was payback for doing it to him."

"Is that how you and your friends like to treat each other? I would think punching someone in the face and then, have them punch you back would not make them your friend."

How did I say Avro wasn't exactly my friend, but also not my enemy. "No, I...forget it. It's too hard to explain. The point is he's not my enemy." Twice he made me say it, twice. Fucking guy. "And I'm technically not sleeping with them. Well, I'm sleeping with them if I ever get back to bed, but I'm not fucking them. Do you see the difference?"

"You lay with them but are not sticking your cock in them. Yeah, I get it." Wilder leaned back on the couch once more, his eyes closing. "I don't know if I could share the object of my affection, but maybe I should try. Do you think maybe she needs more cocks to make her happy?"

I opened my mouth to say that probably wasn't the problem but then decided, nope, I wasn't getting involved. I didn't know who this girl was, and the last thing I needed was to get involved with Wilder's drama, kidnapping, or whatever he had going on. For all I knew, the guy had a Stockholm syndrome fantasy he was playing out. Who was I to stand in the way of a good fantasy coming true?

"I can't answer that question. Shouldn't you get going? What if this object of your affection needs you, and you're not there?"

He shrugged and then smiled. "She won't. I got her watered, fed, and changed her piss pot. She was curled up on the cot and asleep before I left. Plus, I can watch her at any time. See."

He pulled his cell from his pocket and held it up for me. I couldn't see who was in the image from this far away, but the security camera clearly showed someone curled up on their side on a low cot. It was barely big enough for one person, let alone two.

I couldn't believe I was going to ask this and knew I'd probably regret it, but I found my mouth open. "Wilder, have you considered unchaining her?"

"You mean like let her roam around?"

Or run away as fast as she can.

"Yes, that's what I meant."

He lifted his shoulders and let them drop dramatically. "I can't. I keep her chained for her own safety."

That was an answer I didn't see coming. If I'd been a betting man, I would've said he took this girl because she caught his eye. He didn't understand it, so he had to find a way to make it make sense.

"So, someone is after her?"

"No."

"But she's in danger?"

"No."

For fucks sake, I knew this was another rabbit hole of insanity.

"Okay then." This was a redundant conversation, and my brain was screaming it would rather fuck Jace than spend one more second in this conversation. That said it all.

"Night Wilder." I went to turn and then held up a finger. "Oh, and no coming into the bedroom. I don't care about the reason... unless someone is dying, the place is on fire, or you see people breaking in. But those are the only reasons you step foot in the bedroom, especially when I'm having sex." Like it wasn't weird enough that he was sitting listening, I didn't need him propped up in the corner scribbling in his book. "Got it?"

"Sure, but why would I want to?" He screwed up his face, his eyebrows raising like I was the one saying something crazy.

I bit my lip to keep from freaking out. "Just don't." I turned and stomped away. "Fuck, fuck, fuck," I mumbled under my breath and jogged up the stairs. Maybe there was such a thing as Wilder repellent. If not, there should be, and the first can I'd hand out was to the girl he had locked up.

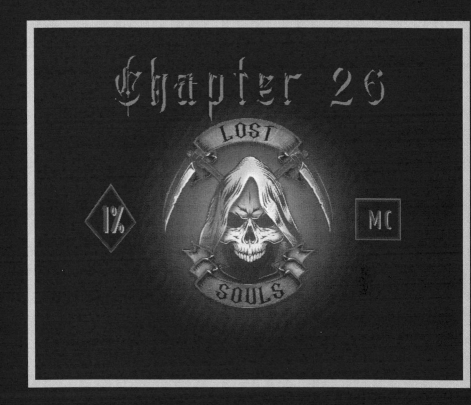

Chapter 26

LOST SOULS

1%   MC

Avro

Everything hurt, yet waking up being held by Jace felt amazing. My eyes fluttered open, my forehead touched Raine's as she slept, and I couldn't help but smile. I looked over at Kai, who was surprisingly still here and asleep.

I was still pissed at him for threatening Jace and me, but Jace said he had the situation handled and for me not to worry. How was I not supposed to worry? We were talking about our lives. We could be sent to prison for the rest of what was left of them.

"You're awake," Jace's soft breath made me shiver as he whispered against my neck. "You okay?"

"Yeah, I'm good."

"I'm sorry again about last night. I wasn't thinking," Jace said, his arm tightening around me.

"I'm good, really, don't worry about it. If I didn't think I could handle it, I would've spoken up," I said, and he scoffed.

"No, you wouldn't," Jace said. My mouth turned up in a smile.

"You're right. I like to push too much."

"Did you tell Raine you need another surgery?"

I stared at her peacefully sleeping face and so badly wanted to touch her but didn't dare with Kai holding her. Last night was a massive breakthrough, but no one knew what today would bring after he woke up in this bed.

"No, not yet. I will. It's not that important," I said. "We've had a lot going on. I just didn't want to...."

"Burden anyone," Jace finished for me.

"You know me too well." I shuffled around and tried not to wince as I rolled over to face Jace. The first rays of the sun peeking through the blackout curtains reflected the silver in his eyes. They were always so intense but held a softness as he stared at me.

"You're not a burden. Why do you even think like that?" Jace cupped my cheek, and I soaked in his warmth.

"I don't know, you know me. I'm a cancer sign. It's in our nature to be emotional," I teased, but Jace didn't smile.

"Tell her. She's not going to care. It's not a big deal."

"I will, I promise. But right now, I'm going to get up, do my stretches, and then make waffles for breakfast. I even got fresh cream to make whipped cream."

"And now I'm picturing licking that off of you. Thanks for that," Jace smirked before gently kissing me. He rolled over and stood to let me up, holding out his hand so I didn't struggle. I tried not to think about being laid up from surgery all over again. It took a huge mental and physical toll last time. It was the reason I hadn't told Raine. It was better not to think about it and put it out of my mind until I had a surgery date. "I'm going to sleep a bit longer while he's still asleep." Jace pointed his thumb at Kai, making me smile. Apparently, Jace didn't trust Kai any more than I did.

Jace grabbed my hand as I turned to walk away. "You sure you're okay?"

"Yeah, why?"

Sometimes I hated that he knew me so well. I was the over-thinker, the worrier, and the one who stressed over everything from bills to what to eat. It was rare for someone to notice as I liked to keep that part of me buried. I was so depressed and worried after the last time I went under the knife that Jace had pretended to be sick for three weeks to come home from tour and help me feel like myself again. I didn't want to go through it again.

I fought the depression every day, battling to get out of bed. I hated it so much. I was scared to end up in that same mental state. The worst was when I overheard someone say, 'Just get over it.' They didn't get it. You didn't just get over it. If they'd really suffered, they would understand that I chose not to let it keep me down, but the pull to hide in my room and never leave was there and poked at me as it taunted my mind every moment of the day. I'd felt like an addict, and the overwhelming sadness was my drug.

"It's not going to be like last time," Jace said as if able to pluck the fears from my mind.

"I know," I said and squeezed his hand. "I'll let you know when breakfast is ready." I walked into the closet and threw on some comfortable clothes before I broke down and poured all my fears at Jace's feet. I hated doing that. It felt like I did it all the time, and as many times as he said he didn't mind, it still bothered me.

Walking down the stairs, I turned toward the workout room I'd set up. It wasn't huge, but large enough for a couple of mats on the floor, a treadmill, and a universal weight machine. Jace liked his free weights, so we made space for a rack of those, and I had wall-to-wall mirrors installed. Grabbing a set of weights, I wandered over to the bench and sat them down to start my arm workout when the white scar on my knee caught my attention.

It seemed glaring to my eye against my tanned skin. I didn't care about the imperfection. It was just another reminder that no matter how well you planned your life, shit always crept up and punched you in the face.

I couldn't believe how nervous I was. Stopping at the large doors of the theatre, I stared at the posters that lined every door. They were all the same. An image of me flying through the air or posing for the camera. I still couldn't believe I'd been chosen to be the headliner. It was my first big gig, and to be the star was crazy to me.

Reaching out, I touched the poster of the death-defying leap I'd practiced for months. I loved flying through the air. This particular show wanted to incorporate traditional circus trapeze, an acrobat routine, and unique dances, as well as the unusual acts of athleticism that a Cirque du Soleil performance was known for. The entire thing piqued my interest from day one.

It was more like a play, the story of a boy dreaming of working in a big top, but his family didn't understand or support him. It followed the boy's life from when he was young and the challenges along the road to following his dreams. It was as if the story had been designed for me. More than once during practice, I'd been moved to tears by the emotion the entire show evoked. I was so proud to open the show in two days, but I wished Jace could be here to see this.

He was, unfortunately, in Germany at his first massive venue. It was a sold-out show, so this was an important week for both of us. He promised we'd talk after, no matter how late it was.

Yanking open the door, I watched as everyone stretched and got warmed up for practice. The sessions were long and grueling, and I'd never been happier. Basketball was never really my thing. I played to do a sport, and Jace was good at it, so it gave us something to do together that our parents had approved of.

Now that my parents had disowned me for 'daring to be bisexual,' I was free to do what I wanted, and I did feel free. If I'd known that the weight that always hung around my neck would be lifted once they knew, I would've done it a lot sooner.

"Hey Avro, you're going to be partnering with Julian today. Maurice is off sick, and we need him well-rested for opening night," Coach yelled when he saw me.

I looked to where Julian was already on the large stage warming up. He was basically my understudy and knew the main parts of the show. He was nice enough, and we got along fine, but I always felt like he was jealous that I hadn't 'paid my dues' in the industry to earn a headliner position.

I may not have been in the industry long, but I was a natural and trained every spare moment. I'd been training from the time I could walk and would practice everything I thought would help me improve my strength, flexibility, and skill. The best was when I talked Jace into doing parkour with me. He wasn't a huge fan of heights, but within a month, I could scale a building. I knew then this was my calling. I wasn't some sloth that had wandered in and got the job cause I knew a producer or something. Normally I was the first to arrive and the last to leave. I'd sit in my small apartment going over what I needed to do and when throughout the night. The only time I took a break was to speak to Jace and catch up.

"Okay, no problem," I yelled and went backstage to get changed. Jogging out, I warmed up with everyone as I reviewed the opening sequence in my head.

"Hey, you good that I'm working with you today," Julian asked as he stepped up beside me.

I gave him a smile that I hoped came off warm and genuine. "Yes, of course, you're a fantastic partner. I've seen you working with everyone."

"True, I am gifted," Julian said and then chuckled, but I didn't get the *feeling he meant it as a joke.*

"Alright, places, everyone. We are going to run through with lighting and sound all day. I want this to feel like the real thing," Coach said.

By the time the first half of the performance was done, my uncertainty about working with Julian had eased. He was not only a great partner, but we were completely in sync with every movement, a perfect mirror of one another, and Coach was calling out how beautiful everything looked. I wondered if Maurice would have a spot to come back to.

My adrenaline spiked as I climbed the tall ladder to the top of the platform, where I would perform the trick that was being advertised all around Vegas. It was what was on the posters. The timing had to be perfect, or I would plunge to the stage below. There was a net lying on the floor that the audience couldn't see. It had an emergency pull in it that if something went wrong, it would snap up and into position to catch me. The first test run to make sure it was working had been terrifying.

Reaching the top, I waved to the fake crowd and smiled before grabbing the fly bar. I knew the movements in my sleep. Julian signaled that he was ready, and we were off. The amount and type of flips before I caught Julian's arms were what made the sequence so dangerous. We took the theme of 'death defying' to a whole new level, and the platform sat twice as high as any other show in the world.

Performers used the ladder and bars on either side to continue to perform as I flew, their vibrant costumes shining under the bright lights. The first release and catch went off without a hitch, and Julian smiled and counted down the release to return to my bar. The next two were equally smooth. I was tight and on point.

We pretended to smile at the crowd again as we caught our breath, and the performer acting as Ringmaster called for silence. We took our cue and once more sailed through the air. I released my bar and did the tight twists that made me look like a spinning bullet before stretching my arms wide in a Superman pose.

Julian was right on cue, and I locked my eyes on his arms, but in the split second, before he caught me, he moved his arms just enough that I missed my grab. One hand missed completely, but the other managed to link the tips of our fingers.

I lifted my gaze to his eyes, and he smirked subtly as his eyes remained wide like he was surprised, "Oops."

There was this moment of hesitation as his finger relaxed, and I began to fall. Julian watched as I plunged to the floor, and the voice in my head screamed that this couldn't be happening.

A burst of fear had adrenaline pumping through my system, and my arms and legs pinwheeled like that would somehow make me fly. I remembered the safety net and relaxed into the position to land safely. I saw the worried faces of the other performers as I dropped like a stone.

Sure enough, I hit the net and bounced high into the air. Like we were taught, I stood up to land on my feet for the second bounce, ready to scream at the top of my lungs what Julian had just done. As my feet touched the net the second time, one side snapped, and that was all it took. The momentum of a twenty-foot bounce and the odd jerk as the safety line broke dropped me at an odd angle onto my left leg.

There was no pain at first, just the sound of a pop and then tearing as my knee bent one way but my body the other as I landed in a heap. I could hear people screaming and shouting and one of the paramedics that we always had on hand telling me not to move. Unable to help myself, I looked down and didn't understand what I saw. Why could I see my heel? Either my leg or spine was backward, and I knew I was in bad shape.

Out of the corner of my eye, I saw Julian running over as if he was concerned, and I screamed and pointed at him.

"You did this. You're evil," I hollered as loud as I could.

Fake tears trailed from his eyes. "I'm so sorry, Avro. It was an accident, I swear," he professed over and over, but I knew better.

That one day, that one man, and that one decision had changed the course of my life forever.

• • •

Bending over, I touched the half-moon line and winced. Sometimes I wished I'd told Jace the truth, told him it wasn't an accident, but I knew what he would do. I'd seen him do it to my uncle, and there wasn't a doubt in my mind he would kill for me again, and I didn't want that for him, me, or our souls. No, it was better this way.

I wanted Julian to pay, but the dark hatred I felt for the man scared me, and I decided to move forward with my life rather than live in the past. As it turned out, I could've gotten a position with the same group but a different show when my knee was healed, but by then, I'd met Raine.

Laying down on the bench, I went through the first half of my arm workout and then sat up and finished it off. I felt better by the time I was done and was tempted to do more, but the others would be up soon, and I wanted breakfast well underway or done. I hated people staring over my shoulder while I cooked, and Jace loved to do it because he knew it would annoy the shit out of me.

Wandering down the hall, I turned into the kitchen and stopped walking as I tried to process what I'd just seen. Taking a step back, then another, I stared into the living room, my eyes searching the corners like this was a great prank. But, it wasn't hiding in any of the corners.

"Jace," I called out. "Jace, can you come here?" I yelled and could hear more than just one set of footsteps running down the stairs.

"What is it? What's wrong? Is it your knee," Jace asked as he looked me over like a worried hen. Raine was next as she stared at my face and then down at my body. They were acting as if I'd just been shot.

"Stop, both of you." I pointed into the living room. "Where the fuck is the couch?"

"Un-fucking-believable." We all looked at Kai, who shrugged as he ran his hand through his hair. "Fucking aliens."

What did one do with that answer other than blink?

Snake

Chapter 27

LOST

1%

MC

SOULS

K aivan

Killing Wilder wasn't an option, but fuck me, I wanted to.

Avro had a meltdown like I didn't think he was even capable of. He searched outside and in the garage, thinking this had to be a practical joke, and of course, I was the top suspect.

I lost track of how many times I said, 'I didn't touch your couch,' and 'What the hell would I even do with it?' Jace checked the cameras, and I covered my eyes, thinking for sure they would see me talking to a random guy in their home and just letting him stay. That would take some explaining. I mean, how the hell did you explain Wilder?

But Wilder had a camera scrambler or some other weird govern-ment tech shit on him. Or he scrubbed the three hours and seven minutes he was here because it was nothing but white snow, which set Jace off. I had to admit. It was nice not being the one freaking out for a change.

Just when we thought Avro was calming down, he noticed the container in the sink and went off, thinking whoever took the couch also ate his food. *How rude.*

"Okay, that's my cue to get going," I said to Raine. She was leaning against me as we stood in the kitchen. We both watched as Jace paced while he was on the phone. Avro was off cleaning every inch of the house, which apparently was his way of calming down.

It was driving me crazy that I felt bad for Avro. I should be laughing and joining Wilder as we sat on it and drank a beer. I should be rejoicing that he managed to piss the guy off, but once the initial anger wore off, Avro seemed beaten down. I could see it in his eyes as clearly as I could see my own reflection in a mirror.

"I'm going to go clean," Avro said, pulling supplies from a walk-in cupboard.

"Do you want me to help," Raine asked.

Avro shook his head and smiled at her, but it didn't reach his eyes. "No, I just need to do this on my own," he said and hugged Raine before disappearing.

"I'm really worried about him," Raine whispered. "What's going on, Jace? I know it's his couch, but it seems like so much more."

Jace poked his head out of the kitchen, making sure Avro was gone before turning to face us. He crossed his arms over his chest and rubbed his bottom lip with his thumb.

"Avro has some control issues if you haven't picked up on it. It comes out in mostly harmless ways, but it started after what happened to him. I've been able to help him through most things, but it got really bad again after his accident, and he refuses to talk about it," Jace said. "He saved for months to get that set and was so proud of it, but it's not just the couch. This made him feel violated." Jace shook his head.

"So, not to be the asshole in the room, but why don't you just buy him a new one? I'm sure you have the money," I said, earning myself a punch in the arm and a hard glare from Raine. Man, she had hard little fists.

"What? It's a good question. He's a rock star, for fucks sake."

"I could, but Avro won't let me. I haven't spent a dime on this house except for my music room. I refused to let him buy anything in there and had a huge fight about that. He wants to do shit on his own. He hates leaning on me, especially financially. I could buy him the whole fucking block if he wanted it. I could build a custom home, but nope. Anyway, I'm going to call the cops. This is the weirdest fucking break-in."

Jace paced the living room as he spoke to whoever picked up at a police station. I'd never called one to find out. We hadn't seen Avro since, and I felt like an asshole, even though I had nothing to do with the couch caper.

I wasn't worried for Wilder, anyone that could carry a freaking couch out by himself without making a noise or leaving a scratch didn't need it, but I had no interest in being interviewed by cops and my name popping up in the parole board system. That was a no-go for me.

"I don't understand this. It's crazy," Raine said, shaking her head as she turned to face me. "This place was supposed to be the safer option."

Leaning down, I whispered in her ear. "Wilder showed up last night, but I swear I didn't know he would take the couch."

When I stood straight, her mouth was hanging open, her eyes wide in obvious disbelief. "What the fuck? Why didn't you say anything?"

"How do I explain Wilder? My possibly unstable and delusional neighbor broke in to make sure I was okay because he was worried about me. He then randomly decided to steal a couch when I went back to bed. Oh, and he's like ex-military, ghost-level shit and already had your house code. But don't worry, he's harmless and thinks he's protecting me or maybe all of us."

"Yeah, okay, aliens seem more plausible."

"Thank you, but…I'll talk to him and see if I can get him to return it." I pinched the bridge of my nose, already picturing how that conversation would go.

"No, don't. That would just add another layer to the violated feeling Jace mentioned. I understand the need to feel safe and in control. I still check my locks multiple times a night when I'm at home. I barely slept, and I'd find a place to hide on really bad nights. I know it probably all sounds stupid to you," Raine said.

I cupped her face and forced her to look at me. "No, I don't think it's stupid," I said and then brushed her lips with mine, loving that she opened up and moaned softly.

Breaking the kiss, I laid my forehead against hers. "You think that if he knows it wasn't some random joke and 'whoever it was' can get back in, it will make the insecure feeling worse."

"Yes, exactly. I'll take him furniture shopping, make a day of it. I know his favorite lunch spot, and there is a sale at one of the stores he likes. I'm just going to spend the day with him."

I nodded in agreement, but I was still talking to Wilder. I had no idea how to get him to understand boundaries, but I obviously needed to make that happen.

"I have a few things that I need to get done today, and I don't know when I'll be finished, but I'll call," I said, grabbing my leather jacket off the kitchen chair and shrugging it on.

"Is that code for I'm going to be killing people today," Raine asked.

"Who says I would do that? Okay, maybe once or twice." I smirked before I sobered and walked back to where I'd left Raine standing. I couldn't tell if she was okay with what I did or not. It wasn't a conversation I ever planned on having with someone. "Are we okay? Are you good with what I do?"

My heart rate picked up as I waited for her to respond. What the hell was I going to do if she said no? Would I force her to be okay with it? Would I quit the MC? Shit...

"Am I okay with you breaking kneecaps and killing people?" She put her hands on her hips and stared at the floor as she nibbled her lip. I knew that look and held perfectly still as she thought.

"Honestly, Kai, I don't know how to feel. It's not like I know much about the inner workings of an MC. Like how do you choose who to go after? Is it you that chooses or someone else that chooses them?" She rubbed at her eyes and sighed. "I don't want to know anything about any of it and don't tell me when you're going because I'll worry myself sick. I want a backup number for someone you trust that I can call if you don't come home. Shit, I need to think about it more. It's not as if I woke up one day thinking this would be an issue and I should have a plan for how I would feel or react."

"That's fair," I said, but I was worrying now.

I didn't want to be like my father or force Raine to live as my mother had. She hated what my father did, and his cheating ate her alive. I watched it with my own eyes, and yet we were trapped. You don't just walk away from an MC. I understood that now, but he could've done things to make them better, and he chose not to. That wouldn't be me.

Other guys in the club had great home lives and still worked with the MC. That was what I needed to figure out how to do. Cause I wasn't letting Raine go, that wasn't even an option in my mind, but I wasn't cut out to work a nine-to-five in an office either.

I wrapped my hand around the back of her neck and drew her in close to my body. Raine's hands slipped around my waist and held me tight, instantly calming the storm that constantly raged in my body.

The scent of her body wash and shampoo drew me in, and I laid my lips against her forehead and closed my eyes. I took a deep breath and let her smell wash over me. The world disappeared when she touched me.

"I can't let you go, Tink," I whispered. "Not ever again, and that should scare you because it scares me. It terrifies me what I will do to keep you." She shivered in my arms, but instead of stepping away like a sane person, she hugged me tighter. Maybe we were both a little unhinged.

The anger simmering under the surface of my skin was ready to lash out at anyone or anything that tried to tear us apart. It didn't matter who it was. I'd rip their beating heart from their chest if they dared to come between us.

But what did you do when that person was yourself?

Snake

Chapter 28

Kaivan

"That was fast," I mumbled as I stared at the number calling on my phone. "Mutt, what do you have?"

"So, just to be clear, we're even once I give you this info. Right?" Mutt said, and I wanted to punch him through the phone. He really was a weasel. It was appropriate that he was in the Weasel Legionnaires.

"Yes, we'll be even until your club fucks up again and thinks they are sharks in a pond when they're really only guppies. Just remember that it will be my face, you see. If you and that MC of yours crosses us again," I growled into the phone.

"We're not, I promise." Mutt's voice was shaky coming through the line.

"Good, now give me the info."

"I couldn't find anything on the Dave Collins guy you mentioned, but I found an address that will interest you. That Father Frank guy is a real nutjob. He started as a motivational speaker for men looking to improve their self-esteem, but it became much bigger. He is at full-blown cult status now, but no one knows where the compound is because either you never see the men that join again, or you do, and they are so brainwashed that they never give up its location."

Great, more good news. "How is this information helpful, Mutt? You mentioned an address."

"Hang on. I'm getting to that." I rolled my eyes.

I looked over to where Roach was freaking out. His angry tone carried on the breeze as he stomped around like a child having a tantrum. I couldn't hear what he and Wilder were saying, but only one topic made Roach that angry...Lane. Hopefully, Wilder wasn't sharing her showering habits, that would send Roach over the cliff.

There was a rattling paper on the other end of the line. "You have a pen?"

"Yeah, go ahead," I said, not bothering to write it down. Memorizing random crap was my specialty.

"It's 555 Catalina Court."

"So, what's this address?"

"When the guy decides to interview the men, he takes them to that house," Mutt said.

"How do you know this? You better not be playing with me, Mutt. I fucking swear, I don't want to have to kill you over this shit."

"Nooo, I promise. The info is legit. I know a couple of guys that, before they joined the club, had interviewed, thinking it was going to be this self-help workshop, but they were taken to this crappy house and videotaped as they answered questions for hours. They decided they didn't want anything to do with his crazy ass, but a lot of others love him."

"What does he want? Power, money...control of the world. What's driving this guy?" I said it out loud but more to myself.

"I don't know, but I do have one more piece of info that is fucked and going to blow your mind. Frank's real name is Francois Hanson, and he has a twin brother. Now get this, the brother was a fucking FBI agent and a serial killer called the Chameleon. He's got an undisclosed number of kills to his name and was like the FBI's most wanted. That right there is some fucked up shit. One brother is a cult leader, and the other a serial killer."

I didn't say anything as I processed the information. Was that why this Frank guy was so cocky?

"So did they catch this Chameleon, or is he still running around," I asked.

"I don't know, man. But that's one family I wouldn't want to be part of. Anyway, no idea when he'll be at the house next, but that was where both guys were taken."

"Thanks, Mutt."

"So listen, I scratched your back. Maybe you can scratch mine and put a good word in for me with your Prez?"

"Not a chance." I hit end on the phone and stuffed it in my pocket.

I was staring at complete opposites as I marched over to the truck. Wilder was leaning back on the truck, taking in the sun's rays, while Roach paced, his face red as he snarled like a dog and mumbled under his breath.

"Dude, calm down before you have a stroke."

"I can't! Do you know what he said to me?" Roach pointed at Wilder, and I shook my head. "That Lane has a boyfriend. A fucking boyfriend. When did she get a boyfriend, and how did she get one? This is not happening. I will cut his cock off with a butter knife if he touches one hair on her head."

"They've already kissed," Wilder said, and Roach went volcanic.

I stepped back as he shook like he was going to erupt. "He's a dead man. This fucking punk is mine."

"He's actually—" Wilder started, and I cut him off.

"That's quite enough info for today, Wilder. Thanks." I glared at him, hoping he would get the message and shut up.

I grabbed Roach's arms and forced him to look at me. "Bro, you know I love you like a brother, right?" He nodded, his nostrils flaring and muscles twitching under my hands. "Great, take this advice from someone who cares if you remain breathing. You need to calm the fuck down and back off Lane's doorstep."

"What? I'm not..."

"Yeah, you are. Keep denying it all you want, but the problem is Hollywood will castrate you if you go anywhere near his baby sister with anything but pure thoughts. She needs to live her life, and you're only supposed to be watching her to make sure she doesn't end up in a dangerous situation. She has your number to call if she gets into trouble."

His body slumped in my hold. "I'm so fucked." His worried eyes met mine. "I can't go near her again, can I?"

"I wouldn't, but I'm not the one with the best friend in jail who is counting on you to keep your cock to yourself. You need to reign this shit in." I shrugged. "Unless you don't give a shit about Hollywood and your friendship anymore."

"I've known that family my whole life. I was at the house playing video games with Hollywood when they brought her home from the hospital," he said. "How the hell did this happen?"

"I don't know, but that's even more reason to stay away. Roach, do you really think she won't see through your I don't like you act? Or Hollywood, for that matter? What if she gets freaked out and tells Hollywood? Just get control for your own sanity." I pulled out a smoke and lit it up, taking my usual two drags before putting it out.

"Take it from someone that has been consumed by a woman for over a decade. The shit will not get better if you continue to stalk her ass."

"I wasn't stalking. I was dedicated to my promise." My brow arched at the perfectly worded statement only a stalker would use. "Okay, fine, I might have been taking it a little too seriously."

"Why are you watching this girl at the sorority when I already am," Wilder asked, and Roach glared at him.

Sometimes I really wish Wilder would learn to shut up. "Remember, Chase asked him to protect the sorority," I said before Roach tied himself into another knot.

"Well, I guess that settles it. I don't need to anymore," Roach said, stuffing his hands in his pockets.

"It's for the best." I laid my hand on his shoulder as he looked down, his face so miserable it was like I'd just told him he was dying.

"You get an address," Wilder asked, effectively ruining the moment. He was right, though. We needed to get going.

"Yeah, I do. Let's roll."

We found the place easily enough. It was a run-down shack on a cul-de-sac, surrounded by mostly abandoned homes and crack houses. Not exactly a warm and fuzzy kind of neighborhood for a man trying to convince people to better themselves. It made me wonder what the fuck this guy was really doing with his members.

"What do you think?" I asked.

We were currently parked across the road from our target. The driveway was in such bad repair that I thought it would swallow the truck when Roach parked. The house wasn't any better, and the badly damaged roof had collapsed. Anyone living inside wasn't gonna be a credible witness.

"Looks like an abandoned shithole. Are you sure this is the right spot," Roach asked.

"Mutt swears this is the joint." I peered up at the sky. It would be dark in about twenty minutes. "I don't think he'd lie, he has nothing to gain, but there is a good chance that Frank no longer uses this location."

"Only one way to find out," Wilder said and jumped out before I could stop him. I didn't even get the button pressed on the automatic windows when he ran across the street and disappeared behind the house.

"That guy is fucking crazy," Roach said, dumping the last of his chip bag into his mouth.

"You don't know the half of it, but I'd rather have him as a friend than an enemy." I pushed open the passenger side door. "I guess we better follow him."

"Oh, you mean you want me to get out and not just be the sexy getaway driver?"

"I think you need a new mirror. Yours is definitely broken." I closed the door as, *asshole*, was yelled loud and clear. I smirked as I pulled my knife and flicked it open. Switching the grip, I held it in my fist and let the flat of the blade lay along my arm.

Walking across the road, I kept my eyes and ears peeled for sirens or any sign of life. The whole street was eerily quiet, like nothing living wanted to stay here, and a shiver raced down my spine. I wasn't much for evil spirits and shit, but everything felt off.

"This place has a bad vibe, man," Roach said, echoing my thoughts. We'd been in some pretty hairy situations together, in places that most would never travel, and his feeling confirmed I wasn't going crazy.

"Agreed."

Wilder jogged around to the front of the house. "This is definitely the place you're looking for." Wilder nodded toward the back. "Follow me."

"Are we really going to follow him?" Roach whispered. The corner of my mouth pulled up in a lopsided grin.

"He grows on you, kinda like a barnacle that just sorta sticks and grows back if you scrap it off."

"That's a horrifying image, thanks," Roach said as he made a gagging face. We rounded the back of the house, but Wilder was nowhere to be seen.

"Over here," he said, waving his arm from inside a tool shed.

"Yeah, definitely not feeling any better about the situation now," Roach grumbled as he pulled his gun.

The shed looked like one you'd pick up at any hardware store for all your lawn crap. It was metal and rusted, with no windows and a single door. Scraggly trees had grown around the sides, and a few vines were growing along the top.

Reaching the door, I looked inside the small space expecting to see Wilder and maybe a pile of bones. Instead, a massive trap door was open with a soft glow coming from inside.

"Fuck my life. I said I wasn't helping you anymore. I should've stuck with that," Roach complained.

"Oh shut up, it's not that bad...." I said and then watched as a spider the size of my hand ran across the dirt and disappeared.

"Right...cause I didn't just see that rat-sized spider," Roach said.

I glanced over my shoulder at him. "You should feel right at home with your fellow insects." I smiled wide.

"I fucking hate you. You know that, right?"

"Are you two coming," Wilder asked as he poked his head out of the ground like a gofer.

"Coming." I waited until he jumped back down before stepping on the steel ladder and making my way down. Roach was close behind me. I looked around the tunnel that was over six feet tall and about the same width. "How is this even possible? I didn't think we could even dig this deep here in Miami?"

"He had the entire piece made from formed concrete, metal, and a silicone substance. Then he had it installed and sealed to keep water from penetrating the cavity. Quite smart, actually, but how all this got done without anyone knowing is the real mystery. This takes a backhoe to dig, a crane to install it, and a massive flatbed truck to move it. This is not a sneak in the night quietly sort of situation," Wilder explained.

"Why the fuck would someone go to all this effort," I asked, following Wilder and his flashlight.

"Not sure, but wait until you see this," Wilder said when we reached the end. All of this was boggling my brain. The door was sealed with a wheel like you'd see on a submarine, and when Wilder opened it to the space beyond, the stench hit us. Roach and I gagged while Wilder seemed completely unaffected.

The combination was similar to the prison laundry I used to wash, but on top of the shit and cum scents was old piss, mold, and something rotting. My nose was assaulted by the worst combination of smells someone could ever put together.

Covering my nose with my arm, I followed Wilder into the basement of a house and assumed it was the one we'd been watching. It was an open space with nothing but darkness. There were no windows, but as Wilder shined his light around, my eyes went wide. Chains and cuffs lined the walls, enough for a dozen people. We reached another hallway with a line of doors that reminded me of solitary confinement at the prison. They were solid metal with a small flap that could be slid open to look inside. The first one we looked in was empty except for a thin old mattress that had seen better days and more chains and cuffs.

There were six doors in total, all the same. The last one had fresh blood on the ground and a smear that couldn't have been more than a few days old.

"What the hell am I looking at here," Roach asked, his voice muffled behind his arm.

"Trafficking, I think, or torture and murder. Each room has a different feature." Wilder pointed to the corner of the room and the tiny camera I hadn't noticed. Then he pointed to the thin lines of wires pulled up like a beast ready to drop from the ceiling. "Those are for electrocution. They can drop and dangle a designated height off the floor. The person here has to stay flat or get zapped, but I'm sure there is more to it. If this were my torture room, I'd let loose a few of those massive spiders or a snake so the person wants to jump up."

I stared at the side of Wilder's face. "You're creepy, man. I like you, but you worry me."

Wilder turned his head to look at me. "Why?"

"Never mind, let's keep searching. I need some clue about where this asshole is hiding. I find him. I find Dave."

The door to go up was locked, but Wilder had it unlocked faster than I ever could. We walked up the stairs quietly, ready for anything.

"Is this the house we were watching?" I looked out a window between a crack in the wooden boards covering the glass.

"Nope, the one behind it. We traveled in the wrong direction, and I bet you won't see your truck if you look out the front."

"This is getting stranger by the second," I said. Doing as Wilder suggested, I looked out the front window. Sure enough, we were facing the wrong way. This was not what I expected.

The place was dated with peeling, floral wallpaper, and floors that were a mix of shag carpet and subflooring. No pictures anywhere, but a new roll of toilet paper was by the shitter, water was running through the taps, and the thermostat on the wall glowed with the temp.

"Hey, Snake, come see this." I left the back room I was looking through and found Wilder sitting at a computer with Roach standing behind him.

"Where did you find the laptop?" He pointed to an air exchange vent, and I shook my head. I would never have thought to look there. Wilder pulled something out of his pocket that looked like a memory stick. The screen glowed and then showed a lock screen. Before I could ask how he planned on getting past that lock, he shoved the stick in the side, and the computer dinged and opened.

"Government encryption decoder," Wilder offered, and Roach and I looked at one another and shrugged. I could kill people with no problem and even make it creative, but this was why I brought Wilder. "These are all files on people, women mostly." He pointed to the long list that went on forever. He opened a file, and even my eyebrow rose with the violent images. A woman's face was contorted in agony as spikes were shoved through her body while someone fucked her. This was a new level of fucked even for me. You couldn't see the attacker's face for the large hooded robe that covered his body, but each image Wilder clicked on was more disturbing than the next.

He went to another folder and another, and it was all the same. Some women had been mangled or burnt but were still alive when these images were taken. One image had candles and strange symbols I didn't recognize drawn on the wall in the background. This Father Frank was more disturbed than I thought. He was using the cover of the cult that focused on spirituality and twisted it into whatever the fuck this was.

"They have dates and names. I'm surprised someone would do that unless they really didn't think they'd get caught," Roach said, pointing to the long list of folders.

"It's their trophies," Wilder answered. "They probably keep something personal as well, but this will be where he comes to relive the kills. Someplace no one would be watching or catch him jerking off or re-enacting it with others."

"That's fucked up," Roach said.

My pulse began to pound hard as a thought occurred to me. "Is there a folder for Raine Eastman?" Wilder and Roach looked at me, and even though they didn't say it, I knew what they were thinking. "I need to know," I said before they could argue.

The little folders went on and on as he made it down to the Rs, and the little cursor hovered over a file highlighted in blue. My fist clenched on the knife, shaking in my grasp.

"Open it," I growled.

"Buddy, you sure you want to see this?"

My eyes snapped to Roach. "What if this was Lane?"

"I know, but...."

"Open the fucking file or get out of my way and I'll do it," I ordered.

Wilder clicked on the file, and the world narrowed in on the photographs on the screen. There weren't as many as the other files, and the photo quality wasn't as clear, but that didn't matter.

There she was, my precious little Tink at fifteen, tied up and naked just like she said. Roach turned around and crossed his arms over his chest, his face as angry as I felt.

Blood and other bodily fluids coated her body. A dark hood was tied with black tape around her neck, but that didn't stop her eyes from gripping me behind the dark material. I could taste her terror on my tongue and acid in the back of my throat as my body revolted against what I saw.

Wilder clicked through all the photos, most were just of her, but some had Jim and Dave. Frank must have been the one taking the pictures.

A sharp pain pierced my chest like I was being stabbed through the heart. She thought this was me. For eleven long years, she thought I did this to her. Fire and ice sizzled in my veins as rage collided with the realization of the horror she'd felt.

"This is a pattern. It's not random. Some of the others have it too, just in different spots," Wilder said, pointing to the six knife wounds on her naked blood-covered stomach. "If she wasn't his first, she was close to it. That's the only reason she's alive. They're not as clean and precise. The cuts were tentative, and he used a different blade than the others. The wounds are smaller in size, and by some miracle, he missed all her major veins, or she would've bled out in minutes."

My body wouldn't stop shaking, and my heart pounded hard in my chest. I gripped my knees as the room swam and took deep breaths to get myself under control. Roach's hands were on my shoulders, but he didn't say anything.

The fear in Raine's eyes that night, when she found me in her house, came storming to the surface of my mind, and I wanted to throw up. That look on her face would haunt my dreams. She was my it, my all, my everything, and these three had destroyed us both.

"Take the computer. I don't care if he knows it's missing. The families of these people deserve closure." I stood and nodded to Roach that I was okay.

"This guy is fucking dead, and when we find him, he's all mine." Wilder and Roach stayed quiet but locked eyes with me. "Father Frank may have signed a deal with the Devil, but I'm the Reaper, and I intend to fucking collect."

Jace

Chapter 29

LOST
1% SOULS MC

J ace

Kai insisted on coming to the airfield with us. I found him extreme and unpredictable most of the time, but he was down-right strange this last week. Kai didn't challenge me or threaten to kill me when I purposely tried to get under his skin. He hardly spoke when we saw him and was more protective and edgy over Raine than I ever wanted to see from an enforcer. I didn't know what was happening, but I would bet money that something set him off.

Raine was splitting her time between us, so we saw Kai every other night, and although he sometimes hung out and ate dinner, it never felt like he was wholly here. He was fine with Raine but would spend most of the time standing at one of the large windows staring outside. I didn't know if this was a residual effect of the night we tag-teamed Raine, but it felt like something else. I hated being in the dark about shit. If he didn't snap out of it by tomorrow night, we were going to have another private conversation.

I glanced out the plane window and watched Raine talk to Kai. He looked panicked, scared she would get on the plane with me and never come back. If he really knew her, he'd know she wouldn't leave unless forced to. She was so much like Avro with her loyalty and undying positivity. Those two were meant to be in each other's orbit, and I was hoping that Raine could get him through his surgery when I couldn't be here.

Kai glanced up at me as they hugged, and our eyes locked. The usual anger brewing in their depths wasn't there. It freaked me out when someone's personality did a one-eighty like this. There was always a reason, and Kai didn't change for sweet, fluffy bunny reasons. He would only have a personality lobotomy if something seriously bad happened.

I looked away first—this was their moment—and answered Allen and the list of questions he was firing at me. They were mixed in with reminders about everything for this evening.

We were supposed to do a concert in Nashville two days ago, but Damon caught the flu and couldn't keep anything down. Not that I wanted Damon to be sick, but I wasn't complaining about the extra time I got. This was the longest stretch I'd been home in years.

"Hey," Raine said, smiling as she walked along the aisle and dropped her carry-on before hanging the garment bag on one of the lockable hooks.

"Hey," I said back. I glanced out the window again, and Kai was still standing in the same spot, staring up at the window. "Did he want to come?" I pointed my thumb out the window. "I mean, he can't come to the awards or anything. But if he's that freaked out about you going to this with me, he can babysit me, I guess."

Raine shook her head before sitting down. "No, I'm not even going to give him that option. He's been...how do I put this?" She bit her lip. "Do you find Kai is acting strange? Like more protective than normal?"

"I have noticed it," I said.

"I wondered if it was because we talked about me moving in with you and Avro, but he said he was fine. In fact, he said it would be safer than living at the old farmhouse so close to the MC property, and he liked that, so I don't know."

She shrugged. "Now that I think about it, they've both been weird. I don't mean they have a thing going on kind of weird," she said quickly, which made me chuckle.

"They've been weird in different ways. I've tried to get them to talk, but neither will say what's bothering them. You're the only one acting normal. You must have some idea what the hell is up. I hate being in the dark." She looked stressed as she stared at me. "I know Avro's knee has been sore. Are we doing too much?"

I sighed and crossed my arms, annoyed that Avro still hadn't talked to Raine, and now I would have to tell her. Probably his damn plan all along.

"If you know anything, please tell me, Jace." She rubbed at her chest. "I'm worried, and it's freaking me out that I'm met with a door slamming in my face the moment I bring it up."

"I know what's going on with Avro, but Kai, I have no clue." I rubbed the back of my neck as I debated whether I should tell her. It should come from Avro, but I wanted Raine to be able to enjoy this experience.

"Avro is acting off. I didn't know if anyone else saw it, so I didn't want to say anything."

The roar of the motorcycle firing up echoed into the plane's cabin, and we watched silently as Kai pulled out into the dark. It was very early, and I wanted to throw my phone as it dinged three more times in a row. Fucking Allen.

"Jace, please tell me about Avro." Raine reached out and placed her hand on my knee.

"I shouldn't. It's not my place to say," I said, and Raine leaned back and crossed her arms over her chest. She was giving me some serious 'fuck you' face, and it was kinda hot. "I'm serious. Avro doesn't like anyone to worry, and I shouldn't say if he hasn't mentioned it yet."

"Jace, are we or are we not all in this together? You made it very clear to me that anything that happened to any of us individually affected us all. I have the right to know."

"Fuck, I hate it when my words are tossed back at me." I leaned my head back against the seat. "Fine, but he may kill me if he finds out I told you."

"I doubt he's going to kill you," she said, shaking her head. "So out with it."

"You know about his knee, right?" Raine nodded. "It started to twinge a few months back, nothing big, just now and then when he'd move too fast the wrong way. He didn't think much of it, just leftover pain from the original surgeries. Then the pain became more frequent. He went to the doctor for testing a couple of weeks back, and he got the call the other night that he needs another surgery. This time they are doing a knee replacement and ACL reconstruction surgery." Raine covered her mouth and swore under her breath.

"What's going on with the knee? Do they know?"

"I don't have technical terms for you, but basically, the bone is breaking apart in the joint." I used my hands to demonstrate Avro's knee and the joint breaking. Raine looked like she was going to cry.

"Oh my god, why is he still dancing at the bar? That has to kill. And why doesn't he want me to know?"

"It's not that he doesn't want you to know. He doesn't want to become someone's problem, and...honestly, I think he's avoiding the topic. The less he talks about it, the less real it becomes."

"So he's opting to stay quiet and pretend he's okay? Jace, come on, that's not healthy," Raine said, and I shrugged.

"I've tried getting him to talk. He's very stubborn when he wants to be. The doc is talking six weeks with zero weight to start and then re-evaluate. That means he is most likely in a wheelchair, then on crutches if all goes well. If it doesn't...I don't know. But stairs will be nearly impossible, so he's been setting up the spare room on the main floor. He definitely won't be able to work behind the bar, and he won't be able to dance. As far as sex goes, I'm guessing that he will be out for a few weeks and can only sit or lay down, so that will bother him too." I ran my thumb across my lip as I pictured the kiss he gave me before I left. I could feel his heart breaking.

I hated that he was going through this for a third time. He didn't like me to know how much pain he was in. When I was home, he'd sneak off to another room. I'd find him silently crying but refusing to take more than one painkiller a day. He was terrified that he'd become addicted. Avro was stronger than he realized, while he always thought he was weak. I didn't get it, but it was another thing he and Raine had in common.

"Anyway, Avro's not taking it very well. That accident was horrible, and his knee was a mess. I was in Germany at the time and didn't get back until two weeks after it happened, but he was...lost, I don't know how better to describe it."

Tears ran steadily down Raine's cheeks as she leaned forward, her hands clasped together. "I feel like such an asshole. How did I not see he was in so much pain? I've been so caught up in my wonderful new bubble with all of you that I just wasn't paying attention." Her eyes snapped up to mine. "Should we even be going on this trip?"

"I have to go, but you can stay if you don't feel like going now. The thing is, Peaches, Avro wouldn't want that. Why do you think he didn't tell you? He doesn't want to be treated differently. It drives him crazy."

Raine slumped back and wiped away the tears. "Is this why he decided not to come?"

"He has an appointment today with the surgeon to go over his surgery plan," I said, and Raine jumped up, her fists clenched tight.

"What? You have to be kidding me? He's going all alone?" I didn't say anything, and she swore and paced the aisle. "I hate this. I have to pretend I don't know when all I want is to be there for him. This is ridiculous. Why are men so stubborn?"

I cocked a brow at her. "Have you ever looked in a mirror?"

"Oh, shut up," she grumbled, making me laugh.

"Look, we are only going for the night. It's why I shortened the trip. We go, do the awards, fly out tomorrow morning, and force him to come clean and accept help. I have to go to this, Peaches. It is an obligation, and I'd prefer to have you with me, but if you want to stay, I won't stop you." I nodded to the Captain and Co-Pilot as they walked in. "But you better hurry and decide. It looks like we're heading out soon."

She nibbled her bottom lip and looked back and forth between the open door and me before sitting down.

"You're right. It's one night, and this way, he won't feel worse that I backed out. Especially since we spent an entire day finding that dress." She looked over at the garment bag. "I thought I was going to kill him. He took me to every store twice."

"I know, you've mentioned it once or twice," I emphasized, and she glared at me.

"You going to turn into asshole Jace again?" She huffed. "I feel like you're a transformer."

"I thought we already settled this. I'm always asshole Jace." Leaning in close to her, I made sure she was wiggling with nervous energy before I spoke again. "And I plan on being very, very much the asshole at the awards. Be prepared to blush for me more than once."

Raine's eyes grew wide, and I heard her swallow. It was so fun to play with her. She'd have the worst-case scenarios running around in her head all flight, and I was sick because I loved it.

"What are you planning?"

The Co-pilot chose that moment to close the door. The lock was loud even over the sound of the engines coming to life. "Too late now. I guess you'll have to wait and see," I said, loving the look of pure horror in her eyes.

This was going to be fun.

Snake

Chapter 30

K aivan

My beer bottle tapped on the top of the bar. The club-house was extremely noisy with everyone back. I couldn't decide if I enjoyed the background noise that drowned out the voices in my head or preferred when it was quiet and my voices kept me company.

"Hey man, what's going on?" Mannix sat on the stool beside me. I looked at my friend and knew he knew about the cult, the house, and what we'd seen. It was all laid bare in his eyes. Roach—that ass —must have said something, and now Mannix looked worried. The only ones that should be worrying were Dave and Frank or Francois, whatever he was going by. I had plans for them, and the images only got worse with each passing day.

"I'm not going to randomly kill anyone if that's what you're asking," I said, staring at his reflection in the mirror.

"The thought may have crossed my mind. You tend to take your pent-up anger out in interesting ways." Mannix smirked, and the corner of my mouth turned up.

"Lately, I've had another outlet for my frustration," I said, and Mannix clapped a hand on my shoulder.

"I'm happy for you, kid."

"No, don't be callin' me that. I thought I'd finally got you kicked of that habit?" I groaned and then laughed. Strangely, being called by the nickname Mannix gave me in prison felt good. I knew he'd done it to remind me of my place but also that my life wasn't over. The guy was like that, subtle with the things he chose to do, but they always had a purpose.

"I remember the first time you mentioned Raine's name. Even then, with all the anger in you, I saw how much you still loved her. That kind of devotion never dies." I drank the last of my beer and pushed the bottle away.

"Is that so? And how would you know?"

Mannix smiled and chuckled a deep sound that always sounded warm and inviting. "Well, I think that will be a story for another night. As long as you're good, I'm good. We're ride or die, remember that."

"Mannix," I said as he stood. I couldn't look at him as I warred with the emotions swirling in my gut. "I would've been honored to call you dad."

"Asshole," Mannix grumbled, and I watched his reflection as he wiped at his face, which made me smile.

"Hey, Snake! Um...isn't that your old lady on the television?" Kickstand yelled over the noise, and just like that, the room fell silent. "Holy shit! It is. What the hell is she doing on that guy's arm? Isn't he some rockstar or something?"

Oh, this was my worst nightmare. If there was a God, he knew how to fuck with me in all the worst ways. I lifted my head to the massive television that typically showed sports or a car restoration show, but nope, not tonight. Of course, someone had to turn to the awards show, and there they were, Jace and Raine, smiling for cameras.

She looked fucking stunning, and my mouth fell open as I soaked her in. She was wearing a shimmery blue dress the same color as her eyes that sparkled under the lights and clung to every one of her delicious curves. It was cut so low in the front that there was a perfect V that left very little to the imagination. The dress was long with a slit up the side, exposing one leg, and showed off the matching shoes. Her hair was styled in an adorable look that showed off her neck and the jewelry I had no doubt Jace bought for her. My mouth ran dry, the shock of her perfection leaving me speechless.

She looked like a queen and as magical as the nickname I'd given her years ago. My heart beat faster in my chest, my breathing harsh as I tried to draw a deep breath. In the bright lights on Jace Everly's arm, she looked like she'd always belonged. And the fear of not being enough tried to claw its way to the front of my brain.

"Let's kill him!" Kickstand yelled, setting off a chain of hollering.

"Yeah, no one touches one of our old ladies and gets away with it." The crowd of a hundred or more stood in a single motion and headed for the artillery room like a wave coming into shore.

"Shit, shit, shit," I mumbled under my breath and slid off my stool.

"Wait!" There were still a few calls for murder, one unsurprisingly coming from Tanner. "I knew she was going to be there," I said and hoped they would leave it at that. I walked around a few tables and turned to face the room, making sure the exit was right behind me for when this hell was over.

"Does that mean she's no longer your old lady," Tanner asked. "Is she fair game?"

I was going to kill him.

"No," I growled in his direction and slowly turned to glare at the massive group staring at me. This felt very much like my drunken dancing on the bar night...what I could remember of it anyway.

"Raine is still my old lady." The group blinked like they were hooked to the same remote control. Fuck they were going to make me say it.

"Well, don't leave us hanging, Snake. What's going on," Chase asked from where he was sitting playing cards.

This felt worse than everyone staring at me on my first day in prison, and that was saying something. I cleared my throat and rolled out my shoulders. My eyes found Roach and then Mannix.

"I'm in a relationship with Raine and two guys," I said, and no one moved.

Roach's mouth hit the floor, and I felt the heat creeping up my neck. It wasn't that there weren't guys in the clubhouse that liked other guys. It was the fact that this was me. I was a jealous, possessive asshole, and I'd made a very loud statement by fucking Raine in here. It was the kind of statement that said my hands only, and that went for inside the club and out.

"So, you're fucking that hot ass woman and fucking the hot ass rock star," Tanner asked, and I rolled my eyes in his direction. "Holy fuck, you are. You're my mother fucking superhero. I want to be you when I grow up. Damn! Where's my foursome ladies and gents," Tanner yelled, and for the first time, I was happy Tanner was crazier than I was because the tension diffused like a balloon popping.

"To be clear, you're good with this," Chase asked, pointing at the television showing Raine and Jace kissing. I may still murder him when they got back for kissing her like that and putting me through this, but I sighed and nodded.

"Yes, sorta, but...." I paused as my feet vibrated. I looked around the room. "Did you all feel that?" There was a soft rumbling sound, and I turned my head to listen. Was this a gas leak?

"Feel what," Chase asked, standing from the table.

"He looks like his head is going to twist right off his body," Tanner joked.

"Not the time Tanner," Chase said before I could. "What do you feel, Snake?"

"There is an intermittent rumbling and...." The floor vibrated again, but this time so did the walls and dirt sprinkled down from the ceiling. "That."

Pulling my gun, I turned and ran down the stairs, taking them two at a time. The entire room was on the move and following behind me. At the next church meeting, I would bring up how this place was a death trap waiting to happen. We needed a second or even third set of stairs.

The sounds were louder down on the lower level, and it definitely seemed like explosions. I pushed open the metal door just enough to peer out and not get shot if this was an ambush.

"What the fuck is going on out there," Mannix asked at the sound of gunfire.

"I'm not sure. Be ready for anything," I said and darted out the door.

When the door wasn't pelted with a rain of bullets, I turned toward the sounds which were coming from the amusement park. That wasn't normal, but it seemed fitting. With Wilder, anything was possible. I stopped in my tracks as an explosion erupted from under the old Teacups ride and watched a screaming man that seemed to be chased by a flying pink teacup. I cringed as the man and the teacup slammed into an old upright support of a roller-coaster before crashing to the hard concrete below. As if to add insult to injury, the ride groaned and bent in half, the top landing on the already still man, effectively squishing him like a bug.

"Wow, that was...."

"Gnarly as fuck," Tanner said. I couldn't even be bothered looking at him.

"What the fuck is going on," I asked no one as my eyes took in the mass amounts of carnage.

How did Wilder get involved with this blood bath? It looked like an invisible hand was tearing apart bodies and decided to sprinkle them all over the amusement park. I'd seen a lot of shit, but never anything close to this.

The ground was littered with pieces of rides while fires burned in every corner of the large park. There was more gunfire and screaming, but it all seemed contained to that side of the fence.

Just to be safe, I yelled, "Stray bullets are an issue. If you don't have a bulletproof vest on, I'd go in and grab one." Some stayed, but most ran back inside. We'd moved a ton of that downstairs since the last attack, so it didn't take long for everyone to be suited and head back out. Beast walked over and handed vests to Chase, Mannix, and Roach.

"Well, at least I know who you love most," I teased Beast.

"I'm coming back with more. Hang on to yourself," he said, not cracking a smile before wandering off. Beast seemed different since Chase came back. It was almost as if the grief of losing his wife hadn't affected him until he no longer had the club's day-to-day to focus on.

I turned my attention back to the ongoing mayhem. There was so much blood and random flesh decorating the ground and rides left standing that I was reminded of what I'd done at the warehouse to that Weasel guy. But on a much larger scale.

All hell broke loose as a large group of men near the back side of the amusement park came roaring out of nowhere on motorcycles, with even more men screaming and running chaotically in all directions. I had a feeling Wilder let them get that far before raining hell on them. It was like they couldn't decide which way to go.

"If a fucking T-rex appears out of the smoke, you're all on your own," Tanner said. "Because I'm gonna ride that bitch."

I glanced over at him and wondered how we'd collected such a pile of insanity in one location. Wilder next door, Tanner came with Chase, and I couldn't forget Ava at the sorority house. Ava was the strangest of them all. We never knew what she was going to do, when she was going to show up, or who she was going to drag in with her.

"It looks like the Desert Vipers," I said as Chase and Roach, now suited up with their vests, stepped beside me. "Or at least what's left of them."

The ground shook like a miniature earthquake as three more explosions went off, much closer this time. We all turned away and covered our heads as we ran from the debris that included large pieces off of motorcycles.

I pointed to the parking lot. "We need to get the bikes inside," I said to Chase as more debris sailed through the air and crashed down on our side of the fence.

"Beast, get a party organized and move the bikes into the back warehouse," Chase yelled, and Beast jumped into action.

There was a growling noise before men started screaming, and what seemed like tall turrets of steam rose into the air.

"Cover up," I yelled.

It felt like rain hitting us, but I knew that wet feeling was not water.

"Oh shit, that's disgusting," Roach growled as he rubbed red dots off his face and flicked a piece of skin off his leather jacket.

Four men on foot were running for our fence, all screaming as if the devil himself was on their heels. I raised my gun and fired two shots taking out the two guys in the middle.

"Don't shoot," the remaining two yelled. "Please don't shoot." Another dropped dead, but I hadn't taken the shot and looked around, realizing it wasn't any of our guys. I knew who it was, but everyone else was looking for the source of the random bullet. The last guy slipped in some blood and landed hard on the ground. He scrambled to his feet, looking like he'd been dipped in red paint.

"Ohhh look, fireworks!"

I jumped at the sound of Ava's sing-song voice. Where the hell had she come from? It was as if thinking about her had conjured the craziness like she was a demon. I looked down at the small woman who was next-level terrifying. I still had no idea how she survived half the shit she did, and what the hell was she wearing? Today she was in a duck outfit like a mascot at a game who wandered away to end up here. I thought Wilder was random, but Ava took the cake and licked off the icing one finger at a time.

Of course, Tanner was in love with her, but she could never remember his name, which never got old. Anytime Tanner was knocked down a peg from his arrogant horse's back was a day to celebrate.

"It's so pretty," Ava said, her mouth making a little O as another explosion went off, and part of another old ride toppled over with a loud groan and then crashed. All I could think was this would give Wilder more places to hide.

"What the hell else are we supposed to do?" Someone yelled.

"Fucked if I know," Chase mumbled under his breath so only Roach or I could hear before barking orders. "Kill anyone that makes it onto our side of the fence unless they want to join us. They'll need to be willing to take their punishment starting tonight. Spread out and stay back from the property line. I don't know how close those explosions will come in our direction."

People quickly dispersed, just as the last guy running for the fence finally made it after slipping and falling on his ass twice more. He gripped the chain link so hard that his fingers were bright white while his eyes were wide with terror.

"This place...it's alive! Help me, please," he begged.

Chase opened his mouth to answer just as a seemingly ordinary bush came to life and jumped on the man. Even though I knew who it was under the cover of the tree camouflage, I couldn't help feeling creeped out as the screaming man was tackled to the ground and fell silent before the bush ran off into the amusement park. If I had a list of shit in my life that I never thought I'd see, Wilder topped it every single time.

"The bush ate that man," Ava exclaimed. "There are killer bushes." She turned and ran off like that was the craziest thing she'd ever seen. That girl was the walking embodiment of 'what the fuck,' and she was worried about a bush coming to life. Fucking ironic.

"Ava, wait up," Tanner took off hot on her heels, and I shook my head.

"Loyal one you have there, Chase," I said sarcastically. Loving the opportunity to get a dig in at him.

Chase's eyes narrowed. "Don't make me tell you not the time or place," he drawled.

I snorted. "Yes, Daddy," I said, sweet as pie, and smiled at him.

"You had to go there and make it weird," Chase countered. "Prick." It was nice to see him flustered for a change.

"Okay, are we going to ignore the fact that a bush just killed a man? Or did no one else other than me and Ava see that," Roach asked. "Please, dear God, let someone else have seen that."

It wasn't often that I got to mess with Roach, and I was tempted to lean over and ask him what he was talking about, but Mannix ruined my fun.

"Yeah, I saw it," Mannix said, and Roach's shoulders relaxed.

"That's good. I look like shit in white straight jackets."

"When the hell were you ever in a straight jacket," I asked.

"I'm just saying it wouldn't suit me. White is not my color." He shrugged as I continued to stare at him. "Besides, for a moment, I thought I was tripping on drugs I didn't remember taking. That would've led to a few more questions."

I shook my head at him. What the fuck was in the water around this place?

"Sooo, two guys huh?" Chase didn't look at me, but I could feel him wanting to smile and joke about my grand statement, 'No one else will touch Raine.'

I turned and looked at Chase. "You know what...." I rolled out my shoulders as a sense of freedom came over me. "Tonight is a whole lot fucked up, and normally I'd take care of it. Just like I've taken care of it for the last one year, three months, and four weeks, minus a day." Chase looked at me. His brow knitted together. "I'd worry about calling in a favor with the guy I'm blackmailing at the cop shop. I'd kill who I needed to keep this shit quiet and organize a proper cleanup, but since you're back...." I squeezed Chase's shoulder. "Have fun. I'm outta here."

"What?" All three of the guys said at once. I never left when there was club shit to take care of. No matter how angry I'd been, I always put the club first, but tonight, I was getting the hell out of here. I had too much toxic shit doing the backstroke in my brain. The last thing I needed was to handle severed body parts.

"You heard me. I'm gone for the night. I'm sick of cleaning up mass amounts of body parts and stressing over this shit. I need a night off." I looked back at the park. "Besides, I think the Vipers have bigger problems than us," I said as an arm landed on the fence, getting tangled in the barbed wire.

I stared at the swinging body part and smiled, unsure why it was so fucking funny. Revving my bike, I rolled up beside Chase, who still looked shell-shocked at the carnage.

"It's good to have you back, Prez. Call Johnson at the local. He'll sort out the paperwork for a price." I looked back at the mess. "He may need a bonus for this one." Smirking, I rode out the gates to get as far away from whatever the hell that insanity was, only to drive by Ava running down the sidewalk in her duck suit and Tanner jogging right along beside her.

Sometimes I really wondered if it was me that was the common denominator because the craziest shit followed me around like a damn dirt cloud.

Chapter 31

Avro

They had already done several cameos and miniature interviews with Jace and Raine. Jace did a great job coaching her because she handled herself well, and they looked like the perfect couple in love. He never left her side, and she kept her hand on his chest. The manicure I'd taken her for looked amazing on camera.

The media sites were eating them up, and Jace was too smooth sometimes. It should worry me how well he lied on camera, but he said it was just part of the persona, part of his act. The story was that he'd kept Raine hidden because she didn't like the limelight, but he wanted the world to know who had stolen his heart and finally talked her into being seen. Raine looked beautiful, and I felt like a total jerk for backing out of going.

So here I was, eating a bowl of popcorn so large that someone could drown in it, drinking a new cocktail I made that I didn't really like, with a bum ass knee, feeling sorry for myself. I had no one to blame but myself. I could've rescheduled my appointment and been soaking in a jacuzzi, sipping champagne as I waited for Raine and Jace, but nope, I had to go and ruin that. I glared at my knee like it had a choice in the matter.

"Why am I such an idiot," I mumbled as the announcer called out the winner of the night's first award. I hadn't been able to pick out where they were sitting yet, but I always made it my mission. I'd lost count of how many times I watched award shows searching out Jace like a game of *Where's Waldo*. I always hated seeing him standing on the carpet with his arm around someone else, but I didn't feel that with him and Raine tonight.

Jace had a good chance of winning one if not two, awards. It was why Allen was so insistent that Jace be there in person. I took another sip of the drink and gagged, tempted to throw it out and start over. Even my skills at making a new concoction were off tonight.

I stood up to make something else when a knock sounded at the back door, which was strange because very few people used it.

Sitting my popcorn on the table, I limped over. I should not have worked behind the bar last night, but I was the only act right now without Raine. My knee was screaming at me for dancing.

I turned on the outside light and peered out the small window. Kai? Did hell freeze over? When I opened the door, Kai was holding a box of pizza and a six-pack of beer, but it was the blood smattering his face and clothes that had me wondering, *what the fuck?*

"I come with a peace offering. It's only pepperoni cause I didn't know what you liked, but the beer is good and cold," he said, holding up the party-size box like I couldn't see it. Who did he think we were feeding?

"Are more people coming?"

"No, why?"

"No reason. This isn't a 'Hey, come over for a beer, but I'm going to threaten you again, type night,' is it?" I leaned against the door jam, not letting him in.

"No, it is a genuine offer," Kai said, but I was still wary.

"So you have no one else you'd prefer to hang out with? Don't you have an entire motorcycle club of friends?"

Kai sighed. "Okay look, I don't have a television, I didn't want to watch the awards in the clubhouse, and the guys at the club are a little busy at the moment."

"Ah! So I'm the last spot you'd come, but you're desperate. Check. Is whatever the club is busy with the reason you're covered with blood? You know you're covered in blood, right," I asked.

Kai looked down and then shrugged. "I didn't do it." His brow furrowed. "I know you don't believe that, but for once, it's actually true. Probably, why I got the huge discount at the pizza joint, though...huh, oh well."

I stepped out of the way to let him in. "You're not sitting on my brand-new couch like that. Give me the pizza and beer, and you can go shower."

"You're serious?"

"Does this expression look like I'm joking?" I said, sarcasm dripping off every word.

"Wow, when did you become the Jace in the room?"

Sighing, I took the pizza and beer from his hands. "Even the nice guy is allowed to have a bad day. There are flannel pants and T-shirts in the dresser closest to the bathroom. Hunt in the closet for a sweatshirt. I don't really care what you wear," I said, biting my lip and forcing myself to walk normally as I turned around and headed deeper into the kitchen.

"Fine, I'll be back."

"Boots off first. Don't think I didn't notice you stomped up my stairs with your boots the other night—no more of that in my home. I don't care how many nights you stay, but I like my stuff clean, and I refuse to clean up after adults," I said, impressed and shocked that I was being so firm. It was the pain making me ornery.

"Fair," Kai said. I was surprised he wasn't arguing and looked over as he undid his boots. I hit bake on the oven and pulled out a pan to heat the pizza. "I'll be five."

"Kai?"

He stopped just as he walked out into the hall. "Yeah?"

"Thanks for the pizza."

"Who said any of it was for you," he smirked, and I shook my head as Kai disappeared.

Wonders never cease. Kai and I were hanging out and about to eat pizza like civilized adults. The world really has gone mad. I got plates ready and poured the beer into tall steins, then grabbed some other snack food from the cupboard as the pizza was heating. By the time Kai jogged down the stairs wearing my clothes, I had almost everything in the living room. I looked at him in my plaid flannel pants and couldn't figure out where I made the crazy turn in my night, but I felt like taking a picture because Jace and Raine would never believe me.

"Thanks, I feel much better," Kai said, taking the plate I held out and then piling it with six slices of pizza.

"Do I want to know what you did with your dirty clothes?"

"You mean they're not to be washed in the sink and laid out on the bed to dry?"

Kai smirked as I glared at him, but he just chuckled and walked away. It took everything in me not to go check that wasn't exactly what he did. Grumbling, I grabbed my plate.

Taking a deep breath, I walked out to the couch. Kai was staring at me with his brows drawn together in confusion. "Why are you pretending you're not limping?"

I blew the air out of my lungs and groaned. "That noticeable?"

"Is water wet?"

"Whatever. I don't want to talk about it. Besides, you've been fucking odd too." I sat my plate on my lap and turned my head to look at Kai.

"No, I haven't," he argued.

"I mean, broody asshole is your go-to, but nah, I'm not buying it. You're hiding something." Kai didn't bother to answer and stuffed half a slice of pizza in his mouth. "Doesn't look like we have anything to talk about then."

"You think he'll actually win something?" Kai was the first to break the silence.

"As good of a chance of any of them, I guess. His agent is pretty certain that of the three awards the group is nominated for, they will win at least one," I answered. "Aren't we a sad, pathetic pair?"

"Speak for yourself," Kai growled, and I couldn't help but laugh. "What?"

"I gotta tell you that you're far less scary when you're in my flannel pants and Jace's band T-shirt."

Kai looked down at himself. "You have nothing else. Do you even buy other T-shirts that aren't molded to your body? Half of them felt like spandex."

"They're for work. The patrons like to see the goods." I smiled, but sadness was tugging at me. I knew I couldn't dance anymore, at least not until after the surgery, and I was given the all-clear, but it could be months and constant pain.

I took a bite of pizza and pushed the troubling thoughts out of my mind for the night. I smiled and pointed at the television as the camera panned across the first few rows, and I was able to spot Jace and Raine.

"There they are." Raine looked slightly intimidated by all the other celebrities around her, but I could only tell because I knew her so well.

"Okay look, I'll show you mine if you show me yours," I said, and Kai's hand stopped moving halfway to his open mouth. It was annoying me that I didn't know what Kai was hiding. It felt big, and I trusted my gut.

"Um...what are we talking about?"

"Please spare me, we've already seen each other's dicks, and I have no interest in fucking you." I took a big gulp of the beer.

"Why not? I'm totally fuckable," Kai said, and I turned my head to stare at him.

"What the hell is going on with you? Actually, forget it, don't tell me. All I want to know is why you've been so quiet and overprotective this week with Raine, and I will tell you about my knee."

"I'm pretty sure you're getting the better end of this deal. What I have is volatile. Why you're limping doesn't seem to hold any real weight." Kai shifted around to face me and kept eating. It felt like we were playing poker. But who had more chips to push into the center of the table?

"I'm assuming this would be our secret. We are not speaking about this to anyone outside of this room?" Kai continued to devour the food, making me wonder how he ate that much.

"Yes, I'd agree to that," I said.

"Then I need something better than your knee," he said.

I watched the television as they ran through commercials and more awards that I wasn't interested in.

"Okay, how about this? I'll tell you how I hurt my knee," I said.

"I already know how. It was during a training session for a circus performance." Kai smirked and polished off the last of his pizza.

"It wasn't the circus," I said and then waved my hand, dismissing the argument. I knew what people thought, and yes, it was a fancy circus, but it was more than that to me. It was theater. It was living out a dream, on stage, under the lights, and being the star. I felt like I could do anything.

"Never mind that. The point is the accident I have told everyone about is only a half-truth. There is a much larger story that not a soul knows about," I said.

"Not even Jace?"

"Not even Jace," I said and turned my head to look at Kai's profile as he watched the television. He rubbed his chin as he thought.

"Alright, I'll tell you, but if Raine hears about this, all the good-will we've built between us over the last week will disappear." The crowd clapped and cheered on the television, but my attention remained firmly on Kai.

"She won't hear it from me, and if Jace hears about what I tell you, then the same goes for you," I offered and turned on the couch to face him. "So, what's going on?"

"You first." Kai grabbed the bowl of popcorn I was eating earlier and ate a handful before grabbing the chips and doing the same. Soon he was surrounded by chips, cheeses, pretzels, and popcorn.

"Would you like a bowl you can mix them in?" I offered. I was starting to wonder if he had a tapeworm.

"Can I just put it in with the popcorn?"

"Sure, I was done anyway." I waited until he was settled before I started.

"The accident wasn't an accident. My normal partner was off sick, but I think he was threatened or paid off to stay home. The guy in his place let me drop from seventy-five feet in the air."

"What the fuck? Did you piss in his cereal," Kai asked.

"So funny. No, of course not. He wanted my spot and was pissed that I beat him out. I didn't die because we had a hidden emergency net that pulled up if one of us fell. Dying in front of people watching doesn't go over well."

"But you still messed up your knee?" Kai picked up single pieces of each snack and popped them into his mouth. I was morbidly fascinated with his eating. Refocusing, I continued with my story.

"I wouldn't have, but shocker, after my first bounce, the line snapped on one of the corner cords, and I landed on my leg all wrong. It bent one way, and I bent the other." I demonstrated with my hands. "That line is designed to handle more than a dozen of us dropping on it at a time. It never should've snapped. The insurance company ruled it an accident, but I know it was sabotage."

"Did you at least get compensated for it?" Kai seemed very interested in my story, which I appreciated, yet...it was weird. Maybe he was actually trying, but I was skeptical.

"They paid for all my medical and this new surgery I have to have. I didn't want to sue since I knew it wasn't the company, but they offered to pay anything I needed to recover, so I agreed."

"Why did you never tell the cops," Kai asked.

"When I was in the hospital after my first surgery, a delivery guy showed up with a large flower arrangement. When I opened the card, there was a picture of Jace with a red line through his face, and on the back, it said, *One word is all that it will take*." I shrugged. "The fact he knew about Jace at all freaked me out. We are always so careful and back then we rarely saw one another."

"Damn, that's cold," Kai said. "Smart and devious, but definitely cold. I get why you wouldn't say anything. What's this guy's name?"

"I don't know if I should say. After I got out of the hospital, I did some digging, and it turns out his family is part of the mafia," I picked up my beer and gulped the rest. "He ruined my life so he could have fifteen minutes of fame. He did like two shows and quit." I shook my head.

"I hate him. I've had two surgeries, and now I need a third to replace my knee and reconstruct my ACL. They're saying two or three months before I'm okay, and that's only if it takes and I'm diligent with my physio. So much pain, and for what? So this guy could say he got to headline in Vegas and then turned his nose up at it." My hand squeezed the glass hard, and I had to take a deep breath before I broke it. "I try to be a good person, Kai, I really do, but this guy...let's just say I wouldn't mind him going missing."

Turning my head, I looked at Kai. He was quiet, his stare intense. "What's his name?

I licked my lips. I hadn't said his name since that day. It felt like bringing bad energy around me if I did.

"Julian Fiore."

"Okay."

"What does okay mean?"

"It means okay. Consider it done. Don't ask questions, don't pass go or collect your two hundred dollars. Just let it be, and it will be taken care of," Kai said, his voice calm.

"You mean you'll...you know?"

"I mean, it's best not to ask questions that you really don't want answers to, but I can say he will be taught a lesson, and you can sleep better at night." Kai tossed a piece of popcorn into the air and caught it like he wasn't just talking about killing someone. I stared at him for a long time as my mind took in and chewed on what he said.

"Thanks." Unsure what to say to that right now, I pointed at him. "Okay, your turn."

"I know who attacked Raine." My mouth dropped open. "I also made sure that one of the three would never breathe again. The other two I'm closing in on, and I found pictures of her assault."

He picked up his beer and took a sip before setting all the snacks on the table. It wasn't so much what Kai was doing that freaked me out. It was what he wasn't saying. He would destroy whoever it was until there was nothing left to find.

"Does Raine know who they are?"

Like I hit a light switch, Kai whipped his head in my direction, his lip curled up, and his eyebrows drew tight as the anger radiated off him. "No, and I want it to remain that way. Two of the three men were people she knew and trusted. She already had to live through thinking I hurt her. I don't want to put any more nightmares in her head."

I nibbled on my lower lip. "I'd want to know, Kai. If it were me, I'd want to know," I said softly.

"Well, Raine is not you, and she's been through a lot. I'm not putting this on her as well. I'll find them, and I'll take care of them. When I'm good and ready, and Raine has had more time adjusting to all of this." Kai demonstrated my home with his hands, but I think he meant all the changes in general. Her growth, not just the new walls around her. "Then I will find a way to tell her, but not before." His face grew darker, like he was casting shadows in the room with his glare. "I will deal with them in my way. I owe her that. I owe myself that, and I won't rest until it happens. You wanted us to have a sharing session and a bonding moment, then there it is. You don't say a word to her about this."

We were quiet after that, and one by one, performers walked up to the stage to accept their awards. It seemed like forever before they called the names of those nominated for Best Rock Song. The announcers on stage made a joke, but I just wanted them to hurry up. My heart was pounding faster as I stared at the television.

"And the winner is...Grimhead Crew!"

"Yes!" I yelled and jumped up, pumping my fist into the air, immediately regretting it as pain shot through my knee. "Fuck" I grumbled as I flopped back down and held onto the joint. But even my stupid knee couldn't stop the happiness or the smile from spreading as the camera swung to Jace and Raine.

He gave her a quick kiss and then walked up with the rest of the band. Of course, Marcus didn't bother with the stairs and just jumped onto the stage. That guy was wild.

Jace stepped up to the podium, and my breath caught. He looked so handsome. He raised the award, and the crowd screamed and clapped.

"Wow, this is an honor. Thank you to all the fans that voted for us. This award is for all of us, all of you. I wouldn't be standing here without my band, but they have unwisely elected me to speak."

He smiled at the camera, and my heart flipped. He'd been nominated so many times but never won. I wanted to dance and cry and laugh. The pride I felt for him when I knew how hard he worked not just on his craft but to come back from all that had happened...he amazed me.

"I'd like to thank this group of guys right here. There are no other people I'd rather be with and spend so much time on a bus with." The crowd chuckled. *"In all seriousness, there are just so many people I want to thank, my agent Allen, the many producers, songwriters, those in the industry that have helped get us to this point, and of course the fans, the list is endless."*

He fell silent for a moment as he looked down at the podium. My stomach churned. It wasn't obvious to anyone else, but he was gearing himself up for something.

"One thing that I learned very early on in my career is that you can't do it alone."

You could hear the fan area chanting: *We love Jace, We love Jace.*

A sexy smile pulled at the corner of his mouth. *"I love you too."*

More screaming but louder now.

"They really do love him, don't they?" Kai said, startling me. I'd forgotten he was sitting on the couch with me.

"Yeah, almost from day one, the fans made it impossible for a label not to notice his talent. He could've done anything. He's always been like that, and it used to make me so fucking mad." I chuckled. "But I've always loved him, no matter what."

Jace signaled for the crowd to quiet down and waited before continuing. *"But I want to come clean on something tonight."*

Everything stopped, including my breathing, as it became eerily quiet. Jace rubbed his chin, and I slid closer to the front of the couch. What was he up to?

"You know, my agent is always making sure I'm in the news, with some sort of drama swirling around me. Some of it is true. I'm not always a good guy."

He dropped his voice and winked as the fan section went insane. The camera swung in that direction, and I thought for sure someone was going to throw themselves off the second-floor balcony. It sounded like he was at a concert as they drowned out everything else. He waited until the, *We love you, Jace* quieted down again.

"But sadly, most of the things you've seen have all been staged to sell more songs. I'm not really that exciting. I mean, come on, me with a Princess?" Jace cocked a brow and smiled before his face grew serious, and my blood pressure spiked.

"What the hell are you doing, Jace? You better not tank your career to stay at home. I will kick your ass," I said to the screen as if he could hear me.

"You do know he can't hear you, right?" Kai held out a new beer for me as he returned from the kitchen. I cracked it and took a swig, not bothering with the glass. I hadn't even seen Kai move from beside me, so engrossed in what Jace was saying.

"Oh, he'll know I'm watching. I always watch. I haven't missed a show he was nominated for."

"You're actually really funny," Kai said, and I looked at him, expecting more from that statement, but he kept his eyes on the television.

"So here's the thing, I'm tired of the lies and the fake drama. I'm tired of the staged photos and interviews. I want all of you in this room and at home to know right now about something real and very important to me. There are two people in this world that I love, and they mean more to me than anything. One has been with me for almost seventeen years, has lived with and watched all this unfold, and still stuck with me. The second person is newer to my life but holds my heart in her palm as equally as the other."

My eyes flicked to the band standing right beside Jace. They were smiling and looking like they knew what was coming, so they had to be in on this. I always knew when Marcus or Damon was shocked. They had easy tells. As the camera panned the room, it was easy to see that Raine had no idea what he was up to. She looked like she wanted to bolt from her seat and run out the doors.

"The first of those two couldn't be here with me tonight, although he wanted to be. I'm going to preface this by announcing that I'm bi-sexual and in a menage relationship." He paused and waited for the collective gasp of shock and then wild cheers to stop.

"Holy fuck, I don't think this is what Allen meant when he said he wanted more drama, Jace. What the hell are you doing?" My hand covered my mouth, and I pictured Allen fainting backstage.

Jace held up his hand to quiet the room once more. He had to be over time by now, but the camera didn't cut to commercial.

"He has kept me going through some very, very dark days in my life. Avro Beck, I'm done hiding you in the shadows. I love you, and I wish you could've been here tonight."

My mouth dropped open. "I think I'm going to pass out," I mumbled. My breathing was as fast as my rabbiting heart.

Kai clapped a hand on my shoulder as he laughed at my terrified expression. "Guess you didn't know what he was up to."

"Now for the second person that I love. All of you just learned of Raine and our relationship, and I know this has come as a shock, as I'm sure

learning of Avro just now has, but Raine, could you come up here for a minute."

The camera immediately found her in the crowd, her image plastered on the massive screens, and I wasn't the only one who looked like they would pass out. Her blue eyes couldn't have gotten any wider, and all the color was drained from her face.

"What is he doing now," Kai asked.

I looked at Kai. "I didn't know about him outing me to the entire world. You really think I know what he's doing now?"

"Shhh, I want to listen," Kai said, and I thought I might just take my chances and punch him again.

Raine stood and walked along the aisle to loud cheers. Damon met her at the bottom of the stairs and helped her up. When she was by Jace's side, her lips barely moved, but I could tell she was asking him what he was doing. He simply linked their hands together.

"I have one more thing to say, and then I promise to get off this stage so you can all get on with your night. Most of you don't know this, but my entire family was murdered a few years ago." There was once more a collective gasp. *"I've managed to keep it quiet until now, but I feel it's important you all know."*

So many shocks for one awards show the media had to be salivating with the headlines.

"I'm sure some of you even saw it on the news, but I'm mentioning this because it would've been easy to allow the tragedy of that loss to consume me, drag me down, and make me turn my back on humanity. I was tempted and held a lot of anger for a long time. On top of that, a close personal relationship with depression almost got the best of me, and I never want any of you to feel that way. The band and I will be starting a help group for anyone suffering, and more will be announced in a few days as we launch this endeavor."

"Is what he said true," Kai asked. "I tried looking him up, but nothing other than his music career showed up."

"He pays to keep it off all search engines, but yeah, his mother, sister, and brother were all shot by his stepfather. If we hadn't left to head back to college, we would probably be dead too. Jace lives with that guilt. It's why you bother him so much. It's not your jerk attitude or the time you spent behind bars or even that you want to be in Raine's life. You remind him of what he lost and how easy it can happen again," I answered.

"Fuck," Kai mumbled. "Don't I feel like the asshole now."

I glanced over at Kai. "You said it."

"Jerk."

I smirked even as my hand shook in anticipation. I chugged the beer but kept my eyes on the screen, unable to look away.

"I want to tell everyone to hold those you love tight, never let them go, and fight for what you want." His eyes turned to Raine. *"This beautiful woman came into my life, and as reluctant as I was in the beginning, I couldn't stop the warmth of her soul from seeping into my heart. I can breathe for the first time in so long, Raine, with you and Avro in my life. You make everyone around you feel loved and safe with your big heart and kind soul. We should all try to be as gracious and loving as you are. This world would be a far better place."*

Jace's hand gripped the little podium, and I could tell he was getting emotional. These weren't just pretty words for the camera. I'd known him long enough to see through the mask and could tell fact from fiction.

"Raine, you make everyone that meets you want to be better without even trying, and I'm blessed that you came into my world. You and Avro are it for me, and I want you to know, in front of all these witnesses, I love you. This world is better for having you in it. I was so lucky to find a diamond like you."

A tear trickled down her cheek, and under the bright lights on stage, diamonds were exactly what the tiny droplets looked like.

"He certainly knows how to captivate everyone," Kai said.

"Yeah, he does."

Jace stepped away from the podium, and it was harder to hear what he said, so I turned the volume on max. He was whispering so low that the mic couldn't pick it up, but I was positive he was warning her that he would kiss her in front of everyone. He was taking a page from my book. I got one hell of an earful for doing that. Jace lowered himself to one knee just as I took a sip of my beer, and it sprayed all over the coffee table.

"What the fuck?" Kai and I said together.

The television suddenly blared at us. *"Raine Eastman, you're the light that will always lead me through the darkest of days and keep me warm on the coldest of nights. You have helped the fire inside of me burn brighter and restored my hope. I thought I'd healed from my family being stolen from me, but I realize now that something was still missing, and you are the piece that has completed the puzzle of my heart."*

"Holy shit," I mumbled. My mouth hung open as Jace pulled a jewelry box from his pocket. I couldn't believe what I was watching. My entire body shook with the adrenaline racing through my system, and I couldn't decipher if I was happy about this or terrified that I'd just been cut out for good. Had I brought us all together to lose them both?

"Raine Eastman, would you do me the honor of marrying me and becoming my wife?"

The cameras zoomed in on her face, and Raine looked as shocked and confused as I felt. I could feel her brain working from here, which gave me hope that this wasn't a plan of theirs that I was cut out of. It was horrible that I could even think that, but Jace always told me what he was going to do, and this was the biggest of big deals. Why had he felt the need to keep this from me?

Raine licked her lips, her face flashing with anger under the shock, and for the briefest of moments, I thought she would slap him and walk off the stage, but that wasn't Raine. She might kill him after, but to make an even larger spectacle wasn't in her DNA.

"Yes, of course, I will," she said, and the entire place erupted with deafening cheers.

Grabbing the remote, I muted the television as they kissed and sat there staring as they cut to commercial

My head slowly turned to look at Kai as he looked at me.

"I'm going to kill him," Kai and I said together.

Raine

Chapter 32

Raine

I was beyond baffled and so angry that I couldn't even form words as I stomped around backstage. I stared at the fancy ring on my finger, terrified to even ask how much it cost because it was definitely more than my house.

I stopped pacing long enough to get a deep breath in, but it didn't stop the shaking. Oh my god, if Kai saw that...I cringed, knowing exactly what he would be like when he found out, even if he didn't see it. I'd be lucky if I lived, let alone Jace. He was a dead man, and I could feel a panic attack threatening.

"Why?" I spun around and growled at Jace. He was leaning against the wall and looked way too relaxed. "Is this a game to you," I asked, and a couple of the stage crew glanced over.

"Come here," Jace said and took my arm. He smiled at everyone we passed, but I was too angry to keep up the act. Pushing through a metal door that led to a stairwell, he looked down before walking up to the next landing to make sure we were alone.

"Talk to me Jace. Help me understand what the hell just happened out there. I can't marry you," I said. It felt like I was going to combust. If I hadn't known better, I'd have said I was melting on the stage. Yes, his words were beautiful and moving, but I didn't even know if they were real. So much of what Jace did was staged. Was I just another act for him to gain sales?

"Why can't you marry me?" Jace crossed his arms, his face the same perfect arrogant mask it always was.

"For starters, we haven't had one discussion about this between us or all of us, and even if I wanted to hop on a plane and fly off into the sunset with you and never see Kai or Avro again, Kai would track us down and kill us both."

"I never thought that. Okay, maybe I did, but we'd bring Avro, but not anymore. I'm not trying to cut them out." Jace crossed his arms over his chest.

"Then what the hell is all this for? Is this just a way to one-up Kai and piss him off? Is that why you decided to bring me? Am I a pawn of drama for you to move around on a board? If it is Jace, so help me, god." I was gearing up for a real rant.

Jace placed his hands on my shoulders and made me look at him. "Stop it, Peaches. Seriously, you look like you're going to pass out."

"Can you blame me? You just proposed to me in front of however many thousands of people out there, and I had no warning at all."

Jace smirked, and it was too sexy for as angry as I was. "First, no one sees a proposal coming. At least if it's done right, they don't. That is kind of the point. Second, it's millions cause everyone watching in their homes just saw too."

My eyes narrowed into a glare, but my stomach flipped at the thought. "Oh god, I think I'm gonna be sick."

Stepping away from Jace, I grabbed the cold railing and closed my eyes. The jittering inside my body wasn't getting better, and it felt like my heart would jump out of my chest. My head swam a little, and I could feel the old panic attack wanting to rear its ugly head. No, I would not pass out. I was stronger than that now. Counting to ten very slowly, I concentrated on my breathing and the seconds between each breath. If Avro were here, he'd help calm me down. Oh no Avro. Wait did he know?

Jace touched my shoulders, but I shrugged him off and stepped away. "Don't touch me Jace." Turning around, I backed away from him until the cool of the concrete stairwell touched my back. "Did Avro know what you were planning?"

"No, no one did because if you want me to be honest, I hadn't planned it myself." My mouth dropped open, and I lifted my trembling hand to look at the ring.

"None of that was real? You made me cry and say yes to a proposal in front of however many people, and none of it was real?" I growled and grabbed the ring to yank it off my finger.

Jace reached out and stopped my hands, cupping them in his. "Stop. I mean it, Peaches. I want to tell you what's going on, but I refuse to talk to this version of you."

"Version of..." My nostrils flared, and I opened my mouth to give him another piece of my mind, but he pushed me up against the wall. The impact shocked me, but not as much as the kiss that followed. I should've been used to the demanding, lightheaded kisses that affected every part of my entire body. My lips moved like he had willed them while my hands gripped his tux jacket.

Every nerve ending was alive and on fire with his touch. I moaned as he deepened the kiss and pressed his body into mine. The air was stolen from my chest as he rubbed his trapped cock against my stomach.

"Fuck I want you right now," Jace growled, his lips still touching mine. "Don't ever take that ring off. I meant every word I said, and it stays on your finger as long as any part of you wanted to say yes. Do you understand?"

I nodded, not sure I could even speak.

"I do love you, Raine. I know it's soon, and I get all the what-ifs and other factors like Avro and, yes, even Kai, but I wouldn't have proposed if I didn't want to marry you."

Pushing himself away from me, he placed a hand on either side of my body, trapping me in place. It reminded me of the first night we met.

I took a shuddering breath and had to look away from his intense stare to think straight. "Then why Jace? Why now? Why like this? Why not tell even Avro? I don't understand."

Jace lowered his voice. "Allen got wind that I've been shopping around to replace him. I didn't like what he was planning and had been arranging for the band lately. Things have been tense. I expected not to see eye-to-eye all the time, but this was different. I wasn't comfortable with the things he wanted me to do." He looked over his shoulder to ensure no one could hear and whispered. "He wanted me to pretend I'd gotten drunk and got this other girl pregnant."

My mouth fell open. "He what? Who?"

"Doesn't matter who, I never let him get that far. I shut him down and told him to forget about it. He'd mapped out how we'd live together for four months, and then she'd pretend to lose the baby, and we'd part ways. It would make a big splash, but this is just too much. A few risqué photos are one thing. This shit he was coming up with was next level." Jace shook his head. "He said as long as it sold records, he didn't care, that everything was repairable, and I could play the part of a broken hearted, wannabe dad." He held out his hands. "I was livid. I mean, that is just...no. Not just for me, it makes a complete mockery of all those who have lost a child. Fuck."

"Shit, I'm sorry. Why didn't you say anything?" I placed my hand on his chest, and his eyes softened.

"I don't lean. I deal. I fix things when they need to be fixed. That's who I am."

There was a whole lot of telling off I wanted to do, but one thing at a time. "So what does that have to do with tonight?"

"After speaking with the guys, we agreed I'd make a few calls and get someone else lined up. I don't know how he found out, but he threatened that if I left him, he'd dig up anything he could on you and release it publicly, making it impossible for us to be together. I know he'd do it too. I could see it in his eyes. I don't know when he turned the corner from having morals to none, but I wasn't following him down that street."

Jace rolled out his shoulder and walked in a circle as he took a few deep breaths. It was easy to see how this was getting to him, and I couldn't blame him. This had to be picking at old memories of his family.

"I decided on the plane, which is why I never spoke to anyone. Besides, even if I had thought of this before leaving, Avro is already dealing with enough. Kai would never have let you get on the plane, and I was unsure what you'd do."

"Son of a bitch. I can't believe Allen did all of this." I groaned, annoyed with myself for not talking to Jace about my gut feeling at the concert. "He was questioning me and promised to find out if I was a gold digger at your concert. Said if I was, he'd ruin me."

Jace glared, and I swallowed hard. "Why didn't you tell me? I asked if he threatened you, and you said no."

I shrugged. "Honestly, I figured you'd blow a gasket. Then he'd have all the ammunition to want me out, make you look bad, or both. I hoped it was better to let the heat die down and have it blow over. Maybe he would end up excited about us. I should've said something, but I thought I was protecting you."

"Guys like Allen don't blow over, not unless you beat them with a big stick first."

"I see that now."

"Anyway, I decided to get ahead of him and his plans. I fired him just before they announced the award winner. Now if he digs up shit, he will look like a petty, bitter ex-employee that just wants to stir up dirt. The millions that were watching will have our back. They will crush him. Having fans has its difficulties, but in a situation like this, there is no one better to have at your back than millions devoted to you."

"But this is a gimmick. Won't your fans just see through what you've done if Allen does do something?"

Jace stood up straight but cupped my chin. "I didn't have time to prep anyone, and yes, this was much faster than I would've done if given the option, but it's not a gimmick. You and what we have are not a joke to me, Raine. I'd be honored if you married me, and I mean that. It's not just placating or pretty words. Avro has always been part of my heart, and now you are as well, and I'm not letting that go. Not for Kai, and definitely not for fucking Allen."

It was not lost on me that he used my name, not Peaches. Butterflies took flight in my stomach, and I tried to picture myself as Mrs. Everly. I smiled and wanted to go all mushy. I mean, who wouldn't? But there were other people in the relationship to consider and there was a gnawing of guilt that was marring the happiness.

"Look, the thing is that no matter what I said out there, we can't get married for any reason without talking to Avro and Kai. We can play it up for the media if you want, but they would be crushed. Not only do I not want to do that to them, but if I'm getting married, I want all of you to be involved," I said.

Jace stepped back and rubbed at his chin. He looked so serious with the furrowed brow and intense stare.

"You're right, I feel the same, but I'm just trying to figure out how to play this."

I grabbed his hands, and they felt so hot compared to mine.

"We don't need to figure it all out now. We can talk about it on the plane and then speak to the guys when we get back. As for right now, we'll go out there and pretend all is normal. What I'm saying is, you don't need to fix it all tonight."

"You're amazing, and I know why Avro fell so hard and why Kai has never stopped. I wasn't certain I wanted anything in my life to change, but you're worth every second of it."

I couldn't stop the blush from spreading. "I can't believe the first time you told me you loved me was on national television." He smirked.

"You always remember your firsts. There is no way you'll ever forget that," he said, tipping my head up and dropping his mouth to nip at my lower lip. "I wish I didn't have one more award to wait for because I've been dying to get you out of this dress all night."

"Now, if it were Kai, he'd have just done it in front of everyone." I teased and loved that, for once, I was getting to poke at him.

Jace's lip curved up. "Don't tempt me 'cause I'm all for it. You must know by now that I love when people watch. Let them drool. Let them hate. I don't fucking care. It all turns me on." Turning my head to the side, he kissed my jumping pulse. "Maybe I should. I'm not sure how I will top that first award speech, and that would definitely do it." He nipped at the sensitive skin, and I shuddered in his hold. "What do you think, Peaches? You want to be my naughty girl and let me fuck you on stage?"

"No amount of begging or pretty words is going to make that happen," I said and then sucked in a sharp breath as his hand easily slipped between the high cut split in the dress, his fingers sliding between my thighs. "Even if you proposed again, I wouldn't do it," I panted as his finger rubbed little circles, teasing me.

"I do love a challenge, Peaches, but you're right. We shouldn't get arrested. At least not tonight. We need to spread out the firsts." Moaning, my hands gripped his shoulders as his finger pushed into me. "Such a good girl not wearing any underwear." Jace sank his finger deeper, and my hands gripped the material of his jacket into my fist. I couldn't even care that it would wrinkle the material.

"We shouldn't be doing this," I said. "What if someone sees us?"

"Then they're going to get a show 'cause I'm not waiting any longer to be inside this sweet pussy of yours. Unzip my cock and pull it out," Jace ordered, his finger never stopping the teasing assault driving me crazy.

"Jace, I don't...."

He stopped any complaint as his lips crashed down on mine, and his finger pressed as deep as it could go. I turned into a panting mess as he added a second finger and swallowed my moans.

"Do it, Peaches, unzip my cock. I know you want it. I will keep you in this fucking stairwell until I get to celebrate with my new fiancé." He smiled. "I'll miss the rest of the awards if I have to, and then I'll tell the media why."

"Are you blackmailing your new fiancé already," I asked, sucking in a ragged breath. He knew exactly what to do to push me toward that sweet bliss and hold off just enough that I couldn't quite get there.

"Call it gentle persuasion."

"This is insane." It might have been, but my hands released the tight hold on the jacket to slide down his body. I already knew he was going commando, it was the deal he talked me into making before we left the hotel, and there was no way he could've walked back out there now. His pants were tented, making it hard to get the zipper down.

I didn't have to reach inside once they were unzipped. That was all the encouragement his cock needed to spring free. I wrapped my hand around that silky, hard length, and Jace groaned.

"Fuck I love it when you touch me, Peaches." My thumb ran over the tip and took the droplets of precum to play with the ring. God, I loved the feel of it. I really wanted all the guys to get one. "Yeah, just like that, fuck, that feels good."

Jace pushed harder into my palm as he pressed me up against the wall. My eyes closed as he slowly fucked my hand until I was begging for more.

"Please Jace."

"Please what, Peaches?" His lips grazed my ear. "You want me to fuck you right here? Spread this tight pussy open and make you cum all over me?" I shivered and moaned. "You're my good girl, aren't you?" I nodded. "Are you going to let me fuck you right now? Say it, Peaches, tell me you want me."

"Yes, I...oh God," I moaned as his fingers picked up the pace.

"What was that, Peaches? I didn't quite catch what you said." I would've told off the arrogant, smirking jerk if I could think straight, but I'd been reduced to nothing more than the feel of his fingers and the need coursing through my body.

"Yes, I want you to fuck me," I blurted out, the words running together. I expected him to make me repeat it, but he pulled his fingers out, and I couldn't stop the excited trembling as he sucked the fingers into his mouth. Everything he did was precise and with intent, and I couldn't look away.

"Gimmie your leg," he said, tapping the one with the slit. I lifted my leg, and his hot hand gripping my thigh made me moan in anticipation. "Move the dress off to the side." Jace's voice dropped, the words coming out like a growl.

My already racing heart tripled in time as I pulled the shimmery material away. I could hear someone talking and getting close to the stairwell door, but if Jace heard, he didn't care. Stepping forward, he teased me for just a second before thrusting in with a groan that vibrated through my body. I buried my face in the crook of his neck and pressed my lips together to keep from yelling out.

As the voice got closer, I realized someone was talking on the phone, and then the door opened. Jace looked over his shoulder, his already dark and intense expression turning into a snarl.

"Get the fuck out, now," he commanded, and I shivered at the tone. I was quickly learning to love this side of him. I couldn't see the person for Jace's body, but the door immediately closed. He turned his heated stare back to me. "Wrap your arms around my neck and hold on, 'cause I'm not holding back." I moaned as I did what he asked. "Fuck I love it when you squeeze my cock like that."

His mouth and the things he said always made me so hot. I was already so close to the edge that it wouldn't take much to push me over. I locked my arms around his neck as he lifted me just enough that my toe was almost not touching the floor. His deep thrusts stole my breath away as I clung tighter to him.

"Fuck, you're always so tight and wet. I can't get enough of you," Jace said. My ass was already pressed into the wall as hard as it could go, and yet Jace was fucking me like he could push me right through the concrete. My body was a quaking disaster of emotions and sensations, quickly pushing me to the peak.

"You gonna cum on me, Peaches? You going to soak my cock and mark me as yours?" I couldn't answer. No words would form, no matter how many times I tried. Jace growled as his hips pounded into me. "Fuck yes, Peaches."

I could only moan as I rode his cock, my body tightening like a spring. I was ready to burst and wanted to scream, but I bit my lip instead.

"I will take my time with you when we get back to the hotel. I want to feast on your sweet pussy until you can't take anymore and then fuck you all over again. You ignite a fire in me, Peaches, and if I don't cum right now, I might burn up and take you with me."

I bit down on his collar and moaned as his pace quickened. His piercing was rubbing me in just the right spot, and with a smothered yell, I came hard. My body arched into his as my arms tightened, and I shuddered with pleasure.

"That's it, Peaches, such a good girl cumming all over my cock. Oh, fuck yes," Jace groaned, his body tensing in my hold, and then I felt him cumming inside me. Something about that sensation always set off smaller climaxes, and the wave I was riding kept going until Jace fell still. He was breathing hard, and I wanted to do it again and not have to head back to our seats.

"I better go get cleaned up," I said as Jace slowly slipped from my body and let my leg drop to the floor.

He smiled wide and stuffed his cock back into his pants. "Oh, no, you're not."

"What? But..."

"I don't care, Peaches. I'm covered in your cum for the rest of the night. So you can sit in mine, besides what you eat right now."

He ran his finger up the inside of my leg and held his finger out to me. His brow cocked, and I opened my mouth, sucking his finger clean. He did it a few more times before the corner of his mouth pulled up in a lopsided grin that showed off the dimple you didn't often see.

"There, that's as clean as you'll get until tonight." He adjusted my dress until it was once more in place.

"You're terrible," I said, shaking my head at him, which only made Jace laugh.

"Maybe, but you love it, and I can't wait to see you out there squirming as everyone stares at you, and you're not sure if it's because you were backstage getting fucked or because you just got engaged."

I glared at him and thought every swear word I could think of, but before I could mouth off, he dropped his lips to mine and kissed me with so much tenderness that it was as breathtaking as when he was demanding.

"I love you, Peaches. I'm proud to have you on my arm tonight." Jace stepped back and held out his arm like a perfect gentleman. There were so many layers to him that my head swam, and my emotions turned inside out.

I put my hand on his arm to see the stunning ring with what looked like a million little diamonds surrounding the large emerald-cut stone. "You're really sure about this? I don't want to be the girl that was proposed to because you were forced to do it."

"I've done many things, Raine, but I wouldn't lie about wanting this. I watched as my mother was beaten down emotionally and physically before her beautiful life was stolen for good. What that taught me, what I want, is a chance at a happy ending, whatever that looks like. You helped complete what was missing in me. Avro knew it from the first moment he met you, and he's been prepping us both for this moment." Taking my hand, he linked our fingers together. "Like keys to my soul, you and Avro hold them all," he softly sang before kissing my hand.

"I love you too, Jace," I said, my body melting at his smile.

Raine

Chapter 33

R aine

Breathing fast as I held the sheets to my chest, I sat up in bed. It was always the same when the nightmares hit. The attack, running down the alley, the pain and fear mixed with the stench of their bodies and the couch, all in vivid detail.

I closed my eyes and took a deep breath as I forced the old images down. I didn't know why they were still creeping up. It was so long ago, and now that Kai and I were in a different place, I thought they would go away for good.

Jace was sound asleep, his two awards sitting on the nightstand, and I couldn't help but smile. He deserved them, and I was so proud as he walked up on stage to receive the second award of the night. We'd celebrated with the band for a few hours after everything wrapped up before coming back here, where Jace had a very loud conversation with Avro before we did anything else. I'd never heard Avro so angry, but he was livid and didn't let Jace get a word in before he hung up on us. If Avro was that mad, how the heck was Kai going to react?

He said we'd deal with it when we got home and weren't letting it ruin our night. It had taken a while, but once I decided Jace was right and let go, our time together was amazing. I'd made the mistake of thinking that Jace couldn't still be able to go that long, but he kept me panting for him for hours until I couldn't even open my eyes or lift my head. I glanced at the clock and realized I'd only been asleep for a couple of hours.

Swinging my legs out of bed, I pulled on his discarded dress shirt, did up a few buttons, and rolled the sleeves. It smelled like him and immediately calmed the last bit of nerves. I checked my phone to see if there were any answers to the texts I'd sent Kai, but all I saw was my side of the convo staring back at me. He was ignoring me. I tried calling, but he wouldn't pick up. I knew he needed space, but if he just talked to me for five minutes, I could set his mind at ease and explain in detail when we got back. Jace was strict about what was put into texts, so I couldn't just lay it all out there, but I expected an *I don't want to fucking talk to you right now*, at the very least.

I padded into the main part of the suite. I'd never seen anything as extravagant as this before and wasn't sure if I liked the lavishness. The sitting room alone could fit my entire house three times over. It was stunning, and there was no denying that, but I'd never lived like this and didn't see the need for all this unused space.

The kitchen was as large as the sitting room and held fancy appliances I doubted ever got used. Grabbing a glass, I hit the ice button on the fridge, and a few clunks later, I had perfectly round ice balls. Holding up the glass, I stared at the shape. Even the ice cubes couldn't be normal. What the heck? I filled the glass and took a long drink of water that felt good as it hit the back of my throat, reminding me that I'd been screaming half the night.

My stomach flipped with the same butterflies as last night, and my lips curved up as I thought about the jacuzzi and then back in bed afterward.

I sucked in a startled breath as I reached the bedroom door. It took a second to understand what was happening, but someone was dressed in all black with one of Jace's awards in their hands raised to strike Jace.

"Jace, look out!" Without thinking, I threw the glass I was holding. After years of throwing glasses and bottles across the bar to Avro, the glass sailed with accuracy and crashed into the side of the attacker's head.

"Fuck," came the deep growl of a man's voice as the glass hit him, and he slammed into the dresser.

"What the fuck?" Jace yelled, his eyes snapping open. He sat up straight in bed as I ran across the room and slammed my shoulder into the startled attacker like I was playing rugby. Whoever the guy was, he dropped the award as the second one on the nightstand toppled over. He held up his arms as I caught him in the knee with my foot, knocking it to the side at an odd angle.

"Fuck off, you bitch," he growled. He could call me whatever name he wanted. I wasn't letting some robber come in and hurt either of us. Gripping his injured knee, he stumbled to the side and tripped over his feet before smacking into the wall and hitting the ground with a thud.

The same kind of blinding anger was taking over as it had when I saw the girl all over Kai at the bar, and I balled my fists, ready to attack again, but Jace picked me up and turned me away from whoever it was.

I was gearing up to complain when I realized I was in nothing but his dress shirt. Jace had his phone in hand, already glowing with nine-one-one on the screen.

"Who the fuck are you, and what do you want?" Jace growled and held his arm out like he thought I would try something again as I stepped up beside him. The guy on the floor laughed and reached up, pulling down the hood. "Allen? What the hell are you doing?"

My eyes widened, and I stared up at Jace, who looked as shocked as I was. "He was trying to kill you. He had the award ready to smash over your head," I said, and Allen's eyes rolled in my direction.

"I should've done it long ago, you thankless prick," he drawled, his words a little slow like he'd been drinking or was on drugs. "And, wouldn't that be ironic? The girl that put an innocent man in jail ends up in jail for murder, but she is also innocent. Well, you're not innocent, but...you get my drift."

I pressed against Jace's arm. "Why are you doing this? I've never done anything to you."

Allen pointed at Jace. "Bullshit, this is all because of you!" I was shocked by the venom in his voice. "He ruined me because of you and the stupidity of wanting to keep you. I told him you'd bring him down, and you will. The fans will learn about your druggie parents and your lies that sent a man to jail, and they'll turn on you. Or how about your interactions with a known motorcycle club enforcer, the one you happened to put in jail?"

"How the hell...."

Jace grabbed my arm, his look telling me not to confirm or deny. I ground my teeth, livid that he dug into my past and tried to twist all the pain I had suffered into a weapon.

"All my clients have left. Jace wasn't happy just firing me, which was humiliating enough, but he had to ruin my career because of his need to have his playtime with you."

Did he think I was a pet? He acted as if Jace owned me with the way he spoke. It was disturbing, but then again, everything about this was disturbing.

"I didn't have anything to do with that. I have no idea why they left," Jace growled. "But, I'm kinda wishing I'd thought of that now."

"Lies! There is no such thing as coincidences," he yelled and began cursing as he tried to pull himself to his feet. I barely recognized him. He seemed so different from the put-together man I'd met initially. "I've lost everything, and it's all your fault."

Allen reached behind his back, and I sucked in a deep breath, not knowing if he was reaching for a gun or a phone. Jace, obviously thinking the same thing tossed his phone on the bed and jumped on Allen, sending the two men crashing to the floor.

I grabbed Jace's phone and realized an operator was already on the line.

"Hello, is anyone still there?"

"Hi, yes. I think he's going for a weapon. Jace and Allen are fighting."

"Go to the door, the officers are there," the woman on the line said, and I sprinted as fast as I could. Reaching the door, I whipped it open, and four officers walked in.

"This way," I said and ran back to the bedroom with the sound of their heavy boots following me. I went inside and got out of the way as they ran over to where Jace now had Allen pinned face down. A small gun no bigger than my palm was on the floor.

I covered my mouth as I realized this man was willing to kill Jace and me. There was lots of noise and chaos as they got him in cuffs, and all the old memories surfaced one at a time. I saw the officers coming to my house when my parents died and giving my statement over and over about my attack. I didn't notice I was crying until Jace wrapped his arms around me and held me tight.

"Shh, it's going to be okay. He's gone. It's just us. Allen is going to go away for a long time. My lawyers will make sure of it."

"Why does this stuff keep happening? It seems like there is something else every time I turn around. He almost killed you, Jace. If I'd been any longer in the kitchen, he would've. I...oh my god." Wrapping my arms around him, I let out the pent-up emotion, my body trembling as the tears fell harder. Jace held me tight, and for the first time, I really felt the connection between us.

Even last night, with everything that had happened and the wild aftermath of the awards show, it was right now, in this quiet moment, that I felt his kind heart and his love for me.

"I can't answer the why, but maybe it's because we all have crazy shit and terrible pasts that we understand one another so well," Jace said, and as I leaned back to look up at him, he wiped away the tears on my face with his thumbs. "Thank you for saving me," he said, laying his lips against my forehead.

"There was no way I was letting him hit you with that thing." I shuddered at the thought.

"Well, I hope you're prepared to save me again," Jace said, and my eyebrows drew together. "We still have to deal with Kai and Avro."

Laying my head against his chest, I groaned. That was one conversation I was not looking forward to having. No matter how we explained it, he would want to shoot first and ask questions later.

Kaivan

I stomped from one end of Avro and Jace's house to the other so many times that there should've been a groove in the tile floor. I needed to sleep, but hadn't been able too all night. Every time I closed my eyes all I could see was Jace down on one knee and Raine agreeing to marry him. It was my worst nightmare coming true before my eyes. I knew I couldn't trust him and I almost had.

The fact that Avro wasn't bitching about my boots screamed what a foul mood I was in. The moment I stopped moving, all I could think about were the different ways I wanted to kill Jace, and there were many. The current fantasy was me cutting him up and turning him into a human shish kebab that I could lower into the water for the sharks.

"They're here," Avro called down the hall where I'd just turned around, and I marched back, my muscles twitching and hands flexing to wrap around his throat.

I rounded the corner as they stepped through the door, and the first thing my eyes landed on was the rock that looked like an ice cube on Raine's finger. It took every ounce of self-control I had not to leap over Raine and onto the man closing the door behind them.

"I fucking warned you!" I yelled, and Raine stepped back. I stopped moving at the terrified look in her eyes. How times have changed. I wanted that look not so long ago, but now it hurt my heart. I opted to point at Jace instead of getting any closer. "I told you if you tried to take her away, I'd destroy you. I thought we came to an understanding. I never wanted to have to use the information, but I fucking will."

"What is he talking about," Raine asked and looked between us.

"What you think is going on is not what happened, Kai, and I'll explain everything if you give me a minute before you try to kill me." Jace looked down at Raine. "Kai and I agreed not to try and pull you in any one direction. We each have dirt on the other that we'd prefer not be shared with the world and have been using it as collateral."

"That's just a fancy way of saying you're blackmailing one another," she said and crossed her arms over her chest. "And here I thought you were actually learning to get along."

"So did I, but it looks like I'm going to fucking need that information after all," I growled.

"Slow your fucking roll, Kai, you don't have the slightest clue what happened, and I'm not trying to pull her away from you or Avro. That's the last thing I'm doing."

"You're fucking liar," I growled, marching around Raine. I gripped Jace by the hoodie he was wearing. "It's been what you were pushing for from the first moment I met you."

"I'm pretty fucking sure I'm not the one that stormed into my home and tore it up and waved a gun around threatening to kill you, or have you forgotten that you almost shot us all?" Jace yelled, and I hated the reminder of how close the gun had come to going off and taking Raine forever.

"Now, get your fucking hands off of me," Jace growled but continued to hold his hands up and didn't touch me.

"What's this bullshit? Fight me, you asshole," I said. Jace stood his ground but didn't touch me, and my heart raced faster.

Raine shoved her arms between us, and I snarled at her, my anger shifting and dividing as it rose like an inferno and then tumbled in on itself, only to reform again.

"You agreed to marry him? How could you do that?" My world was narrowing in as I stared down at her. So many years of love and pain were welling up inside of me, and I couldn't think straight looking into her big blue eyes. "After everything we've shared, how could you just decide to say fuck it and turn your back on me? How could you leave and never come back?"

"Whoa! What are you talking about? I'm not turning my back on you. Kai, I'm right here. I came back," Raine said, her eyes searching my face.

"Yeah Kai, we are standing here in front of you on time, exactly when we said we'd be back," Jace said, and the sound of his voice was grating on my nerves.

"Stay out of this. This is all your fault." It was a good thing that Avro said I had to leave all weapons outside because if I had my gun, there was a good chance I would've shot Jace. The image of him bleeding out was so vivid in my mind that my fists tightened until they cracked, and still, he didn't look away or move. "You think you're so fucking smart, don't you?"

"Kai, let Jace go. You don't know what's going on. Let him explain what happened."

"Why, so you can pack a bag and fuck off to wherever you want? So you can have me tossed in prison again. That's what you want, right? You want me out of your life for good. You want to pack a bag and run off to your sister's."

Raine shook her head. "Kai...I don't have a sister. What is happening right now?"

I pushed away from Jace to give Raine my full attention. I pointed my thumb at Jace. "It's pretty obvious who you've decided to choose. I knew this would happen. I knew he'd get to you with his fancy plane and concerts around the world. That you'd be swayed by the five-star restaurants and decide you'd rather not stay at the club-house and with me."

"No, of course not. I don't care about money or fancy things. You know that about me. Do you really think I'm that shallow? And what club are we talking about?"

"I knew it, I knew you'd decide to leave me alone for however long without checking on me, and now you come back and expect me to forgive you." I snorted in disgust. "Now you have the cost of everything I own on your finger."

I stomped away from them, needing to put space between us before I did something I'd regret or that landed me in jail. My head was pounding, and a sharp pain was throbbing behind my eye. I couldn't show weakness. You never showed weakness to your enemies. I whipped around to glare at the three sets of eyes trying to stare me down. They were trying to corner me. They'd been waiting for this moment to attack me.

Raine took a step toward me. "Kai...are you okay? I'm not sure what's happening, but you're not making sense," she said. She kept walking in my direction, and I backed away like her hands were poison.

"So, you're saying we're done?"

"What? No. Of course not. What is going on with you? Kai, you're really worrying me right now." Reaching out, Raine laid her hand on my chest, and her brow pulled together. "I love you. I don't want to leave you. Do you hear me?"

"Don't look at me like that." I stepped away from her until her hand fell away. "Your eyes are all full of concern like you fucking care about me. Lies on your tongue that you spill so easily."

"Kai, seriously, what the fuck is going on," Jace asked, his worried voice just as grating as his cocky one. Really him speaking or breathing at all. As I looked at him, my head started to spin.

"I warned you not to divide us. I promised you that I didn't care who crashed and burned. Now she's dead."

"Who's dead? Kai, are you okay," Avro asked and stepped up to my side. "You're really not making much sense. Come sit down. You're all sweaty like you're going to pass out."

"Don't touch me," I jerked away from Avro, my mind for just a moment seeing Red's hand on my bicep. I shook my head to erase the image. What was happening? My head was light, yet my limbs were so heavy it was an effort to point at them.

"Why are all of you looking at me like that? I'm fine. It's all of you that are the problem. I knew this was all a mistake. You can't go into that area without getting hurt, and now the three of us are here together. I had to kill him. It could never work" I stumbled sideways away from them, planning to leave out the back door and never return.

"Kai, stop this." Raine was walking toward me, holding out her hands, but when she touched me, it felt like I'd been burnt, and I jerked away. My mind was clouded with overlapping images, and I ran my hand through my hair, trying to decipher what was real and what wasn't as they merged.

"I said, don't touch me," I grabbed at the door jam to the kitchen, but when I took a step, I tripped on something and landed heavily against the wall. Of course, they took advantage of my weakened position, and all three of them descended on me.

"Don't touch me, no, don't touch me...I'll kill you," I said, or at least I think I said it, but I didn't feel my mouth moving. The pounding in my head worsened as I slid down the cool surface to the floor.

"I said...stop touching me. Stop hurting me, please. No, I don't want to go," I said, and it all went dark.

Raine

Chapter 34

R aine
    I was waiting outside the backdoor for Roach to arrive. Something was going on with Kai, but I didn't know if he could go to a hospital. The worry was eating me alive.

"Hey, are you okay," Avro asked as he stepped outside and wrapped his arm around my shoulders. I leaned into his warm body and shook my head no.

"I'm scared. I expected the anger, but it was like he was talking to someone else part of the time or multiple people...shit Avro, what if something is really wrong with him? I just found him. I can't lose him all over again. I know you two don't like him, but...."

"Shhh, stop. First, you're not going to lose him. Kai is a tough SOB. Second I don't hate him. We actually got along well until the proposal, but that's beside the point." He sighed as he kissed the top of my head. "There is no point stressing or worrying until we know more."

I wished I could be as optimistic as Avro, so many strange and terrible things had happened already. For Kai to come back into my life and, then something might be wrong with him...I couldn't even let myself go there. I wanted to fall to my knees and beg whoever would listen to help him.

"I hope you're right," I said as a black truck pulled into the back lane and parked in the driveway. Two men got out. The driver I recognized, but I didn't know the second man. Roach opened the back door and then walked over.

"Hi, thanks for coming," I said. "I just didn't know who else to call."

"You did the right thing. We have a club doctor who has all the best equipment needed to make sure Snake is okay," the man I didn't know said. He held out his hand, which was as large as my face. "Nice to meet you finally, Raine. My name is Mannix. I have heard a lot about you." I shook his outstretched hand.

"I'm sure not all of it has been nice," I said, and he smirked but didn't confirm or deny it.

"Nice to meet you. I'm Avro." Avro held out his hand for Mannix to shake next.

"So what happened," Roach asked, crossing his arms over his chest. I didn't like the way he was staring at me. It felt like he was blaming me for this happening to Kai. I already held enough blame in my heart. I didn't need this.

"I don't know. One minute he seemed fine but angry. The next, he was arguing, but it felt like he wasn't really talking to us, and then he slowly collapsed to the ground. His pulse was racing, and he was clammy to touch. We got him to the couch and covered him up, then I called you immediately. He's breathing, and his pulse has slowed, but he hasn't woken up."

"Where is he," Mannix asked, and I tore my eyes away from Roach's hard stare.

"He's just inside in the living room," I pulled open the door and led the way to where Kai was lying on the couch, murmuring something while Jace sat in a chair watching him.

"Well shit, you're Jace Everly," Mannix said and smiled. "Nice to meet you." Jace stood, and the pleasantries started all over again.

I stood by the door out of the way, and Roach leaned down and whispered. "You had to know something like this would happen," he said.

I looked up at him. "Excuse me?"

"The very public proposal and you accepting. You had to know that it would send Kai into a tailspin. Why would you do that to him?"

Crossing my arms, I glared at Roach. "You have no right to ask me that. You also have no idea what's going on or why."

"You're right, I don't, but that man is my brother, blood or not, and this shit you have going on, making him play house with you and two other guys, is bullshit."

Roach walked away before I could say anything else, but I was seething mad. Why was it that he thought he got a say in our relationship?

I watched as Mannix and Roach picked Kai up, and my stomach churned to see him like this. Kai was so strong. I expected the anger and to see him fired up, but this was different. Had I pushed him too far? It wasn't like I set out to hurt him. I loved him with every fiber of my being.

"I want to come with you," I said as they approached the living room door.

"Not a chance," Roach said, and I was ready to punch him.

Mannix glared over his shoulder at Roach before turning his eyes on me. Mannix had a calming personality that reminded me a bit of

Avro, but where Avro wasn't commanding or liked to be in charge, Mannix's entire aura screamed that he was the man to talk to, and everyone listened.

"Even though Roach has terrible bedside manners, he is right. It's better if we take him to the club doctor alone, but I will personally call you the moment we know anything."

Avro placed his hands on my shoulders as if silently telling me to let it go. I nodded even though I wanted to argue until I was blue in the face. But this wasn't about me. This was about Kai and a doctor seeing him as quickly as possible.

"Thank you," I said, and Roach rolled his eyes.

"Don't do that," I growled at him.

"I said what I said, and I stand by every word. The reason Kai is like this is because of you," Roach said.

"Roach, knock it off," Mannix ordered. "I will call you, but we need to get going." They walked out the back door, and we watched as Kai was loaded into the truck, and they drove away.

Stepping away from Avro, I began to pace, unable to sit still. "So, I take it Jace filled you in?"

"Yes, I'm sorry I blew up and didn't listen last night. I think I'm part of the reason Kai is so agitated." I turned to look at him, and he ran his hand through his hair. "We were both here watching the awards when the proposal happened. We were understandably shocked, hurt, and pissed. We stayed up all night talking and arguing, and then I had the blow-up phone call with Jace, and I think we fed off each other's anxiety. Not a great combo."

"Shit," I moaned. "I should've kept calling until he picked up." I rubbed my face. This whole thinking about so many people at once was harder than it looked. I turned to Jace, who was staring out the window. "You've been awfully quiet. What are you thinking?"

"I don't know. It's been an intense forty-eight hours. I was threatened, I proposed, was almost killed in my sleep, and now this.

I'm going to go play and hopefully pump out a new number-one song." He faked a half-hearted smile. Jace was doing that closed-off thing, and I wanted to hit everyone and scream. I might still scream just because it would make me feel better.

Jace stopped walking when he reached me. "I'm sorry about Kai, I may not like him, but I don't want to see him in a bad way either, you know?"

I nodded. "I know, and I know this will blow over when he understands why you did it and that we're not just making plans without him." Jace looked down to the ground and then back up into my eyes. The look gripped my heart and twisted. His face wasn't covered with the arrogant mask, and the sadness laid bare was trying to break the last piece of my heart that was already fracturing.

"Technically, with Allen going to jail, we don't have to get married or pretend to be engaged if you don't want to. If this is going to cause a huge issue with Kai, then we can figure out a way to spin it," he said.

"I wasn't planning on backing out of the agreement we discussed last night. Is that what you want?"

Jace raised one cocky eyebrow. "You already know the answer to that question. I've told you how I feel and what I want. Once you decide, let me know." Jace sauntered away, his hands stuffed in his pockets, and Avro and I were left staring at one another.

"What the fuck?" I resumed my pacing. "Why can't things just be calm? I don't understand why my life is like a hurricane. It goes out to sea, then comes back into shore to destroy everything, then swirls away only to do it all over again."

Avro shrugged. "I don't have any answers to that. I'm sorry, but I have an idea that might help ease the tension and get you out of the house while we wait to hear about Kai."

"What's that," I asked as I walked past where he was leaning against the wall.

"Let's go pack some of your things and bring them over. I know you still had reservations about moving in full-time, but—"

I held up my hand and cut Avro off. "No, let's do it. I need the distraction, or I'm going to go crazy waiting to hear about Kai," I said as the sound of the piano drifted down the stairs. "It seems we all need a distraction."

Avro grabbed his keys, and although the drive to my house was quiet, it felt good to get out, and it felt even better to be around Avro, who'd always been the buoy in stormy waters I clung to.

Pulling up, I stared at my postage stamp house and knew this was the right decision. This place never felt like home. It was a pit-stop, a place to hover while I tried to get my shit together. So much had happened in a very short time, but I'd learned that I was stronger than I gave myself credit for. I was more adventurous than I ever thought, and I had enough love in my heart for three of the best people I'd ever met. I loved them all and would protect them fiercely.

Kai needed to be okay, and I would find a way to make him see that public engagement or not—he was my heart. I loved Avro and Jace, but I wouldn't do anything without Kai involved in the decision. We were two souls destined and fused together long ago.

We walked into the small living room, and I quickly surveyed the furniture purchased at thrift stores or garage sales. None of it was anything I wanted to keep.

Avro's fingers trailed down my arm as he passed, but before he could get far, I pulled on his hand and brought him to a halt. "Why didn't you want to tell me about your surgery?"

Avro's gaze went from shocked to annoyed. "Jace can't keep his mouth shut."

"Don't get angry with him. He told me something you should've." Avro ran his hand through his hair and looked away from my eyes. When he didn't say anything, I knew I would have to poke at him. "Start by telling me how your appointment went yesterday?"

He shrugged and tugged my hand so we could sit down on the couch. "Surgery is set to happen in two weeks. I already took care of the paperwork yesterday to have you come back to Eclipse and explained that your family emergency was a false alarm."

"That's it, business as usual?" I curled up on the couch, leaning my elbow on the back as I stared at the side of his face.

"I just want everything to be ready, and I knew you'd want to head back to work. Look, I didn't say anything because I hate talking about it. I'm going to be useless for months. Just a bum sitting around at home, feeling sorry for myself." Avro rubbed at his eyes. "I know, it's not true, but I won't be able to do even the simplest things easily, things we all take for granted. Like how awkward it is to sit on a toilet and wipe your butt." He smirked, making me smile. "Or doing laundry, making a meal, and taking a shower. Hell, even sex is a problem. I will be useless, and it's a horrible feeling."

Reaching out, I ran my hand through his soft hair. I really did love this raven color. It was so striking with his amber eyes. "Avro, you're never useless. Would you ever think that of anyone else that you saw on crutches, in a wheelchair, or anything else for that matter?"

"No, of course not," he said, his eyes had gone wide with the horrified expression.

"Then why are you placing these unrealistic expectations on yourself and thinking about yourself so negatively?" He pressed his face into my hand.

"I don't know. I'm not a great patient, I guess. I prefer to look after people than be looked after, and with this, I'm going to need help, and I'm so scared to fall back into the dark depression I had before. It's like this monster looming and waiting to strike when I'm at my weakest."

I scooted closer to him, and he turned his head to look at me, so I stole the opportunity to kiss his way too-tempting lips. Avro was so tender and sweet with everything he did, and I knew that if Kai had found me years ago before Avro had helped me trust again, then I wouldn't have been able to handle everything that happened since. Avro pushed me to find my strength and believe in myself. Breaking the kiss, I touched our foreheads together.

"That's not going to happen. Things are different this time. Now that Jace is rid of Allen, he's planning to be around more, and I'm here. You always let us lean on you, so it only seems fair that you lean on us. Besides, I'd look cute in an apron and nothing else."

Avro laughed, his eyes lighting up. "Now, that is definitely worth having a bad knee. I just hate that I've leaned on Jace so much over the years. For so many different things, it feels like it's all I do."

"So what. Do you realize how much Jace and I need and lean on you with things that have nothing to do with your knee or how well you can do doggie style?" Avro chuckled. "I mean think about it. Who is it that Jace calls whenever something is bothering him, when he's excited about news or needs advice? It's you. Who helped me feel safe around men and helped me open up to even having a relationship? That was also you. Who took me shopping for the perfect dress for last night? Who has given me countless pep talks, made me laugh, or anything you do just by being you. So you can't work for a few months, we will be fine. So you can't cook everything you want. It gives you time to look up more recipes you can try. Don't stress. We'll get through this together."

I ran my thumb down his cheek and then over his lips, which should be on a magazine cover.

"I get all that I do, but..." He sighed. "I'm scared and don't even want to say it out loud." He closed his eyes and took a deep breath that shook his whole body. "What if I never dance again?" He opened his eyes, and they were filled with so much worry. "I was lucky I healed as well as I did last time, and my knee is still falling apart. Dancing may seem like nothing to everyone else, but to me...to me, it's the lifeline to my sanity. If that's taken away, what do I have left?"

"I hate to sound like the positivity queen. Especially when I feel anything but and would be just as scared as you are right now if roles were reversed. But… what I do know is that you're Avro, which means that no matter what is thrown at you, you will find a way around it or will figure out a new passion to throw yourself into. I'm not saying it will be easy. I'm just saying you have so many options you can't dream of yet. Dancing may end up reserved for at home, but no matter what, you will be okay. I'm making it my mission."

I smiled and kissed his cheek, then the side of his neck, and his hand snaked around my waist.

"Is that so?"

"Oh, it's very so," I said, slipping my leg over his lap to straddle him. Avro pulled me as close as I could get to his body, the warmth he radiated instantly blanketing me. "But, no more not telling me important things like your knee."

Cupping my face, Avro licked and nipped along my lower lip until I opened for him. Just like the first time he kissed me, the tenderness and emotion behind the kiss wiped everything else away. For a few moments, the world was perfect with candy canes and gumdrops.

"I promise to tell you everything from now on," Avro said, breaking the kiss.

"Do you want to tell me what this dirt is that Kai and Jace have on one another?"

"Nooooo, how about we leave that for another day when we can all talk about it," Avro said, and I could agree with that. It made sense to have them tell me themselves.

"That seems fair enough, but I do want to know." He ran his hands through my hair, and I moaned. He had a magic touch.

"Good, because I suddenly have other things on my mind."

"Is that so? Like what?" I teased and wiggled in his lap. He drew in a sharp breath that ended with a groan.

"Like getting you out of these clothes. Might as well christen the house before you leave it." No one could pull off a sexier and more inviting grin than Avro.

"I think I could be talked into that."

Chapter 35

Avro

It felt like forever since I had Raine all to myself, and I wasn't wasting this opportunity. I was pretty sure that even if we told Raine about my uncle and what happened, she would find a way to move past it, but the worry wormed its way into my mind. If she left...no, I couldn't let that happen again.

Ever so slowly, I pulled down the zipper on the hoodie she was wearing. She loved these, and I didn't know how she wasn't always melting in the heat. I smiled as Jace's band T-shirt was revealed underneath. I couldn't have planned for their connection to be this strong if I tried.

Raine pulled the hoodie off her arms and tossed it aside before pulling the T-shirt over her head. A strangled groan tumbled from my mouth as I stared at the black lace bra.

"You're so sexy," I said, my thumbs playing over her nipples, already hard and calling to me. "I have no idea how I managed to wait so long to taste you. I craved to feel your touch every night."

"Truth?" I nodded, and a pink blush spread across her cheeks. I wanted to eat her up. She was so adorable and sexy. All wrapped up in this beautiful package. "I'd dreamed of kissing you for months," she whispered like that was the most intimate thing we'd shared to date. "Every time you arrived at work, my heart would beat faster. I worked hard to keep the feeling suppressed so you wouldn't notice me staring."

Nothing could wipe the smile off my face. "You have no idea how much I love hearing you say that. Not the suppressed part, of course."

"I still can't believe this is real," Raine said and slowly pushed herself to her feet.

"I'd always held out hope this was where we'd end up. I admit I hadn't been prepared for a few of the other surprises along the way," I said and stood, but the pain in my knee flared, and I grimaced.

Raine wrapped her arm around my waist. "You good?"

"Yeah, just moved too fast. I have to keep reminding myself to go slow. I'll be fine." Cupping her face, I smiled, and her eyes filled with mischief.

"I have an idea," Raine tugged at the bottom of my shirt, and I lifted my hands and arms so she could pull it off. "I'm going to take your jeans off, and I want you to lay down on the couch for me." Her smile was wicked and promised a lot more than a hot kiss. I was so ready for all of it.

"I will in a minute. I just want to look at you. You make my heart sing, Raine. I feel so complete having you and Jace. I can't believe I'm going to say this, but I really don't mind Kai either." I looked down at Raine's hands on my arms and let go of her face to look at the ring Jace had given her.

"It's beautiful, isn't it? I mean, it's massive, which scares the crap out of me, but I don't know how he got one so unique so quickly." Raine's eyes told me she'd already made up her mind, even if she hadn't realized it yet.

"So he didn't tell you?"

"Tell me what?"

"This is a family heirloom. He found it in a bank deposit box when his mom was killed. There was a note with it that said it was to go to him, her eldest son if anything ever happened to her. It was his great, great grandmother's ring, and with each generation, something was added." Raine's mouth dropped open as she looked at the ring again. "All true, I swear. When I first saw this ring, it was just the emerald cut center, with two little side diamonds. Now it has the soft blue stones and a new ring of diamonds around it. He had someone put that together for you."

"For me?"

I laughed hard. "You are the one wearing it."

Raine's cheeks flushed a bright red all over again. "I mean, he didn't have it done like this and was just waiting to give it to someone. Not that...that wouldn't be special, but...I'm totally botching this question."

"No, I know for a fact he hadn't changed it before, but how he had it done so quickly...well, that's a Jace question. Knowing Jace, he made friends with a jeweler at some point and called in a favor." I ran my thumb over her fingers. "I'm happy you said yes, and when Kai finds out, he may not be great with it, but he will understand."

"I'm not so sure about that," she said, her face falling. "You know I'm not marrying Jace unless you're all involved, right? He explained that to you?"

"Yes, and Kai will get it too, even if it takes a hot minute. I just have a feeling about it."

Raine smiled. "See, here you are again, cheering me up. Now for once, do as I tell you to and take your damn clothes off and lay down."

"Yes, ma'am. That is one order I will never decline." I stripped as fast as I could and stroked my cock as I stared at Raine taking her time to get undressed. It was sweet torture to watch her, yet I'd spend all day doing it if given the opportunity. "Fuck girl, I swear you make me so hard. Do you have any idea how many nights I went home and ached as I thought about having you?"

My eyes followed her as she bent over, pushing her sexy little underwear down her legs. "I don't know what I would have done if you broached the topic sooner, but I'm suddenly picturing really hot phone sex." I groaned, my cock throbbing in my hand. "Now lay down, or I'll put my clothes back on."

"Damn, you've been hanging around Jace too much," I teased as I eased myself onto the couch and laid down like she told me to.

"Are you complaining," Raine asked as her bra unclipped and fell to the floor.

"Fuck, no."

I expected her to straddle me, but instead, she turned around, and I groaned as I realized she was getting in position to sixty-nine.

"Oh fuck, yes," I said as her sweet pussy hovered above my mouth. Grabbing her hips, I pulled her down onto my face and loved Raine's immediate moans and whimpers.

"Yes Avro, it feels so good." I held her tighter, burying my tongue as deep as I could. I was addicted to her. My tongue feasted on her while her breathy moans were a feast for my ears.

I growled into her pussy as her hot mouth slid around my cock. The silky feeling of her lips and tongue swirling around my sensitive head made my hips thrust into her mouth to get deeper.

"Fuck Raine," I moaned loudly as she bobbed faster on my aching shaft. She cupped my balls and gently massaged them, driving me wild. I sucked her clit into my mouth like a piece of candy, and

Raine's cry of pleasure sent a shiver racing down my spine. Raine moaned and moved back and forth on my mouth as she pressed harder into me.

"God Avro, you're going to make me cum too fast...ah, oh fuck too late, I cumming," she yelled. I swirled my tongue on her clit and sucked harder until she was cumming in my mouth as she screamed my name. I was ravenous for more, and even as her hips bucked with the sensitivity of her orgasm, I held on tight and buried my face deeper.

"Ah! Oh, so not fair, you're too good." Raine said. I was a whore for praise, I could admit it, and I would have her craving my mouth on her pussy. When she laid her head down at night, I wanted my face to be who she pictured between her legs.

"Mmmm," I moaned as she sucked me back into her mouth. Her hand and mouth worked in perfect rhythm as she bobbed her head in time to the stroke of my tongue. We were entirely in sync, and as her body shuddered, I knew she was as close to her second orgasm as I was to cumming. I tried to push the desire down, but I was failing and felt the release pushing past my restraint.

Raine's body quivered as her sucking got faster and more desperate. I growled and bucked my hips up to meet her mouth. She rubbed my balls and then ran her finger along the sensitive skin to my ass. My legs spread further to give her more room, the pleasure of her exploring fingers driving me insane.

"You like that, huh? You want me to do this?" Raine asked and pressed harder on my back door. I groaned loudly as I sucked on her clit hard. "Fuck Avro! You have the best tongue," she said, and my pride swelled along with my cock.

"Cum for me, Raine, cum for me again, and I'll let go." Her hips started to rotate in quick circles. I followed and found the spot she wanted me to lick.

"Yes, oh, yes," the words tumbled from her mouth, even with my cock still in hers. Her body tensed as she sucked hard on my cock, and a wet finger pressed into my ass.

I couldn't hold back and yelled as I came, the first shot so intense it almost hurt, but in the most delicious way possible. With a final flick of my tongue, Raine came as well, and we were left moaning and panting as we drank each other down.

Raine collapsed on my body, her tongue lazily licking at my spent cock.

"Fuck I could eat you all day," I said, and I meant every word. I was tempted to see if I could make her cum a third time, but my knee was starting to throb.

I closed my eyes and gave her the same treatment, making sure every last bit of her release was licked up and earned a few sighs.

"I don't want to get up, but I guess we should get a few things packed," I said, and Raine nodded.

"If I could move."

I laughed as she moaned and slowly stood. She was always stunning, but her entire body was flushed, with her cheeks a bright red, and I loved that I put that look of pure satisfaction on her face. There was nothing more satisfying.

"On the bright side, we can always try another knee-safe position when we're done packing," I said, wanting to throw packing out the window and just fuck the rest of the day away. It seemed like a perfect stress killer.

"I could definitely be talked into that." The corner of Raine's mouth pulled up in a devious grin as she pulled on her underwear. "Shit, I wasn't even thinking. I don't have any boxes."

"That's okay. I'll get some. I know a place not far from here that sells them, and I need to go to the hardware store anyway. The faucets in the lower level bathroom are shot, and I need to get a new set," I said, slipping my T-shirt over my head. "Why don't you start organizing what you want to take and what to throw out?"

"I like that plan. Can you grab me a coffee when you're out?"

"Sure." I finished tying my sneakers and stood. I quickly used the washroom to clean up and then met Raine at her door. "I'll be about forty minutes, I think," I said and gave her a kiss. "I love you."

The smile that always lit up a room beamed up at me. I never wanted to let her go, but it was just the hardware store and coffee. I'd be back soon. Sighing, I kissed her again. "I love you too."

Snake

Chapter 36

K aivan

Bang. Bang. Bang.

The beer bottles exploded, and I covered my ears to block the sound, but after being out here for the last one hour and eleven minutes, I couldn't stop my ears from ringing. Father held out his gun to me. "That son, is how you shoot a gun."

"I already told you I don't want to shoot a gun. They kill people," I said, annoyance with this day seeping into my tone. I didn't see his hand coming, but I felt the crack as he smacked me across the face and knocked me to the ground.

"What did I tell you?"

I held my cheek, my eyes stinging, but I refused to cry. My father said that only women and pussies cried, and I wouldn't be either. I glared up at my father. I wanted to ride my bike or surf with my friends, but he told me

I needed to learn to be a man instead. What did shooting a gun have to do with being a man?

"Come on, get up. You're still a fucking terrible shot," he said. "Such an embarrassment."

My father's friends from the motorcycle club and their sons laughed as they drank off to the side. They were all older than I was. The youngest of the group was five years, six months, and nine days older than me. None of them wanted me to hang around, and I didn't like them either. They all wanted to be like their dads and be part of the motorcycle club. I had other interests that didn't involve riding around on a Harley and hanging out in a smoky clubhouse.

Mom hated that my father was always gone, and I'd heard them arguing when he was home about sweetbutts. I didn't know what they were until he dragged me to the club to hang out with the other kids for events like Tony's birthday. I quickly learned what they were and what they did when Tony's dad got a sweetbutt to suck his dick for his eighteenth birthday in front of all of us. Of course, my father smiled and said he'd do better for me on my eighteenth. Whatever that was supposed to mean.

I glanced over as they made jokes and laughed. I hated that they always came when my father dragged me out here into the middle of the swamp with the bugs, snakes, and other strange crap. We'd all take turns shooting empty bottles like it was the best thing ever, but I could think of at least ten things I wanted to do instead.

Pushing myself to my feet, I dusted off my hands on my jeans and took the gun that felt heavy compared to my plastic water ones. He pointed his hand toward the target of bottles set up on wooden stumps. For just a moment, I wondered what it would be like to turn the gun on him instead of the bottles. Would he treat me like a man, then?

"Now shoot, and try to hit something this time. The only thing that isn't safe from you is a barn wall," he said, then laughed with multiple voices echoing.

As I raised the gun to shoot the bottles, the stumps and swamp disappeared.

I blinked and stared down at my mom's body lying on the living room floor. I looked at my hand, but the gun was gone, and I dropped to my knees beside her.

The roar of a motorcycle was loud, and I could just make out a man on a bike outside. His laughter was almost as loud as the bike as he rode away into the dark.

"Mom, how can I help?"

"You, you killed me," she said, her voice wet, blood dripping from the corner of her mouth.

"No, no, it wasn't me." I pressed on the wound, but she batted my hands away and started to laugh. "Mom, stop it. I need to stop the bleeding."

"You're a killer, you've always been a killer, and it's what you will always be," she snarled as she pushed my hands away again. "I should've left you with your father years ago. Now look at me. It's all your fault."

Tears streamed from my eyes as I pushed myself away from her body. "It's not true, Mom, it's not true, don't say that," I cried, the tears making it impossible to see.

"You couldn't save yourself, just like you couldn't save Raine." I whipped my head from side to side to see who said that. "Your father was right. You destroy everything you touch."

"Who said that?" I pushed myself to my feet and glanced around the garage filled with boxes. It felt like I was in a crazy game of hide and seek.

"Oh, come now boy, you must recognize my voice. I was part of your life for five years. Five long terrible years where I had to put up with a useless sack of shit like you."

I marched down one long row of boxes and equipment that seemed to go on forever, but when I turned at the end, no one was there.

"Just admit it, Kaivan. Admit that you were never going to be able to

save Raine from me that night. You stayed home and let her take your beating for you."

"Shut the fuck up, that's not what happened," I yelled and pushed over some boxes in the direction of the voice. More laughing reached me, and the anger churning in my gut erupted. I slammed my shoulder from side to side and knocked the two stacks down until there were no tall objects to obscure my view.

Dave stood by the garage door without a shirt, zipper down on his dirty jeans, and a knife in hand. "She was always going to be mine that night, Kaivan. You sent her to me, and mmm, was she ever good. That sweet little virgin pussy."

Roaring, I ran at Dave, and he calmly walked inside the house with a smile as he slammed the door. Maniacal laughing was loud in my ears.

"What happened to Raine was all your fault. You have no one to blame but yourself," Dave said through the door as I beat my hands and feet off the metal until my knuckles bled. Breathing hard, I dropped to all fours, my eyes stinging with more tears.

"Don't cry, boy. Cryin' is for pussies," I looked up at the gruff voice and stared into Red's cold glare.

"What the fuck do you want?" I pushed myself to my feet, and he took a step back. "Last I checked, I was off limits to you."

He licked his lips. "Were you, though? Were you ever really off limits?"

"What the fuck are you talking about?" My hands clenched into fists as my gaze flicked to the two men hovering in the doorway.

"I have it under good authority that Mannix lied. You weren't already part of his gang when he came into the bathroom. Technically, he stole from me, not the other way around." Red ran his tongue over his teeth, accentuating the gap where a tooth was missing.

"Is that so? I don't know your source, but they don't know shit. You seem to have a recurring issue with that. Maybe you need a new informant." I would go to my grave telling that lie until it manifested into the *truth. There was no fucking way I'd ever let Red know that he had some-thing on Mannix or me.*

Red's nostrils flared, his eyes narrowing into slits. "You're full of shit and just as mouthy as the day you arrived. You haven't learned a thing."

"What I've learned is that you're not as big as you like to think you are. You've already lost control of the cigarettes, and I'm working on cell phones next. Soon you'll be nobody. Nothing but the raping piece of shit you are."

Red rubbed at his bottom lip and chuckled low like he was amused, but I knew he was seething inside. Controlling the cigarette import and export was massive. He'd taken a huge hit when I got the guards on my side. That had taken some work, but it was paying off.

"One of these days, you won't be so lucky, and I'll be there waiting," Red said, his eyes promising he wouldn't let this go.

A sharp pain stabbed me behind my eye, and I grabbed at my head. Opening my eyes, I shivered from head to toe as I stared down at Red, a mangled and bloody mess on the floor. My hand was shaking so hard it was hitting the side of my leg.

"Fuck, Kaivan, what the hell did you do? You said you wanted to rough him up a little," Steve, the guard said as he came in and looked down at the bloody corpse. "Give me the weapon, now."

Lifting my hand, I realized I was clenching a shank in my fist, once white, now a bright red. Steve held out his hand, and I dropped the blade into it.

"What the hell happened? I need an answer," he looked over his shoulder at the sound of a door closing and the echo of more guards coming.

"He...he...." I looked up at Steve. "He knocked me out, and when I came to, he was...um...it was self-defense," I managed to say, and Steve shook his head.

"Fuck, go on, get out of here. The cameras to the east wing are off, go

shower and leave your clothes in the garbage. I'll get rid of them. But, Snake, after this, we're even."

I glanced down at Red's still face, his pale skin glowing even against the white tile. His head turned in my direction, and I took a startled step back.

"You may have killed me, but you'll never be rid of me. Death sticks to you. I will forever cling to your mind," he said.

"Kai, get the hell out of here," Steve said.

"Did you see that?" I pointed at Red, whose head was perfectly still once more.

"No, they're almost here, go, now," he whispered, his voice harsh.

I took off and ran along the hallway he told me to take and tried to ignore the pain in my body and the humiliation in my soul. Stripping, I stuffed the bloody jumpsuit into the garbage and got in the shower, not caring that the water was ice cold.

With my eyes closed, the icy water pelted me in the face, and I let the tears I'd been holding back fall. Death did cling to me, and no one was safe around me. Everything I touched was corrupted or died. The Devil had marked me at birth to live and breathe, walking among souls already lost. I felt it. I wanted to deny it, to push it away, but eventually, everyone turned on you or died.

"Do it!" My eyes snapped open, and Raine was screaming at me. I stared at the gun in my hand pressed to her chest.

"No."

"Do it," she screamed again as tears streamed down her beautiful face. "I've wasted so much of my life being scared. I can't be that person again. So do it, 'cause I'm done. My heart was ripped from my chest in that warehouse. You might as well destroy my soul too."

I wanted to yell no, that I loved her, that I'd always loved her, but I stood there staring at her saying nothing, my mouth refusing to move. Each tear that slid down her cheek was like a knife to my chest.

"Do it," she whispered.

Bang

Raine stumbled back, her hands going to her chest as blood poured from her and soaked the front of her hoodie. I looked at the gun and then back up to her scared eyes.

"You...." Raine collapsed, and I dropped the gun and grabbed her body before she hit the floor.

"No, no, no. This is not happening. Help her," I yelled at Roach and the two other men in the room. "Why are you just standing there? Help her. Call 911, get me towels, do something." I smoothed back Raine's hair, her hand cool to the touch as I gripped it in mine. "No, Tink, please, it was an accident. I didn't mean to. Please help her," I pleaded again with those standing around, but still, no one moved. They just looked away.

"I love you, Tink. Please stay with me, don't go, don't leave me. Please, I'm sorry." Tears poured down my cheeks, and the pain of her fading eyes ripped out my heart as if she were using her hand.

"I...love...you," she said and then went still.

"No!" I wailed and gripped her lifeless body to my chest, rocking, unable to manage the pain.

"Please."

"What are you crying for, boy?" Red and my father squatted beside me as I held Raine tighter.

"Go away," I yelled at them.

"He still doesn't get it," my father told Red.

"Nope, he definitely doesn't."

"Get what?" Both sets of eyes turned in my direction.

"She was already dead, boy. The moment she met you, the reaper took her soul. Everything you touch is tainted. You're a stain on this earth, and you killed her."

"No, it's not true," I said, but everyone, including my mom, stood around nodding at me.

"Ah!" I screamed and grabbed the gun off the ground. I didn't hesitate as I put the barrel in my mouth.

Bang

My eyes snapped open as I gasped for breath. I didn't know where I was, but I grabbed for Raine, and she wasn't there. There was enough light coming in the window that I recognized my room. I struggled to remember what happened, but all I could see was her fading eyes and the blood all over my hands. What had I done?

I hadn't cried in years, but the tears streamed down my cheeks in relentless lines as I struggled to breathe against the growing pain in my chest. Grabbing the pillow she used when she slept here, I gripped it hard and buried my face in the fabric. I clung to it like I'd clung to her body as the sobs wracked me.

I heard the sound of boots and didn't even care who saw me. My life wasn't worth living if she was dead...if I took her life. I could still taste the metal of my gun in my mouth and would've reached for it if Roach hadn't appeared and gripped my face in his hands.

"Let go..." I pushed at him, but he held me harder. "I killed her. I killed my heart," I said, and he shook his head.

"No, you didn't. Look at me, bro. Raine is okay."

"What?"

"I said, Raine is alright. You didn't hurt her. The doc was here. He said you'll be fine. The stress and lack of sleep brought this on."

"I don't care about me. You promise she's alive?"

"Yes," Roach said, letting go of my face and groaning as his phone rang. He pulled it from his pocket, and I realized it was mine. "This guy never gives up. How do you put up with him?" He hit a button and sat the phone down.

"What? Who?"

"Avro. The guy keeps fucking calling," Roach said.

"Why?" I asked, pushing myself up in bed. Everything ached. Whatever I went through left me feeling like I ran a marathon and then did a round with Mike Tyson.

"I don't know. I didn't answer."

"But Avro never calls me," I said. "Give me my phone."

"The doc said that...."

"I don't fucking care what the doc said. Give me my phone," I growled.

"I don't get it, man. Why are you torturing yourself, allowing them to be in a relationship with you and Raine? I couldn't do it," I looked at the fifty missed calls and then up at Roach.

"I'd do anything for her. That's all there is to it. I'd survive longer without my beating heart than if you took her from me." Roach shook his head like he just couldn't understand. Of course, he couldn't. He'd never loved someone so much they made his blood sing. They became his world.

"Why didn't you answer any of these?"

"I had more important things to worry about, like what the fuck was wrong with you. Besides, Raine was pestering us to let them know how you were before we took you from their house. I may not have bothered to call when Mannix asked me to."

"Why?"

"She hurt you. She fucking deserved it. She can wait a little to find out what's wrong. It won't kill her."

"Fuck man, I swear if something is wrong," I mumbled. I was about to hit the voicemail and listen to the messages when it started to ring again.

"Avro?"

"Kai, thank God. She's gone, she's gone, something happened," he rambled, but I sat up straight and was on the move. Whatever was going on with me could fucking wait.

"Slow down. What do you mean she's gone? Raine took off again, like last time?" I grabbed my leather jacket off the door handle, not slowing my pace. I knew Roach was following, the sound of his boots heavy behind me.

"Fuck Kai. No, not like last time." He sounded like he was hyperventilating. The one thing I'd learned about Avro, he was pretty fucking chill. It was Jace and I that freaked out. To hear the terror in his voice had me gripping the phone tighter.

"Then what happened?"

"After you were taken away, Raine was really upset. I offered to come to her house and pack some of her stuff to keep her mind occupied. I went to get some supplies from the hardware store, and when I got back, she was gone."

"But not like last time?"

"Kai! No!" Avro yelled into the phone. I could hear Jace in the background telling him to take a breath, but his fear spiked my adrenaline, and my heart pounded against my ribs.

"Then how?"

"Give me the phone," Jace said, and there was swearing, but Jace came on the line. "Kai, she's been taken by someone. There were signs of a struggle, and her phone was smashed on the floor. The door was open when Avro got back, but who the fuck would want to take Raine? Is this because of me and the proposal? I just can't see a fan doing this."

I stopped dead as an ice-cold dread snaked down my spine. "No, it's Frank."

Snake

Chapter 37

LOST

1%   MC

SOULS

8:31PM

K aivan

Jace stood in the doorway when Roach, Wilder, and I pulled up. His body language seemed calm, but as his silver eyes found mine, I could tell he was on the same edge as me. I turned to Roach as we parked in front of the house, and before I could say a word, Wilder hopped out and jogged up to meet Jace. I'd never admit this out loud, but I felt better having Wilder along. My nerves were shot, and the tremors that started when I learned she was taken had only gotten worse over the last twenty-one minutes.

"Roach, go see if any of the neighbors saw anything," I said. It was probably a long shot. In this neighborhood, people kept their drapes drawn tight and never talked. Not wanting to get involved was a standard MO.

"What am I supposed to say? I'm your friendly neighborhood biker. Just checking in to see if you saw a girl being kidnapped?" I glared at him.

"Just say you're her cousin or something and that you were coming to help her move. I don't care what you say. Just see if they saw anything. If they have a door camera, I'll pay for the footage."

"Fine, whatever," he said, and I grabbed his arm before he could move.

"What the fuck is your problem?" I growled.

"Honestly?" I nodded. "Since the moment you found Raine, it's been nothing but stress and drama. You've been out of your mind, agitated in your skin, anger rolling off you in waves to the point that we're all terrified to go near you. This love or obsession, whatever it is the two of you have with those guys, is toxic as fuck for you. I'm worried you don't see it. I'm worried that without meaning to, Raine will drag you so far down the rabbit hole away from your sanity that there will be no coming back." He turned his eyes away from me and gripped the steering wheel hard.

"I will do whatever you want. I will help however you want 'cause, at the end of the day, you are my ride-or-die. I have some serious reservations that I haven't voiced to be supportive, but the way Mannix and I found you earlier...." Roach turned his head to stare at me again. "It scared the fuck out of me, and you know I don't scare easily."

"Earlier wasn't just Raine. It's been building for a while." I rubbed at the back of my neck. "All the shit, the old memories, the pain that I buried...that crap decided it was coming up faster than projectile vomit. The dream was...fucked. Point is, I get your concern, and coming from you, I respect it, but it's also not your call. So if you want to continue to be my ride-or-die, get the fuck out of the truck and stop wasting time. I love Raine, and if Dave and Frank have her...you saw what they will do to her. You good if that happens?"

"No. No, I'm not. You're right. Let's go," Roach said, hopping out. Getting out of the truck, I jogged toward the front door of Raine's small house.

I got Roach's concern. We'd been looking out for one another since he was arrested and tossed in the same block as the rest of the wild animals. When I saw him and Hollywood, I recognized myself —five years earlier when I was thrown to the wolves—in their terrified expressions. I immediately brought them in before anyone else could, and we'd become kill for one another tight. But he needed to get on board with what I chose to do with my life.

Raine may have laid down what she wanted, but I had the choice to be part of it or leave, and I chose to stay. If I was completely honest with myself, I didn't mind Jace and Avro in her life. They were like those sticky vines that just kept growing on you. The engagement was a crazy shock, and maybe seeing that brought on whatever the fuck that dream shit was, or maybe it had been building for years and would have happened no matter what.

Regardless, I felt clearer, and so much of the anger and jealousy I'd been carrying around like a weighted vest had fallen away. Now it was replaced with a paralyzing fear I was trying really fucking hard to ignore so I didn't lose every last marble left in my head.

I stepped inside the house as Wilder came down from upstairs.

"What can you tell me?"

"They're correct. She was taken. It was quick, so there was more than one person, or they subdued her somehow." Wilder bent over and picked up the smashed phone. "My guess is drugged. The guy left this upstairs on her pillow."

Wilder handed me an instant photo of Raine tied up and laying in the bed of a pickup truck with tape over her mouth and her hands and feet tied together. Anger so volatile burned in my veins. If they touched one hair on her head....

Flipping the picture over, I read the short note:

Payment for taking something important to me,
so I'm taking something important to you.
Stop looking, or more people you care about will end
up the same way.
JJ

She looked asleep, but I knew better. I handed the picture to Jace, and he growled. I knew exactly how he felt.

"How did you find this? We searched upstairs and didn't see anything," Jace asked, his eyes glued to the picture.

Wilder shrugged. "I looked."

Jace looked up at Wilder, and if I weren't so afraid for Raine, I would've laughed at his confused expression. I now knew what I looked like talking to Wilder.

Roach stepped into the doorway and blocked out the sun. "If someone saw something they aren't saying. Most didn't answer the door." I nodded.

The fear that started when I heard Avro's panicked voice was swirling around in my gut, and I had to push it down and lock it up tight. I could deal with the demons in my head later. For now, they needed to take a back fucking seat.

I glanced at Avro sitting on the couch, his head in his hands as he leaned forward on his knees. His eyes were trained on the floor, and he looked like he was caught between throwing up and having a panic attack.

"Hey, I need you to know before anything else that the proposal wasn't to take her away from you. I can tell you all about the why later, but I needed you to know that, and—"

I held up my hand to stop Jace. "I don't care. None of that is important right now." Jace nodded. "All that matters is getting her back and killing the fuckers that took her."

"Fair enough," Jace said.

"Both of you going to be good with that?"

"Killing them?" Jace asked. He looked at Avro, who lifted his head, and there was a conviction in his eyes that reminded me of the day he came to my house to tell me Raine was gone the first time.

"I don't care what happens to them," Avro said, and we locked stares as we shared an understanding. Whatever happened after we left this house was never to be spoken of to anyone. No cops, no other friends, no drunken nights out and rambling to others because you couldn't deal. It was 'lock it up tight and throw away the key' kind of shit.

I glanced around the small home that seemed extra tiny with the five of us in it and spotted her backpack sitting in the corner.

"Fuck," I growled. "I don't know how to find her."

"We'll track her, but we're going to need a lot more weapons," Wilder said, and I blinked in confusion.

"Her bag is sitting there. How do you propose I track her?" I pointed at the black backpack. "I only had one."

"A tracker? On Raine? Damn man, you're brave. If she found that out...," Jace said, and I glared at him. "What? I didn't say I was going to say anything, just that it's ballsy, but it explains how you found her so quickly."

"We will track her like normal." Wilder tilted his head as he looked at me. "With the other trackers."

"What other trackers?"

"The ones I put on her," he said matter-of-factly, and I wanted to kiss him for doing it and punch him for the same reason.

"You put more trackers on Raine?"

He nodded. "Yes, a bag is okay, but as you can see, it can get left behind. I slipped one into the sole of all her shoes."

Roach whistled. "That's smart. Fucked up, but smart."

"So why do we need more weapons?" I asked, ignoring Roach's shocked appreciation.

Wilder held his phone out to me, and I took it. The screen showed what looked like an overhead view of a really large farm. "What am I looking at?"

"That's where they took her. It's a property about an hour outside the city, but if you zoom in, you'll see the armed men. There is also a security gate with four watch towers. This must be where they take those they decide to keep long term," Wilder said.

"So, who are these guys, and why would they want Raine," Jace asked, and Avro spoke before I could answer.

"They're the fucking guys who attacked her years ago and sent Kai to prison. He's been hunting them down," Avro said. "My guess is you were getting a little too close to finding them, and they've taken her as collateral or punishment."

"Yes, that would be my assumption, as well," Wilder agreed.

"There had to be a camera in the house. We should've sat on it to see when Frank fucking returned." My hand clenched into a fist as I kicked myself.

"Let's go. We need to ride out," I said, and Wilder grabbed my arm and shook his head no. "Don't fucking shake your head at me. I'm going."

"No, you can't, at least not yet. You will be dead before you ever reach the gates. We need a plan and a lot more firepower. I have trusted you with all my questions, but this is my arena. Attacking impenetrable targets and staying alive is what I do best." Wilder let go of my arm. "If you want her alive, and you alive to be with her, then you need to listen to me."

I glanced around the room, and no one else was disagreeing. "Every second Raine's there...they could be doing anything to her," I growled at him, my heart hammering hard.

"True, but if you go alone or with just a few of us and no plan, the chance of success is still zero, but now we are dead and cannot help." His face was void of all emotion, just like it always was, and for once, I wished I could be like him. Not feeling this terror as it tried to choke me out would have been welcome.

"If it makes you feel better, I do not think they will kill her until tomorrow around mid-day."

I swallowed. "Why?"

"All the newer images on the laptop, the lighting is the same. It is as if they wait until the exact same time of day." My left hand shook and I squeezed it into a fist to keep my shit together. There was so many other things they could do to her in that amount of time. "We will get her back alive, is that not what is most important?"

He was right. I slammed the door on my fear so I didn't do something stupid. "Fine. What's the plan?"

LOST SOULS CLUBHOUSE - 2:04 AM

Kaivan

The five of us stood around a large map of the property as Wilder placed pieces from a Risk game on the paper. If the situation were different, I might have laughed at the man moving tiny game pieces around dressed in full camo. His face was painted, and Wilder was strapped with everything from knives to grenades.

I truly thought Avro and Jace would back out, but neither had wavered in their conviction, which earned them points in my 'They're not terrible' book.

Leaning over the table, I focused on my entry point as Wilder reviewed the plan for the last time.

"What the fuck?" Chase's voice echoed as he slammed the door open. Chase, Mannix, Beast, Tanner, and some of the other guys walked into the room and stared at us. "What the fuck are you doing?"

I pushed myself up straight and squared off with my Prez. He wasn't keeping me from going, and I was taking whatever weapons I wanted. I'd earned the right after all the blood, sweat, and hours I'd spent keeping this place safe.

Chase's eyes were narrowed as he glared at me. The muscle in his jaw was twitching as we squared off.

"Answer me, Snake. What the fuck do you think you're doing?" He turned his head to look at Jace and Avro, and even though he knew who they were, he didn't comment.

"I'm going to save Raine. She's been taken, and we're going to get her back. You can't stop me from going, and I'm taking what I need for weapons. If you try to stop me, Chase, you can consider this my official resignation."

Chase shook his head, his brows knitting together. "Why the hell would I try to stop you from going and getting your old lady?"

"The way you came in here, I thought..."

"Well, you thought wrong. I'm fucking pissed off that Roach was the one who texted me what was going on and not you. We're your fucking family. Get that through your head. If your girl is in trouble, we'll all get her back." Chase stepped forward until he could put his hand on my shoulder. "I promised you that I'd prove I was back for good, but more than that, you need to believe that not everything will go to shit. We'll get her back safe. Now, what's the plan?"

I couldn't bring myself to say anything as the room filled with people. Mannix gripped my shoulder on the way past, his eyes locking with mine. He gave me a single nod, and emotion clogged my throat, making it hard to swallow. The world felt like it was painted with blood when it came to my life, but a glimmer of hope sparkled among the gore.

Words that Mannix had said over the years played on a loop in my mind. Even though I'd been part of the MC, it wasn't until now that I felt like I belonged. I turned to see Wilder jump up on the large table and hold up the map as he organized groups to hit the target locations.

"Sorry, but as soon as I saw what we were up against, I texted Chase and told him what was happening. I knew you never would," Roach said.

"Thanks, man."

"We'll get her back," he said before walking away.

I once saw a quote that said love was stronger than revenge, and I spit on the sentiment. I called it a false truth, a fake fact that people liked to say and hide behind when they were too weak to take care of their business.

Tonight, I realized I may have missed the true meaning behind the quote. It wasn't that love was stronger than revenge...love fucking fueled it like gasoline to a naked flame, and I planned on scorching the earth to get back what was mine.

Raine

Chapter 38

Raine

I shivered, my body cold. The kind of cold that seeped into your bones and made you ache from the inside out. I tried to move or even open my eyes, but my body wouldn't respond. Not my arms, legs, or eyes. My brain raced through the fog as I tried to remember what happened. Was I in an accident? Was I paralyzed?

That didn't make sense because everything hurt. My toes to the top of my head felt like I'd been beaten. The last thing I remembered was going to my house with Avro and kissing him on the couch. We were going to be packing...I think. Pieces of our time and conversation were coming back to me like little images floating by, and I had to grab them, or they would disappear again.

"You got her?"

The remaining fog was instantly wiped away. My heart stopped and then pounded so hard that it felt like it would rip from my chest. I knew that voice. I could never forget that cold and calculating rasp as sharp to my ears as the steel blade he shoved into my stomach. My body trembled, or I thought it did. I still didn't feel like I was moving except for tremors under my skin.

"Yes, but I don't know if anyone saw me. It was a shit time of day to take her, but she was with some guy, and I had to wait for a good moment."

Dave.

It all came rushing back. The doorbell rang, and Dave stood there in tears apologizing for tracking me down, but Irene was in the hospital, and her dying wish was to see me. I didn't want to go without Avro, but when I turned to grab my phone to call him, something sharp stabbed me in the side of the neck, and everything went dark.

"It was worth the risk. You did well, Profit Dave," the man who haunted my dreams said.

How had I ever thought this man was Kai? Hearing his voice again, he sounded so different. There was no comparison, yet for so long my mind had conjured Kai's face and voice every time I thought about the attack.

Did that mean Dave was one of the other men? My stomach flipped and churned with images of him on top of me. I had to push it aside quickly, or I would vomit, and I didn't think I could open my mouth. My pinky twitched, so whatever he'd given me was slowly starting to wear off, but there was no way in hell I was letting them know.

I needed to be smarter than I was at fifteen if there was any chance of getting out of this alive. The two men talked, but none of it was about me, or anything that made sense, and my mind drifted to the men in my life.

If I didn't escape, then what? Would they think I took off again and they just couldn't find me? Or would my body be dropped off somewhere like a discarded bag of garbage, and that's how they would find out?

"When was the last time you re-administered the drugs?"

"Forty minutes ago, just like you asked."

"Excellent. Take her to my wives. They will know what to do. This one needs to be cleansed before the ceremony," the man with the terrifying voice said.

How long had I been here?

"I'll make sure she's ready, Father," Dave said, and if my mouth could move, it would've fallen open. There was no way this other man was his real father, was he supposed to be someone spiritual?

"Good, and be careful the drugs you gave her should be slowly wearing off. We want her able to scream for the ceremony." There was a loud bang, but I remained still even though the adrenaline coursing through my body spiked. "Isn't that right, Raine?"

I tried so hard not to react, but the fear made it nearly impossible. My lungs stopped working for a few seconds, and the man Dave called Father chuckled. I realized then that I was in a cell, and they were both very close. My skin crawled like I was coated in a million insects, even though I was pretty sure there were none.

"She is starting to hear us. Get her prepped quickly. I'm excited to complete the ritual that started so long ago," Father said as he moved away from the cage, his voice getting quieter.

The sound of keys and the scrape of a door reminded me of those old medieval shows and the cells where they kept prisoners. This wasn't much different. I was being held and would be put on display. It might not be a guillotine coming for my head, but that would've been better than whatever these men planned.

I'd already suffered in their clutches once before and barely survived. There was no doubt that if they completed this...ceremony, there would be no coming back.

Rough hands gripped me and picked me up, and as much as I wanted to strike out and make my escape, I couldn't move anything other than my little finger. He stank of sweat and sausage as I was pressed against Dave's meaty body. My stomach rolled again, and to keep from being sick, I counted his steps and tried to follow which direction he went.

"You know, Raine, I was content to let you live your life and never see you again. You were never the intended target that night, but Kai...he needed to be taught a lesson then, and he needs to be stopped now."

They were after Kai that night. What the hell had they planned on doing with him if they got him? I couldn't even fathom the pain they would've caused him, and for the first time, I was happy that they had gotten me instead. Kai would've fought until they killed him.

"But, if I'm honest, I have to admit that I'm excited to finish this and maybe get to fuck you again. You did have a sweet pussy, and it ruined me forever. The only thing that satisfies me now is the taste of a sweet young thing like you were."

Was he really blaming me for him being a sick piece of shit? Oh, hell no. I'd taken on way too much guilt over my life. There was no fucking way that I was allowing him to blame me for his twisted fantasies. He was my foster father, someone that I thought at least cared for me on some level. But it was obvious now he was nothing more than a child molester looking for the right opportunity.

There was a loud knock on what sounded like wood, and I realized we were at a door.

"You want to know something else?" *Did I really have a choice?* "Sometimes when I stroke myself, it's your screams I hear and your pussy, I imagine."

And when I thought about what you did to me, I fantasized about ripping your cock from your body.

The initial terror was still there but slowly shifting into something else. Something far more lethal, and if I got my hands free, I would make my fantasy come true.

"Come in, Profit Dave, we have the bath prepared," a female voice said. What woman in their right mind would willingly choose to say here? "You can place her in the bath. We will look after her until it's time."

I wanted to scream as Dave sat me down in the water. It was so hot that I was positive it would burn the skin off my body. When he released me, my head lolled to the side, and no matter how hard I tried to lift it, it wouldn't budge. It was like my brain had been disconnected from my body, and none of the controls worked.

"Thank you, Profit Dave. We will summon you when needed." The same female voice said.

"You have been chosen for a very special ceremony. You must feel honored," a new female voice said.

Honored was not how I felt right now. Terrified, creeped out, and angry were all words I would use, but honored was not on my list.

"She is very beautiful. Could we ask to keep her?" A third woman chimed in with a sweeter sing-song voice. What was I a pet? Keep her? The women were more terrifying than Dave or the Father.

"No, we have been given our instructions. We know what we must do. Let's not question the Father's wishes. He does know best," the first woman said.

"Yes, Deist," at least four other voices said in unison. The water around me splashed and moved, and I would've jumped out if I could when multiple hands touched my body. I smelled something flowery and figured it must be soap as the woman directly behind me rubbed the silky lather across my chest and over my breasts. Her fingers softly twisted my nipples between her fingers until they were hard.

"You do have pretty little buds," she said, and squeezed them harder. "To bad we don't have more time." She spent all her time playing with my breasts and would've sworn that she was sucking on them.

Battling back the fear to be able to think straight was almost impossible as time ticked on. They didn't miss a single spot and even held my leg above the water to do my feet. I fought against the drugs and could twitch two fingers now, but it was still not enough. A hand slid between my thighs and rubbed along the sensitive folds of my pussy.

"Check to see if she is satisfactory for the Father," the woman behind me said as she continued rubbing my nipples. I wanted to stand up and yell at them to leave me alone. The finger massaging my pussy slid inside, and once more, I was violated. If I wanted to fuck multiple women, I wanted it to be my choice, not the demand of some lunatic. Instead of feeling dirty or tainted like before, I got angry. No angry wasn't a strong enough word, I wanted them all dead. I didn't care why they were like this, I just wanted them to be wiped from the earth for good.

"If we were allowed, I'd keep you," the one who asked earlier said. She had a distinct voice. "You have a very tight womanhood and I would've enjoyed tasting you. Father will be pleased."

And if I could, I'd cut your tits off. Now get your finger out of me.

I wanted to scream and rage. My foot suddenly flexed, and one eyelid parted slightly. Suddenly I didn't care about the woman and her finger anymore. The only thing that mattered was my body's movements. They were tiny, but the more parts I could move, the greater my chance of getting out of here in one piece.

With my partially opened eye, I glanced at the women leaning over the tub as they touched me with hands, sponges, and coarse scrub brushes. It was hard to focus at first, but one of the women leaned closer, and it was a good thing that I couldn't make a sound. Her neck and the side of her face were carved with patterns and symbols, the scars deep enough to stand out from the rest of her unmarred skin. The closest comparison I could think of was an old Star Trek episode, but those people were supposed to be aliens.

I focused in on the symbol near my eye and it looked like a round circle with a star in the middle and the outline of horns that turned into the letter Y.

Maybe I'd judged them prematurely. Maybe staying here wasn't a choice. Maybe they were victims like me, but the crazy got to them one mutilation at a time.

My body felt raw and sore everywhere by the time they were finished. I thought they would call Dave to get me out of the narrow tub, but instead, they all picked me up at once and laid me out on something hard. I made sure not to try and open my eye any further, but I couldn't help wanting to know that was going on. As if I was a child, they dressed me in a white robe, the material itchy against my sensitive skin.

The first woman, whom the others called Diest, opened the door. "She is prepared for the next stage."

Next stage? How many stages were there? No, this was good. The longer they kept me from going to this Father guy, the better. With each passing second, I felt more of the drug wearing off.

Dave once more picked me up and carried me out, and again I laid like I was dead across his arms. He walked me into another room and put me on a bed where a man in a dark grey outfit chanted and waved smoke over my body that smelt like weed more than anything else. Were they trying to get me high now? I held my breath for as long as possible and only took shallow breaths.

"She is ready to receive the mark," Dave said.

I felt like I was traveling through terrifying magical doors, each one more confusing than the next, but this last stop was where the real panic began to set in. The room was stifling, and as Dave laid me on the uncomfortable table, I noticed the wood-burning stove in the corner. It looked like one you'd see at a hunting cabin on television, but the long black piece of metal the man pulled out was another matter.

Dave pulled up my sleeve as the other man walked toward me with the glowing cattle brand. I recognized the symbol from the side of the girl's face, and it dawned on me they weren't cut. They'd all been branded. I didn't want this, I didn't want any of this, and I tried to command my body to roll off the bed, but other than a few more jerks from my feet, my body didn't respond.

No, no, no

As the man got closer, my legs twitched up to my hips, but it wasn't enough, and a moment later, that bright red poker touched the outside of my shoulder. I screamed, but the sound came out like a weird moan, and the scent of burning flesh tainted the air. Searing pain radiated down my arm, and the room swam.

I braced against the pain, my teeth clenching together.

"You like that, Raine? Feel the evil inside of you leaving your body?" Dave asked. He'd completely lost his mind. There was no other explanation because to believe any of this was a way to cleanse me of evil was ludicrous.

The second man took the brand away, and my head spun more. The pain was immense. I thought I knew what pain was, but I wasn't prepared to have my flesh burned off.

No, you cannot pass out.

Don't pass out.

Dave picked me up again, humming as we walked. His gate had changed from earlier. He walked slowly and deliberately with each exaggerated stride. I flopped around in his outstretched arms and knew I would look asleep or dead to anyone watching, but inside, I was trying hard not to come undone and lose focus on my opportunity.

The humming grew louder as more voices joined in, and a shiver raced down my spine. It was hard to see my surroundings while hanging upside-down, but it was dark with the soft glow of flickering candles and a single sun spot that glowed like a beacon.

There were a lot of people. The humming was so loud that it felt like a thousand voices together as the sound vibrated through my body. I could just make out the bottom edge of what had to be black robes as they swayed against the floor.

This was a cult.

The way Dave and the Father addressed one another, the group of subservient women that Father had called his wives—cleansing, chanting, branding, and now more people in robes.

Dave stopped walking, and my head flopped to the side as he placed me on something cold and hard. My fingers felt like they were touching rock, and the earlier fear I'd managed to control threatened to take over once more. I was in a hysterical fog, trapped inside my body like an animal trapped in a cage, but the cage was my flesh and bones. I didn't need to see to know I'd reached my final destination.

The hum that had turned into a chant reached the end, and the room fell silent. I could feel the tears sliding down my cheek as the weight of my reality settled on my chest. Even if I could get free, this wasn't like the warehouse. There were dozens of voices. I didn't know where I was. I had no weapon, and my body still couldn't respond. With every passing second, more would tingle and twitch, but it wasn't enough to get up and run or fight my way through a crowd of any kind, let alone those hell-bent on making me a sacrifice.

More tears spilled from my eyes and felt cool on my skin as they fell and dried on my cheeks. For eleven years, I'd lived in constant fear of those that had hurt me. Eleven years I blamed the wrong man, and the moment I let myself live and breathe and believe in love and a happily ever after again...they struck. I'd let my guard down and never suspected who the real culprit was. Did Irene know what Dave did? Did she even care? It didn't matter, but so many questions swirled in my head.

It was like they were waiting for the moment I let my walls down to take me and finish what they'd started. The feeling was coming back to my jaw, and my teeth chattered. The longer no one said anything, the more scared I became. I should've been happy that no one touched me, but not knowing where they were and what they were doing was somehow worse.

"Today is a special day," Father said. His loud booming voice pierced my heart with more terror than I ever thought possible, and all I could think about was my guys.

Kai. The first love of my life, the other half of my soul. I could so clearly see our chance to rebuild the future that had been stolen from us. I could feel his hands and how he made me feel protected and safe.

"Today, we will complete a ceremony that was interrupted and left uncompleted. A circle that should have brought us more power from the beginning." He said, and I tried to block him and the crazy out.

Avro. The sweetest man I've ever known. Who was there for me through so many terrible nights and helped me step out of my shell with his unwavering patience.

"By completing this circle, we will feed evil one of its own, and just like a snake eating its tail, its mouth will be too full to bother us and our righteous path that only God can see."

Jace. The way he commanded everything and pushed me hard to step out of the shadows of my fear and become who I wanted to be. Our short time together had shown me there was so much more I wanted to do before it all ended.

This man who claimed to be a Father, a man of God, was no more than a charlatan. The world needed fewer people like this. People who twisted religion into whatever they wanted it to be, whatever served them. They were wolves in sheep's clothing who planned on stealing everything from me—the potential laughs and smiles, the soft touches and stupid arguments over who ate the last cookie. I wanted it all.

My jaw clenched tight, and my shoulders twitched, the muscles firing and coming to life as Father kept talking. Those in the room would call and answer during parts of his ludicrous speech. They had held me down and taken what they wanted, but not this time. I'd fight to my last dying breath.

The room fell silent, and all I could hear was the pounding of my heart and the woosh of air leaving my lungs.

I couldn't stop my whole body from jerking as someone touched my leg. What felt like fingers traveled along my body until a hand gripped my chin.

"And so we meet again, Kitten," Father whispered close to my ear. I no longer wondered what the Devil sounded like. This man had walked straight from hell and into this room.

"Your death was stolen from me once. Your friend Jim couldn't stomach it any longer and called the paramedics. He was weak and undeserving of the robe, but there is no one here to help you today, Kitten," he whispered so only I could hear. "I'm going to enjoy every second of this."

The only Jim I had known was Dave's friend, who was like an uncle to me. My body revolted against the thought that not only Dave but also Jim could do that to me. No other explanation made sense.

He took a deep breath, smelling my skin, and both my legs spasmed and jerked on the table. "Oh yes, you do smell so sweet. We will all fill you with our godly seed to wash away any lingering darkness before your demon body is sacrificed."

"You're..."

"What's that, Kitten? I didn't understand that demon tongue of yours."

My eyes fluttered open, and I stared into the eyes of the man who had worn another's face for too long. His dark eyes felt like they were penetrating my soul and trying to steal it from my body. I hated him. I hated everything he did to me, everything he stood for.

"You're...a...dead...man," I whispered and then swallowed down the dry and smoky taste from the candles in the room.

Father smiled at me, but it was cold and calculating. I could see in his eyes he was envisioning me screaming in pain. There was an edge to his stare that had all my instincts screaming *serial killer* dressed up in religious robes. My hand twitched at my side, and I tested my fingers. They all moved.

"You're still the same, Kitten. I see we didn't break you well enough. Not to worry, we will tonight," he said as he pulled the red hood over his head.

I tried to lift my arm, but it only raised slightly before flopping back to the stone. I was panting hard when he finished lighting the rest of the candles.

"Profit Dave, begin the shackling process."

"Yes, Father," Dave said and stepped up to pull a thick chain and leather cuff from under the table.

"No...don't...touch...me," I growled and coughed. I tried to yank my leg away, but it was heavy and slow. Dave grabbed it easily, holding it in place while he fastened the cuff. I felt an intense combination of panic and rage as Dave gripped my second leg.

The leather was securely in place, and Dave moved toward my arms when we heard a scream that froze everyone. I glanced up at Dave and Father. They looked worried. Or was it just my hopeful imagination?

Like a switch was hit, the sound of gunfire could be heard. The distinct roar of not just one but dozens of motorcycles echoed through the room, and my bottom lip shook.

"Go, all of you, go and fight. This is our home, kill all who try to take it in the name of all that is holy," Father yelled.

As soon as everyone left, Father turned his glare on Dave. "Did you let them follow, you fool?"

He dropped to the floor, and I could just make out the top of his head. "No, Father. I'd never do that. I was careful."

The screams were getting louder along with the gunfire, and an explosion erupted outside. The entire building shook, toppling over a couple of the candles. The shrieks of women reached a new level as they ran into the room where we were and kept going toward the back of the building. Father looked around and then down at Dave.

"Guard her. I'll be right back." Father looked at me, and our eyes locked.

He wasn't coming back.

He was a weak man who hid behind the men and women he manipulated to get what he wanted—the thrill of the kill. I'd gotten away once and could see the emotion in those dark eyes, he was torn, but his self-preservation won out. He sprinted in the direction the women had run.

Dave went to one of the doors and stood to the side, staring out. He didn't consider me a threat, but that was his mistake. I tested my shoulders, lifted my arms, and squeezed my hands to make sure everything worked. I wanted to scream as I forced myself into a sitting position while all my muscles slowly came to life and burned worse than the brand on my arm.

I kept an eye on Dave while my fingers fought with the leather buckle attached to the cuff on my ankle. My fingers were moving but didn't have much strength, and I was sweating by the time I got the first one off. Another explosion shook the building, and a tall candelabra toppled over, hitting the wood paneling along the edge of the room. Within minutes the dry wood caught fire.

My hands shook harder, and I bit my lip to help concentrate on loosening the second cuff. Dave turned and looked over his shoulder in my direction, and there was a brief pause before his brow furrowed.

"What the fuck do you think you're doing?"

A scream rippled up from the depths of my body as I pulled on the strap three times before the buckle gave way. Dave growled as he stomped toward me, and not caring how much pain it caused, I rolled off the other side of the table and landed hard on the floor. I winced with the impact, but something shiny caught my eye. A small table had been set up with various tools for the ceremony, which was really public torture.

Not hesitating, I reached out and gripped the handle of the cere-monial curved knife. The metal felt cool in my palm, and a sense of empowerment washed over me as a hand grabbed my ankle. I screamed and kicked out violently with my heels, catching Dave in the chin with my foot.

"Let go of me!"

My eyes locked on the large hand wrapped around my ankle, the fingers pressing into my skin. Those fingers had gripped me like this once before, but there was no way it would happen again.

11:13AM

Kaivan

The transport truck pulled up to the meet with something loaded on the back. Wilder jumped out of the driver's seat while

Avro got out the passenger side and undid the straps holding the massive canvas covering in place. I stared at the shape.

No...this couldn't be what I thought it was, could it?

"Did they bring a fucking tank?" Roach asked.

Before I could answer, the last strap was freed, and my eyes bugged out at the sight of the massive tan-colored tank.

"I believe they did," I said.

"Wow." I looked at Jace and his surprised expression. "I mean, I knew Avro had family in the army, but I was not expecting this as the favor he asked for," Jace said.

"You and me both."

"Do you think they robbed a museum," Roach asked.

"Anything is fucking possible at this point."

The long line of motorcycles and men waiting for the gates to be opened all stared on as Wilder climbed inside and Avro dropped the ramps down.

Avro walked over, his knee looked like a football with all the supports he had strapped in place, but he wouldn't even consider being left behind.

"Well, that should take their gate down," Avro said as he wiped his hands off.

I didn't give him time to think about it and grabbed him, pulling him into a hug. He held himself perfectly still but then slowly hugged me back. "Thanks, man. I don't know what you had to promise to make this happen, but thank you." Pulling back, I gripped Avro's shoulders.

"Don't look at me like that. I didn't do it for you. I did it for Raine," Avro said. "I'd do anything for her, but...you're welcome too," he tacked onto the end, making me smirk.

Wilder popped out of the top hatch as the tank pulled up beside us.

"Remember, wait for the signal. It will be a big boom. Let's move out," Wilder yelled, and the hatch slammed down. The hair stood on my neck as the powerful machine took the lead the rumble and sound of tracks screaming how lethal it was.

The four of us jumped in Roach's truck and waited for the signal. My nerves had been bad the whole way here. Nothing seemed to be moving fast enough, and the anxiousness made me jumpy and irritable. Now that we were here, a sense of calm had washed over me. The part of me that loved the kill was ready for what was coming, and I wouldn't stop until Dave and Frank were both six feet under.

An explosion went off, the sound of the tank unmistakable, and the truck shook.

"Fuck," I mumbled as smoke rose into the air. That was our cue.

Roach pulled out along with dozens of trucks and an even longer line of motorcycles. All the guys were riding with their guns out, ready for action.

We crested the rise just as the tank smashed into the second watch tower. The people inside tried to hang on as the wooden structure crashed to the ground. The long barrel of the tank's gun swung in the direction of the last tower on the far side of the property, and even though I knew it would be coming, the sound of it going off and the large tower exploding was something I'd never forget.

Roach sped through the gate, clipping a guy running with the front of the truck before speeding across the property to the furthest building on the east side. Cranking the wheel, the ass of the truck slid on the sand before coming to a stop.

"Be careful."

Nodding, I hopped out and ran for the building, looking for a door. One burst open, and two men in black robes ran out. They didn't see me, and I shot them as they ran toward some vehicles parked on this side.

Grabbing the door, I pulled it open and listened, but I couldn't hear anyone coming with the noise out front. Slipping into the dimly lit building, I looked up and down the hallway, not sure which way to go first. I couldn't say why, but I chose the hallway leading to the back of the large steel structure.

I wasn't sure what I expected to find in a cult compound. Maybe a few old farmhouses, a couple of sheds, or a barn, but not something that could double as a jet hanger. Poking my head around the corner, I didn't see anything, but the quiet was eerie.

I paused when I heard a scream, and not just any scream. That was Raine. I knew her voice like it was my own. Not caring how many were in the way or what danger I was running into, I sprinted for the sound as a crippling fear held my heart.

I turned the corner and ran past a few open rooms. A man came running out of one with a fire poker held above his head. I didn't slow or lose my stride as I fired my gun, and he dropped to his knees. I ran around him, not caring if he lived or died. Raine's hysterical screams were all the fuel I needed to put one foot in front of the other.

Bursting through the doors, I ran into a large circular room. The place was on fire at the far end, but it was moving, and it wouldn't take long for the entire building to go up in flames.

My panic reached a new level when Raine's screams echoed in my ears, but I couldn't see her. Running toward the stone slab in the center of the room, I saw something moving and whipped around the end, only to skid to a stop.

Raine was covered in blood, with only her beautiful blue eyes showing through the mask of red. She straddled Dave as the knife she held stabbed into his chest and stomach, even though he was long dead. He wore a black robe like the other men had on, but it was open, exposing his naked body. There was a deep gash across his face showing off the bone. His hands and cock had been severed, and most of his insides were lying around him, but still, Raine screamed as her hand moved in a blur.

Putting my gun away, I inched around so she would see me better and got down into a crouch.

"Raine," I said, but she didn't respond. I knew this level of anger and fear, it made you delusional. She wasn't here in this room. She wasn't anywhere but the room inside her mind playing a movie all its own.

The flicker of flames caught my attention as they licked up the far wall. We needed to get out of here.

"Raine," I tried louder this time, but her wild eyes remained locked on Dave's face. Each plunge of the knife sent blood flying in all directions, his limp body rocking with the harsh blows as she tore him apart.

"Tink!" I yelled, and her hand paused in the air, even though her eyes stayed looking down. She was panting hard, her chest heaving, and her arm shaking violently. "Tink, it's me. Look at me, baby. It's me, Kai. Look up at me."

Her big blue eyes slowly lifted to meet mine, but her hand remained raised above her head. "That's it, keep looking at me." I touched my hand to my chest. "Do you see me? It's Kai," I said, and she blinked a few times. "Tink, we need to go. The building is on fire." I ever so slowly held out my hand so I didn't spook her. Dark smoke drifted in our direction and I coughed as some of it reached my nose. "Give me the knife, Tink."

I coughed a few more times, the taste of smoke itching the back of my throat.

Raine looked down at the man she was straddling and then up at me.

"Kai?"

"Yeah, it's me, Tink. We found you. Jace and Avro are outside. But we need to go."

"He tried to hurt me." She sniffled. "I had to do it. I couldn't let him hurt me again." Her voice hitched, as her bottom lip trembled.

"I know, I'm so fucking happy you did." I kept my hand stretched out and took a deep breath as her arm lowered one inch at a time. "He's dead. I promise you killed him, and he's not coming back, but we need to go." She looked at Dave's face again. "Give me the knife."

Hand trembling, she held out the blade that was dripping red and whimpered as she let go of the handle. I stabbed Dave through the eye up to the decorative hilt. Raine's body slumped, and she looked like she would fall over. Reaching out, I gripped her under the arms like a small child and stood in a single motion.

"Kai," she cried, her arms wrapping around my neck, her body shaking uncontrollably as she clung to me. "You came for me." I hated that even a shadow of doubt existed in her mind.

"Always." I held her tighter. "I'll always come for you." Her crying got louder, but she kept mumbling how much she loved me over and over.

Marching for the door as the fire spread, I kept my eyes open for other threats. I hadn't seen Frank on my way in and hoped that Roach or someone else found him, but I wouldn't be surprised if the coward found a hole to crawl into the moment the fighting started.

The shooting outside had stopped, but I still poked my head out the door to check that all was clear before stepping into the mid-day sun. All those we captured were on their knees with their hands zip-tied behind their back. I didn't know what Chase planned on doing with them, but if it were left up to me, I'd make sure an example was made of them.

"I'm going in, now fucking let go of me," Jace growled as Avro, Roach, and Chase held him back.

"Snake will find her," Roach said, but Jace looked ready to throw down with the three men.

"The fire is getting bigger. What if something happened to them? Let go," Jace roared.

I took a moment to appreciate Jace. He sure didn't act like a celebrity. He was as ornery and ready to fight as any of the guys in the club. I had come to terms and was at peace with them and our relationship. They'd proven their loyalty to Raine, and that was good enough for me. The rest we would figure out.

Before they all ended up in a brawl, I whistled, and they looked over. The relief was evident in their eyes as Avro and Jace ran in my direction. They didn't even wait for me to put her down before we were wrapped up in a hug.

Roach caught my eye, and he shook his head. I knew what that meant. They didn't find Frank.

"I love you guys so much," Raine said.

"We love you too," Avro said. "We were all so scared."

"I didn't think I was ever going to see any of you again," she said, breaking down into sobs that shook her body.

I didn't know what this relationship would look like six months or even a year down the road. What I knew was that all the shit I'd been worrying about didn't matter. All I cared about was Raine. The rest would sort itself out.

The building behind us exploded, and a large pillar of smoke snaked its way up into the sky, blocking out the bright rays of the sun.

In a way, we were back to where it all started, and even though I never wanted Raine to have to defend herself, I hoped it helped her sleep at night, knowing that she'd gotten her revenge. She deserved to see them all burn in hell.

I glanced around at the burning buildings and for trees beyond that. This wasn't over. One day I'd find Frank, and I'd make him pay.

Two down, but still one to go.

Raine

Epilogue

THREE MONTHS, THREE WEEKS, AND THREE DAYS LATER

R aine

I stared at the stunning, simple wedding dress in the mirror before slipping my arms into the leather jacket. Turning to see the back, I smirked at the Lost Souls emblem.

"Are you sure you want to wear a leather jacket for your wedding," Emma, the seamstress, asked.

Smiling, I took it off and turned for her to unzip the dress. "Yeah, I really do. It'll still be ready next week?"

"Yes, all the minor adjustments will be complete." Emma smiled as I walked into the changing room to get dressed. I glanced at the ring Jace had given me and then at the other two rings on the same hand. I looked like I was diamond-obsessed, but fair was fair.

Kai wanted the middle finger for his black diamond arrangement. He said it was a classic fuck you to the social norms.

Avro chose my index finger, and now my hand was worth a fortune and could be used as a weapon.

I kept Jace's on my wedding finger. It had taken the jeweler a while to get the blood off it and put it back together. My overwhelming happiness quickly fell as I pictured it coated in blood. Looking up at the mirror, I couldn't help but turn to stare at the mark on my arm.

I ran my fingers over the area. The brand had been a firm ridge before Jace found a plastic surgeon willing to fix it. Once it was fully healed, I would get a tattoo to finish covering it up.

Dave's face haunted me, but what I'd succumbed to haunted me more. I still remembered everything from the hours I was in Frank and Dave's grasp, and so many times, I woke up in a cold sweat with Dave's mangled body taunting me. I jerked my fingers away from the spot as I felt myself slipping down that hole. I hated to think about that day.

I pulled on my jeans, sneakers, and my Grimhead Crew T-shirt. Shockingly, Jace had added a small reaper to the artwork for Kai. He might be the biggest jerk of the bunch, but he could be a marshmallow that left you breathless and shocked. I turned my mind back to the ceremony next weekend.

We'd decided that I wouldn't officially marry any of them. At least as far as the courts were concerned. But after much arguing, we decided on a fake lavish wedding for the social media sites and a promise ceremony with all three of my guys. The entire motorcycle club was invited, and Chase was handling the service. I'd seen him a few times at the clubhouse and learned almost everyone's name. I was still scratching my head over how Chase ended up with Naomi.

She was bit much and we all backed out of the room whenever she arrived.

Roach and I made up. I did end up punching him in the face and told him he would never cut me out again, but he deserved it, and luckily it made Kai laugh. I loved talking to Mannix. He was a wealth of knowledge and wisdom that touched my heart. Kai told me that Mannix helped protect him in prison, and I'd forever be grateful to him for that.

Kai was still just as broody and domineering as he always was, but it had shifted. He was relaxed at home, loved to cuddle, and was letting me in on some of the shit he never shared with me before. He joked around with Avro and seemed to enjoy the constant banter with Jace. I still didn't want to know what he did as an enforcer. It was probably wrong of me to turn the other cheek and ignore it, but so did all the other wives. It was a conscious choice we all needed to make. If I wanted to be with him, I needed to decide what was more important to me, and it always came back to the same answer. I loved Kai more than I cared about my moral compass or my soul after I was dead.

We'd finally gotten Avro to cave and talked into selling his place, and now we were all chipping in to revamp a mansion where all of us could live. It was best to have neutral ground to start fresh and build new memories. I thought it might break his heart since he'd worked so hard to buy it, but since we found the ideal location and he was helping with the remodeling and interior design of the new house, he came around. Of course, we all knew everything was going to be overly labeled.

I'd decided to go back to school rather than work at Eclipse. It was never my dream job. I loved it there because of Avro. He decided he couldn't go back once he got the all-clear, especially with the world knowing he and Jace were involved. Avro shocked me by deciding to be the band's new manager. No one was more suited, with his organization, ability to tell people no—and still sound like it was a maybe—to talk his way into venues for performances, and come up with fun photo-ops and stunts for the band's social media. You've never seen someone more protective, and he kept a tight hold and eye over Jace's finances to make sure no one was taking advantage of him or the band. It was the perfect match, and Jace seemed calmer. His newest songs were all at the top of the charts, and he was home more than ever.

I had to do some serious self-reflection to understand what really made me happy. I wanted to help people, specifically those traumatized or in the system. I had firsthand knowledge of the struggles, and if I could help even one person, that was what I wanted to do. What that job looked like was still undetermined, but it felt right.

Jace and Kai were scaring me. I wasn't sure I liked them getting along. They still sniped at one another and would take every opportunity to piss the other off, but I never felt like it would turn into a fight like it did before. There was an underlying respect now that wasn't there previously.

I grabbed my purse and other bags from the mall and walked out to the front of the store.

"See you next week Emma," I called out.

"See you later, Raine."

I shouldered open the door and did the usual sweep of my surroundings. It always felt like I was still being watched. I was kidnapped twice and almost saw Jace killed, so I found myself looking over my shoulder again, and I hated it. Kai kept telling me it was normal. Avro told me to give myself a break. Jace...well Jace was always pushing me emotionally. But I still had the fear that Frank was hidden around every corner.

Avro was finally walking and working out now. He'd offered to come with me today, but I didn't want him to see the dress and all the other purchases, like their gifts, I'd gotten for the ceremony.

Stuffing all the bags in the trunk, I wandered around the car and hopped into the driver's seat. I couldn't figure out why I'd waited so long to get my driver's license. The feeling of freedom it brought was undeniable. Something thumped as I pulled out of the parking spot, and I jumped. I looked in the back seat, my heart racing, only to find that it was the container of windshield wash I'd picked up earlier and forgot was there.

"Shit, I meant to put you in," I said to the blue liquid as I tried to tame my racing heart. My teeth ground together, the anger seeping in. Whenever I jumped like a scared rabbit, I was angry afterward. Smacking the steering wheel, I finished pulling out and drove to the exit.

"I need to find a way to get over this."

I got over jumping at my shadow once, and I wouldn't let what happened at the ranch hold me back or keep me scared. He didn't get that kind of power.

My cell phone rang, and I hit the answer button, a smile already on my face at the sight of Jace's name.

"Hey there," I answered. "All okay?"

"Define okay," Jace said as something crashed in the background. I could clearly hear Avro and Kai yelling at one another.

"Oh shit. I thought we were past all this. What's wrong?" My heart sank thinking they would be on bad terms for the ceremony.

"Let's just say I'm never agreeing to us doing any of the final renovations again. These two can't make their mind up about anything, and now the brand-new faucets don't work. Avro is blaming Kai 'cause he bought them on clearance, and...anyway. I know it's a lot to ask, but just to keep world war three from breaking out in here, can you please go and pick up a couple of new sets for the bathrooms?"

"I swear to god, Kai, you never listen!" Avro yelled, and I cringed. Avro never yelled, which meant he had to be pretty fired up.

"Yeah, of course, I'll head to the hardware store close to home. I'll get there before they close for the night." I glanced at the time, knowing I'd be cutting it close since they closed at six, and it was already almost five, but I flicked on the turn signal and headed that way.

"Thanks, I'll keep them from killing each other. Fucking children." Jace hung up the phone, and once more, it was like the world had turned upside down. When had Jace become the calm one, and Avro and Kai argued? Men...

"Are you kidding me?" I grumbled when I saw the yellow caution tape blocking off a huge section of the parking lot for repaving. Of course, it was crazy busy, and I found a single parking spot around the corner of the building. "Unbelievable," I said as I pulled into the lone spot at the end.

Sighing, I got out and did my usual sweep for the boogeyman, but there was only the sound of workers, birds, and cars on the road —no sign of any monsters lurking.

It took forever to find and match the right faucets to the images that Jace sent. I swear it was like they were hidden on purpose. Then I ended up stuck in a massive line to check out, and I swear if I got to the front and they said they were now closed, it wouldn't just be Avro going postal.

Bags in hand, I marched for the car. Food was next on my list. The old kitchen was ripped out, and we still had weeks to go before it was functioning again, so I was picking up pizza. I still hadn't found as good of a spot near us as Terry's, but Jace was begging to invest in an expansion. He might get Terry to cave, which was amazing and dangerous. The last thing I needed was a pizza place I could eat at every day within walking distance from the new property.

My phone rang as I got to the trunk of my car, and I stuffed my hand in my pocket. It was like a trap as the rings caught, and I couldn't get my hand back out. The gates to the back of the store opened, and I glanced over my shoulder as a large cube truck left with product.

I didn't hear the other vehicle coming up until the whir and bang of a sliding door opening made me jump. I turned around just as gloved hands grabbed me.

"Ah!" I screamed as I was whipped off my feet. I pulled on my hand but still couldn't get it free, and my other hand was weighed down by the plastic bags around my wrist. "Let go of me," I managed to yell as I was tossed in the back of the van. The door slammed shut, leaving me in complete darkness inside the window-less box.

No, this couldn't be happening again. How fucking unlucky can one person be? I rolled to the end of the van and banged into the back, the faucets banging into me as the van peeled out. The loud squealing of the tires and the rough bump and sharp turn told me we'd just pulled out on the main road.

I'd handcuffed myself.

This was unbelievable.

I was always so careful.

Shaking out my wrist, I got the bags off and then fought with my pocket to free my hand and the cell phone I was after in the first place.

Jumping to my feet, I stumbled from side to side but made my way to the front and banged as hard as I could.

"Frank! Let me out of here," I screamed. Unlocking the phone, I tried Kai first, but it just beeped busy. How the hell was that possible? I tried Jace, and the same thing happened. "Fuck," I mumbled under my breath.

Bang, bang, bang.

"The Lost Souls will hunt you down and kill you! You're a dead man."

Bang, bang, bang.

There was no response other than to turn a corner so fast that I fell to my knees.

"Dammit," I growled with the sudden impact, which was more disorienting than painful. I tried the phone again, including 911, and nothing worked. Could this guy really have a cell jammer? What the fuck? I seriously wanted to know how I managed to piss this guy off so fucking much. He'd tortured me twice now and was aiming for round three.

Standing, I tried hollering again. "Snake will rip your fucking balls off your body while you're still breathing. Let me out of here!"

It was no use. There was zero response, and I was wasting my energy. The vehicle drove on, even when I hit the walls and screamed like a banshee. My throat and fists were sore. The fear that hadn't hit at first with the anger flowing became a crippling terror that wanted me to curl up in a corner and cry.

I tried to figure out where I was taken, but as the ride dragged on, I lost track of the turns and how much time went by. My thumb ran over the rings, and I let myself have a moment to think about Kai, Jace, and Avro. Our worlds were all so different, our traumas significant and fears just as great. Yet we managed to come together and became a unit that worked.

I wiped away the tears running down my cheeks. I wasn't giving up. Frank had taken too much from me, and there was no way that I was letting him take anything else. Even sitting, I braced myself so I didn't fall over as the van turned sharply and began driving over a rough road. We were going slowly now. It felt like an unmaintained service road or a really long driveway.

We had to be getting closer, and my pulse spiked, the blood pumping through my veins as I pictured the fight I would have when those doors opened.

The van made a wide sweeping turn and then started to back up. The sound of the reverse alarm was loud inside the empty cargo area.

I got ready to spring the moment the sliding door opened. Thump, thump, thump was all I heard as the van shut off and doors on the other side of the dividing wall opened and closed. I listened hard, trying to track their movements, but I was startled when the back doors suddenly opened.

The setting sunlight poured into the back half of the van, but no one charged in to grab me. I didn't know which was worse. If someone had rushed in, I was prepared to fight, but all the hair stood on the back of my neck, and a cold dread raced down my spine as everything remained quiet.

"Raine Eastman, get out of the van," a loud mechanical voice bellowed. It sounded like he was using a PA system or something. So my hope that they just decided to take me for a joy ride and leave me was definitely not happening. I glanced at my discarded bags of faucets and wondered if I could use one as a weapon, but all those zip ties they used to hold them to the cardboard would be impossible to get off.

"Now, or die sooner," the voice announced.

Swallowing hard, I took a tentative step toward the open doors, and as I got closer, I realized that we were in the middle of nowhere. All I could see were trees and grass. With each step closer, I shook a little more, but still, no one reached in and grabbed me. What the fuck was this guy doing? My brain raced as fast as my heart as I tried to piece this newest torture together.

Poking my head out of the back, I saw no one. It was completely silent aside from the sounds of nature. The main issue was a fence taller than the van, complete with barbed wire running in each direction away from where it was backed up. With a quick look, I could tell that the van just fit, like this entire thing had been designed to screw with someone. As strange of a time as it was to have a movie flashback, all I could picture were the raptors in Jurassic Park being dropped off in their enclosures.

"Get out of the van. This is your last warning," the voice was really loud now, and as I stepped down and looked around, I spotted the speaker on the top of a pole, but still no sign of actual people.

I'd been expecting almost anything, but this...this I wasn't prepared for.

"Now run. If you make it through the forest to the other side, your sins will be forgiven, and you will live. If not...then the demons chasing you will finally catch up."

My eyes swung to the forest. Holy shit. My heart pounded so hard I thought I would pass out.

"You will have a five-minute head start. Three, two, one...go."

I bolted away from the van and glanced back only once, and it only confirmed that there wasn't another option out.

Slow your breathing.

I kept saying to myself as I reached the edge of the tall trees and veered to the path that looked like it was used for biking. Even though it would keep me in sight, I could move faster, and there was less chance I would trip over a vine and fall.

I was plunged into shadows, and the cool evening air made me shiver. The sound of a twig snapping off to my left had my head whipping in that direction. I couldn't see anything, but the trembling in my body told me someone was out there. A yipping sound to my right spiked my heart rate, and when whoever was on my left answered, I knew I was being chased down.

My feet moved faster, and I whipped around a slight bend in the path.

"Get her," the same mechanical voice growled.

"You have nowhere to go," a second voice chimed in.

"I'm going to fuck you so hard," the first one said.

Even though it was getting darker, I could see the gap in the trees. The voice had said if I made it to the other side, I would live—if I could trust that voice. Who knew what Frank really had waiting for me? I glanced around for anything I could use as a weapon, but there were no sticks or branches. I didn't even see any rocks bigger than pebbles you'd skip at the beach.

"Whoop, whoop," the voice to my left said. I looked over and almost screamed as I stared at a black and white devil's face, such a contrast to the surroundings that it practically glowed. The crashing of the person on my right getting closer drew my attention. That person wore the same mask, but this one was black and red.

Fear gripped my throat, making breathing difficult, but I pumped my arms harder for the last few feet to my only hope of freedom. Out of my peripheral vision, I saw the masked men getting closer and knew they were toying with me. Even though I was terrified to run through this gap and find out what was on the other side, it was my only chance.

Holding up my arms to ward off a couple of dangling vines, I burst through the gap into the open grassy area.

"What the?" I gasped as I looked around at the massive backyard and the house I recognized. There was a fancy gazebo with lights hanging all along the edge and off the railings. It was easy to see the man leaning against the entryway with a blue and black mask, no shirt, and jeans.

My pace slowed as my brain tried to understand how I ended up at home. I screamed as arms gripped me around the waist. Instead of tackling me to the ground, the man swung me up into his arms. I reached back, ready to hit him, when all the tattoos on his chest, including my name, caught my eye.

"Kai?"

"Hey, Tink," he said and chuckled.

"Are you kidding me right now?" I looked at the second guy laughing under his mask and knew it was Jace. "I'm going to kill all of you, I swear."

"I did like the part where you wanted me to rip off the guy's balls while he was still breathing," Kai said, and I could feel him smiling at me. "You know me so well."

"You three are unbelievable. I should lock you out of the house."

Kai laughed hard. "You could, but I'd just have to ask Wilder for the key I'm sure he already has made."

The corner of my mouth pulled up. Wilder and his crazy appearances had grown on me. He loved it when I made chocolate chip muffins and would sit and talk for hours, then suddenly disappear as if he'd never been there.

"That is true," I said as we walked up the steps to meet the masked man in blue, who was definitely Avro.

"Okay, then tell me what the hell all this was about?" I held my hand out to the forest as Kai set me on my feet. "I thought I was dead, you bunch of jerks." I was annoyed, but as they closed the screendoor, a different kind of tremor raced down my spine. No one could deny that they looked as sexy as any sinful fantasy. They stood shoulder to shoulder, shirtless with matching black jeans and those masks that promised dark desires.

"You've been having nightmares about being taken again," Avro said.

"And you kept saying you wanted to get over it," Jace said.

Kai stepped forward and wrapped an arm around my waist. "Now, when you think of being kidnapped, the dream will end with the three of us. We are your monsters tonight, ones you'll never get out of your head."

I licked my lips, I wasn't sure this would be in any medical journal anywhere, but I couldn't deny that this was definitely a better outcome to have floating around in my head. I looked over my shoulder to our new home and then around the large gazebo that could easily hold a party. I had no idea when they installed this without me seeing it, but a smile tugged at the corner of my mouth. It screamed Avro with all the lights and a large bed with a million pillows. The pizza I was supposed to get was piled on the table, and there was a built-in brick oven and fridge. This was incredible, a small oasis away from the house.

"You did all this for me?" My eyes went to their jeans. No strip club anywhere could compete with this show.

"Yes. We would do anything to help you, but there are rules tonight," Jace said. I watched as they finished stripping together, and I pulled at the shirt I was wearing, overheating from more than just the run.

"What kind of rules?" I crossed my arms but knew I would play whatever game they had in mind. They were way too tempting, and the surge of fear had left a lasting hangover effect of excitement that made me rub my thighs together.

"Kai is going to be in charge, and the three of us are going to do what he says, no hesitation, no questions asked."

If I hadn't been chased through the woods a few seconds ago, I would've said that those words coming out of Jace's mouth were the most shocking thing to happen. Although Kai and Jace had learned to share me on occasion, this was the one time it felt like anything could happen.

"Don't look so shocked," Kai said. He leaned down and growled into the side of my neck. The strange mask was terrifying, yet as the glacial shivers started, so did the twin inferno that licked up my body from between my thighs. I gripped his shoulders, loving the feel of his muscles flexing under my touch and his hard cock pressing into my stomach.

"Alright, I'll play the game." I bit my lip in anticipation.

"Such a good girl," Kai said, the sound devious from inside the mask.

He grabbed the front of my shirt, and I gasped and moaned as he pulled hard and sent buttons flying in every direction. I felt his eyes on my body even though I couldn't see them, and it was still as intimate as any touch.

"That's much better."

Kai stepped back, and my chest was heaving like I'd gone for another sprint. He casually walked over to a chair off to the side and sat down. I wanted to take a picture of him naked like that, his cock standing up with that mask on. Not even the hottest day could compare to the sight of these three intoxicating men. My heart was full, and my life was nowhere near what I imagined. It had turned out so much better than I thought possible or deserved.

But I was never letting go.

- Would you like the rest of this spicy scene? If so, then leave a review on Amazon. When Surrender reaches 250 reviews, I will release a BookFunnel to all those that have reviewed and signed up in the link attached to have the rest of this scene. Review Link
- If you'd like to see the conclusion to the story of Father Frank, then be sure to keep a lookout for the next duet in the series – Hollywood's story - Showbiz and Fealty
- If you'd like to see the conclusion of Happy Harris, the man that murdered Kai's mother, then be sure to keep a look out for – Wilder's duet – Warfare & Dissention by T.L. Hodel
- Would you like to know more about Father Frank, aka Francois Hanson, and his twin brother? – Then make sure to read the Buchan Brother's Duet – Unhinged Cain by Brooklyn Cross and Twisted Abel by T.L. Hodel

THANK YOU

Thank you to all those that decided to pick up this book and read it. It is only with readers continued support that Indie Authors, such as myself, are able to keep writing which is why your reviews mean so much to us. If you enjoyed this book, please consider leaving me a review.

ABOUT THE AUTHOR

Writing is not just a passion for me. It is a lifeline to my sanity.

I have always loved writing but suffer from severe dyslexia and short-term memory retention issues. I struggled in school while I worked every night on re-training my brain.

I was frequently treated like I would never succeed, and I found myself putting my love for writing on a shelf.

Even at the age of six, I found it easier to communicate with animals than people, which was a big reason why I was drawn to dressage horseback riding. I remained focused on my passion for riding until I had to step away from the competition world for personal reasons.

Today, my desire for writing and storytelling has been rekindled. I have published multiple books and will never let anyone or anything hold me back again.
I am a proud romance author who offers my readers morally grey heroes, a ton of spice, epic journeys, and redemption stories.

Brooklyn Cross

-Follow Your Dreams-

Below are the links that you can use to find me if you'd like to follow me on my social media platforms.

Book Bub: <u>Brooklyn Cross Books - BookBub</u>
Goodreads: <u>Brooklyn Cross (Author of Dark Side of the Cloth) |</u>
<u>Goodreads</u>
TikTok: <u>Author Brooklyn Cross (@authorbrooklyncross) TikTok |</u>
<u>Watch Author Brooklyn Cross's Newest TikTok Videos</u>
IG: <u>Brooklyn Cross (@author_brooklyncross) • Instagram photos</u>
<u>and videos</u>
FB Group: <u>Crossfire - A Brooklyn Cross Reader Group | Facebook</u>